ALASTAIR LUFT

ONE KINGDOM UNDER HEAVEN

Black Rose Writing | Texas

First printing

This is a work of fiction. Names, characters, businesses, places, events, and incidents are either the products of the author's imagination or used in a fictitious manner. Any resemblance to actual persons, living or dead, or actual events is purely coincidental.

ISBN: 978-1-68433-697-5
PUBLISHED BY BLACK ROSE WRITING
www.blackrosewriting.com

Printed in the United States of America
Suggested Retail Price (SRP) $20.95

One Kingdom Under Heaven is printed in Sabon

*As a planet-friendly publisher, Black Rose Writing does its best to eliminate unnecessary waste to reduce paper usage and energy costs, while never compromising the reading experience. As a result, the final word count vs. page count may not meet common expectations.

For Katherine,

The future is yours.

ONE KINGDOM UNDER HEAVEN

CAST OF CHARACTERS

Malcolm's Team

Malcolm Kwong – Former US Navy SEAL

Mary Woo – Former US Army Intelligence Support

David Nip – Former US Navy SEAL

Gleb Chudinov – Mercenary, former Russian Spetsnaz

'Wolf' Schlosser – Extreme outdoor adventurer, Former UK 22nd Special Air Service Regiment

Ismail Khoja – Chinese-Uighur political activist, husband of Gul Dilmurat

Gul Dilmurat – Uighur political activist, wife of Ismail Khoja

Aziguli Khoja – Daughter of Ismail Khoja and Gul Dilmurat

Chinese

Zhao Guoqiang – General Secretary of the Communist Party of China, President of the People's Republic of China

Jiang Gaoli – First-ranked Vice-Premier of the State Council

Wang Qiao – Secretary of the Central Commission for Discipline Inspection

General Fan Qiliang – Chief of the General Office of the Central National Security Commission

Air Force General Chen Jihua – Vice-Chairman of the Central Military Commission

Ling Chunlan – Premier of the State Council

Zhang Qishan – Chairman of the National People's Congress Standing Committee

Xu Huning – Chairman of the National Committee of the Chinese People's Political Consultative Conference

Lu Weidong – First-ranked Secretary of the Central Secretariat

Others

Admiral Donald T. Couzens, III – Commander United States Special Operations Command

Lieutenant-General Stuart Fletcher – Chief of Joint Operations, UK Permanent Joint Headquarters

Lieutenant-General Ed Wilton – Chief of Joint Operations, Australian Defence Force Headquarters Joint Operations Command

Major-General Yuri Alekseyev – Commander, Russian Special Operations Forces Command

Major-General Astrid Ødegård – NATO, Allied Command Operations

Toshiro Kobayashi – Civilian, Japanese Self-Defense Forces

Meirav Arens – Civilian, Israeli Institute for Intelligence and Special Operations

"There's a level of admiration I actually have for China. Their basic dictatorship is actually allowing them to turn their economy around on a dime."
–Justin Trudeau

ONE

18 DECEMBER 2029

T he assassin sat on a straight-back chair in the concrete walled room and did not look around. He stared at his hands instead, shackled to a metal table. His hair hung in his face and he had dried blood on his cheek from a cut on his forehead and his left eye was dark and swollen. His chest rose and fell in a controlled rhythm. He kept his gaze on his hands and his face betrayed no sign of any kind that hours ago he'd failed to kill the General Secretary of the Communist Party of China.

• • • • •

General Fan Qiliang studied the assassin through the one-way mirror. The man would not have stood out in any part of Beijing except, perhaps, for his evident physical shape. Which was no doubt why he had been chosen.

Fan had not been invited to that morning's meeting of the Central Politburo. As the Chief of the General Office of the Central National Security Commission, he was not entitled to attend, so instead he'd taken breakfast with several colleagues while the Central Politburo discussed desired outcomes for the annual Economic Work Conference. He'd been eating congee when the suicide bomber self-detonated and killed half of the Politburo Standing Committee. That had been three hours ago and now he was here.

The assassins had almost murdered the entire Standing Committee from what he could gather. It was even rumored that the Uighur terrorist Ismail Khoja had been among them. Audacious, if true. The death count was not yet final although it was already known that First-ranked Vice-Premier Jiang Gaoli was among the dead. The sole assassin to survive was the man in the interrogation room and somewhere in his head with its iron-flecked hair lay the answers to how a team of murderers had penetrated the defences of the Great Hall of the People. Although for General Fan, it wasn't hard to guess.

•   •   •   •   •

Fan had known there would be trouble when Vice-Premier Jiang briefed how America would be removed as a competitor. Almost a year ago. Wang Qiao, the Secretary of the Central Commission for Discipline Inspection, had been there too.

The general shook his head in disbelief. "This will bring nuclear war."

"Perhaps," Vice-Premier Jiang said. "More likely, the Americans will finally be forced to confront their decline. They are not as strong as they think."

"It is no matter. They will retaliate."

"General, for all of Chairman Zhao's faults, the plan is a good one," Secretary Wang said. "It will take the Americans by surprise. By the time they are able to act, they'll find themselves short of allies, and we'll be poised to reclaim our rightful place in the world."

"We must be prepared."

"We are." Secretary Wang placed a hand on his shoulder. "We are all prepared to do what we must."

Fan pondered Wang's unspoken request for support and also the potential rewards if they were to succeed. Then he nodded.

•   •   •   •   •

General Fan considered whether the assassin could cause yet more harm. It would appear that a complete catastrophe had been averted, however, it was well known that disasters did not walk alone. He found it difficult to believe that a man who could infiltrate the Great Hall of the People would not have a plan in the event of his capture and he did not like that the assassin looked no more bothered by his predicament than if he'd had his wallet picked. He wondered if it would not be better to have a guard shoot the man in the head.

Bootheels clacked on the concrete floor and Fan looked over to see General Chen Jihua approaching. A dark red stain sprawled up the leg and lower part of General Chen's blue air force tunic. "You're injured."

General Chen stopped beside him at the one-way mirror. "The blood is Premier Ling Chunlan's. She was beside Jiang Gaoli."

Fan's eyebrows rose. "Both of them?"

Chen nodded and then coughed and pinched the bridge of his nose.

"And Chairman Zhao?" The passage of power would be messy if Chairman Zhao Guoqiang died along with Premier Ling and First-ranked Vice-Premier Jiang.

"Unhurt." General Chen nodded at the assassin. "He wants to question him."

"Absolutely not," Fan said. "We will transfer the assassin to Qincheng and conduct the interrogation there. The convoy will arrive in minutes."

"It can wait."

"The interrogation must happen while he is still in shock from capture."

"That is why the Chairman is on his way here as we speak."

Fan blew air out his nose. "To waste his time questioning this man?"

"A man who killed half the Standing Committee."

"The Party needs the Chairman to lead," Fan said. "Not pretend he's an interrogator."

"He needs to question this man to do so."

"Perhaps the Chairman was more hurt than you know. Perhaps he suffered an injury to his head."

"My head is fine."

The generals turned as one and snapped to attention before Chairman Zhao Guoqiang. The Chairman was dressed in a clean suit that belied he'd been the target of an assassination attempt a few hours prior. Chairman Zhao strode up to the two generals. "Open the door."

General Fan glanced at his colleague. "I don't recommend –"

"Must I repeat myself?"

Fan reached up to resettle his glasses. "*Lingdao*, please reconsider. We have professional interrogators at Qincheng. We can extract anything he knows. You must tend to the Party and the country. The people need you." He looked again at General Chen for support. "The cell is only a temporary holding area. He may still be dangerous. It would be reckless to risk harm to yourself."

"Have you finished?"

"*Shi*."

"Open the door."

Fan stood fast for a moment and then nodded to a nearby guard.

"And General?" Chairman Zhao said.

"*Shi*?" Fan had started to step back and now he paused and then stumbled out of Chairman Zhao's way.

"Don't make me repeat myself again."

· · · · ·

General Fan followed the Chairman into the room and strode over to the assassin. "On your feet, cur." The assassin did not move. Fan waited several seconds and then nodded at the door. A guard sprang into the room and grabbed a clump of the assassin's hair.

The assassin grimaced and fought to stand against the chains which bound him to the table.

The guard pulled the assassin farther off-balance and Fan leaned close. "You will answer when asked a question."

"Release him," the Chairman said.

The guard froze and Fan glanced back at Chairman Zhao, who stood across the table and behind the other chair. The guard looked to Fan for direction and the general nodded. The guard shoved the assassin back into the chair.

"What is his name?" the Chairman asked.

"He hasn't told us."

"What is your name?"

General Fan's face hardened. He nodded at the guard once more and the man punched the assassin in the ear.

"Stop that," the Chairman said.

The guard's hand paused in mid-air. This time when he sought guidance from Fan it was the Chairman who answered.

"Touch him again and I will have you shot," Chairman Zhao said and then sat across from the assassin. "What is your name?"

Fan's lips pressed tight together. "*Lingdao* –"

"Malcolm Kwong."

"Leave us," Chairman Zhao said.

Fan bit his tongue and backed out of the room. He returned to stand at the one-way mirror beside General Chen. "He is making a mistake," he said as the door closed.

Chen smiled. "It is his right, *Tongzhi* General."

"The future of our people plays out before our eyes and he ignores his duties."

"He has steered us well so far."

Fan watched the Chairman and the assassin stare at each other and did not reply.

• • • • •

Malcolm did not avert his gaze.

Chairman Zhao Guoqiang sat across from him with his fingers interlaced on the table and watched him with an expression that did not change. The same expression Malcolm had seen in hundreds of pictures. Malcolm considered that when one stared into an abyss, the abyss stared back. He could not have said if a minute or an hour had passed.

Zhao leaned back and rested his hands on the arms of the chair. "You failed."

"Did I?"

"I'm still alive."

"As am I."

"For the moment."

"Just like you."

Zhao blinked and leaned forward to rest his elbows on the table. His hands clenched in fists. "You will tell me who sent you. You will tell me how you accomplished this attack."

"Why would I do that?"

"I will give you the death that you seek."

"I think that's coming one way or the other."

Zhao's smile did not reach his eyes. "You may feel differently over time. Death will be withheld long after you have been reduced to a grovelling mongrel."

Malcolm said nothing.

"Who sent you?" Zhao asked. "Why did you try to kill me?"

. . . . .

It had taken Malcolm hours to notice time had stopped on a snowy winter's day in January, almost a year ago now. He no longer wore a watch and he'd been so deep in the West Virginia woods that he'd missed the flashes of light that had brightened the sky along the Eastern Seaboard. The same flashes seen in the Midwest and the South and on the West Coast. When the shadows had grown with the onset of night he'd dug the watch out of his backpack to find the hands stuck at five minutes after three. The watch's digital display was blank. His phone wouldn't turn on nor his GPS.

It took a month to walk from West Virginia to New Jersey. He arrived at the start of a hundred-year blizzard that was no different than the year before.

He never found his wife and son. Neither they nor the SUV were at their ransacked house. He supposed they would have been on the Turnpike coming home from daycare when the attack happened and he made his way there. The roads and highways had not been cleared, the wreckages had been pushed to the side and that's where he eventually found Amaelia's silver Volkswagen Tiguan. The front end crumpled and blood on the steering wheel and a cracked booster seat on the back bench.

When the lists of the dead began to be published, he found their names.

. . . . .

Malcolm sat in silence. The questions had stopped for the moment and the quiet dragged on. He counted the seconds in his head. Tried to count. His thoughts wandered and he struggled to catch himself and regain focus on the Chairman and start the count anew and then his mind would slip loose once more to seek refuge in half-remembered conversations and skies painted every shade of yellow and orange and red.

And sand.

Always the sand.

The door to the interrogation cell opened and a guard scurried in and slid a piece of paper onto the table. Chairman Zhao skimmed the page and glanced over Malcolm's shoulder and then waved the guard out of the room. The hint of a smile appeared at the corners of the Chairman's mouth although he hid it well.

"Malcolm Kwong," Zhao said. "Former Lieutenant-Commander in the United States Navy. Former SEAL. Until recently, employed at Appalachian Wilderness Survival."

Zhao rotated the paper and slid it across the table.

Malcolm glanced at the page, a printout in English of his biography and headshot from the company website. He put a finger on the paper and slid it back toward Chairman Zhao until the manacles that bound his wrists grew taut.

"An assassin in the employ of the United States of America," Zhao said.

"I'm retired," Malcolm said.

"I assume we'll uncover similar information about the other members of your team. Although it might take slightly longer since all we have is their bodies."

"They were also retired."

"You are a former American service-member and as such, I shall consider this attack an American act of war. In the absence of other information, I must assume the assassination attempt is synchronized with a follow-on attack. Accordingly, I will direct the People's Liberation Army to retaliate immediately."

The Chairman pushed away from the table and the chair legs scraped along the concrete floor. He stood and slid in the chair and then stared at Malcolm. "Since I believe the United States has still not recovered from the attack earlier this year, I would expect our forces to prevail." He turned and signaled for a guard to open the door.

"You're making a mistake. My team and I did this on our own."

"Do not waste my time." The door swung open and the Chairman strode out into the hallway.

"You know it's possible. It's happened before," Malcolm called. He struggled to his feet and his chains rattled. "Why do you think we needed Khoja?"

After a moment Zhao reappeared in the doorway.

Malcolm held the Chairman's gaze. "Things are not as straightforward as you might think."

"The simplest explanation still tends to be the correct one," Chairman Zhao said.

"Then let me provide it."

"And why would I believe anything you would say?"

"Because I no longer suffer from perplexities."

The Chairman snorted. "Perhaps. I suppose you also know the biddings of Heaven."

"That depends on your willingness to listen."

"Do not think that quoting Confucius makes you more believable." The Chairman drew a deep breath and then exhaled and leaned out the door. "General Chen. Direct the Joint Staff and service chiefs to prepare a retaliatory attack against the United States. It will not be executed until I give the order."

General Chen's voice sounded from the hallway. "At once, Chairman. Your guidance?"

The Chairman shifted his gaze to Malcolm. "All options on the table. Go." He walked back into the room and sat down once more at the table. "Now, *assassin*. I will give you one chance. What you say may possibly save lives although I suspect many more will die because of you."

"I fear that more will die regardless."

"That is your choice."

"And yours."

"So be it. The path of virtue is difficult to follow, yet I can only do my best until I die."

Malcolm lowered his gaze and dipped his head toward the Chairman. "Then let us begin."

• • •

General Fan's forehead almost touched the one-way mirror. Alone at the viewing window since General Chen, the senior officer on the Central Military Commission, had left to attend to the Chairman's orders. In Chen's absence Fan had ordered the section of soldiers posted in the hallway to be silent so he could concentrate on what transpired in the cell and had grown so engrossed that when a man cleared his throat behind him, he started in an undignified manner. He stepped back and found himself face to face with Secretary Wang Qiao. Fan straightened his tunic.

"Comrade Secretary," he said.

"General." Secretary Wang came to stand beside him and peered into the interrogation cell. "The American assassin."

Fan shifted to make space. "*Shì*."

"One of their famous SEALs."

General Fan's jaw muscles tightened. "Your sources."

"My sources, General." Wang smiled. "I was half-expecting a wild savage from what I was told. But seeing him now, I'm confused. I would think any self-respecting PLA soldier could best this cowardly assassin with his bare hands." He turned and spoke louder. "Although perhaps it would take three airmen."

A few of the soldiers snickered and Fan silenced them with a glare and then looked at Secretary Wang. The bull neck that rose from the impeccable suit. The widow's peak of jet-black hair that capped a face too young for a man who'd competed to be General Secretary in the last leadership convention and finished second. "He seems to have done quite well to me," Fan said. "Good enough to infiltrate multiple assassins and a suicide bomber through layers of security to attack the Politburo in the heart of the Great Hall of the People."

"Yet he failed none the less."

"I understand it was your good fortune to not be present when the attack occurred."

Wang raised a finger. "As previously arranged with Premier Ling. She was sorely unqualified for her position – Zhao Guoqiang should not have picked her – but even she recognized the Economic Work Conference functions well enough without input from my commission. Better, perhaps."

"I meant no offence, only to offer that it is difficult to assess an attack's success when not on the battlefield."

Wang's smile disappeared. "And yet even with the assistance of the great Ismail Khoja, this assassin still could not achieve his goal."

"Your sources no doubt gave you that information as well, Comrade Secretary. Did they neglect to mention this hapless assassin killed Vice-Premier Jiang?"

"Of course not. Do not point out the obvious, General." Secretary Wang drilled his finger into Fan's chest. "The death of Jiang Gaoli is a great loss, but the target was clearly Chairman Zhao, whose reckless policies invited this retaliation and, in doing so, cost us the most unrecognized mind of his generation."

"As I said, I meant no offence."

"Then be clear with your words," Wang said. "Chairman Zhao should not be alone in a room with an assassin that just tried to kill him."

"I told him as much," General Fan said. "But he is the Chairman."

Wang closed his eyes and spoke in a slow and steady monotone. "Which is why he is needed to provide guidance to the Party and the country. This," he nodded at the glass, "is not where he should be."

"With respect, the Chairman provided guidance. General Chen is preparing options for a retaliatory attack."

"Without any authority to execute no doubt, and while Zhao Guoqiang himself sits in this room listening to lies. A wonderful plan."

Fan resettled his glasses. "Comrade Secretary, not much of today has gone according to any plan. At this point, we must be flexible. Exploit opportunities as they present."

Wang graced General Fan with a thin smile. "The Russians are fond of saying that our generals lack imagination and think intelligence equates to regurgitating quotes. I'd thought you were different. That's why I supported your nomination for the Security Commission. Perhaps I was wrong."

Fan stiffened. "You were not."

"Then get Zhao out of that room so we can salvage this day."

"And how shall I do that?"

"I trust you'll figure it out. In the Chairman's absence, I will consider our options and coordinate the Party's response with General Chen. You are undoubtedly right, an opportunity exists within this situation. We must simply find it. Until then, try not to let this sideshow become more of a distraction than it already is." Wang began to walk away and then stopped and half-turned. "The world, and America in particular, is waiting for our next move, Comrade General. We must have the courage to act." Secretary Wang continued on his way and his men fell in behind.

General Fan watched Wang depart and then resumed his watch at the one-way mirror. He should have had the assassin killed when he had the chance.

• • • • • •

Secretary Wang Qiao strode through the underground hallway trailed by his aide, Cai Chunhua, and several soldiers. They rounded a corner and passed an alcove that housed a portrait of Chairman Mao and seized with sudden inspiration, Wang stopped to examine the painting. A black-and-white image of the Chairman in his trademark grey tunic suit peered at him and Wang studied the well-known face and then stepped back to appreciate the hallway.

He rarely came to Beijing's *Di Xia Cheng*, the miles of tunnels and underground city built to withstand a nuclear attack from the Soviet Union. This part of the tunnel system was unexceptional. Poured concrete floor. Red carpet runner and white-painted concrete walls that met at a barrel-vaulted ceiling hung with fluorescent lights and tubes of wire. Wide enough for four men to walk abreast.

"Impressive, isn't it?" he said to his assistant.

Cai stood at his side and frowned at the spartan walkway.

Wang smiled. "We could travel beneath the city to the heart of *Zhongnanhai*, where the tunnels are big enough to hold columns of tanks. Even into the Western Hills at one point." He resumed walking. "The power of the people, when correctly marshalled, is humbling."

Never mind that farther from the heart of *Di Xia Cheng* the tunnels were flooded and filled with garbage and shit and citizens and migrant workers alike. People who'd abandoned the world above. Those tunnels had been cut off from these ones.

Cai kept pace at his side. "Comrade Secretary, the General –"

"Fan Qiliang?"

"*Shi*. A lot depends on him."

"You wonder if he can be trusted."

A faint blush appeared in Cai's pale-skinned cheeks. "Only if he is up to the task."

"Fan is ambitious. That ambition will lead him to do the right thing, even if we share different goals. Do you understand, Cai Chunhua?"

Cai bowed his head. "With respect, please enlighten me."

Wang clasped his hands behind his back. "General Fan is a soldier first and a Party member second. Like many soldiers, he is inherently conservative and understands that the course Chairman Zhao has set introduces too much change in too short a time. The Americans are desperate. They will not stop until they find themselves restored to the top of the system they've dominated for so long."

"They do not know when they have been beaten."

A smile warmed Wang's face. "Would we?"

Cai bowed his head once more.

"The Americans are many things, but not cowardly. They will not accept defeat easily," Wang said. "What's more, we have other enemies and this attack may give them confidence. As I warned, Zhao's impatience led him to overreach. We must hope he has not jeopardized our potential to realize our complete rejuvenation."

"The Chinese Dream," Cai said.

"*Shì.* However, to preserve that dream, we must also preserve the system in which we have risen. We have learned the form. We are about to master the form, and only then should we break the form. The Chairman must be made to see that. General Fan understands all this."

"Then he can be trusted."

"Yes." Wang snorted. "And no. Fan Qiliang also believes the reason our progress has slowed in recent years is because we've strayed from socialist ideals."

"And not the trade conflict with the Americans?"

"Or the pandemic, or the drought, or our aging population, or any number of more valid reasons. Yes, I know it makes little sense, but he is convinced of his simplistic reasoning, just as he is convinced that the answer lies with the PLA."

"I did not realize the PLA had military solutions to all of these challenges."

"The Americans have an expression, 'to a man with a hammer, everything is a nail.'" Wang shook his head. "General Fan has no real solutions. He believes the PLA should be elevated to a status equal to the Party so it can better safeguard the precepts of communism. With those values secure, all our problems will go away."

"How do you reason with such a man?"

Wang's smile returned. "You listen to him, and agree with his argument, and then remind him that it is unseemly for generals to line their pockets through kickbacks in defence contracts. And that there are a number of other generals waiting to take his place."

Cai's eyebrows rose. "He could not have been so stupid."

"He could and was, among other things. All to support his mistress." Secretary Wang's smile disappeared. "Still, you raise a good point. Fan Qiliang is a good soldier, but he may see today's events as an opportunity to maneuver. He would be wrong."

They'd reached the stairwell that led back up to the Great Hall of the People. Wang paused and swept a relaxed hand toward the tunnels. "Do you know what is truly impressive about *Di Xia Cheng*? The amount of effort that was wasted." He waited until Cai's gaze shifted. Then his outstretched hand lashed out at his aide's face and stopped a hair's width from the younger man's temple.

Cai stumbled into a crouch with fists held before him, ready to block a blow.

Wang dropped his hand. "Inefficient, Cai Chunhua. We need to practice more."

Cai straightened and bowed his head.

This time Wang returned the bow. "We must always seek to eliminate wasted effort, whether in our movements or our plans. That is one mistake Chairman Mao made, and Fan might make the same mistake. Return to him and ensure that his efforts are aligned."

"Yes, Comrade Secretary." Cai pointed at one of the soldiers to follow him and together they set off down the hallway.

Wang straightened the cuffs of his shirt and watched his aide walk away and then entered the stairwell and climbed the concrete steps two at a time. The tunnels had grown oppressive and confining and though he knew that black clouds loomed heavy, he would not stray from what must be done.

Dawn would break again. Of that, he was sure.

TWO

APRIL 2029

MALCOLM'S STORY

Malcolm hunkered down among the moss-covered trees and watched a lone man pick his way along the dried riverbed. Fog hung heavy and thick in the woods and whenever the man kicked over a rock the mist absorbed the sound. The two were separated by thirty feet or so and the man hadn't yet seen Malcolm hiding in the greyish-green bush. Nor did it seem he would. Malcolm had been in the wilderness too long for that.

He'd wandered the streets in and out of his New Jersey neighborhood for days after he'd found his wife's SUV. Hoping the death rolls were wrong. That Amaelia and Oran were simply waylaid and not already buried beneath the lime-drenched soil of a mass grave. He didn't eat. He didn't drink.

On the third day he collapsed.

He awoke in the Newark Beth Israel Medical Center. An IV in his arm and nurses who needed his cot for other patients. When he could stand on his own he checked himself out. Which is to say he pulled out the IV and got dressed and left. The next conversation he had with another person was when he arrived back at the Appalachian Wilderness Survival School. The facilities deserted and he'd tracked down the owner to tell him he was back and then topped off his fuel and water and disappeared into the bush. That had been two weeks ago and he'd been in the woods ever since.

The man now stood abreast of Malcolm. A little over fifteen feet away and six feet down the bank. The man's bald black head glistened sleek from sweat and mist and not for the first time he cursed and drew up and wiped his brow. The veins in his neck stood out as he squinted around the haze and then he cursed again and hitched his backpack and trudged on.

In a minute the man would be lost in the fog. Malcolm would melt back into the trees and forget the outside world that had intruded into his sanctuary. And that would be for the best. He could find his way back to the log cabin deep in the bush where he was prepared to spend the next year or longer.

Except the man had made all this effort to come out here and find him.

Malcolm straightened and his upper body emerged from the bush. "Admiral," he called out.

The man twisted and his right hand went for a hip-carried sidearm that wasn't there.

Malcolm slid down the bank into the riverbed. "What brings you out here?" he asked.

Admiral Donald T. Couzens III spat a wad of tobacco juice. "Come to ask you the same damn thing."

• • • • •

Malcolm replaced the pot on the rock set inside the campfire and then leaned back on his haunches. He cradled a cup in both hands, stared into the flames and sipped the bitter camp coffee. So hot it scalded his tongue. He did not flinch or grimace and instead blew on his cup and waited for the man seated across the fire to speak.

"Nothing you could have done," Couzens said. The Admiral pulled a tin of chewing tobacco from his shirt pocket, flicked it twice and then topped up the wad in his lower lip. "Hell," he said, "if you'd been with them, you probably would have died too."

"With respect, Admiral, if that's supposed to make me feel better, you'd best try again."

"I don't need you to feel better. I need you to stop feeling sorry for yourself."

"I'll give you an E for effort."

"Like hell. Everything I do is all-in."

"Of course. How could I forget?"

"Shit, Mal." Couzens spat tobacco juice into the fire and then looked away and wiped sweat from his head. "What are you doing out here? Playing drums at night or some other New-Age bullshit that's supposed to help you heal?"

"I don't much care for music."

"Christ," Couzens said and then snorted. "This isn't how I wanted this to go."

Malcolm sipped from his cup. Closed his eyes and savored the sting of the near-scalding coffee.

"I'm sorry about Mel," Couzens said. "And your boy."

"Amaelia."

"What?"

"Her name's Amaelia. She hated when you called her Mel."

Couzens sighed. "That's just how I talk, Mal. Malcolm. You know that."

"Our son's name was Oran."

"Owen?"

"Oran." Malcolm drew out the syllables. "Ore. Ahn. Oran."

"That what you named him?"

"You're not very good at this, are you?"

Couzens shook his head. "And you don't make things easy." He stood and poured his coffee into the fire and then placed the empty cup on a rock beside Malcolm. "At least I'm trying."

"Good for you, sir. Glad I could be there for you." Malcolm picked up the cup and poured in a capful of water from his canteen. "Probably time you were on your way though. Say hi to the boys for me."

"Goddammit, Mal. Tell them yourself."

Malcolm had begun to rinse the cup and now he paused. "I don't think I heard you right."

"We need you back."

Malcolm thought about that for a moment and then tossed the dirty water from the cup onto the ground beside the campfire.

• • • • • •

Malcolm hadn't intended to resign.

He'd had one month left as a squadron commander. Had led his team across half of Africa and the Middle East and that was only his latest assignment. A trail of bodies behind. The enlisted joked that he'd spent so much time in the sandboxes that were Iraq and Syria that he'd earned the right to vote there. He wore it as a badge, one of many and worth more than most. He'd never failed. Except for the few he hadn't brought home, and they were never far from his thoughts.

His accomplishments hadn't gone unnoticed. He'd been chosen. He would go back to school. Learn the theory of war and then be a flag aide to an admiral. There'd be a Pentagon tour and then he'd be assigned to a SOCOM job where he'd run ops from a desk instead of from the field.

And then the reward.

Command of America's most storied counter-terrorism unit.

He'd been deep selected. By then Rear Admiral (upper half) Donald T. Couzens III, the squadron commander when Malcolm first made the teams fourteen years ago and who would, in turn, be in charge of SOCOM by the time Malcolm's path returned him to Dam Neck. A warrior's path, the one thing he'd ever excelled at, and for which the nation was grateful.

And the unborn baby on the ultrasound image stored in his phone would grow up a stranger.

Like father, like son.

He'd written a letter. Asked the Admiral for a chance to catch his breath and pay back into the family. An investment to be withdrawn in later years, with interest. The letter had been returned along with a note from Couzens, the Admiral's distinctive scrawl no doubt written with one of the executive fountain pens he preferred. The Admiral allowed himself few conceits. The pens were one of them. *Not a pen*, he would say, *a writing instrument.*

The note, like Couzens, was to the point.

APPROVED. BE ADVISED, HOWEVER, THAT THIS WILL HAVE LONG-TERM IMPACT ON YOUR CAREER. I NEED WARRIORS TODAY. IF THIS IS STILL WHAT YOU WANT, THEN DON'T LET THE DOOR HIT YOU ON THE ASS ON THE WAY OUT – DC3.

Malcolm hadn't.

• • • • •

Now it seemed the door had reopened. Five years later and six miles from the nearest civilization.

"Did you hear what I said?" Couzens asked.

Malcom poked a stick into the dying embers. "There's nothing wrong with my ears."

"Just with what's between 'em."

"Not interested."

"Come again? Don't think I heard you correctly."

"There's nothing wrong with your ears either, Admiral."

"You haven't even heard the plan."

"Must be a good one to come all the way out here."

"We're going to war, Mal. The call's gone out. Every able-bodied pipe hitter needed."

"Maybe you missed it, Admiral. The war has come and gone. News flash, we lost."

"You swore an oath, Mal."

Malcolm ran a hand through the dark earth and cupped the soil in his palm.

"To train for war and to fight to win," Couzens said. "To defend those who can't defend themselves. To be a common man with uncommon will to succeed. To answer your Nation's call. Any of that sound familiar, Mal?"

"I'm not a SEAL anymore, Admiral. Maybe you missed that as well."

"It don't matter. This is war, and your nation is calling."

Malcolm let the dirt trickle between his fingers and then he picked up his cup and poured the dregs onto the dying coals. Steam hissed into the air. "Nobody's home," he said. "Leave a message after the tone."

Couzens squatted at his side. "I get that you're hurting, Mal. We all are. But this is war. That's why you can't stay out here. You're too good to leave on the bench and somewhere in there is the man who single-handedly saved his team in Syria. The same man who went into the Sahara and came out with Abou Zeid. The Uncatchable. That's the man I need right now. Or this war will get worse. It will escalate and get out of hand and it will consume everything we've ever known."

"Beep," Malcolm said.

Couzens sighed. "What the hell do you want, Mal? You want me to beg? I guess you've earned that much."

The fire was more or less out. Malcolm scuffed the ashes with his boot and gathered the pot and cups. "I want you to leave," he said and then knelt and stuffed the cookware into a mesh pouch.

"You can't bring them back. You know that, right?"

The mesh pouch went into the backpack.

"Will you stop that?"

Malcolm cinched the backpack's drawstring tight.

Couzens grabbed Malcolm's wrist. "I said stop that."

He drove his shoulder up into the Admiral's chin. Couzens flew back and fell to the forest floor and in two steps the sole of Malcolm's boot pressed down on the Admiral's throat. The Admiral gagged and clung to Malcolm's foot. Writhed in the dead leaves like a pinned snake. Malcolm stared at him and then ground his boot into the Admiral's neck. The Admiral's back arched up and out of the twigs and Malcolm noted the reaction with dispassion and began to speak.

"Listen carefully, Admiral," he said. "You don't tell me what to do. And I'm not here to bail you out. I don't owe you anything and you have nothing that I want." He corkscrewed the toe of his boot up and under the Admiral's chin so that Couzens was forced to look at him. "You understand?"

Couzens grimaced and nodded as much as his head could move around the boot.

Malcolm watched the old man struggle a moment longer and then removed his boot from the Admiral's throat and returned to his backpack.

The Admiral's coughs filled the clearing. "I hope that made you feel better," he said.

"I didn't hit you hard enough for that."

The Admiral flopped onto his side and fought to his feet. Decayed leaves on his clothes and dirt from Malcolm's boot on his neck and up onto his cheek. He stood and rubbed his jaw and watched Malcolm busy himself at his backpack.

"What the hell are you doing out here, Mal?"

The backpack zipped close. "Living within my means," he said.

Couzens considered him and then shouldered his own pack. He began to walk away and then paused and looked back. "You're wrong, you know. I can give you what you want."

"And what's that?"

"To go out like a warrior." Couzens tossed a thin yellow envelope onto the ground and then set off down the dried riverbed.

• • • • •

Malcolm squatted and stared into the mist where Couzens had disappeared. A tick crawled up his pant leg and he flicked it off and then slit the envelope open with his belt knife. There were three papers inside. He pulled out the first and read it. His face darkened. He stood and began to pace around the campfire. He reread the report and then he pulled out the second paper and stopped dead. When he looked up, he half expected to find Couzens standing on the edge of the clearing, watching him, but he was alone.

He dug into the envelope and pulled out the last item. Thicker and smaller than the others. A photograph. He held it between his thumb and forefinger and stared at it for a long time.

When he'd seen all he could see he knelt by the fire and poked around the ashes until he unearthed an ember. He held the edge of the first document to the coal and blew first gentle and then hard and coaxed the spark into a flame that shot up and licked his fingers. He dropped the page into the firepit and fed in the other papers and the envelope into the flames.

Then he watched the fire feed on the reports and the findings and on the flaming torch and red ellipses that formed the logo of the Defense Intelligence Agency and when all that had burned, he watched the fire consume the face of the one man that had escaped him.

And as the flames burned, he thought about what he needed to do.

• • • • •

Malcolm flew into Bishkek in late-August.

It was a bright morning. The mercury had set records in the Kyrgyzstan capital for two weeks straight with no end in sight. He waded into the torpor of Manas airport, claimed his bags and then cleared customs. Plodded through an ambling crowd that clogged the barely air-conditioned main concourse and out onto the walkway beside the waiting taxis and the cars and the SUVs that arrived and departed. He shielded his eyes and scanned left and right and then took shelter in the shade of a concrete overhang and dug for the pre-paid SIM card he'd purchased in the airport.

A silver Toyota Fortuner stopped at the curb nearest him and a woman got out. She wore a high-necked tank top with jeans. Her jawline was thin and V-shaped and she passed for Kyrgyz but probably wasn't. He watched her from the corner of his eye and she stood in front of the SUV and perched her sunglasses on her forehead and stared at him. She smiled when he looked up and he noted it did not reach her eyes. He nodded at her and turned back to his phone.

"Hello, Malcolm," she said. "I'm here to pick you up."

He considered her in more detail. "Have we met?"

"I'm Mary."

"I was expecting David."

"Change of plans," she said and then pointed to his twin duffels. "Need help?"

He stooped and picked up the bags. "I can manage," he said.

Mary watched him and then dropped her sunglasses back into place and opened the back hatch. She closed it after Malcolm had stowed the bags. Then she tossed him the keys.

He snatched them in mid-air. Stared at them and then stared at her.

"It's better if a man drives," she said and smiled once more. "In case we get stopped."

He watched her enter the passenger side and then he got behind the wheel and turned on the engine and eased the SUV south onto Manas Airport Road toward the center of Bishkek. His driving steady and confident despite never having been in Kyrgyzstan. Then again, he'd always been more comfortable on roads where traffic laws were more of a suggestion. To the south the Kyrgz Ala-Too mountains were painted orange and white and the shadows crept into the spaces between the peaks as the sun rose.

"What happened to David?" he asked when they were on the highway.

"He went ahead. Wolf went with him."

"Who decided that?"

"I suggested it and everyone agreed. Take this exit." She pointed at a sign for the A365.

"We were supposed to travel together."

"It made sense for David to go in advance to get things ready."

"I wanted us to cross the border together. One time only."

"David said you wouldn't like it, but this way we have a smaller footprint, which has always worked for me. Plus, the Russian said the Chinese don't like big groups."

Malcolm glanced at her and her face was serene. "David must trust you."

"More importantly, I trust him," she said. "We worked together a fair amount after you got out."

He looked back to the road.

"You have interesting friends, Malcolm Kwong," she said. "What's the Russian's story?"

"Ask David. He was there."

"He doesn't talk much about what you guys did before."

Malcolm drove on and said nothing.

"So?" Mary asked.

"Gleb owed me a favor. I called it in."

"Must have been a big one."

"Something like that."

"And Wolf?"

"If he hasn't told you, then it's not my place."

"Oh, he has," she said. "I just wanted to confirm how much he was lying."

They followed the A365 east along the border with Kazakhstan. Past Bishkek the traffic died to a handful of vehicles. Through the village of Chuyskoe and along the shores of the Orto Tokoy Reservoir and into the Terksey Ala-Too mountains until they reached the town of Kochkor a few minutes before one o'clock. They stopped for lunch at the Retro Coffee Bar and then drove on and arrived in Naryn two hours later. The hillsides north and south of the valley were brown hardscrabble and the river that divided the city was barely deep enough to cover the rocks. Mary directed him to a small hotel where she'd arranged for separate rooms and he dropped off his bags and went for a walk about town and then took to the hotel's restaurant where he ate mutton and dumplings. Later on, in his room, he sat in bed and scrolled through pictures of Amaelia and Oran on his phone. Deleted the images one by one until the only photo he had left was a dog-eared wallet size picture he carried in his pocket.

• • • • •

They stayed in Naryn for three days. He walked up and down the valley and grew less and less out of breath on the hills. Although he spoke little Kyrgyz, he got by with his limited Russian, and he soon found it rare for all but the most observant Kyrgyz to give him a second glance. Like it had always been for him. He ate at street booths around town and stopped for tea at cafés and took his suppers with Mary in the hotel. She did not ask to accompany him during the day and he did not offer. He was not surprised she spoke fluent Kyrgyz to the hotel staff. At night he studied his maps and read what books he'd found. Checked his supplies and then laid on his bed and stared at the ceiling until he slept.

On the third night a new guest appeared at supper.

The man would have been tall in any country. He towered over the locals. He had a thick, Slavic brow and hair that looked like he'd cut it himself. Malcolm sat with Mary and ordered naan bread and tea and watched the man argue with the bartender. The man spoke loudly and knocked over a small glass on the counter and the bartender scurried into a back room while the man glared around the room. His gaze settled on Malcolm and Mary and his eyes narrowed. The bartender returned with a bottle and showed it to the man and the man seized it and grabbed up the knocked-over shot glass and walked across the room and slammed bottle and glass onto Malcolm's table.

Malcolm tore off a piece of naan. "Still have a way with locals, I see."

"And you still can't help sticking your nose where it doesn't belong." The man spoke with a heavy Russian accent.

Malcolm snorted and then stood. Grinned and clenched the hand of the other man so hard their forearms shook. "Good to see you, Gleb."

"And you."

"What was that about?" Malcolm nodded toward the bar.

"That?"

"With the bartender."

Gleb looked back at the bartender and then his head raised slightly. "Oh. That." He grunted and turned back to Malcolm. "Idiot tried to pawn off home brewed vodka. They all do." Then he drew a circle in the air near his temple.

"Well, join us for supper."

"I've already eaten." Gleb sat at an empty chair.

"Besides vodka?" Malcolm returned to his seat.

"If that's what you'd call it." Gleb nodded at Mary. "I'm glad to see you again," he said and offered her the bottle. "Drink?"

Mary smiled and nodded. "I thought you'd never ask."

Gleb's eyes widened and then a smile spread slow across his face. He looked at Malcolm. "I like her," he said. "She has good sense. Except for her taste in men." He overturned an empty glass and filled it with vodka and handed it to Mary.

Mary made a face at the Russian and then took the glass. "What about you, boss?" she asked and looked at Malcolm.

Gleb raised his drink to Mary and then took a sip. "He won't have any," he said. "He is boring."

"I'm surprised you left Syria," Malcolm said.

Gleb's gaze met Malcolm's over the shot glass. "No point making money if I don't live long enough to spend it," he said. "And since you Americans all crawled under a rock, there are no cowboys with balls big enough to rescue me." The Russian pronounced cowboy as if the word caused him pain.

"If it helps you get over it, we would have aborted that mission if we'd known you were one of the hostages."

"Ha-ha."

"Is that what happened?" Mary asked. "You rescued him?"

"Good times," Gleb said and saluted Malcolm with his shot glass. "Good times."

Malcolm returned the salute with his tea cup. "Yeah," he said. "I guess."

Gleb looked at Mary. "And what about you?" he asked. "Just going to sit there?"

Mary raised her glass. "I thought you boys were having a moment."

Gleb leered. "Even if we were, there'd be room for three," he said.

"In your dreams, big guy," Mary said and sipped from her glass. "In your dreams."

"Good times," Gleb repeated and then downed his vodka. He returned the glass to the table and refilled it and then cradled it in his hand and scowled into the vodka. "For some reason, I have this feeling what you have planned will not be good times. The desert –"

"The desert is the easy part," Malcolm said.

Gleb snorted and downed his vodka and filled the glass once more. "Then, my cowboy friend, I can tell you that I don't want to know what else you have planned."

"You will," Malcolm said. "Takes two months to get to Beijing."

Gleb held up a hand. "I said I didn't want to know."

• • • • •

Malcolm wanted to depart the next day for Kashgar.

But Gleb had made arrangements for a few days later. The timings could not be changed and to do so would confuse the Kyrgyz and the Chinese officials and the tour company that would pick them up on the Chinese side of the border. Might even jeopardize getting across the Kyrgyz border into China completely. They may as well enjoy the vodka while they could.

They waited two more days and then left Naryn at dawn with Gleb at the wheel of Mary's SUV. Passed a checkpoint south of the city and crossed the Chatyr Kul Basin and arrived at Torugart a few minutes past nine o'clock. To the east the Tian Shan mountains loomed crisp and stark under a deep blue sky along the border with China. Gleb wove their SUV past a snaking line of cabover trucks that clogged the road and stopped at the red-and-white striped boom barrier of the Kyrgyz border control post. Beyond the barricade sat several one and two-storey buildings in the shape of a hollow square.

Gleb pointed to the open space between the buildings. "We will leave the vehicle there."

"Aren't we taking it with us?" Malcolm asked.

"Impossible. The rental company will pick it up in a few days and we will get into a vehicle provided by the tour company that arranges crossings. Assuming we get through."

"With the right permit you can take a vehicle across," Mary said from the back.

Gleb grunted.

"Then again, what do I know?" Mary asked. "I've only inserted covert teams into half the countries on earth."

"Ever do that at the Torugart Pass?"

"Never needed to."

"Then as I said, impossible."

A Kyrgyz guard in camouflage fatigues raised the boom barrier a few minutes after ten o'clock and waved them inside.

"On time today," Gleb said and drove through the gate. "A good start."

Another guard stood where the road entered the hollow square. The guard was stocky and carried a rifle slung from his shoulder. He directed Gleb to an open space and Gleb drove ahead and stopped and then the stocky guard shouted at them in Kyrgyz and made them stand beside the vehicle. Three more guards arrived. The guard who was giving the orders yelled at the newcomers and then the bags were pulled from the SUV and opened for inspection while the stocky guard shouted anew at Gleb and Malcolm and Mary.

"What does he want?" Malcolm asked.

"Proof that we have transport in China," Gleb said. He rummaged in his messenger bag.

"Why's he shouting?"

"Because I'm bigger than him." Gleb withdrew a paper and handed it to the guard and replied in Russian.

The guard scanned the paper and nodded and disappeared into the main building. By the time he came back the inspection was done and the contents of their bags lay in heaps on the gravel. The guard motioned for Gleb to join him and the two spoke in Russian.

Gleb's voice grew louder and he frowned. The guard shook his head and Gleb turned to Malcolm and Mary. "Give me your passports," he said.

"What's wrong?" Mary asked.

"The driver on the Chinese side hasn't arrived yet. The Kyrgyz will clear us through, but we'll have to wait at the border crossing."

They handed over their passports. The guard stamped them and handed them back and said they could put their clothes back in their bags and then returned to the main building. It was past eleven o'clock. Mary raised the SUV's tailgate and sat on the edge of the trunk.

Around noon the stocky guard reappeared and told Gleb the driver had arrived on the Chinese side. While they talked an elderly, leather-faced Kyrgyz drove up in a Toyota Hiace minivan. The guard shouted and pointed at the minivan and they loaded their bags and got in and drove back out onto the road. The guard smiled and waved and grew small and distant as the road climbed into the mountains and the Chatyr Kul Basin fell away behind them. Ten minutes later they reached the border.

It was closed.

A black metal gate topped with spikes stretched across the road and the gate was secured with a padlock and chain. Concertina wire along the sides of the road boxed them in and on the Chinese side of the border stood a glass-lined observation tower covered with cameras. The driver honked the minivan's horn. Honked again and minutes later a Chinese border guard marched to the gate and the driver got out. They spoke and then the guard walked back to the observation tower.

"The crossing is closed," the driver said when he returned to the vehicle.

"When will it open?" Malcolm asked.

"When they've finished eating."

"When will that be?"

"When they're done."

The driver parked in an open space on the Kyrgyz side of the crossing. The arid mountains stark and brown all around them against the blue September sky. Malcolm and Gleb got out and stood beside one of two concrete monuments that marked the border. A grey pillar rose from a tiered, red-marble base and the number '51' had been engraved on the pillar in red letters beneath a Chinese crest.

Malcolm checked his watch. "Already one o'clock," he said.

"It's possible we don't get across today," Gleb said.

"I thought you'd made arrangements."

"I did. This is how it is." Gleb shrugged. "If we don't get through, we try again tomorrow."

"Tomorrow is the weekend."

"Then we try on Monday."

"I don't want to wait until Monday. I want to get to Kashgar today."

"The desert will still be there."

Malcolm snorted and began to circle the monument.

"David, and Mary, and Wolf, and me," Gleb said. "An interesting team for a desert crossing."

"Wolf knows more about deserts than anyone in the world."

Gleb pulled out a flask and took a sip. "And the others?" he asked. "What are they the best in the world at?"

Malcolm paused and turned to stare out over the valleys. On a barren hillside across a gorge there was a Chinese flag built out of painted rocks. "I thought you didn't want to know."

"I don't care who you're planning to kill in Beijing. My concern is the desert."

"I never —"

"David, for instance," Gleb said. "Your old second in command. He is no doubt good at many things. And of course, he's Chinese. Also good. But crossing deserts? I don't think so."

"You don't need to worry about David. Or Mary."

"No, not that one. She's smart." Gleb smiled and raised the flask toward the minivan. "Smarter than you, anyways."

"She's not your type."

"They're all my type." Gleb ambled over to Malcolm's side. "It's called the Taklamakan for a reason."

"'The Desert of Death,' yes, I know what it means."

"Then you know it deserves the name."

"Just get us across."

"The route —"

"Through the middle, Gleb," Malcolm said. "Through the middle." He looked over his shoulder and nodded at a Chinese guard who now stood at the gate. "Time to go."

The guard informed the Kyrgyz driver that a party of Chinese Communist Party officials would soon arrive from Kashgar and then the gates would open. They unloaded their bags from the Hiace and waited. Forty minutes passed and then a white Mercedes van drove up from the Chinese side and stopped near the tower. Three middle-aged Chinese men in suits dismounted from the van and an officer from the observation tower scurried down to meet them. The officer bowed to each man and pumped their hands and dispatched guards to fetch bags from the Mercedes. Another guard was sent to open the gates.

Malcolm and Gleb and Mary waited beside one of the monuments while the officials and their impromptu entourage passed through the gate. They watched the border guards load the bags into the Kyrgyz minivan and then help the men take their seats. Then the ancient Kyrgyz driver put the Hiace in gear and drove off back the way he had come. When the Hiace was lost from sight, the Chinese guards waved Malcolm and the others across to the empty Mercedes van on the Chinese side of the border.

Gleb led the way toward the Mercedes and pulled open the driver's door. "Feng," he said in accented Mandarin when he saw the driver. "Where's Ling?"

Feng hunched over the steering wheel. "I drive," he said.

Gleb pointed at Feng's head. "I said I wanted Ling to drive."

"I drive."

Gleb swore in Russian and slammed the door shut on Feng's protestations and stomped to the back of the van.

"What's wrong, big guy?" Mary asked as she placed bags into the van.

"The tour company that arranges the border crossings did not send the driver I wanted," Gleb said. "It will be a rough ride."

When the bags were loaded they got in and Feng began to drive. It took thirty minutes to cover the ten kilometres to the Chinese customs clearance area where a guard ordered them out of the van and demanded their passports and papers. Other guards tore open their bags and rifled through their clothes. The guards were efficient and after fifteen minutes they were allowed to continue.

Feng drove deeper into the mountains. The road hugged the sides of steep valleys and was potholed and washed out and would have been a white-knuckler with a good driver. Feng was not a good driver.

Two hours and eighty kilometres later they rolled into another checkpoint. The guards took a cursory look at their papers and waved them on and fifty minutes later they arrived at the Chinese Immigration post at the junction of the Torugart and Irkeshtam border crossings. Gold Chinese letters gleamed on the white brick face of the building. It was almost six o'clock.

Feng parked in a vehicle search area and they were directed out of the van. They stood around and at last a guard took their paperwork and passports. Malcolm began to unload bags for inspection but the guard dismissed him and then stamped the passports and handed them back. The bags had just gone back in the van when a voice called from the other side of the search area.

"What took you so long?"

Malcolm turned and stared at the well-groomed Chinese man with the youthful face and sad eyes and raised a hand in greeting. "Gleb wanted to sight-see in the mountains," he said.

Russian curses came from inside the van.

The man waved at a guard and got a nod, and then hopped the concrete Jersey barrier that surrounded the search area and strolled forward.

Malcolm extended his hand. "Great to see you, David."

David brushed off Malcolm's hand and grabbed him in a hug. "I thought you'd never get here. I will never listen to Mary again."

"Was being stuck with wee Wolfie that bad?" Mary asked from the side of the van. She stuck out her lower lip and pretended to wipe away a tear.

David shook his fist at her. "You have no idea," he said and he pounded Malcolm on the back once more and then released him. "It's good to see you again. You ready, boss?"

Malcolm nodded. "Ready."

•　•　•　•　•

Malcolm rode with David in a separate van the tour company had provided and it was after dark by the time they arrived at the Radisson Blu Hotel in Kashgar. They checked in and doubled up in rooms. Gleb talked his way into the hotel's business class lounge and later snored all night so that Malcolm barely slept.

The next morning found Malcolm in a tea room several blocks from the hotel. Over the following days David paraded in a number of guides from the tour company. All Uighur men with creased faces and eyes distant as the bleak horizons in that desert land. They were mostly old.

All but a few had trim facial hair and the traditional 4-pointed *dopa* hat. One had a beard to his chest in defiance of the reinstated ban that targeted Islamist extremism and prohibited long beards and the wearing of veils in public places. Most lied about their experience. One turned out to be a taxi driver and had never even touched a camel.

Gleb joined them mid-afternoon of the second day. He took a seat beside Malcolm and shortly after the few Uighurs that were in the café stood and walked out. David threatened to call the tour company and they ignored him and so he gave up and sat across from Gleb.

"Thanks, Gleb. You scared them off," David said.

"Me?" One of Gleb's eyebrows rose.

"They all left when you showed up, didn't they?"

"They should worry about the police. Not me."

"Maybe they don't see it that way."

"Then they are fools. There are Chinese police at every intersection looking for trouble. There is only one of me."

"Same time as yesterday," Malcolm said.

"What?" David asked.

"They all left this time yesterday, too," Malcolm said. "Just not at once."

"You sure about that?"

"I didn't notice the exact time, but I'm pretty sure."

Gleb checked his watch. "Three o'clock," he said.

"About right for this time of year," Malcolm said.

Gleb cocked an ear. "No *muezzin*."

"Must not have been one of the restrictions that were lifted," Malcolm said.

"You guys are not making any sense," David said.

"They're at prayer," Malcolm said. "Defying the government crackdown on Muslims."

"I thought the Chinese had backed off on that."

"They did, after the attacks five years ago. Looks like the reforms didn't stick." He stood and stretched and then picked up his tea. "They'll be back."

"Almost no point," David said. "I thought there'd be more."

"How goes the camels?" Malcolm asked.

"Wonderful, wonderful. The Wolf is very happy," Gleb said.

"I've known Wolf since his days in 22 SAS. Before his whole extreme adventurer days. The only time he's ever happy is when he's getting something for nothing."

"So, I lied." Gleb rested one forearm on the table and rested his chin in his hand. "The tour company cannot understand why we need so many camels."

"It's a long trip," Malcolm said.

"We know that. They don't."

"And we can't exactly tell them we'll be in the Taklamakan for over two months," David said.

"They don't expect to see the camels again," Gleb said.

"What about the people?"

Gleb shrugged. "The camels are more valuable."

"They can buy more," David said. "Twice as many for what they're charging."

"You do not understand," Gleb said. "Even if we told them, they would not believe the Taklamakan can be crossed."

"It can," Malcolm said. "Tourist expeditions go into the desert all the time."

Gleb leaned back and folded his elbows across his chest and his chair creaked. "They stay within a day's ride of the edges," he said. "That's what I thought you had in mind. That's what anyone would think. Not straight across all seven hundred miles."

"And the Chinese know where those expeditions are, at all times," Malcolm said. "Do you think that works for us?"

Gleb stared at Malcolm and then grunted.

Malcolm sipped his tea. "Break it into pieces," he said. "The Mazar Tagh mountains are a quarter of the way. We can do a quarter of the way."

"That is over hundred and fifty miles."

"Then worry about today," Malcolm said. "Today, we hire some camel handlers. Tomorrow, we join Wolf in Makit."

Gleb sighed. "That does not reassure me."

"One day at a time, Gleb. One day at a time. Tomorrow we leave for Makit."

· · · · ·

In Makit Malcolm took possession of eighteen Bactrian camels selected by Wolf, the animals stabled in a corral assembled from welded lengths of rusty steel pipe. The desert began where the makeshift fence ended and he stared out over the sands while Wolf complained about the camels and the tour company and the Uighurs and the Chinese and how everything that wasn't British was shite. Wolf was taller than Malcolm, had his brown hair cut close and his body had the same lean hard edges.

"These sorry-looking beasts aren't the worst I've seen, mate, but they're as close as it gets." Wolf adjusted his wrap-around shades and smoothed his manscaped beard. "Paid an arm and a leg, too, that's the worst part. Tossers." He spat on the ground.

"Good work," Malcolm said.

"I always do good work," Wolf said. "You know that."

"That's why you're here."

Wolf snorted. "I'm here for the bloody bragging rights after we cross the Taklamakan. No more, no less. Got it?"

Malcolm smiled and nodded.

Wolf lit a cigarette. "Where are the others?"

"At the compound checking out the gear."

"It's rubbish."

"I'll go take a look."

"Suit yourself, mate."

David had rented a small compound within a ten-minute walk from the corral and Malcolm headed here next to inspect the supplies provided by the tour company. Tents and sleeping bags. Camel saddles. Plastic water cans. Rations. Shovels. Straps and rope and firewood. Sacks of camel fodder and empty sacks in which to load everything. Strewn in piles across a dirty courtyard.

He found Mary amid the mess and squatted beside the tent she'd spread out on the ground. "How does everything look?" he asked.

Mary traced her fingers along the seams of the tent. "Honestly?"

"There can't be any other way."

She glanced at him and then back at the tent. "Like it was last used during the Long March."

"Will it get us through the desert?"

She paused and then nodded. "It'll take some work."

He set Mary and David on to the equipment. Patched the tents and cut strips of cloth to jam the tops of the jerry cans. Replaced straps on the frames that would hold the baggage onto the camels.

The camel handlers arrived the next day. Eight Uighurs. One youth who was not old enough to shave and one elder who could have predated the desert itself. Skin and bones and silence. A stocky Uighur named Musa who seemed to be in charge. Malcolm put them to work with Gleb and Wolf and the camels. Load. Unload. March discipline and how to hobble and tie together packets. Which camels could carry the water and which would spit and kick and fight.

He did all of this and more. Plotted the route. Calculated times and distances and where they might find oases in the desert whose name meant one could get in but not out. Avoided the Chinese soldiers clad in riot gear who owned the streets and befriended the plain-clothes police who asked questions and followed them whenever they left the compound. He studied the weather and tracked the days as September became October and gave little thought to what came after. He wanted the desert behind him before winter came and yet knew it to be foolish to begin while summer still scorched the land.

And then the day arrived for their departure, half a year since Couzens had found him in the West Virginia woods.

• • • • •

He let the Uighurs leave to say their good-byes. Called the other four together the day before the departure and splurged for a hot meal from a local restaurant. Laghman and lamb kebabs and fried eggplant and black tea scented with cardamom and saffron and rose petals. They did not talk. Ate and ate and shovelled up the scraps with Uighur flat bread as if they did not know when they would eat again. And still there was food.

When he could eat no more Malcolm pushed back from the table and surveyed the team. He read the confidence in a calm nod from Mary. Gleb's face already browned and weathered. Strained yet stoic. Wolf did not return his gaze. He'd moved on to David when Wolf spoke.

"Why cross the desert at all?"

Malcolm did not reply.

Wolf shrugged. "I mean, there are perfectly fine highways that go around." He drew arcs in the air with his hands.

"Too many checkpoints on the highways," David said.

"Bollocks," Wolf said. The word erupted. As if he'd kept it in and could contain it no longer. "You want to get to the other side of the Taklamakan, yeah? Go around it."

David looked to Malcolm and received no help.

Wolf downed his beer. Wiped his mouth with the back of a hand and looked to the Russian. "Gleb. Speak up, mate. We talked about this."

Gleb stared at his untouched glass of vodka. When he spoke, his voice was steady, matter-of-fact. "The water will be a problem," he said.

"The water." Wolf slammed the table and the plates clattered. "We don't have enough water."

"There's nothing new in that," Mary said.

"We're carrying as much as we can," David said.

"That's the point, innit?" Wolf said. "It's not enough. It's never enough, believe me."

"We can dig," Mary said. "There's water under the surface, we just have to – "

"Great fuckin' plan, that," Wolf said. "Hope to find water." He thrust a finger at Mary. "But you can take your positive mental attitude and shove it, yeah? Hope's not going to find us water."

"Watch your mouth," David said.

"Oh, the muppet talks." Wolf raised his eyebrows and spread his arms. "Or is her hand so far up your arse you can't think for yourself?"

David shot to his feet and his chair clattered onto the floor.

Malcolm raised a hand and the room stilled. "It's okay to have second thoughts," he said.

"Christ almighty, second thoughts?" Wolf ran a hand over his head. "Third and fourth thoughts, more like it."

"I thought you wanted the bragging rights."

"There isn't enough water. And there's no backup plan to find more."

"You'd be the first to cross the Taklamakan since Blackmore."

"Blackmore had an external support team that supplied him. We don't. At this rate, we'll end up like old Sven Hedin instead, drinking camel blood and our own piss."

Malcolm thought about that. "Gleb?"

The Russian did not flinch from Malcolm's gaze. "There is a lot left to chance."

"Chance is a good thing. Isn't that what you say?"

"Because I can always improvise." The Russian nodded to the eastern wall beyond which waited the dunes and the rocks and the heat. "There is no improvising out there."

Malcolm sipped his tea and stared at the scraps on his plate. "Anyone who wants to back out, can," he said and then looked at Wolf. "But we're going *through*. Not around."

"For the love of Christ," Wolf said. "I'm not getting paid enough for this."

"You're getting paid?" Mary asked.

David and Gleb smiled.

Wolf shook his head. "Barmy. The lot of you," he said and then stood up and pointed at Malcolm. "I'll get you across the desert. But if it becomes every man for himself, I'm the one who's walking out. I can promise you that." He glared at David and Mary and then stormed from the room.

Malcolm waited until Wolf had gone and then looked around the table. "Anyone else?"

Mary and David shook their heads. Gleb opened his mouth and then shut it and picked up his glass.

"Gleb?" Malcolm asked.

"I will miss the vodka," the Russian said and downed his drink. "That is all."

"All right then." Malcolm stood and pushed in his chair. "Early start tomorrow. Get some sleep if you can."

He walked out and into the room where he kept his gear. Sat on his cot and unlaced his boots and stared at his half-filled backpack. Then he took up a dog-eared copy of *Conquering the Desert of Death* and removed the photo jammed between the pages. Amaelia smiled up at him, a wide brimmed hat on her head and a sun shawl over her shoulders. Oran between her legs. He brushed a finger across Amaelia's face and then traced the line of surf that raced up the beach and wondered what the sand in the desert would be like. If it would itch and scrape and scour.

If he would even feel it.

•   •   •   •   •

Malcolm rose hours before the dawn. He gathered his bags and made his way to the corral, sweating by the time he arrived. Late fall and still over 20° degrees Celsius before the sun had come up if the thermometer on his watch was accurate. He wiped his brow and then checked and rechecked his map while David and Mary ferried over equipment and supplies. When Gleb and Wolf arrived with the handlers, he set aside the map and helped load the first camel. He had started in on a second when shouts came from farther into the corral.

One of the camels refused to kneel. The Uighur who held the camel's lead rope tugged and yanked and the animal tossed its head and grunted. A second handler struck the animal on the knees with a stick. The camel's cheeks bulged and its lips pulled back and it gobbed a wad of undigested food onto its attacker. The Uighur snarled and hit the camel in the head. Struck it again and again until Wolf wrenched the stick from the Uighur's hand and clubbed out the man's legs.

The Uighur thrashed on the ground and Wolf jammed the end of the stick under the man's chin and stretched him out. "How do you like it, mate?"

The rest of the Uighurs watched as the man on the ground fought against the stick. Wolf drove it deeper into his throat and the man gagged. One of the younger handlers stepped forward and the Uigher called Musa placed a hand on his chest.

Wolf waited for the man at his feet to stop moving and then pointed at the other handlers with the stick. "Next one who beats a camel in anger gets the same treatment, yeah?"

The handlers said nothing and at length Musa nodded.

Wolf stepped back and allowed the handler to regain his feet. Then he gave the unruly camel a smart rap on the side of its knee. The camel knelt and Wolf stood beside its head and scratched its ear. "And I'll call you, Andy," he said. "Not the smartest, but tougher than shit."

They cursed and shoved and wrestled with the remaining camels. When each animal was loaded it was led off and tied together with others until by the end there were three packets of six.

Malcolm divided the team among the packets. Wolf at the rear with Musa. Mary and Gleb in the middle. David with the lead packet and the rest of the Uighurs split evenly. He searched faces and received nods or thumbs up and he nodded in return and then made his way to the front of the caravan.

He removed his compass from inside his shirt and studied the picture of Amaelia and Oran newly taped to the cover. His wife with their son held to her chest. He lingered a moment and then shot the bearing and when he was done, he tucked the compass away and forced himself to take the first step.

He would not fail.

Could not fail, however things turned out.

· · · · · ·

The sun had breached the horizon and the dunes were painted orange and red and scarlet. The camels cast long shadows that stretched out behind as Malcolm led the caravan into the Taklamakan. No wind and soon enough no sound except the grit beneath their feet and the creaks and groans and grunts of the equipment and the camels. His boots sank into the sand so that he had to fight for every step.

After the first mile his calves ached. After the second they screamed. The same agony etched on the faces of those in the lead packet. A blank expression akin to shock and which grew more intense as the sun rose and sweat rolled down their faces and their backs and even the camels seemed to oppose them.

The packets lagged and the caravan stretched out and after the third mile the last packet had become a thin shimmering line in the distance. He thought of the seven hundred miles to go. Seven hundred miles and the dune mountains that ruled the desert's interior far ahead.

Seven hundred miles.

Every last one under the unblinking sun.

· · · · ·

At noon Malcolm halted the caravan in a wide flat.

Five hours in.

Six miles.

The dunes loomed ominous around them. He plodded up a forty-foot sand hill while he waited for the caravan to close together and at the top, he pulled out his binoculars and surveyed the land in front. Waves of sand ran in unbroken parallel lines from north to south. He saw that to head due east would drive the caravan up the face of every dune and yet to snake a path through the shifting maze meant the caravan would cover twice the distance. More.

And the dunes would only get bigger.

He turned and trained the binoculars back over the caravan. The camels were spread over more than a mile and the third packet had bunched up and stalled and fallen farther and farther behind. He watched until he saw the packet move and by then the lead packet had gathered at the base of the dune beneath him.

He slid down the sand and ordered a break for lunch. He pulled David aside while the Uighurs ate. Asked how he was doing and together they made the rounds of the Uighurs and camels and then did the same when the second packet arrived.

Wolf led the last group into the impromptu camp an hour later. Said nothing to the Uighurs that were with him. Sat by himself and pulled out his canteen and a piece of flatbread. Musa brought up the rear and glanced once at Wolf and then had the other handlers picket the camels and break out their rations.

Malcolm studied Wolf for a moment. He said nothing as the Brit tore chunks off the flat bread and wondered if the Brit would speak first.

"Suppose you want to know what happened to us," Wolf said after a minute.

Malcolm picked up a handful of sand.

"Fuckin' frame fell off one of the camels," Wolf said.

Malcolm made a loose fist and let the sand trickle out the bottom of his hand. "How?"

"How?" Wolf's eyebrows rose. "Because those arseholes can't tie a knot."

"And whose fault is that?"

Wolf pointed at him with the canteen. "Don't start, mate. We've lost two bags of feed."

Malcolm scanned the faces of the Uighurs. Saw that all except Musa refused to look at Wolf. Their flat, black eyes and weathered faces. "Can they tie a knot now?"

"Damned right they can."

"All's well that ends well, I guess."

Wolf spoke around a mouthful of flatbread. "How far have we come?"

"Six miles. Give or take."

The Brit snorted. "We should be headed more to the south. We want that highway close."

"Even if I wanted to, we can't. Not now."

"And why, pray tell, is that?"

"There's a no-go area south of us I want to avoid," he said and then glanced up at David who'd come to join them and knelt slightly apart. "Everything all good?"

David nodded. "Not a very talkative bunch," he said.

"You should have heard them an hour ago." Wolf swigged from the canteen and then replaced the lid. "And what's this no-go area? First I've heard of it."

"It's a re-education camp," Malcolm said.

"For who?" Wolf asked.

"The Uighurs."

"And here I thought the Chinese were well sorted," Wolf said and shook his head.

"What are you talking about?" David asked.

"You can't 're-educate' this lot. They haven't been educated in the first place."

The muscles in David's jaw clenched. "Not sure they'd see it the same way," he said.

"Piss off," Wolf said. "Who gives a fuck what they think? If it were up to me, I'd drop in at this camp and trade these numpties for some that might have half a brain between them. We'd be better off."

David's face darkened. "It's a concentration camp, you asshole," he said.

"That'll do," Malcolm said and placed his hand on David's shoulder.

"Then maybe the Chinese aren't so daft after all," Wolf said to David.

"I said that will do."

Malcolm held David back and stared at Wolf until the Brit dropped his gaze. "We leave in fifteen minutes," he said. "Be ready."

"I'll be ready, mate. Count on it."

Malcolm stood and waved David away and looked around the faces of the Uighurs in Wolf's packet. All except Musa with their heads buried in their lunches.

"The route doesn't change," Malcolm said.

"Your bloody loss."

"That's right. It's my loss, because I'm the boss." He waited for Wolf to say more and was disappointed. "Be ready to go in fifteen minutes," he said and then left Wolf to sit in the sand.

• • • • • •

There were still hours of daylight when Malcolm halted the caravan in a wide depression at the base of two Euphrates poplars in full yellow bloom. He had David and Wolf and half the Uighurs unload and feed the camels while Gleb and two other Uighurs set up camp and began supper. Then he gathered Mary and the last two Uighurs and had them fetch shovels. He led them to a large white crusting spread on top of the sand near the poplars and they began to dig.

The hole caved in again and again and every foot gained in depth required two feet or more dug in width. The hole was around four feet deep when David came to observe. He squatted on his haunches beside the hole and watched the group dig.

"Come to take a turn?" Mary asked.

"Wondering why you're breaking your backs on the first day."

"Can't take water for granted," Malcolm said.

"Musa says there are lots of places to find water over the first hundred miles," David said. "It's the eastern part of the desert he says we should be concerned about."

"Don't you have camels to see to?" Mary asked.

"All done. I'll say this for Wolf, he doesn't mess around. Think I'll check on supper instead." David stood and headed for the camp fire.

"Better yet," Malcolm called after him, "why don't you get the camels unhobbled?"

"What for?"

"We just hit water." Malcolm tossed a shovel-full of damp sand onto the ground near David's feet. "Supper can wait. Let's get the animals over to drink and the jerry cans topped off." He tossed aside the shovel and scrambled out of the hole. Clapped David on the shoulder as he strode past. "And close your mouth," he said. "Makes you look stupid."

• • • • •

In the morning they loaded the camels. Coaxed and prodded the animals one by one toward the baggage and stores where they were brought to their knees. Then on went the baggage frames to be secured by a girth and rope and twine. The loads came next. Under Wolf's direction the tamer camels took water. Sturdier camels took tents and personal gear and food, which left the skittish animals for pots and pans and fuel and any supplies that could afford to be lost or damaged. When the loads were on, the frames were re-centered and girths retightened and when all this was done and the loads secured the camels were led aside and tied into packets.

The morning grew long.

Malcolm stepped off as soon as the first packet was ready. Left Gleb and Wolf to shout and bully the camels and Uighurs of the second and third packets into a semblance of order. He kept his thoughts on the march, impatient to get moving as he forced the morning's route past the two Euphrates poplars and through dunes that seemed to have grown during the night. One step after another. His mouth already dry and yet he left his canteen untouched. Forced himself to see how long he could hold off before he dipped into the two litres of water that was the day's ration.

He traversed a gap between two parallel dunes and climbed the gently sloped windward side of another. At the top he spied the glint of sunlight reflected off metal to the east and knew it would be the blades of the turbines in the world's newest and largest wind power plant. An installation not on his map, but which the shopkeepers in Kashgar had freely mentioned. He reached for his binoculars and then a commotion of shouts and groans came from behind and he turned in time to watch the second packet fall apart.

The third camel in the group threw its head back and forth and steadily dragged the packet off the line of march and up the steep face of a dune Malcolm had bypassed. The handlers at the front and rear of the packet yelled and beat the camels closest to them and those animals grunted and spat. Mary grabbed for the halter of a camel trying to break away. The animal stopped and then the camel's girth strap loosened and its baggage frame slipped halfway off its back.

The third packet had come into sight now and a tall figure broke off and loped through the sand. Gleb, except he was too slow. The load of the rogue camel crashed to the sand and the ropes that held the second packet together came apart. Mary clung to the halter and then lost her grip and disappeared into the sand beneath the camel's feet. The animal broke away and two other camels from the second packet followed.

Malcolm called a halt and ran back to Mary. Sand clung to her face and her hair and she had sand in her shirt and an angry red welt on her arm where the camel had trod on her. He stayed with her while the others corralled the loose camels. The animals had not gotten far although it still took an hour to gather them and reset the supplies.

A full morning to travel little more than two miles.

Malcolm made his way back to his place at the front of the caravan. Gleb grabbed him by the elbow and towered over him. The Russian's breathing was heavy and his face puffy and splotched red as if his rage would break out through the pores of his skin.

"Don't ever start before all the camels are ready again," Gleb said. "Or we'll leave you here in the desert."

Malcolm bore the Russian's glare and then shrugged off the hand that held him tight. Turned his back and ignored the gazes of the Uighurs and everyone else and slogged toward the front where he resumed the march.

• • • • • •

Days blurred together. Mornings began with a cold breakfast in the greyish pre-dawn light, powdered oats flavored with the dried fruit and nuts they'd picked up in Kashgar. The energy bars saved for later. Then the camp would be torn down. The camels would be brought to drink if they'd found water the night before and then led off to be loaded and tied into packets. Malcolm would check the map and the GPS and wait for David to signal that everything was ready.

Then they would march.

After the first mile Malcolm would call a ten-minute halt so loads could be checked and tightened. Ten minutes would become twenty and sometimes thirty and then the caravan would continue. Three hours until a brief stop for lunch. Three to four hours more in the afternoon during which the last hours would be spent with an eye for the white crusts of salt that signaled water.

Camels broke free no matter what they did. On good days once. On bad days three times or more. They learned which camels could lead a packet and which must be tied in the middle.

Sand got into their boots. It got into the collars of their shirts and the seams of their pants. Worked its way into their armpits and knees and groins where it mixed with their sweat to chafe and cause raw aching sores. It found its way into their boots and caused blisters to break out on their feet.

Gleb and Wolf oversaw the camels and the bags at the end of the day's march. Either Malcolm or Mary would lead a team to dig for water and the remainder would help unload and set up camp. Supper duty rotated until it became clear David alone could make a passable meal. Wolf declared that David had missed his calling and nicknamed him Ramsay.

Malcolm forced them to dig each night. Sometimes they found water. More often they did not. Once they found water so brackish the camels could not even drink. Two liters a day was not enough. In the middle of the night Malcolm would bolt upright with his hamstrings cramped hard and tight and he would sit and massage his legs and think about their dwindling supply.

The sole respite from the heat and the dust and the wind came at the end of the day. The sun would sink into the horizon and color the sky orange and red and indigo. Then the shadows would devour the land and in the brief window before darkness fell, the desert air did not sear nor freeze but instead cocooned them in calm warmth. David would joke with the Uighurs around the fire and when the night cold began to bite they would retire one-by-one to bedrolls and sleeping bags.

Eight to ten miles every day.

• • • • •

On the eighth day the wind changed. It blew stronger and felt almost moist. Even the docile camels stubbornly fought the handlers. Three animals broke free of their packets in the morning alone. Gleb yelled at the Uighurs and David yelled at Gleb and the Uighurs yelled at each other. Wolf cursed everyone and everything with the misfortune to cross his path. When the third camel had been recovered Malcolm called a halt for lunch.

Two miles in four hours.

The afternoon march had barely started when Malcolm heard a yell from behind. He turned and saw the second packet stopped and that the Uighurs had begun to hobble the camels. Mary stripped bags from one of the animals and then the first packet began to do the same.

Malcolm spied David in the first packet and yelled at him. "What's going on?"

David did not look up from where he struggled to hold the halter of a camel. Malcolm opened his mouth to yell again when one of the Uighurs pointed to a thin line of black and yellow and red that spanned the northwest horizon. The line grew thicker and darker as Malcolm watched, spread to their flanks and by then he had to squint against the dust and sand in the air.

He slid down the dune and ran for the first packet.

The Uighurs had the camels hobbled by the time Malcolm arrived. He pulled a tent from one of the bags lashed to the animals. Dragged it to the leeward side of a dune and threw it up while the sky overhead darkened from blue through yellow to sickly orange. He wrapped a *shemagh* around his face and scrambled to help with another tent while the wind roared. They'd barely finished when a wall of sand blocked out the sun. He and David and one of the Uighurs dove inside the tent and then the storm was on them.

The fabric walls snapped and stood taut and David had to lean close and shout to be heard. "Did everyone get inside?"

"I don't know."

David reached for the zipper that held the tent door shut.

Malcolm grabbed his arm. "We have to ride it out," he shouted.

"We have to check on the others."

"You'd never find them."

David tried to pull away and Malcolm struggled to hold him. He put his free hand on David's shoulder in case the other man fought him and put his mouth at David's ear. "It's a sandstorm," he said. "We rehearsed this."

David paused.

"Tell me," Malcolm said.

"Each packet puts up two tents."

"And?"

David released his hold on the tent's zipper and met Malcolm's gaze. "We get inside and wait it out," he said and then eased back to sit cross-legged on the floor. He did not look away from the tent door.

Malcolm loosened his grip and waited to see what David would do. "It'll be all right," he shouted into David's ear. "The big storms happen in spring, not fall."

"This isn't a big storm?"

"No." Malcolm felt the tension ease in David's body and he let him go. He saw the Uighur, a twenty-year old named Esa, about to say something and Malcolm shook his head. Esa closed his mouth and they sat in silence while the storm raged and sand piled up on the sides of the tent.

• • • • •

The winds died in the late afternoon.

Malcolm crawled out of the tent and into a land turned upside down. Yellowish sand hung thick and oppressive in the air and obscured all but a small orb that was the sun. He dug out the other tent from the first packet and left David and three of the handlers to look for camels and bags while he saw to the rest of the caravan.

Baggage frames with their loads attached lay fallen along the entire line of march. Half buried as if abandoned for years. He arrived at the second packet to see Gleb and Mary emerge from a tent and by the time he made it to the rear of the caravan Wolf had already taken out a search party. Everyone had made it into a tent, although ten of the camels had wandered off. They did not recover the last animal until the sun had long since set.

They camped on the spot.

Malcolm abandoned the nightly search for water. The storm had covered any salt crusts although that was but one part of the reason. The other part he did not understand. It was a feeling. A festering bitterness he sensed in the team as they tracked down camels and gathered bags. It was more than frustration, which might have been put to work. Disillusionment, maybe, even shock, at how easy it would be for the capricious desert to end their journey.

They lit no fire that night. The meal was cold and silent, vegetarian ration packs they couldn't be bothered to heat. By the time they made for their tents, the storm had blown over and the sky was full of stars. The temperature dropped and one by one they fell tired and shivering into restless sleep.

Malcolm dreamed of Amaelia.

She sat on a rug before a fireplace in a cottage he knew had been destroyed in the hurricanes of '26. He wished he would never wake and when he did the sun had risen and the camp had been packed. He bolted upright and found Wolf sitting on a backpack with a cigarette in hand.

"Got your beauty sleep, did you?" the Brit said.

"You should've woken me." He kicked out of his sleeping bag.

"Your mum wouldn't let us," Wolf said and nodded at Mary. "Said you looked too peaceful." He dragged on the cigarette and allowed the smoke to escape out his nostrils.

Malcolm looked at Mary and she met his gaze and then turned back to the camel she was loading.

"Girls," Wolf said and shook his head.

• • • •

They continued on for the day.

And the day after that.

Up and down dunes which had grown into mountains of sand hundreds of feet tall. They no longer found even traces of vegetation. Only sand. As far as could be seen beneath the merciless sun that seared them from on high. Always forward. Then late morning on the eleventh day out from Kashgar, Malcolm crested a four-hundred-foot dune. There had been no way around. He paused at the top and let the hot breeze blow in his face and stared off to the east. He squinted and shielded his eyes. Pulled out his binoculars and after a minute or two decided he was not imagining the shimmering line of mountains enshrouded in the heat haze that hung across the ranks of dunes.

He checked his map as the caravan closed up to him. Traced the unfamiliar mountain names that were the lone landmarks for miles around.

Hami Tagh.

Guten Tagh.

Mazar Tagh, from which the mountain range drew its name. He'd circled an unnamed mountain in the middle of the range and it was this point that he studied when David joined him. Malcolm offered the binoculars without a word and pointed in the direction of the mountains and waited.

David glassed the horizon. He stood for a moment and then lowered the binoculars. "Is that them?" he asked.

"Yes."

"We did it."

"Almost. A few days to go."

"Don't rain on my parade."

Malcolm chuckled and David joined in and then Malcom could no longer hold back. Laughter gripped him and his eyes teared up and then David mimicked Wolf's voice. Called him a tosser and said he'd better not waste any water and Malcolm laughed even harder. They leaned on each other and laughed until Mary walked up from the second packet.

"Are you boys finished?" she asked. Her words were tempered by a smile that played around her lips. "We're kind of all waiting on you."

Malcolm straightened and took a deep breath and then took back the binoculars and stowed the map. "We should make the leeward side of the mountains tomorrow," he said. "Then the going will get easier."

David shielded his eyes and stared at the mountains. "Finally," he said. "Something to look at besides sand."

"Not going to get closer while we stand here, though," Malcolm said. He shouldered his pack and slid down the far side of the dune.

"You really think Khoja's in those mountains?" David asked.

"He's there."

"And you think he'll listen to you?"

"He's there."

· · · · ·

The following day they reached the leeward side of the mountains. The dunes shrank and the land became baked and hard and they made good time. By the end of the day Hami Tagh loomed to their north with its red and brown outcroppings in stark contrast to the yellowish ground and hazy sky. Like the mountain might not be real and yet it was real enough to suffocate any breeze so that they marched as if in an oven.

They found no water that night.

The next day they reached the end of Hami Tagh and entered a small gap in the mountain range. Another day and another ten miles behind them.

No water again.

A silent urgency propelled them past Loes Tagh in a single day. Fourteen miles closer to the Hotan river on the east side of the mountain range and as much water as they could drink. The Uighurs began to smile and sing and the camels strained at the ropes and Malcolm had to fight to hold the pace steady.

On the fourth day out of the sand dunes they entered a horseshoe-like valley of rocky hills at the feet of the unnamed mountain on Malcolm's map. Sandy slopes along the base gave way to jagged rocks and cliffs so that the mountain seemed to stab up out of the desert like a knife. Malcolm halted and scanned the hills with the binoculars while he waited for the caravan to close up in the box canyon. Studied what looked to be a path that ran around the east side of the mountain.

David led the first packet into the valley and left the Uighurs with the camels while he joined Malcolm. "Lots of daylight left," he said. "You see water or something?"

"No."

"Then why are we stopping?"

"Because we found Khoja."

David shielded his eyes to peer at the mountain's peak. "All the way up there?"

"No. There." Malcolm pointed at the base of the mountain. To what he'd initially taken to be a small cairn beside the trailhead.

"Jesus. You've got to be kidding me. Is that him?"

"Yes."

"How long do you think he's been watching us?"

"Long enough."

"What do you want to do?"

Malcolm stood still and then raised his arm to the sky. Left it up and nothing happened and he began to lower it and then the cairn moved and raised an arm in return.

"Let's invite him for supper," Malcolm said.

• • • • •

Malcolm arranged himself on the sand and stared through the flames at the man on the other side of the fire.

Ismail Khoja, the Chinese-Uighur terrorist or freedom fighter depending on perspective, had a neatly trimmed beard and his disheveled black hair was flecked with grey and hung to his shoulders, other than the section gathered in a topknot. He wore a loose cotton shirt with mandarin collar and over top of this a cotton coat that hung to his knees. A folded band of light brown cloth bound the coat at the man's waist. He sat cross legged and the tails of the coat covered his knees and he held a cup of black tea scented with cardamom that David had prepared. A half-eaten plate of rice mixed with raisins and dates sat beside him and every minute or so he would take a piece of almond-laced nougat from a nearby bowl.

Malcolm and Khoja sat alone. The others waited at a separate fire and the Uighurs sat in small groups on the edges of the camp from where they stared at Khoja and whispered to each other. Malcolm ignored them all.

"Ismail Khoja," Malcolm said.

The old man sipped his tea.

"I've known you for some time, although we've never met," Malcolm said in Mandarin. He selected a length of wood from his pack beside him. Took up his knife and began to carve off small chunks. "I first heard of you in Syria. A rumor, that was all. The Free Opposition called you the Chinese ghost. *You Hun Ye Gui,* that's what David and I called you."

Malcolm repositioned the wood and continued with the knife. "We tracked you in Mali, but it wasn't until South Sudan we started targeting you," he said. "Came close a few times."

Malcolm could not tell if the old man listened. Or if he'd even moved since he'd tasted the tea.

"I remember one time in particular." Malcolm blew shavings from the end of the wood and then held up the stick to inspect the dragon's head that had taken shape. He made several fine cuts with the point of the knife and began to work the middle of the wood.

"We were after an al-Shabaab target in Bakool." Malcolm paused to drink his own tea. "We came in low and quiet off the ships. Landed about twelve miles out and humped the rest of the way. We were inside the compound before Khalaf even knew we were on the ground. Got him and everyone else without a shot fired, one of the rare missions in Somalia where everything happened the way it was planned."

Malcolm looked up and wondered if it was his imagination that the old man had leaned forward.

"I remember tearing apart a room and finding a pair of shoes beside a bed," Malcolm said. "Cheap canvas slip-ons. The kind Bruce Lee used to wear." Malcolm did not waste a glance at the old man's feet which he knew would be covered by the coat.

Khoja sipped his tea and then cradled the cup in his lap. "You've come a long way for my autograph," he said.

Malcolm brushed away wood shavings with his sleeve. "I've come for your help."

"Huh."

"At the time I never understood what you were doing in Syria all those years ago. Or Africa, for that matter. And then five years ago the Uighurs rose up across Xinjiang."

Malcolm inspected the wood against the light of the fire. Blew away several splinters and went back to work. The knife had not slowed although the pieces of wood that fell to the sand had become smaller. "For a time, I thought they might succeed," he said. "I even heard of an assassination attempt on the Xinjiang Party Secretary, reports that the Party itself might fall. And always, in the background, rumors of an unnamed Chinese insurgent helping the Uighurs. A ghost. And then," Malcolm said as he lowered the wood to stare at Khoja, "as quick as the uprising began, it ended. And here you are."

"As good a place to be as any other."

"Why did you stop?"

"Timing."

"Timing," Malcolm said.

"It is important to perceive the right moment to press an attack. And just as important to recognize when that moment does not exist."

"Are you saying you could not have succeeded?"

"What I said was that the moment did not lend itself to the delivery of an effective blow."

"I don't believe that," Malcolm said. "You had the Party itself on its back foot."

"What you think is of no concern to me."

"You gave up."

Khoja shrugged. "The moment passed," he said.

Malcolm took up the wood once more. "It has come again," he said and this time he did not imagine that the old man leaned closer.

"What do you want?" Khoja asked.

"I told you."

"My help."

"Yes."

"You had a better chance at my autograph." Khoja drained his tea and set the cup on the ground and rose to his feet. "Thank you for the meal," he said and turned.

"I'm going to finish what you started."

Khoja paused. "Who has sent you?"

"I'm here of my own free will."

Khoja turned and the firelight illuminated his face and burned in his eyes. "That's what we all think."

"Please sit down," Malcolm said, "and I'll tell you how it will be done."

Khoja remained standing and his face didn't change and when it seemed he might turn and walk away he instead resumed his seat. A divot appeared in his brow as Malcolm talked and his frown grew deeper and then there was silence.

"Impossible," Khoja said when Malcolm had finished.

"Not with your help." Malcolm still worked the wood although now he preceded every move of the knife with a studied gaze. Each cut assessed after he'd finished. The seconds stretched out and it would seem as if he was done and then the knife would move again.

"If I could do what you ask, I would have done so already."

"You cannot succeed by yourself."

"I would not be so sure."

"As you said, if you could do so, you would have."

"There are others I could draw on."

"None with my skill."

"And I must take your word for that?"

Malcolm held up the carving. He inspected it end to end and then returned the knife to its sheathe. "Even if there were others," Malcolm said, "as you said, the moment was not right." He stood and walked around the fire and held out the carving to Khoja.

The old man stared at the offering and then accepted it with both hands. Held it up and turned the wood so the firelight reflected off the dragon's mane and the scales of its skin and the talons of its feet and the spines that graced its back. He traced his fingers over the snake coiled around the dragon's neck and up to the snake's head with its fangs buried deep into the dragon's throat.

"We would be entering the dragon's lair," Khoja said. "Where they have the advantage."

"You've been there before," Malcolm said. "And they're not expecting us."

"Perhaps." The old man sat with his legs crossed as before. He held the carving and alternated between staring into the flames and at the snake which had brought the dragon low.

Malcolm sat back down and waited. The fire grew low and he added wood. Sparks shot into the air and then the old man stood.

Malcolm stood as well and gestured to the other fire. "Please," he said. "There is more food."

The old man held up a hand. "I must go," he said and began to return toward the mountain.

"Will you help?" Malcolm called after him.

"I will let you know in the morning," Khoja said and then passed into the darkness beyond the edge of the firelight.

• • • • •

Malcolm woke the team before dawn.

They ate a cold breakfast and then struck camp and loaded the animals. Malcolm worked alongside Esa. Together they held a baggage frame on a camel's back while David tightened the girth strap.

"Do you think he'll show?" David asked.

"Wouldn't you?"

"I'm not a sixty-year-old Chinese terrorist hiding out in the desert." David grunted as he wrestled the braided girth into position. "What do we do if he doesn't?"

"Plan B."

David paused and then glanced up at Malcolm. "There's a Plan B?"

"There's always a Plan B."

David held Malcolm's gaze and then his eyes narrowed and he snorted. "Great," he said and bent to the girth once more. "Plan B is we make it up."

"Good old Plan B," Malcolm said.

The camels had not yet been tied into their packets when Mary flagged him down. "You're going to want to check this out, boss," she said and pointed at the mountain.

Malcolm wiped his forehead and looked in the direction she'd indicated. Spotted not one but three figures on the spur that jutted out from the mountain's base. He recognized Khoja in the lead.

The caravan stood ready to march by the time the group arrived at the remains of the camp. The camels shuffled in place and chewed their cud and watched in disinterest while the old man strode up to Malcolm. The two others flanked Khoja on either side and Malcolm saw that they were women.

"I will help you," Khoja said.

Malcolm bowed his head. "Thank you," he said. His gaze shifted to the woman to the right of Khoja. On either side of her weathered and creased face hung twin braids of hair. Thick as ropes. The braids draped over her shoulders and onto her chest and the woman held her chin high and stared at him as if the entire desert belonged to her. "I don't remember talking about anyone else," he said.

"My family have come to say good-bye," Khoja said.

"I understand." Malcolm bowed his head again. "We can leave some food and supplies."

"There is no need. They will come with us."

"What?"

Khoja shrugged out of his pack and handed it to the second woman and then nodded to the camel train. The woman took the pack and the hood that covered her face fell away and Malcolm saw that she was barely an adult. Her thin jawline mirrored that of the older woman and her skin was pale and smooth and she looked as if the wind might carry her away and yet she held the old man's pack without difficulty. Like the other woman, she met Malcolm's gaze with her chin raised. In her big eyes he saw Khoja and a glimpse of Amaelia and the flesh of his forearms grew cold and broke out in tiny bumps. The women walked toward the closest packet of camels and Malcolm let his gaze follow them and then caught himself and turned back to Khoja.

"I will not be separated from them until it is necessary," the old man said.

"When will that be?"

"When it is necessary," Khoja said and then walked off to help attach the bags to the camels.

Malcolm stood and did not move even when David came to stand at his side.

"Everything okay?" David asked.

"Fine."

"Who are the women?"

"His wife and daughter."

"That won't complicate things at all."

Malcolm turned and studied the women as they loaded the bags. Saw the same grace and fluidity in their motions and that neither had wasted movements. Like tigers might move if cursed with human bodies. "I know," he said.

"Thank God for Plan B," David said.

"Good old Plan B."

. . . . . .

The ground continued to be flat and rocky and they made eighteen miles that day. Malcolm stayed at the front and Khoja came up to walk with him twice. Once in the morning and once in the afternoon. The old man said little.

The women started the day with the trail packet and by mid-morning had drifted to the front. They spoke even less than Khoja although Mary was able to extract their names. The older woman was called Gul Dilmurat and the younger one Aziguli.

On the second day out from where they'd met Khoja, they reached a gap in the mountain range. The next mountain, Guten Tagh, rose several miles to the south-east and Malcolm angled the route to keep the range to their north. No sooner had he changed course then Khoja appeared at his side.

"Head north," the old man said. "Then due east."

"That's the windward side. The dunes will be bigger there."

"Yes."

"It will take twice as long."

"Yes."

"We need to make up time, not go slower." Malcolm pulled the map from his leg pocket and spread it in front of the old man. "The Hotan River is only a few days away at this bearing," he said. "Just past Mazar Tagh."

"That is true. It is also why the northern route is preferable."

"That makes no sense."

"I would think it would be obvious."

"It's not."

"It is preferable because it is harder."

Malcolm stared at Khoja and then shook his head. He folded the map and replaced it in his pocket and began marching toward the south-east.

"Because it is harder, there will be less chance of meeting other travelers," Khoja called out.

Malcolm spun and waved a hand at the sand and the rocks and the mountains in the distance. "Do you see anyone else?" He waited and then turned his back and walked.

"Not here," Khoja said. "But if we keep to your route, we will."

Malcolm slowed. Forced himself to stop once more and face the old man.

"The fort at Mazar Tagh draws tourists from all around," Khoja said and then shrugged. "But perhaps you know better. Perhaps you've lived in this desert your whole life."

Malcolm hooked his thumbs in the shoulder straps of his pack and considered the old man's words. He sipped from his canteen and then pulled out the map and located the dot that represented Mazar Tagh. Left his finger on the paper and then inhaled deep through his nose and stowed the map and led the caravan north. Khoja beside him.

Within an hour the flat and rocky ground had disappeared beneath the sand. Malcolm could see the dunes waiting in the distance. Eager to swallow the caravan once more and his feet grew heavy although his step did not falter.

He was not surprised when David shouldered between him and Khoja.

"You're leading us back into the dunes," David said.

"I know."

"That wasn't the plan. We're supposed to stay in the leeward side, that's what you said."

"Khoja told me to go this way."

"With all respect, Khoja brought his wife and daughter on a trek across the world's worst desert. His judgement leaves a lot to be desired."

Malcolm kept walking.

"Wolf is losing his mind back there," David said, "and he's got a point. The dunes will be bigger and built up against the base of the mountains." David gestured to the north. "Look. You can already see that's the case."

"He's right," Khoja said. "We should head north for the rest of the day and then turn east to avoid the worst."

"Or," David said, "we can angle south-east again and get back on track."

Malcolm kept to the bearing. "Perhaps you know better, David," he said. "Perhaps you've lived in this desert your entire life."

David's mouth shut with a snap. Then he turned and shoved past Khoja to head back to his place in the caravan. Malcolm stopped and watched him go and then shared a look with the old man. Neither spoke and after a moment Malcolm resumed the march.

Khoja beside him.

• • • • •

They walked north and then north-north-east for the rest of the day. Followed a narrow corridor amid dunes that swelled to hundreds of feet high. The next day they turned east. Three more days.

Late on the afternoon of the third day Khoja called for a halt.

"We can't stop here," Malcolm said.

"The Hotan River lies up ahead."

"I know. That's where we're going."

"Wait here. I'll call for you," Khoja said and stepped off before Malcolm could reply. In minutes he'd disappeared into the dunes to the east.

The caravan closed up and Gleb came to the front. "Why did we stop?"

"I'm waiting for the old man."

"Where did he go?"

"To scout the river. I think."

"He didn't tell you?"

"He told me to wait here."

"Not a bad idea," Gleb said and drank from his canteen. Swished the water around his mouth and then spat it onto the ground. "How much do you trust him?"

"You should go check on the camels."

"He reminds me of my dad. Little bit."

Malcolm glanced at the Russian. "In all the years I've known you, I've never heard you mention him."

"He was a soldier, a good one. Also a tyrant, a drunk, and a terrible gambler. It is because of him that I learned how to fight."

"So this is not a good thing."

Gleb snorted. "As I said, how much do you trust him?" The Russian turned and paused. "You've got visitors," he said and then tramped toward the rear of the caravan.

Malcolm turned to see Gul and Aziguli. A few feet behind him and he'd heard nothing. He nodded in greeting and then faced the east to watch for Khoja.

The women came to stand on either side. The sun beat on his neck and the wind rose and he caught a hint of fragrant lavender.

He thought of Amaelia. How she would cook shea butter and lye and almond oil and then would add lavender buds and green zeolite clay which she would send him to one of two stores to buy. He would joke that it would take a lot of home-made soap to save the environment and she would reply that one had to start somewhere. Then he'd find himself at the store with a list of ingredients he'd never heard of and couldn't find without help. And her hair would smell of lavender and cardamom. So too the soft skin behind her ears and at the base of her neck and on their pillows and their sheets and –

"There," Gul said.

He blinked. "Where?"

She pointed at a gap in the dunes where Khoja waved at them.

Malcolm turned and spied David in the first packet. He whistled and when he had caught David's attention, he gave a thumbs-up and then stepped off. Gul and Aziguli kept pace a few steps behind and he'd walked for a minute or so when Gul spoke again.

"You never answered the question," she said.

He stopped. "Excuse me?"

"How much you trust him." Gul walked past and did not even look at him.

"Enough," he said. "I trust him enough."

"That is not an answer."

"I traveled all this way here for him, didn't I?"

"No. You didn't."

"Then what did I come here for?"

"The same reason everyone comes to this desert."

"And what's that?"

"To run from truths they can't face."

• • • • • •

Malcolm stopped at the edge of a small escarpment and peered out over a depression several miles wide. Scrub and brush dotted a gentle downhill slope that ended at a thin growth of Euphrates poplars along the Hotan River.

A third of the way across the desert.

He stood straighter. Breathed deep and allowed himself to appreciate the break from the monotonous sand until movement caught his eye. He squinted and scanned the basin. On a small plateau on the far side of the river he spotted a caravan of ten or twelve camels.

He dropped to one knee. Held up a hand so the packets behind him would not crest the ridge and then pulled out his binoculars and glassed the valley. Khoja came into view. Waved from across the river and was joined by a man from the other caravan who embraced him with both arms. The men separated and Khoja waved again. Malcolm stood slowly and then raised his arm in response.

Khoja gave one last wave and then walked beside the other man toward the river's edge.

Malcolm continued to watch through the binoculars and did not lower them until David joined him on the ridge.

"Everything okay?" David asked.

"There's another caravan here."

"The surprises are getting old."

"Tell me about it," he said and began to lead the caravan toward the river. "Be ready for anything."

He joined Khoja and the other man at the river. The two spoke in Uighur and Malcolm waited to be acknowledged. When it became obvious he might wait the rest of the day, he cleared his throat.

Khoja frowned and made a show of folding his arms behind his back and then faced him.

"You want to tell me what's going on?" Malcolm asked.

Both men stared at him and then the stranger clapped Khoja on the back and departed in the direction of the foreign camel train. When the man was out of earshot Khoja squatted by the river and dipped a hand into the water. "This is our resupply," he said. "We will replenish our food and water and perhaps swap out a few camels, although we do not have much time." Khoja cupped a handful of water and poured it over his head.

"Who is this man?"

Khoja poured more water over his head.

"I asked you a question."

"And I did not answer."

"Can this man be trusted?"

"Do you have a choice?" Khoja stood and began to walk after the other man.

Malcolm grabbed Khoja by the shoulder and spun the old man to face him.

Khoja stood still. Glanced once at Malcolm's hand and then back at Malcolm as if he'd seen him for the first time.

"Tell me what's going on," Malcolm said.

"This man is an old friend," Khoja said. "He has helped my family and I survive in the desert and has agreed to help once more. At great risk to himself. The highway is a few miles to the east and while we can pose as tourists here for a few hours, we are far to the north of where the tour companies normally travel. We must be across the highway tonight."

It was not lost on Malcolm that while the old man talked, he'd reached up to cover Malcolm's hand with his own.

"Is that enough for you?" Khoja asked.

Malcolm stared into Khoja's eyes. Felt the tips of the old man's fingers alight on the pressure points that would allow him to turn Malcom's wrist and arm against him. Like being touched by a whiff of smoke. "For now," he said and let the old man go.

Khoja stared at him a second longer and then turned and walked up the bank.

The caravan arrived and Malcolm ordered the camels unloaded. They took food and water from the other caravan and swapped out five animals. Two had gone lame and not been able to carry a load the past few days. The others had raw sores on their backs and legs from chafing of the ropes and baggage frames. Wolf and Musa had about unloaded the last of these camels when Wolf began to gag. Let go of the baggage frame to shake tiny flecks of white from his hand. The frame slipped from the camel's back and crashed to the sand and pungent ammonia filled the air and on the length of the camel's bare hump wriggled thousands of maggots. They dropped from the animal's back in clumps and Wolf's face went scarlet and he cursed Musa and the Uighurs and had to be restrained by Gleb.

Too soon the sun began to set. They hurried their goodbyes and marched out of the valley. At the top of the eastern escarpment Malcolm all but stumbled over the G217 Highway. Sand obscured most of the road and not a single vehicle was in sight. He pushed on into the desert on the other side and by the time the moon rose, the mountains and Hotan river and the highway lay miles behind.

A dream already begun to fade into the sand.

• • • • • •

They headed east-south-east for three days. Through mountainous dunes and monotonous days that differed in degree by the sun's position in the sky and the burdens of daily routine.

On the fourth day Malcolm walked past an ancient and long-dead tree. Bone-white and devoid of branches. Malcolm slowed and the first packet closed up and the camels grunted and strained at the ropes that held them together and the sounds pushed him on. He tripped over the slipface of a dune and tumbled down the leeward slope and there in a wide depression bounded by sand on all sides were the remains of several buildings.

"Let us stop here for the day," Khoja said.

Malcolm could not recall hearing the old man approach. "It's only mid-afternoon," he said and in the shadows of the ruins the words felt heavy.

"It will do us good to have a few extra hours of rest."

The site was sheltered and the nearby sand crusted white. The first packet marched into the camp and the voices of the Uighurs rose and quickened. They pointed at the ruins with wide eyes even after Malcolm ordered them to set up for the night. He helped unload the camels and the Uighurs fumbled with the straps. Baggage tumbled to the sand and for once Wolf did not berate the handlers. When the animals were unloaded and hobbled Malcolm cut the team away. Within minutes, they'd scattered into the ruins and he was left alone. He double-checked the animals and then followed the voices into the ruins.

Nearest the camp were the outlines of four squarish buildings staked out by decayed wooden posts. Beyond these stood three additional buildings with still-intact walls of baked mud and brick. The Uighurs paced the perimeter of these buildings and would not enter. Malcolm poked his head into the largest of the buildings and found Gleb and Mary hunkered near a pile of pottery shards. Dried and brittle rattan divided the interior into rooms and Malcolm stooped to pick up a dried husk that might have been a shoe. He turned it over and brushed sand from the cracked leather. Then he set the shoe where he'd found it and walked deeper into the site.

A hundred yards past the buildings he came across Khoja. The old man stood beside a ten-foot tall tree trunk thicker than a man could encircle with his arms. The tree rose out of the sand in the middle of a squared space enclosed by a low wall and the far side of this courtyard ended at a building with a domed roof. Half-buried in a dune that climbed the building's rear wall like oversized prey stuck in the throat of a serpent.

Malcolm moved to Khoja's side. "What is this place?" he asked.

"A temple."

"A holy place."

"The remains of a Buddhist empire."

"How old is it?"

"Three thousand years. In the past there was a large oasis nearby."

"Where the Keriya River is on the map?" Malcolm asked.

"Perhaps, although I do not think so. We will reach it tomorrow and you can judge for yourself."

Voices came from behind and Malcolm turned to see Musa and several Uighurs at the edge of the wall. Their talk was fast and excited and they smiled and pointed at the temple and greeted Malcolm and then noticed Khoja. The old man had moved to the far side of the tree. When the Uighurs saw him, their faces grew serious and they became silent and disappeared back from where they'd come.

"Why do they avoid you?" Malcolm asked.

"They believe I betrayed them."

"But you led the uprising."

"They believe it made them worse off."

"Because it brought back the camps."

"The camps never closed. Nor did the curfews and the inspections and the disappearances stop."

"Then what changed?"

"They no longer had hope of escaping China's rule."

A sound from the domed building drew Malcolm's gaze and then Gul and Aziguli emerged from its interior. The women stared at him and then came to stand by Khoja.

"We have paid our respects," Khoja said and faced him.

"To the dead of this fallen empire?" Malcolm asked.

"Has not the lives of everyone who lived ended in death?" Khoja asked and then took Gul's hand and together they walked in the direction of the camp while Aziguli trailed behind.

Malcolm waited until he could no longer see them and then entered the temple.

• • • • •

The air inside the temple was cool. A ray of sunlight filtered through a hole in the high-vaulted ceiling and brightened a swept and tidied interior. There were pottery fragments on the floor and a finely woven basket stacked neatly in one corner and several engraved wooden tablets in another. Malcolm walked deeper into the building and stood before a faded mural on the rear wall. The sole thing of value not carried off in the pillaging the Swedish explorer Sven Hedin had begun in the late 19th Century.

In the middle of the mural sat a cross-legged man or woman in front of a spoked circle. The figure wore a robe and had dark hair pulled into a topknot and to its left stood a bare-chested warrior with a toga held loose in one hand and a club above its head in the other. Malcolm's gaze roamed the length of the mural and he felt the weight of bygone eras press in upon him. As if the creators of the mural reached across the ages with some message he did not understand.

A shadow fell across the mural and he started, looked over his shoulder to find Khoja's daughter Aziguli silhouetted in the temple's entrance. He watched her enter the temple and then turned to face the mural once more.

"What do you think it means?" he asked.

"Nothing," she said.

"It must have meant something."

"No longer."

"But it has survived."

"Its meaning has not. That died with those who created it. That is the message."

"I guess," he said. He stared at the mural a few seconds longer and then continued around the room. Knelt to pick up the remains of a clay jug and was not reminded of an ancient civilization that reached across time, but rather a pottery wheel in the basement of the last place he'd called home.

"Although I know some who would disagree with you," he said.

"Who?"

He picked out a pottery shard from the floor and held it in his hands. Closed his eyes and cradled his memories as he ran his fingers over the piece of clay. Felt it crumble to dust beneath his touch. Opened his eyes and placed the fragments on the floor. "Nobody," he said. "It doesn't matter."

He stood and headed for the temple's door.

"You will only make things worse," Aziguli said. She'd moved to stand before the mural.

He paused in the doorway.

"Rulers cannot allow themselves to be challenged," she said. "And the ruled must accept their place."

"I would not expect you of all people to hold such a view," he said.

"My education has been complete."

"And what of your culture? Your people?"

"What good are traditions with no home in which to practice them? They are like this temple. Empty. Meaningless."

"And what good is a home with no traditions? They are worth fighting for. That and our families."

"You are wrong," she said. "The only battle worth fighting is for the pain to stop."

He stared at her and then turned. Took a step out of the temple and then paused and looked back. "It is you who are wrong," he said. "The future is worth fighting for. Our families expect nothing less."

"Does yours?"

His mouth shut with a snap and then he turned and left her alone in the temple.

* * * * *

They did not find water that night and in the morning, Malcolm led them on.

After several hours, the dunes gave way to a rocky bluff that overlooked the Keriya River. Their steps grew light and they picked their way down into a small valley where they found a parched riverbed. Malcolm sent out a search party and had David sink two exploratory holes. Sand flew into the air at a frantic pace and the holes went deep and dry and empty.

As if water had been no more than a long-dead rumour in that place.

Hours later they gave up, continued up the other side of the river valley. Within a mile, they were once more lost among sand dunes hundreds of feet tall.

No water the next day.

Nor the next.

On the fourth day out from the ruins they uncovered a trickle of water. Six feet down in a hole that collapsed twice and buried an older Uighur named Kirim up to his neck. Malcolm dug a sump at the bottom of the hole into which Gleb placed a bucket and the water seeped over the lip. When the bucket was half full, Gleb handed it up to Khoja.

The old man cupped a handful and raised it to his lips. Tasted it and then spat it out and let the water he held fall to the sand. "Not even the camels can drink this," he said. He kicked over the bucket and then walked away while the water drained back into the hole.

Gleb knelt and placed his canteen in the sump and drank when it had filled. His face scrunched and he supressed a gag and then drank again.

"How is it?" Malcolm asked.

"I've drank worse."

"At least run it through a purifier."

"They are broken."

"They can't all be broken."

Gleb glanced at him and snorted.

"That was top of the line equipment," Malcolm said.

"They were not designed for the desert."

They brought over the camels and the animals grunted and fought and refused to drink. Two or three put their mouths in the bucket and lifted them out again with no more than their noses wet and so Malcolm reduced the water ration to one liter per day per person and shared the remaining portion with the animals.

The next day the dunes grew to four and five-hundred-feet high. The hind legs of the camels trembled as they plodded up crumbling hills and the handlers pulled constantly on the ropes to drag the beasts along. One camel knelt and it was half an hour before it moved and not until half its load had been redistributed.

In camp that night they found water beneath the sand and again it was too brackish for any except Gleb to stomach and even he gave up. They poured the meagre water they had into buckets and offered it to the camels. The animals grunted and shoved and knocked the handlers aside. When the camels kicked over the buckets, the Uighurs beat the animals with their sticks while the water drained into the sand.

Wolf launched into the mix of men and beast. Threw Musa to the ground and then the Uighurs turned on the Brit with their sticks. Gleb grabbed one of the Uighurs in a headlock and another by the back of the neck and then Malcolm stepped in.

"Get a hold of yourselves," he yelled and dragged Wolf out of the fray by the collar of his shirt. "Let them go," he said to Gleb. He waited for the Russian to release the men he held and then he glared at the group. "We have enough to worry about without fighting each other," he said.

Wolf snorted. "Not too quick on the uptake, are you? These animals start dying soon. Just like I told you." He shook himself out of Malcolm's grip and stuck a finger in his face and then frowned at Gleb. "What's wrong with you?"

Gleb stood hunched with both hands held to his stomach. Then his eyebrows rose and he ran toward the dunes in an awkward and bow-legged gait.

"Great," Wolf said. "The big, stupid fuck has the trots."

A groan came from Gleb's direction and Esa smiled.

"Don't laugh, it could be you," Wolf said and then shook his head. "Best get these animals taken care of as much as we can. Come on, lads."

In silence the Uighurs began to hobble the camels.

Malcolm pulled Wolf aside. "You really think the camels will start dying?"

"Look at them, mate."

"It hasn't been that long since we last found water."

"We're working the shit out of them every day. That means they have to drink more."

"All right."

"I tried to explain this to you."

"I said all right." Malcolm stood with his hands on his hips and stared around the disorganized camp and then met Khoja's gaze. The old man stared back from where he sat beside Gul and Aziguli. "How much farther can they go?" Malcolm asked.

Wolf held the halter of a camel so it could be hobbled. "Couple of days. Three maybe."

"Then we'd better hit water soon."

• • • • •

The next day the pace slowed. Malcolm's compass hung around his neck by its lanyard and bounced off his chest as he trudged along. The temperature soared into the mid-nineties despite it being late October and he counted the minutes and hours between sips from his canteen. He had stared so often at the now-faded picture of his family taped to his compass that at times he could imagine they walked beside him. He knew they were not there and yet if he closed his eyes, he could hear their footsteps beside him. The memories of their voices in his head.

A hand fell on his shoulder and he started. Tensed and twisted away from the grip and had to struggle to recognize Mary and not Amaelia.

"You all right?" Mary asked.

"Of course," he said. "What is it?"

"There's a break in the caravan."

"Where?"

"Last packet."

"What happened?"

"Not sure."

He called a halt. After thirty minutes the third packet had come no closer and he began the long trek to the last packet where he found Wolf on his back. The Brit's head rested on his cast-aside pack.

"What's the holdup?" Malcolm asked.

Wolf did not open his eyes. "Gleb," he said.

"Where is he?"

"Other side of that dune." Wolf waved to the north.

Malcolm took a step in the direction Wolf had pointed.

"Be careful not to get any on you, mate," Wolf said. "He's shat himself twice today already."

Malcolm paused but did not know what to say. He continued over the dune and on the far side he spied Gleb about halfway down. The Russian stood bent over and bowlegged. He held his pants below his waist and took a step and then groaned and dropped his pants and squatted. His face turned red and a vein bulged in the middle of his forehead.

Malcolm waited a few seconds and when Gleb showed no signs of standing he moved closer. "How you doing?" he asked.

Gleb mumbled a curse in Russian.

"Listen, big guy, you need to keep going. We're almost out of water."

"Fuck you," Gleb said and slurred the words.

"The highway's only a day or so ahead. We'll find water there."

Gleb spat. His saliva a long dribble that hung from his lips.

Malcolm watched the Russian struggle to wipe his mouth. "Never thought I'd see the day you quit," he said and then headed back toward the caravan.

"Where are you going?" the Russian called after him.

"We're moving on."

"Fuck you! I'm sick."

"Then you shouldn't have drank that water. Khoja told you it was bad."

"I'm sick!"

Malcolm stopped short of the dune's crest and looked back. "When I reach the front of the caravan, we're leaving," he said. "I hope you're with us."

He left Gleb there and walked back up the line. Wolf raised his head off the sand when he passed.

"What's the word?" the Brit asked.

"We're moving on."

"We're leaving him behind?"

"He'll come. He's got no other choice."

• • • • •

They reached the S165 Highway late in the afternoon of the next day.

The wind was at their backs and grey clouds had gathered in the west when Malcolm crested a dune and spotted a band of green in the distance. He dug out his binoculars and the line came into focus as two or three rows of trees and bushes on either side of the highway. Farther out from the road the ground had a grid-like appearance. As if squares had been drawn in the sand. He followed the pattern north and south along the highway and he was still studying the grid when Khoja appeared beside him.

Malcolm offered Khoja the binoculars. The old man took them, held them up and adjusted the focus wheel and slowly scanned north and south.

"Your friend is quite sick," Khoja said.

"He's been through worse."

"That does not change the seriousness of the situation."

"We'll figure it out."

"I hope so. There is nothing beyond this highway until we reach the end of the desert."

"I'm not leaving him here."

"He will slow us down," the old man said.

"I said I'm not leaving him here."

"And what of your mission?"

"That's for me to worry about."

Khoja handed back the binoculars and then pointed at a spot to the north.

Malcolm aimed the binoculars along the line of Khoja's finger and a service station filled the lenses. "That could solve a lot of problems," he said.

"If you accept the risk," Khoja said.

"Will there be water there?"

"Yes."

"Will there be enough?"

"Yes. There's an underground irrigation system for the vegetation along the highway. There will be a pumping station, probably in the back."

"What else do you think they'd have?"

"Basic goods in the store," the old man said.

"Fresh food?"

"Probably not. But there will be an attendant who lives onsite. They will have something."

"Medical supplies?"

"Possibly."

Malcolm considered his options as Khoja waited and then lowered the binoculars. "I think we'll risk it," he said.

"Are you sure?" Khoja asked.

"No," he said and shouldered his pack. "But I don't see what else we can do."

Khoja nodded.

Malcolm took a few steps and then glanced over his shoulder. "I meant to ask," he said, "what's that grid on the sand?"

"Hay."

"Hay?"

"Hay stalks to be exact."

"What does it do?"

"Stabilizes the sand."

"How far does it go?"

"The entire length of the highway."

"All 400 miles?"

"Yes."

Malcolm turned to stare once more at the highway. "That must have taken an incredible amount of work," he said.

"Great things can be accomplished when individual parts are subordinated to the whole," Khoja said and then turned away and began to walk.

• • • • •

Malcolm led the caravan toward a blue shed the size of a large shipping container near the back of the gas station. There were two other buildings on site, a long, squat structure covered with metal siding, and a building with a large billboard on the roof which Malcolm took to be the store. The blue shed at the back of the site had a red roof and two darkened windows and the doors were locked. From within came the muffled chunks and clanks of a motor. He figured it must be the water pumping station. While the caravan gathered into the open space at the back of the gas station, he walked around the building and discovered a water faucet on the far side with a hose attached.

He had David tap the water supply while the others hobbled the camels and then began to unload buckets and the empty water jerry cans. A man in a bright yellow shirt and blue pants exited the rear of the store. The man stood and watched as they filled buckets and the camels pushed and shoved and guzzled water and then disappeared back into the building.

Mary looked up with a bucket of water in each hand and glanced at the building where the man had appeared and then at Malcolm.

"I'll take care of it," he said.

He left David and Mary to oversee the resupply and made his way to the front entrance of the gas station's store. As he walked past the squat building with metal siding, a woman emerged and stood in the door with a bundle clutched to her chest. He paused and they stared at each other and then the cry of a baby pierced the silence. The woman shifted the bundle to her hip and re-entered the building and closed the door. Malcolm stood for a few seconds longer and then the wind picked up and the sand began to blow and he kept going toward the gas station's store.

The gas islands at the front of the gas station were sheltered by a massive red canopy emblazoned with the PetroChina logo. There were no vehicles and the pumps appeared deserted. He spotted Aziguli beside one of the pillars that held up the canopy. Her back was to him and her robes and hair billowed and whipped in the wind.

He glanced at the store and then went to Aziguli. Stood beside her and stared out at the highway and the trees and vegetation that lined the road and thought of how Amaelia would have been impressed that anything could be brought to grow in the harsh terrain.

"My father says there is an underground ocean beneath the desert," Aziguli said.

"That's where the pumping stations get the water."

"*Shì.*"

"Hard to believe."

"Except the trees survive and hold back the desert."

"Must have taken a lot of work."

"You cannot imagine."

The wind gusted and carried a lock of her hair into his face. He closed his eyes and brushed the strands aside and thought of countless times Amaelia's hair had slipped between his fingers. Then he opened his eyes onto the dust covered trees and the sand dunes beyond. "I once heard we already have solutions to most of our problems," he said. "What we lack is the will to put them in place."

"Who told you that?"

"My wife."

"Where is she now?"

"Dead."

"I'm sorry."

"Me too," he said. "Me too."

A cabover truck pulling a trailer full of scrap metal limped down the highway from the north. He watched the truck and then turned and headed for the building with the billboard.

"Where are you going?" she asked.

"To pay for what we take."

"They will not have a price for it."

"I find that hard to believe."

"That does not make it any less true."

"Then I'll give what I think is enough."

"There is only one thing they'll accept, and it's not in your power to give."

"And what's that?"

"Their lives."

He frowned. "They have nothing to fear from us," he said.

"That's not what they think. They think we're going to kill them."

"Why would they think that?"

"Because they've been dead since the minute we stopped here."

• • • • •

Malcolm found Khoja already inside the store.

The old man wandered among rows of dried noodles and Pocky and White Rabbit candy and bags of Pringles and Lay's chips. Malcolm stood across a shelf from him and watched him take and then open a bag of roasted green peas.

"Found everything you were looking for?" Malcolm asked.

Khoja selected an orange-colored pea from the bag and popped it into his mouth.

Malcolm glanced at the counter. The man in the yellow shirt and blue pants had put on a red hat and waited in front of a shelf of cigarettes. Hands folded at his waist. His gaze was downcast and averted and yet Malcolm guessed the man watched everything through his peripheral vision, like some hunted animal alerted by a predator in its midst.

Khoja ate another roasted pea and strolled toward the counter and Malcolm kept pace on the other side of the shelf.

"I won't let you do this," Malcolm said.

"You have no choice in the matter," the old man said.

"If you think this will cover our trail, it won't."

"Do all Americans feel the need to lecture on that which they know nothing about?"

"You're going to draw attention to us."

"Do not be naïve."

"This will get out of control," Malcolm said. "And once you start –"

The door to the building opened and Malcolm glanced behind to see Mary.

"Boss, we have a problem," she said.

"I know," he said.

"I don't think you do," she said. "There's a truck driver out there who's seen the camels."

"That's okay," Malcolm said and looked back at Khoja. "We're all going to go our respective ways. Aren't we?"

Khoja stepped up to the counter and set down the half-empty bag of roasted peas. "You said you would accept the risk of stopping here," he said. "What did you think I meant?"

"It's my risk to assume. Not yours."

The attendant reached across the counter for the bag of peas and Khoja grabbed the man's hand. Held it tight and watched the man squirm and his face go pale.

"Let him go," Malcolm said.

The old man did not move and the attendant continued to struggle.

Malcolm reached for Khoja's wrist and as he did the old man drove his free hand into Malcolm's gut. He gasped and grasped for Khoja's arm except the old man's hand had already gone to Malcolm's belt and stripped him of his knife.

"Boss?" Mary asked.

Malcolm shook his head and Khoja leaned close.

"I wonder if you're as ready to die as you think you are," the old man said and then the blade flashed and a thin red line appeared across the attendant's neck as if drawn by felt marker. The man stood with his mouth agape as the cut parted in a trickle of blood. The trickle grew and blood spurted onto the counter and then the man gagged and clutched his throat and collapsed to the floor.

Malcolm turned his face as the attendant's legs spasmed and his feet kicked against the counter. Squeezed his eyes shut like he could drown out the sounds and then the main door creaked open and he looked up to see a bald and portly middle-aged man in a white t-shirt enter and stand behind Mary.

He lunged for Khoja.

Except the old man had already sent the knife toward its target.

The blade tumbled end-over-end and light glinted off the metal. Through the air and over Mary's shoulder to embed in the truck driver's neck with a wet thunk. The man gurgled and took a step backward. Clutched the hilt of the knife newly sprouted from his throat and slumped against the door and slid to the ground.

Khoja turned from the counter and Malcolm grabbed the old man by the shoulder. He began to yell at the old man and then pain rocketed through his wrist and up his arm and drove him to his knees.

The old man stood over him and wrenched his arm tighter. "I suggest you reflect on what sacrifices you're prepared to make," Khoja said and twisted Malcolm's wrist even farther. "And once you have done that, resolve your heart to follow through."

Malcolm gasped at the pain. Put his forehead on the floor and when it seemed like the old man would rend his arm from his body he was instead released.

"It is not the knowing that is difficult, but the doing," Khoja said and then walked out.

Mary rushed to Malcolm's side and helped him to his knees. "You okay, boss?" she asked.

He shook his head and glanced over to where the truck driver lay on the floor. A puddle of blood already pooled on the floor beneath the body.

"We have to go," he said.

•   •   •   •   •

The camels had all been watered, the jerry cans filled and all but reloaded when Malcolm and Mary hurried around the back of the gas station. Gleb and David stood apart from the animals and Malcolm was near on top of them before David looked up and smiled.

"Can you believe Gleb actually found a bottle of cipro?" David asked and then saw Malcolm's face and his smile disappeared. "What's wrong?"

"We're leaving," Malcolm said. "Right now."

"Got it," David said and whistled for the attention of the Uighurs. The handlers looked up and David circled a finger in the air and turned to walk away and then glanced at Mary. "What happened?" he asked.

Mary shook her head.

"Where's Khoja?" Malcolm asked.

"I thought he was with you," David said.

"I sent him to check the store for drugs," Gleb said and tapped several pills out of a bottle and into his mouth. Washed the pills down with a swig from his canteen and grimaced. "The old fool never came back," he said.

"Yeah, well, I wouldn't hold your hand over your ass waiting," Mary said and headed toward the lead packet of camels.

"What are you talking about?" David asked and then turned to Malcolm. "What happened?"

"How long before we can leave?" Malcolm asked.

"Wolf's loading the last packet now," David said. "The first two can go any time."

"Then let's go."

"What about that truck driver?"

Malcolm stopped and met David's gaze. "He's dead," he said.

"What?"

"Khoja killed him. The gas station attendant too."

"Holy shit."

"So, now we have problem," Gleb said.

"We will if we don't get moving," Malcolm said.

"We'll be out of here in ten," David said and ran off toward Wolf. Gleb moved to follow.

"Gleb," Malcolm said.

"*Da?*"

"You said Khoja never came back."

"*Da.*"

"Where did you get the drugs?"

"The old woman."

"And where did *she* get them?" Malcolm asked.

Gleb shrugged.

"Where did she get them?"

Gleb nodded across the courtyard. "Why don't you ask her?"

Malcolm peered over his shoulder to the building where he'd seen the woman with the baby. Saw Gul Dilmurat exit the building and close the door and take two steps and then stop. He stared at her and she returned his gaze and then she strode toward the caravan. Moved to walk past him and he grabbed her by the elbow.

"Are they dead?" he asked. The wind gusted and blew sand into his face and his eyes watered.

Gul's face did not change.

"Deny it," he said.

"I will not."

"A mother and her child," he said and his eyes narrowed.

"I do not have to explain myself to you," she said and pushed past.

He clung to her elbow and she whirled and raised her hand to strike him and then her gaze flickered over his shoulder and she hesitated. He turned and saw Khoja watching them from under the canopy that sheltered the gas pumps. Aziguli beside him and his hand on her shoulder.

"Do not talk to me about the pain of women and children," Gul said and threw off his hand. "I know more about this than you could understand in a lifetime."

He let her go. Watched her walk away and then glanced back to find that Khoja and Aziguli had disappeared.

* * * * *

Malcolm stood among the trees on the far side of the highway and watched the last of the camels cross the road. He waited until the animals had disappeared through the thin line of brush and then peered back at the gas station and the abandoned truck and the dunes built up on the horizon where dark clouds had gathered. He took out his compass and could not look at it and did not turn when footsteps sounded in the sand behind him.

"The storm will soon be upon us," Aziguli said.

"I know," he said.

She waited in silence and her hair blew in the wind. Drifted into his face and smelled of lavender and the last thing he wanted to think of was his dead wife. "You should go," he said.

"The world moves forward," she said. "We either submit or are overrun."

He thought about that. "To what end?" he asked.

"The only one that matters. To be worthy of our responsibilities."

He inhaled deeply and the hot desert wind burnt in his nose. "I should not have come here," he said. "This place is a wasteland."

"You are wrong."

"I am not," he said. "The desert will consume all of this. The wind and the sand will take us away and we'll never come out and maybe that's for the best."

"Here is potential."

He snorted. "What do you know, anyways?" he asked.

She reached out and cupped his chin. Guided his face so he looked at her and then spoke. "I know that the bamboo stands upright amid the mountains steep," she said. "And that the wind that scours this desert is the same one that helps boats skim the waves of the oceans."

He stared into her eyes and felt the heat of her fingers on his face and then she released him. Headed in the direction of the caravan and then stopped and glanced back.

"The wind is picking up," she said. "In an hour, you won't be able to find our tracks." She held his gaze a second longer and then passed between the trees.

He watched after her and then turned and looked out over the way he'd travelled. Breathed deep of the desert air and stared at the gas station and then scanned up and down the highway with the trees that had defeated the desert. Last of all he looked at the compass in his hand and the picture taped to the cover. He brushed Amaelia's face with the back of a finger and then tucked the compass into his shirt and marched into the desert to the east.

THREE

18 DECEMBER 2029

Geneeral Fan Qiliang snapped his fingers and pointed at the cell door. "Open it."

The guard outside the cell hesitated. "The Chairman –"

"Open the door." Spit sprayed from General Fan's mouth and his voice rang in the corridor.

The guard flinched and fumbled with the door and barely had it open when Fan barged past to stand inside the doorway. The heads of both the Chairman and the assassin swiveled to stare at him. General Fan thrust out his chin and clasped his hands behind his back.

"Well, General?" Chairman Zhao asked. "What is it?"

"*Lingdao*, you must stop this interrogation."

"I have not finished."

"It has not even begun. All this man has done is lie."

Zhao turned to study the assassin.

"At this point, we must consider who gains the most from this lengthy session," Fan said.

"Continue," Zhao said.

General Fan entered and stood at Zhao's right hand. "We have already determined he is an American. This was therefore an American operation. They would not be so foolish as to launch an attack like this without coordinated follow-on action. Even now, they are almost certainly exploiting the confusion they have caused."

A slight crease appeared between Zhao's eyebrows. "This is not new."

"Except that all this coward has done is add to the confusion, which is now his goal." Fan stalked closer to the assassin. "*Lingdao*, this man's mission to kill you failed, thankfully. However, he can continue to damage our country by keeping you here, feeding you misinformation. The country and the Party need its leader to provide stability. You cannot do that from this room."

"I'm the best judge of where I should be."

"Then consider that this man has so little respect for us that he feeds us lies that are easily disproven." Fan backhanded the assassin across the face and the crack of flesh on flesh echoed loud in the room. "What fool would infiltrate China by crossing the Taklamakan?" He slapped the assassin again.

"General."

Fan froze with his hand in mid-air.

"I can't think with that noise."

. . . . .

Chairman Zhao Guoqiang tapped a finger on the table and studied the assassin. The cut over the man's right eye had reopened and a fresh trail of blood trickled down his cheek. The assassin had made no move throughout the General's beating and he continued to sit in the same position now. Silent.

General Fan paced near the assassin's chair. Clasped his hands behind his back and then across his chest and looked at the door and then at the assassin and then at the floor.

"Control yourself, General," Zhao said.

General Fan halted beside the assassin and faced Zhao. "It is you who must control yourself. Had you not undertaken this reckless attack on the Americans, we would not be in this situation."

Zhao grew still and shifted his gaze to the general.

He did not like what he saw.

General Fan swallowed. "Forgive me, *Lingdao*, but had we continued to follow Chairman Deng's basic policy, hidden our capabilities and bided our time, the Americans would have done our work for us. As the Russians collapsed before them."

"This is not the time, General."

"They had over-extended and were in the process of failing." Fan threw up his hands. "All we had to do was wait. Continue to build our strength and then take their place. And we would have been saviors, as we were during their debt crisis. We could have rebuilt the global system and they would have thanked us."

"Enough."

"Vice-Premier Jiang was correct, and now you continue to worsen your mistake. We had time –"

Zhao sprang to his feet and slammed the table with both hands. "What time do you think we had?" His chair clattered backward to the floor and his voice rang in the enclosed space of the cell. He held Fan with his gaze and let the echoes die and then stood tall and straightened his suit jacket. "Had we waited for events to take their natural course, we would have watched our best opportunity to recreate *tianxia* disappear. A unified world of order and tranquility among all humankind, that is my vision. Not this petty competition for advantage between states that currently defines our international relationships and prevents us from achieving *taiping shengshi*. Global peace and prosperity, General, that is something Chairman Deng did not foresee. Could not have foreseen."

"Do you really believe that?" the assassin asked.

"Be quiet," Fan roared and backhanded the man across the face.

"That is enough, General Fan," Zhao said. "Control yourself."

Fan stood over the assassin and seemed about to hit him again when he turned to face Zhao. "With respect, *Lingdao*, your rash actions have jeopardized our position of strength."

"General, what you and most of your peers fail to realize is that you have become comfortable in Chairman Deng's defensive mindset. You have forgotten that only offense can deliver victory. This is why your precious PLA must always be subordinate to the Party. The affairs of state are beyond you."

General Fan's face reddened. "*Lingdao* –"

"Silence," Zhao said. "Your lack of awareness and control dishonors you, as well as the uniform you wear."

Fan's mouth snapped shut.

"Worse still, you know nothing about what you speak. Go amuse yourself with your tanks or your mistress and leave the business of governing to your betters." Zhao picked up his chair and resumed his seat across from the assassin and then glanced once more at Fan. "Have you grown deaf, General? You are dismissed."

"Then you shall have to relieve me of my duties as well."

"General Fan, do not be so arrogant as to think that you have been met with no warm reception. In your case, it is the opposite, and while your incompetence has been useful in other ways, those days are numbered."

The general breathed deep and slow. "If you won't listen to me, then at least consider those who've died at this man's hand." Fan walked to the door of the cell. Paused and spoke over his shoulder. "Vice-Premier Jiang mentored you and now lies dead. As does Premier Ling. You speak of dishonor, and yet you disgrace their service by ignoring your responsibilities."

"You are relieved, General Fan."

Fan bowed his head. "As you command, *Lingdao*. I will leave you here with your foolish conceit and go to the War Council to inform General Chen he will act in my stead until a successor is chosen."

"See that you do."

"And I will request that Secretary Wang talk some sense into you."

"Wang Qiao is not in control."

"Then who is?" General Fan asked and stalked out of the cell.

• • • • • •

The door shut behind General Fan with a heavy thud.

He stood in the hallway and a vein throbbed at his temple. He closed his eyes and inhaled deep through his nose and then removed his glasses and wiped away a fleck of spittle from one of the lenses. Ignored how the guards avoided looking at him and resettled the glasses on his nose and then gestured for his aide.

"What did he say, General?" asked Secretary Wang's lackey, Cai Chunhua.

Fan did not dignify the question with a response and instead spoke to his own aide.

"Stay here and oversee the situation until I return." He glanced at the guard posted outside the interrogation cell. "Do not open that door until I come back," he said. "Nobody goes in. Or out."

The guard's eyes flickered to the side and his mouth half opened.

The vein in General Fan's head throbbed again and he ground his teeth and stalked toward the guard until their chests almost touched. "I repeat, do not open that door for anyone but me. You will repeat the order and acknowledge that you have understood."

"General." The voice came from behind Fan.

"What?" Fan asked and continued to glare at the guard.

"General, you have been relieved of your duties."

Fan stared at the guard a few seconds longer and then slowly turned. The lieutenant-colonel in command of the guard detachment stood alone in the middle of the hall.

"General Fan, please step away from the cell," the lieutenant-colonel said.

Fan stared at the guard commander and then scanned the faces of the other soldiers in the corridor. Peered at the guard by the interrogation cell and noticed the man returned his gaze but would not look at the lieutenant-colonel. Fan resettled his glasses once more and then strode to stand in front of the guard commander.

The man shifted from foot to foot. "General," he said, "the Chairman –"

"You there," Fan said and pointed at a soldier standing by the wall of the corridor. When the guard looked at him, Fan nodded at the lieutenant-colonel. "Arrest this man."

The soldier glanced at the guard commander and did not move.

"General –" the lieutenant-colonel began.

"I said, arrest this man," Fan yelled.

The soldier still did not move.

The aide, Cai, spoke. "Soldier, I speak with the authority of Secretary Wang," he said. "The General gave an order. You will obey."

The soldier glanced at Cai and then stepped away from the wall to wrestle the lieutenant-colonel's arms behind his back. When the man was secured, the soldier paused and looked to General Fan for more guidance.

"Put him in one of the other holding cells," Cai said.

The soldier led away the guard commander and General Fan grunted.

"Very good," he said and then turned to his aide-de-camp. "Stay here. See to it that my orders are followed. Chairman Zhao has lost his mandate."

"General." His aide-de-camp bowed his head. "Where will you go?"

"To find Secretary Wang," he said. "He is the only one to show common sense in this debacle and he will understand what to do." He nodded at Wang's man, Cai, and the two of them headed down the corridor.

"And what will happen to you, General?" his aide-de-camp called out after him.

General Fan paused. "What happens to me is not relevant," he said and then straightened his tunic and kept walking. "All that matters now is that the People's Liberation Army is ready to execute the will of the people. Trying times lie ahead. We must not be afraid of sacrifice."

·   ·   ·   ·   ·

Back in the holding cell, Chairman Zhao Guoqiang drummed his fingers on the table. He thought about what General Fan had said. It was not the first time he'd heard those accusations. He'd considered them from time-to time himself, yet his conclusion was always the same. His strategy was the right one. Indeed, it was the singular strategy with any chance of success, although it grew tiresome that even his own officials did not understand his intentions. He stilled his restless hands and frowned at his own lack of control and then pushed back from the table and rose to his feet.

"Have we finished?" the assassin asked.

Zhao's gaze flickered to the man. He sat as before with hands clasped in their manacles and his face downcast. The one change was that the fresh blood on the assassin's cheek had begun to dry.

"The General may have his faults," the assassin said, "but passion can surely not be one of them. He seems like a man who will do what he thinks is right."

"I do not need your advice," Zhao said.

"My apologies." The assassin dipped his head. "I did not mean to be familiar."

Zhao studied the assassin a second longer and then turned to walk out of the cell.

"Khoja told me that a battle is like a dance," the assassin said. "Events naturally happen that knock an artist off-balance. The difference that marks a student from a master is knowing how to reset."

Zhao paused. "A wise statement," he said and looked over his shoulder. "And because of that, I believe he most likely said it. Only a Chinese warrior would have this wisdom." He walked back to the table and pulled out the chair and sat down. Then he clasped his hands together in a mirror image of the assassin and glared at the man who'd come to kill him. "You cannot stop China from reclaiming its rightful status."

"I understand."

"Do you?"

The assassin lifted his head and met Zhao's gaze.

"America has never recognized China as its equal, much less its better," Zhao said. His voice grew sharp and his frown deepened at his continued lack of control and the whole time the assassin did not move and Zhao became aware that this angered him further. "But you will learn. America is as a comet in the night sky. Burning fast and drawing attention while it can be seen, but gone as quick as it appeared. China is as the North Star, and when the comet has gone, the rest of the heavens will remember their positions."

The assassin did not avert his gaze and Zhao saw a spark of defiance. The room fell silent and the two dueled without words or actions and at long last the assassin looked down.

Zhao allowed himself to glance at the wall behind the assassin. He let his gaze pass over the curved MicroLED screen that displayed timelines and backgrounders and locations from the assassin's story, personal information as it became known. Everything controlled and updated and fact checked by analysts in an adjacent room.

"You will continue," Zhao said.

The assassin bowed his head.

FOUR
NOVEMBER 2029

MALCOLM'S STORY, CONTINUED

They continued due east after they left the gas station. Trekked for two hours until the sun went down and then set up camp in the pitch-black. They were back on the move before first light the next day.

A week passed.

They trudged over the dunes and baked beneath the sun and watched their supplies dwindle. Night after night they dug for water. More often than not the holes were dry. Their faces grew skeletal. They became so silent that the sound of human voices was almost as rare as water and the map showed another hundred and fifty miles of barren expanse until the eastern edge of the desert.

Two weeks at their current pace.

On the morning of the tenth day out from the gas station they awoke to ice in the jerry cans.

"You're fucking kidding me," Wolf said. He stuck a cigarette in his mouth and stomped on the plastic jerry can and it cracked up one side and water and ice trickled out onto the sand.

David scrambled to save the remaining water and Gleb pulled Wolf aside.

"Get your fucking hands off me," Wolf said. He pushed the Russian away and flicked his cigarette at him.

"Go tear up your teddy bear somewhere else," David said.

"Shut it," Wolf said. He took a step toward David and then Gleb placed a large, meaty hand on the Brit's chest. They glared at each other and then Wolf sneered and walked off.

Malcolm stood to one side. Watched Wolf leave and then shared a look with Mary.

"Starting to have your hands full with that one," she said.

"Today I'm more concerned about *that*," he said and nodded at the thin line of dark clouds marshalled on the western horizon.

"Think we should stay put for the day?" she asked.

"Probably," he said. He considered what that meant and then shook his head. "But we can't afford to lose another day."

· · · · ·

The storm harried them throughout the day.

In the early afternoon Malcolm dropped back to curse and coax and coddle the lead packet up a five-hundred-foot-tall dune. The legs of the camels shook and one animal sank to its knees and wouldn't get up and it occurred to him the animal might have the right idea. He pushed the thought aside and yanked on the lead rope again and this time the packet began to move.

At the crest of the hill he stopped to catch his breath. The wind whipped his shirt and he had to shield his eyes from the sand to see out across a two-mile wide valley to the east. On the far side of the valley rose another ridge as high as the one where he stood. Higher. He leaned on the lead camel and dropped his gaze into the valley and saw a narrow band of trees some half-a-mile long wedged north-to-south among the low-lying dunes.

"Water," he said.

He hauled the lead packet over the dune's slipface and down its leeward slope. The two Uighur handlers in the lead packet crested the ridge and must have seen the trees as well because they began to shout and then one began to sing. The camels strained at the ropes and halfway down the dune they began to drag Malcolm along. He shouted and dug in his heels and the camels tossed their heads and spat and fought him the rest of the way down the hill.

He called a halt at the edge of the trees and told the Uighurs and David to unload and picket the camels. It was early afternoon and they had hours left in which to march and yet the sun had become hazy and faint behind a cloud of dust and the wind blew strong even in the shelter of the valley. Under the darkening sky he walked around the valley's basin and thought it would hold the entire caravan.

His route brought him into the grove of trees and he sought out the white crusted sand that would herald water. Noticed most of the trunks were bleached white and stripped of bark. What branches the trees had were jagged and dry as talons and clawed into the sky. Long dead stumps poked out of the sand with rounded tops like fingers and when he kicked one it was hard as rock. Harder. The hair on his forearms stood up and tingled and he returned to the lead packet and looked for the rest of the caravan.

The second group stretched across the flat ground near the base of the dune. Khoja and Mary held the lead camels tight by their halters and Gleb struggled with a camel at the rear. Malcolm pulled out his binoculars and scanned the top of the dune. Saw Aziguli and Gul appear and then watched the lead camel of the third packet crest behind them.

The camel tossed its head and fought its Uighur handler whose yells were lost to the wind. The other camels bucked and dragged their handlers over the crest. Wolf fought with an animal in the middle of the packet whose load hung from its side. He seemed to regain control and then the handler in front tripped and lost his grip and fell on his face. The first and second camels broke away and then one near the end as well. Then Wolf fell beneath the camels and the animals began to barrel down the dune's leeward slope.

Toward the two women who walked in front.

Malcolm shouted and waved his arms and could do nothing as the camels broke into line abreast. Gul's head turned and then Aziguli's. The women froze and then Gul pushed Aziguli to one side and followed close behind. Plowed across the hillside until the wave of sand that rolled ahead of the camels engulfed them and then they disappeared under the hooves of the stampeding packet. The camels ran on and halfway down the dune an animal in the middle tripped and plowed into the sand. The other animals pulled up short and then another one fell and the packet collapsed in an avalanche of tangled hooves and necks and baggage.

• • • • •

Malcolm found Aziguli on her knees beside Gul. She held her mother's hand and wiped hair and sweat from her forehead. He knelt on Gul's other side and then Mary was there. She pushed him out of the way and tossed a briefcase-sized nylon pouch onto the sand near Gul's head.

"Where is she hurt?" Mary asked.

"She can't breathe," Aziguli said.

Malcolm stood behind Mary. Watched over her shoulder while she leaned over Gul.

"Gul?" Mary asked. "Can you tell me where it hurts?"

Gul winced and grunted and gasped in a series of short and ragged breaths.

Mary put a hand on either side of Gul's face and peered into the woman's eyes and then walked her hands down Gul's shoulders. Stopped at Gul's chest. Tilted her head to one side and then placed her fingertips over Gul's heart and prodded.

Gul screamed.

"You're hurting her," Aziguli said and swatted Mary's hand.

"We need to know how bad she's hurt," Mary said.

Another person ran up and then Khoja knelt at Gul's feet. "How bad is it?" he asked.

Malcolm turned to him. "We're not –"

"It's flail chest," Mary said.

"Are you sure?" Malcolm asked.

"Yes. See how the left side of the chest sinks when she inhales? I need to roll her over."

"Won't that make it worse?"

"I have to stabilize the chest until I can get something on it. Moving her onto her side is the best I can do."

"Do it," Khoja said and moved beside Mary.

"Put your hands here," Mary said. "And here. Very slowly on the count of three."

"How can I help?" Malcolm asked.

"Get me a pillow or a jacket. And a tent fly. And shut that camel up. Ready?"

Malcolm looked toward the valley floor. Halfway down the dune a camel thrashed on its side. Wailed and frothed at the mouth and tried to stand on a leg snapped below the knee. Wolf held the camel's lead rope and fought to hold it still while Musa worked to cut loose its baggage frame.

Malcolm headed down the dune. "Wolf!" he called. "Bring up a tent fly."

"Not him," Aziguli said.

Malcolm glanced over his shoulder.

"Not him," Aziguli said. Her top lip pulled back so her teeth were bared.

The old man put a hand on Aziguli's shoulder. Shared a look with her and then looked down the hill. When he saw Wolf, his face hardened and he shifted his weight as if to stand.

"I need you to focus," Mary said. "On the count of three. One."

Khoja's gaze shifted to Malcolm and Malcolm shook his head.

"Two."

The old man's lips tightened and then he settled back into the sand.

"Three. Now."

Gul's scream pierced the air.

Malcolm grabbed two of the Uighurs. Had them strip a jacket from one of the bags and locate a tent and take everything to Mary. Malcolm yelled at David to get the camp set up and received a thumbs up in return. He saw that Gleb had rounded up most of the camels and also that the wind blew ever-lengthening trails of sand over the ridges around the valley to make a brownish haze that threatened to block out the angry sky above.

He rushed back to Mary and stood ready to help as she directed the Uighurs to unroll the tent fly. Poles were slotted along the edges of the fly and it was placed beside Gul. Mary positioned one of the Uighurs at

Gul's hips and the other at her chest and Khoja at her legs. When everyone was in place Mary moved to cradle Gul's head.

"Ready?" Mary asked and received wide-eyed nods in return. "Now."

Gul screamed again. Convulsed into the fetal position and Khoja held her legs and then she went limp and silent. Mary secured the fly around Gul's body and had the Uighurs pick up the front corners and then led the litter down the hill. Khoja and Aziguli held hands and trailed behind. Chased by the sand and the wind and the echo of Gul's scream.

The procession passed Wolf and the wounded camel and Khoja stopped. He seemed about to talk and then Malcolm shouldered between him and Wolf. The old man stood for a second longer and did not look up and then he and Aziguli continued down the hill.

Malcolm watched them go. "What happened?" he asked.

"Nothing," Wolf said.

"Nothing?"

"I got carried away, mate. That's all it was," he said. "And if I were you, I'd worry about the crocs closest to the boat."

Malcolm cleared his throat and glanced at the camel. "Can it be saved?" he asked although he already knew the answer.

"No."

Malcolm knelt beside the injured camel. Did not let his gaze linger on the white spurs of bone that jutted from its leg. He stroked the animal between its ears while its eyes rolled back in its head and streams of thick spit dangled from its mouth.

"This changes things," Wolf said. "We'll be lucky to ride out the storm, never mind the next few days."

"You let me worry about that," Malcolm said and freed his knife from its sheathe. He held the blade against his leg where the camel couldn't see it. Cooed and made soft sounds and thanked the animal for its service. He shifted so the animal could not kick him and then pushed the camel's head into the ground. The animal strained and grunted and its hind legs flailed and then Malcolm dragged the knife across its throat. Hot blood gushed onto his leg and he sat and waited while the camel's life bled out into the thirsty sand.

The wind chased them down the slopes. They reached the valley floor and placed Gul inside a tent with Mary and Khoja. Malcolm set David to boil water and then the sky disappeared into a yellowish haze and drove them all to retreat into what shelters they had put up. Aziguli sat outside the tent that held her mother and would not leave and Malcolm threatened to carry her. She yelled and pushed him away and Khoja poked his head out of the tent and whatever he said was carried off from all except Aziguli. Her face grew still and then she nodded and allowed herself to go with Malcolm.

The storm blew the rest of the day and into the night.

Malcolm and David sat with Aziguli and the sides of the tent snapped in the wind. Around midnight the door unzipped and Mary and Khoja jammed their way inside. They all sat cross-legged on the floor and their knees touched. Their faces haggard and worn in the light of their headlamps.

"How is she?" Malcolm asked.

"All right," Mary said. "For now."

"Who's with her?"

"Musa."

"One of us can go," Malcolm said and nodded at David. "Or Gleb –"

"No," Mary said. "I'll be going back soon."

"As will I," Khoja said. "But first we must talk."

Mary looked at Malcolm. "She needs medical attention."

"How badly?" he asked.

"She'll die if she stays out here."

Aziguli's breath caught and Khoja reached out to squeeze her knee.

"How much time do we have?" Malcolm asked.

"Depends on the internal bleeding," Mary said. "She's strong, though, so maybe half a week. I hope I'm in half as good shape at her age."

"Where does that leave us?" David asked.

"Qiemo is due south," Malcolm said. "Two, maybe three days pulling a litter."

"We can split up," David said. "Send a team to drop off Gul, they resupply and meet us back here."

"We cannot stay in this location," Khoja said.

"Why not?"

"There is no water."

David frowned. "We're camped beside a forest. There has to be water."

"There is not," Khoja said and his gaze shifted to Malcolm.

Malcolm thought of the dead and petrified trees and had a feeling Khoja was right.

"You can't know that," David said. "Besides, it's only a few days. We have enough water to last that long and by then the packet will be back with a resupply."

"If they come back," Malcolm said.

"Correct," Khoja said.

"Then we all go," David said. "We all go and we figure out transport in Qiemo."

"Qiemo Town is small and there are many Chinese," Khoja said. "A caravan this size will not go unnoticed."

David snorted. "So, like I said, where does that leave us?"

"Let me think," Malcolm said and he rested his chin on his hands and stared down at the floor of the tent.

"Do you hear that?" Khoja said.

"Yes," Malcolm replied.

"Hear what?" David asked and cocked his head to one side. "It's all quiet."

"That's his point," Malcolm said. "The wind has died down."

"I'll take that as my cue," Mary said and unzipped the door. "Come on, Aziguli. Let's go see your mother."

Mary crawled out into the blackness and Aziguli followed and frigid air flowed into the tent until Malcolm closed the tent flap.

"Cold out there," David said.

"It'll get colder," Malcolm said and sat down once more. He folded his hands in his lap and cleared his throat and then looked up at Khoja. "Ten days," he said.

Khoja grunted. "Maybe less."

"Let's say ten. Add two more to get to Beijing. That takes us into December."

"*Shì.*"

"Cutting it close."

"*Shì.*"

"How much time do you need?"

"I will succeed in whatever time is available."

"That's not what I asked."

Khoja sighed and reached for the tent door. "It is you who must decide."

"She's your wife."

"And she gave her word," the old man said and unzipped the door. He crawled out the opening and poked his head back into the tent. "As did I."

· · · · · ·

Morning came desolate and cold and Malcolm decided to split up the team. One group to Qiemo Town, the other to Beijing. They would not rejoin.

Gleb and Wolf and two of the Uighurs would head to Qiemo Town with Gul. He, Khoja, Aziguli, Mary, David and the remaining six Uighurs would continue east. Three camels were set aside for the trip south and with these animals went the baggage frames they'd mended with twine and the shovels with the cracked handles and anything else that had outlived its purpose. Musa and Gleb built a makeshift litter from the remains of a camel saddle. David led a search for water that found nothing, so they pooled what was left and loaded the empty jerry cans for the trip to Qiemo. The remaining fourteen camels were split into two packets of seven and onto these animals they loaded most of the water and the food and also the tents and sleeping bags for the cold nights ahead.

They worked in silence.

The wind had receded but not died. It hissed through the branches of the petrified trees beside their camp and the Uighurs cast their gazes downward and would not look at each other as they prepared for the day's march. Malcolm asked Musa what was wrong and the Uighur said they believed the forest to be haunted. That the wind carried the voices of the restless dead who'd entered the desert and never left.

By mid-morning the two caravans were ready.

They loaded Gul into the litter and tied it behind one of the camels and then Malcolm left Khoja and Aziguli to kneel at Gul's side while he gathered the rest of the team at the front of the three-camel caravan. They stood in a tight circle. Malcolm flanked on one side by Mary and David and on the other side by Gleb and Wolf.

"You have everything you need?" Malcolm asked.

"Of course," Gleb said and smiled. "Are you sure you will not wait for us to rejoin you?"

Malcolm shook his head. "You and Wolf were always only going to help us get through the desert," he said. "We can make it another ten days on our own."

"I don't have my money," Wolf said.

"You have a story money can't buy," Gleb said and took in the caravan and the desert with an outstretched arm.

"Stuff it, mate. I'd rather have money."

"Can I take Mary instead?" Gleb asked.

"Not a chance," Malcolm said and held out his hand.

The Russian pushed Malcolm's arm aside and wrapped him in a bear hug. Lifted him up and then set him down and rested his hands on Malcolm's shoulders. "My debt is paid," he said.

"And then some. Thank you."

"Are you sure you won't reconsider about Mary?"

"I wish I could."

Gleb's smile broadened and he turned to Mary and shrugged. "I tried," he said and stepped back from Malcolm and held open his arms.

"Thanks, big guy," Mary said and the Russian hugged her and then moved on to David.

"Wolf," Malcolm said and extended his hand.

"I'm not kidding about the money," the Brit said.

"It's been taken care of."

"Then it's been a pleasure," Wolf said and walked off to stand by the second camel in line where he turned and whistled at Gleb. "Enough, you teary-eyed Russian," he said. "Let's go."

Gleb winked at Malcolm and then picked up the rope of the camel in front. Looked back over the caravan and his gaze lingered on the litter and the kneeling figures of Khoja and Aziguli. "I still think the girl should come with us," he said. "To be with her mother in the hospital."

Malcolm frowned and followed Gleb's gaze.

"She stays," Khoja called out and then rose to his feet.

"I wasn't talking to you," Gleb said and then glanced at Malcolm and shook his head. "Like my father," he said. "Remember that."

"She will not leave my side," Khoja said and squeezed Aziguli's shoulder and then headed forward along the line of camels.

Malcolm considered the idea and then shook his head

The Russian shrugged. "As you wish," he said and then turned to watch Khoja.

The old man had stopped beside the two Uighur handlers and held his hand over his heart. He bowed and the Uighurs dipped their heads in return and then he left them. Did not look at Wolf and stopped in front of Gleb.

"She's in good hands," Gleb said. "We'll get her to Qiemo in one piece."

"Either way, I have made my good-byes."

Gleb opened his mouth and then closed it again. He nodded at the old man and then yanked on the rope of the lead camel and began to walk. The caravan followed.

Except Wolf.

The Brit stopped in front of Khoja while the camels marched on. Stared at the sand and the animals and everything else and then looked the old man in the eyes. The old man said something Malcolm did not hear and Wolf's upper lip curled and then he dropped his gaze and shoved past to catch up with the caravan. He took two steps and then Khoja grabbed him and metal glinted in the old man's free hand.

"No!" Malcolm said and sprang forward. Too slow once again and could do nothing but watch as Khoja jammed the knife to its hilt in the back of Wolf's head.

Wolf gagged and his body became rigid and the old man held him under one arm and eased the Brit to his knees. Put his mouth close to Wolf's ear and whispered while the Brit's hands opened and closed.

Malcolm pulled on Khoja's shoulder and the old man resisted. Twisted the blade and Malcolm pulled again and Khoja yanked the knife from Wolf's head and the Brit's body went limp on the ground. Malcolm spun Khoja and lifted him off the ground by his shirt and stuck his face close to the old man's. "Why?" he asked. "Why did you do that?"

Khoja glanced behind Malcolm and then Aziguli came to his side. Her lips pulled back from her teeth and her eyes moist with tears. She stood over the Brit and the wind whipped her hair about her face and she spat in the sand and then met her father's gaze. Stared at him and then walked off to the east to be joined by Musa and another Uighur.

Malcolm lowered Khoja but did not let go. "Whatever happened," he said, "you didn't need to do that."

"You would say that to me?" Khoja asked. "You, who've come halfway around the world to murder a man who had a hand in hurting your family?"

Malcolm stared at Khoja and did not answer and the old man sneered.

"Then walk away," Khoja said. "Go back to America and forget whatever it was that brought you here. But do not ask me to turn the other cheek."

Malcolm felt Mary's hand on his arm and he released his grip on Khoja.

The old man straightened his robes. Shifted his gaze to Mary and then back to Malcolm. "Remember that bitter sacrifice strengthens bold resolve," he said. "And we will need all our resolve for what lies ahead."

"Get out of here," Malcolm said and the old man hesitated and then bowed his head and walked after his daughter. Malcolm watched him go. Then he looked down and saw that Wolf's blood had stained his boots.

"Jesus," David said. "I can't believe that just happened."

"But it did," Mary said. "So, what now?"

Malcolm looked up from Wolf's body. Saw Khoja with his arms around Aziguli and knew he had no choice.

"Boss?" Mary asked.

"We carry on," he said and looked from Mary to David to Gleb. "We carry on."

· · · · ·

Malcolm led the caravan to the east.

Always to the east.

December arrived on their fifty-second day in the desert and the temperatures dropped even more. They slept in two to three layers of clothes and shivered through the night in the thin sleeping bags chosen for weight instead of warmth. When they woke, their knees and hands and hips were stiff and creaky like corpses birthed from the grave. The jerry cans froze solid each night and even the days seemed frigid. Malcolm began to look forward to the daily march so he could fend off the coldness that leached into his body.

Then a week later, the dunes ended. Petered out over the course of a day from hundred-foot swells to a skiff of sand that dusted the rocky ground and Malcolm let himself stop. By now he did not need the map to know that the desert continued another sixty miles and yet here at the sand's edge it felt like the terminus had been reached. Even with the desolation stretched out flat before him. He shifted from foot to foot and then caught a flash of reflected sunlight in the distance and pulled out his binoculars. Scanned ahead and located the solar power station at the exact place it was supposed to be.

The vehicle was there as well. A faded red van at the base of a row of industrial size solar panels in the north-west corner of the installation. They found the keys in the center console, also where they were supposed to be. David eased the van between the panels to where Malcolm had stopped the caravan and they began to strip gear from the camels. A bag or two each in the van and the jerry cans and frames and everything else would go south with Musa toward the town of Ruoqiang.

Malcolm found the camel that held his carry-all. He worked loose a strap that bound the bag to the frame and heard two pairs of footsteps behind him. "What is it?" he asked.

"We need to talk," David said.

"I'm listening."

"Mary and I have been thinking about this for a while, from before the caravan split to be honest, and both of us –"

"Aziguli should leave with the Uighurs," Mary said.

Malcolm stopped. He glanced at them and read the resolve in Mary's face and then returned to his work. Freed the strap and his bag fell to the sand. "Why is that?" he asked.

"You know why," Mary said. "She's a liability. There's no room for mistakes in Beijing."

"Compared to out here?"

"An amateur can't get us compromised in the desert."

"I see," Malcolm said. "David?"

"I agree with Mary," David said. "Having her along endangers the mission. Plus, Khoja's the one who knows how to infiltrate the Great Hall. We don't need her."

"The old man made it clear they're a package deal," Malcolm said.

"Then leave them both behind," Mary said.

"You feel that strongly?"

"Yes," Mary said.

"And how do you plan on getting into the Hall?" Malcolm asked.

"We can check out the tunnels ourselves," David said.

Malcolm refastened the strap that had secured his bag. "We don't have time," he said. "There are miles of tunnels."

"Not where we're going," David said.

"Forget the tunnels," Mary said. "Go with only one access."

Malcolm stared at his carry-all and considered the idea as if he hadn't thought of it already. Always the same conclusion. "There's no margin for error," he said and stooped to lift his bag. Stood and faced Mary and David and then glanced to where Khoja stood on the other side of the caravan. "And we didn't come all this way to put our eggs in one basket," he said and headed toward the van.

"What about Wolf?" Mary asked. "And the gas station. Are we supposed to pretend those things never happened?"

He came to a stop. "Yes," he said and then walked on.

. . . . .

They loaded the bags into the van while the Uighurs stood in a silent semi-circle around them. When the vans were loaded, Malcolm walked down the line. Bowed to each of the handlers and took their hands in both of his and thanked them. He wished Musa luck and told him to take care of the camels since they were his now.

Then the goodbyes were done.

They piled into the van to be confronted by the reek of their nearly two months of built-up sweat. Crammed in shoulder-to-shoulder after the expanse of the desert. They rolled down the windows and David drove while Malcolm stared at Musa and the other handlers through the rear window. They stood, stoic and still, and finally Musa raised an arm.

Malcolm watched until they were swallowed by the dust.

David followed a dirt trail that bordered the solar installation until it connected with a paved road headed east. This road connected to the G218 National Highway and here they turned north. Travelled thirty minutes or so until they crossed the S214 Provincial Highway where they went southeast. Hit the G315 and headed east.

David drove for the rest of the day and they took turns at the wheel through the night. They reached Aksai at dawn the next day and continued past Dunhuang and Guazhou, the land flat and barren, a rocky extension of the desert. Past the Gansu Wind Farm on the east of Yumen City. The wind turbines rose gigantic against a pale blue sky where the three-bladed rotors made slow and ponderous turns. They stopped in Jiuquan City to steal a few hours of sleep in a hotel and in the morning they continued. The Qilian Mountains rose to their south, the forest covered slopes the first time they'd seen green trees in months. Onward they drove, through the Hexi Corridor, through the city of

Zhangye, past the pagoda-like South Gate of Wuwei and then east on the G2012 which ran along the southern edge of the Tengger desert.

"God, I thought I'd never have to see another desert again," David said from the driver's seat.

"I kind of miss it," Mary said.

"Of course you'd say that," David said. "Let me guess, you miss the challenge."

"You know me," Mary said. "I'm always game for going up against something infinitely stronger than me."

"And beating it," David said.

Mary smiled. "And beating it."

David looked at Malcolm in the rear-view mirror. "What about you, boss? Anything you miss about the desert?"

Malcolm watched the dunes pass by from his seat in the back. He remembered the howl of the wind and the grit of the sand against his skin. How it chafed and forced him to squint and how, if he let himself, he could at times imagine his wife and son in the sand ahead of him.

"Boss?"

Malcolm blinked and glanced at David. "What?"

"Miss anything about the desert?"

"No," he said and then stopped his hand on its way to a compass he no longer around his neck. Then he looked to his side to find Khoja looking at him. "The emptiness," he said. "I miss the emptiness."

The old man said nothing and they drove on.

They paralleled the southern edge of the Tengger desert into Zhongwei and then left the sand behind and turned south. Carried on past Guyuan and through the shadow of the sacred Kongtong Mountains in Pingliang, then into Shaanxi Province. They spent the night in Xi'an and the next day they got on the G5 highway and headed northeast. Past the Terracotta Armies beneath a clear blue sky and south of the manufacturing hub of Tiayuan. In Shijiazhuang they took the G4 north through Baoding and the farmland and low hills outside Beijing. At the suburban outskirts of the city David gave a small cheer, which turned to curses shortly after when he was forced to navigate them through the traffic of the urban districts. Finally, late on the day of the 11th of December, they arrived in the heart of old Beijing.

• • • • •

Malcolm woke the next day before dawn.

He stared at the ceiling and could not get his bearings and then David grunted in his sleep and he remembered. They'd wandered for hours along narrow lanes and streets, the historic *hutongs* of the old city. Deep into alleyways so tight in places they could not even walk abreast. He had at last turned to Khoja to lead them to the tiny residential courtyard where they'd spent the night. The three men slept on cots in the *siheyuan's* living room and Mary and Aziguli shared the bedroom.

David grunted again and Malcolm glanced over. He saw David asleep on his side and an empty bed space where Khoja should have been. A muffled bump came from the direction of the kitchen and Malcolm rose in silence. Pulled on a shirt and pants and padded toward the sound to find Khoja before a cast iron kettle on a hot plate.

Khoja did not turn around. "I'm getting noisy in my old age," he said.

"Nobody else heard," Malcolm said.

"Tea?"

"Please."

Khoja poured the tea into bluish-back bowls and handed one to Malcolm.

He nodded his thanks and sipped the tea. Burnt his tongue and winced. His gaze flickered to Khoja but the old man had not moved. They drank their tea and did not talk and when his bowl was empty, he reached for the teapot.

Khoja blocked his hand and then he took Malcolm's bowl and set it beside his own on the counter. "Come with me," he said and walked out the door into the small courtyard beyond.

Malcolm followed the old man into the narrow laneway, which was clogged with bicycles and motorbikes up against the brick walls. They walked past the tight packed doors of other *siheyuan* until the alley emptied into a larger laneway that was perhaps the width of four people side-by-side. The grey façades of doors and brick walls mixed with bright red lanterns hung outside red painted doors. They headed down the laneway until it emptied into an even bigger street that wound among two-storey buildings with electrical cables strung through the air in between. The pre-dawn sky began to lighten and men and women on three-wheeled bike carts clattered along cobblestone streets beside rickshaws that stood empty and ready for the day. After several minutes the street ran beneath an arch in the middle of a red-painted wall that spanned the road. The wall was topped with glazed golden roof tiles.

They passed through the arch and Malcolm looked up as they walked underneath. "Where are we going?" he asked.

"To see what we're up against," the old man said.

They continued on and Malcolm guessed they were headed north. Past an open park where a troop of people swayed and shifted from stance to stance in unison to music they alone could hear. They stopped at a food stand and bought two servings of *jianbing* and walked while they ate. Across a wide thoroughfare beyond which towered *Zhengyangmen*. The massive brick wall of the southern gate into Beijing's Inner City soared and transformed into pagoda-like tiers topped with green-glazed tiles and it was here that Malcolm understood their destination.

They skirted the Archery Tower and took the long tunnel through the heart of the Gatehouse. The tons of brick and stone pressed down upon them and then they entered Tian'an Men Square. Past the boxy columned building that was Mao's Mausoleum and the clay sculptures of heroic Chinese with rifles in hand and arms raised and chests bared. The Great Hall of the People loomed on the western side of the square and the National Museum flanked them to the east and any of the buildings would have been imposing on its own. They passed through the shadow of the high granite Monument to the People's Heroes in the center of the square with its bas-reliefs of Chinese resistance through the Century of Humiliation and Malcolm grew small and silent.

The square opened up beyond the obelisk-like Monument and Khoja led them to a crowd at the north end of the square. They pushed into a mass of people that surrounded a small dais with a flagpole fenced off behind a chain-link barricade. Bugles sounded from across Chang'an

Avenue and Khoja pointed to a group of soldiers who paraded out from the Tian'an Men Gate to the north. They carried rifles with long bayonets and their white-gloved hands cut crisp lines across their bodies as they marched into position around the dais. The air was clear and cold and the shouted commands of the honor guard carried across the square. Then the flag of China ascended the flagpole while the gathered crowd snapped pictures. When the flag was up, there was more shouting and then the honor guard marched back across Chang'an Avenue and through the Gate of Heavenly Peace while the attendant crowd broke up.

Khoja and Malcolm turned and headed back south through the Square. They stopped at the base of the Monument to the People's Heroes and Khoja clasped his hands behind him.

"Have you seen what you needed?" the old man asked.

"It's a start," Malcolm said. He pulled out his phone and snapped a picture of the Monument and then faced to the west and the Great Hall. Stared at the building through the phone's screen. "Uniformed police throughout the square and on all the bordering streets," he said. "Soldiers at all the buildings. I'd expect there will be more next week."

"There will be," Khoja said. "And you missed the plain clothes police."

"You didn't let me finish."

"By all means."

"There's also the CCTV," he said and nodded at the lampposts that ringed the square and the cameras mounted beneath the lights. "And I would guess hundreds of police and soldiers within a minute's notice."

"That is a conservative estimate."

"What did I miss?"

"The drones."

"Of course," Malcolm said and glanced to the sky. "Stupid mistake."

"Do not waste your time looking," Khoja said. "It is easier to assume you are watched at all times."

"Will the Square be locked down?"

"No, although as you said, there will be more police and soldiers."

"A hard nut to crack."

"Perhaps harder than you thought."

"That happens sometimes."

"It is not too late to walk away."

Malcolm lowered his phone and breathed deep of the chill morning air. "Yes. It is," he said.

Khoja snorted. "So brave," he said and headed toward Mao's Mausoleum.

"That why you never carried out your attack here?" Malcolm asked.

Khoja paused and then looked back. "As I said, it was a matter of timing."

"If you say so," Malcolm said and watched Khoja walk off.

· · · · ·

They returned to the *siheyuan* where Malcolm gathered the others. He sat with Mary and David at a small table in the kitchen while Aziguli made tea and Khoja rested cross-legged on the cot where he'd spent the night.

"The Work Conference is in one week," Malcolm said. He pulled out a tourist pamphlet he'd taken from a stand near the square and spread it out on the table. Pointed at the landmarks with a pencil as he spoke. "This morning, Khoja and I checked out Tian'an Men Square. Security is tight, as expected," he said. "Checkpoints on all the entrances to the square itself and a heavy police and military presence."

"More than Kashgar?" Mary asked.

"Yes," Khoja said.

"You weren't in Kashgar," David said.

"He's right," Malcolm said. "Although it's less overt."

"How so?" Mary asked.

"There are more cameras and the police are mostly plain-clothes."

"Any idea what the security will be like next week?" David asked.

"The Great Hall will be the most secure place in China," Khoja said.

"Well, that's great," David said and crossed his arms. "Okay, so now what?"

"More reconnaissance," Malcolm said. "First the Great Hall and then the tunnels."

Aziguli set empty bowls on the table and began to pour tea.

"We also need to put our gear together," David said.

"That's where Khoja comes in," Malcolm said.

"Oh, yeah?" David asked. "He gonna take care of that like he handles everything else?"

"Better," Khoja said and rose from the cot to take a bowl of tea.

"I can hardly wait for the trail of dead bodies," David said.

"Is that not why you have come?" Khoja said.

"Enough," Malcolm said. "Let's stay on task."

"Boss, what do we know about the schedule for the Work Conference?" Mary asked.

"It's a two-day event," he said. "The Standing Committee meets briefly on the first morning to confirm the agenda and then the entire Politburo will meet. That's followed by opening ceremonies, which should include the complete Communist Party Central Committee."

"How many is that again?" David asked.

"Close to four hundred, not including hangers-on."

"Lot of people."

"Which narrows down where things will happen in the Great Hall," he said. "The Central Committee is too big for most of the meeting rooms, and too small for the Great Auditorium, so the opening address will most likely be in the third-floor auditorium."

"What about the Standing Committee and the Politburo meetings?" David asked.

"That's what we need to find out."

"What happens when the opening address is done?" Mary asked.

"The delegates move to the Jingxi Hotel for working sessions."

"So, that's confirmed," she said.

Malcolm pinched the bridge of his nose. "The Jingxi is not an easier target, Mary."

"Yeah, come on, Mary," David said and made a face. "Can't you be happy with the Great Hall?"

"I know, we've been over this," Mary said. "And I still feel the same. The Jingxi offers better options for us to get out."

"And you have a point," Malcolm said. "However, the fact remains that the only place we can nail down the Politburo in one place is in the Great Hall. At the start and end of the conference."

"That's no good if we can't get in," Mary said. "Or if we can't find where they're meeting."

"That's why we're going to check out the Great Hall," Malcolm said. "And we'll have the location beforehand. Right, Khoja?"

The old man slurped his tea and made no sign that he'd heard.

David sighed. "How do you want to tackle this?" he asked.

"Mary and I will take the Great Hall," Malcolm said. "You and Khoja will start mapping the tunnels."

"Aziguli will go with you to the Great Hall," Khoja said.

Malcolm coughed.

"No chance in hell that's happening," David said.

Khoja nodded at Aziguli and the girl moved into the bedroom. Came back with a rolled-up scroll of parchment and Khoja helped her unroll it on the table.

"What do you see?" Khoja asked.

"Come on, boss, how long do we humor this guy?" David asked.

Malcolm leaned in and pored over the paper. Glanced at Khoja and then returned to the scroll.

"What do you see?" Khoja repeated.

"Tian'an Men Square and all the surroundings," he said.

"And another," Khoja said and nodded again to Aziguli who unrolled a second and smaller scroll on top of the first. They held down the corners while Malcolm squinted at the lines and sketches and said nothing.

"I don't get it," David said and a frown darkened his face. "What is this?"

"It's the Great Hall," Malcolm said.

"I thought we didn't have a floor plan," David said.

"That's what this is though, at least the start of one," Malcolm said and then met Khoja's gaze. "Isn't it?"

"*Shì*."

"Where did you get this?"

"Aziguli drew it," Khoja said. "From my description."

"How did you do this?" Mary asked. "Photographic memory?"

Khoja nodded. "That is why she will go with you to the Great Hall."

"She'd be better use mapping *Di Xia Cheng*," Mary said.

"She will do that also," Khoja said. "The Great Hall will come first."

"It's good, I'll give her that," David said. He leaned back in his chair and put both hands on top of his head. "But I still don't like it. It should be Mary."

"She will not jeopardize the mission," Khoja said. "I trained her better than that."

David closed his eyes and sighed and then looked at Malcolm. "If she can draw so well, then have Mary describe it to her when you get back," he said. "I mean, are we seriously considering sending Khoja's daughter on target reconnaissance?"

Malcolm stared at the map and then looked at Aziguli. He saw Gul in her eyes and Khoja in the way she stood. Felt a patience beneath the demurity that reminded him more than anything of a pit viper about to strike. "What do you think, Mary?" he asked.

Mary traced her fingers over the lines and layout of the floor plan. "I think we need all the help we can get," she said. "I say we give her a chance."

"You know what I think," David said.

"And you, Aziguli?" Malcolm asked. "What about you?"

Her eyes flickered and she glanced at her father and then met Malcolm's gaze. "I will help however I can," she said.

"You'll do what I say?"

She waited in silence and then nodded. "*Shì*," she said.

Malcolm stared at her and then turned back to the map. "All right then," he said. "We'll go tomorrow morning. For now, let's see about getting some supplies."

• • • • •

Malcolm and Aziguli woke at dawn the next day and retraced the route to Tian'an Men Square. A dusting of snow had fallen in the night and their footsteps were dark and grey on the white-covered streets. They bought breakfast at a street vendor and then strolled along Guangchang Side Road on the west of the square. Shared steamed buns and drank tea and observed the metal and concrete barricade that ran the eastern front of the Great Hall. Men in dark suits stood at intervals of a few meters the length of the fence. The men wore dark sunglasses and wireless in-ear headphones and their jackets bulged at the chest or shoulders from concealed weapons. Beyond the barricade were the steps to the Great Hall's entrance, lined with policemen in dark green trench-coats, peaked forage caps and small caliber machineguns in hand.

Above everything loomed the Great Hall of the People. Grey and solemn and coffin-like. The building was topped by red flags that snapped and stood taut in the wind. The bronze doors and windows of the eastern entrance shrouded in shadows against the cold morning light by the eaves of the main gate so that the national emblem on high gleamed bright like a cyclopean eye.

"Not the best-looking building, is it?" Malcolm asked.

"It is considered an architectural wonder," Aziguli said.

"Oh, yeah? By who?"

"The Chinese."

"The people?" he asked. "Or the party?"

"There is no difference."

"Isn't there."

Aziguli seemed about to reply and then closed her mouth and Malcolm let it drop.

They walked along the perimeter fence to the tourist entrance on the southern side of the Great Hall. No one was in line and Malcolm paid thirty renminbi each and they were permitted to walk through the unplanted gardens on the east side of the Great Hall. Up the main steps where they were dwarfed by gray marble colonnades wider than the height of a grown man and through the entrance onto bright red carpet where they met a bank of walkthrough metal detectors and guards. They screened through the checkpoint and a guard gave Malcolm a pat down while two others smiled and laughed with Aziguli and then they moved into the Central Hall.

Malcolm slowed and then stopped. Raised his face and turned in a circle to behold the marble floors and red carpets and tapestries and paintings of blooming trees and cranes in flight. Enough to decorate an Olympic-size sports field. He stood like that for some time and then Aziguli led him up one of two staircases to the second-floor balcony.

They stood before a painting of a tranquil river woven between mountain peaks and bucolic villages and then spotted a set of huge double doors into the Great Auditorium. A guard blocked them at the entrance and directed them to a similar set of doors farther along the hall. Malcolm nodded and they walked down the concourse and another guard glanced at them, then smiled at Aziguli and allowed them into the Great Auditorium. They moved inside and stopped and then gazed up at the ceiling and the illuminated red star that shone within a galaxy of lesser lights.

"Do you still think the building is unimpressive?" Aziguli asked.

Malcolm dropped his gaze to look at her. Her face basked with light from the stars. "I never said it was unimpressive," he said.

"It symbolizes unity."

"Whether the people want it or not."

The trace of a smile ghosted across Aziguli's face and then they walked on, guided by ever-present ushers and under the constant watch of various guards. They went on through the other parts of the building open to tourists, the Main Auditorium and the Congress Hall, the Beijing Hall with its deep red carpet and mural of the Forbidden City, and the cream-colored walls and chairs of the Jiangxi Hall with its paintings of mountains and golden pagoda-like castles. They saw the Banquet Hall in the north wing of the building, and several more offices and halls in the south wing whose names Malcolm could not remember. Throughout, they kept track of which rooms were open and which were off-limits until they found themselves back in the Central Hall.

"Did you get all that?" Malcolm asked.

Aziguli nodded. "*Shì*," she said.

They passed back out through security and down the main steps. The air was cool and bit through their clothes after the oppressive warmth of the Great Hall.

"What will you do after you have finished?" Aziguli asked.

He glanced at her and they continued on through the barren gardens toward the visitor entrance. "I haven't given it much thought," he said.

They walked in silence and then Aziguli took his hand. Pulled him to a stop and held him with her gaze. "It is your hope that there will not be an after," she said.

"This is not the place to discuss it," he said.

"It is written in your eyes."

"We should get back," he said. "We have work to do."

"What if you don't succeed?"

He stared at her and waited and then saw that she would not move until he'd answered. "Then I'll have done everything I can to avenge my family," he said. "Can we go now?"

She remained where she was and then nodded and they walked on. She rested her hand in the crook of his elbow and together they passed out the visitor entrance. Skirted Guangchang Side Road and found themselves beside the Qian Men subway station to the south. They stopped to look back out over the square and Malcolm could barely make out the Tian'an Men Gate at the far end.

"Do you know what *Tian'an Men* means?" she asked.

"My parents told me," he said. "The Gate of Heavenly Peace."

"That is the short translation."

"There's another one?"

"'Receiving the mandate from heaven and pacifying the dynasty.'"

"I see."

"When it was built in the Ming Dynasty, it was called *Chengtianmen*."

"'Gate of Receiving Grace from Heaven.'"

"Yes. Destroyed when Li Zicheng was defeated and rebuilt by the Qing Emperor Shunzhi."

"That's when it was renamed?"

"Yes."

"How do you know so much about the history?"

She let go of his elbow. "As I said, I have been properly educated."

"You were in one of the camps," he said. "Weren't you?"

Wind gusted through the square and she turned to him and her eyes glistened. "We can go now."

He led her south past Qian Men and reentered the twisting streets of the *hutong*.

"There is much that can go wrong with your plan," she said.

"There always is. We will be ready."

"I mean if you succeed."

His pace faltered. "That is not my concern," he said.

"Would your wife feel the same? That is, as you said, why you are here, is it not?"

He did not answer and instead continued to walk until Aziguli drew up short. He took a few more steps and then stopped as well and stood with his back to her.

"You have given no thought to what the Party will do," she said.

The wind gusted and blew and he set himself against the cold.

"Or perhaps you have," she said, "and decided it does not matter."

"Given the history of your parents, I'd have thought you'd understand."

"The Party is bigger than the Politburo. It will survive."

"It is welcome to try."

"And what about those who will live through what comes next?"

"What about them?" he asked and his voice shook. He breathed deep and glanced back at her and his hands clenched into fists as he spoke. He stared at her and he saw Amaelia and the next time the wind blew he welcomed the cold. "What about them?" he repeated.

Aziguli raised her chin and met his gaze and did not flinch. "What do you think the Party will do when they discover my father among the attackers?" she asked.

"Your father would not be here if he did not think this was the right thing."

Her eyes moistened and she blinked and then shook her head. "My father cannot be trusted," she said and walked past him.

He let her take several steps and then called after her. "You're the reason he never completed his attack," he said and she came to a stop. "Aren't you?"

"As my father says," she said, "it was poor timing."

"That's not good enough," he said.

She turned and gazed at him and her face was calm and resolute. "My father gave in to his emotions," she said. "And he will do so again. That is his nature."

"That does not seem like the Ismail Khoja I've come to know," he said.

"Then you have not paid attention," she said and trudged deeper into the network of alleys that would take them back to the *siheyuan*.

· · · · ·

The days and nights of the next week blurred together.

Malcolm worked out of the living room of the *siheyuan* to control their preparations. He had Khoja lead the first scouting trip into *Di Xia Cheng* and then David took over. Aziguli went to the underground as well after she had finished the floor plans of the Great Hall and needed no more than two trips to sketch a map David claimed could make her rich.

Khoja flitted in and out at all hours and would summon Mary or David to accompany him without notice. A succession of terse phone calls and dead drops and foot mobile meetups in the labyrinthian *hutong* streets and every inch of space in the *siheyuan* began to fill. They took possession of disposable cell phones and clothing and radios with ear-bud microphones and a modified shoulder-carried news video camera. A 3D printer and identification cards. Electronic passes and enough paperwork to create two new identities each. At a night-time live drop with a man in a custom-tailored suit and a police bodyguard, they were given a footlocker-sized reinforced suitcase. Khoja said the man was Chinese mafia and the case was heavy enough to need carrying by two people. They rolled the case back to the *siheyuan* and inside they found Chinese-made bullpup submachine guns and semi-automatic pistols. Boxes of ammunition and grenades and explosives and thin, goo-filled shirts that squished and stretched and hardened to steel when hit.

None except Khoja were familiar with the Chinese guns and Malcolm had the old man run them through the weapons daily. Load and unload drills and all the ways the weapons could malfunction. Malcolm had them study the maps of the Great Hall and the tunnels and double-checked their identification and paperwork and he did the same and practiced with the television camera.

And then it was the day before the Work Conference, a week after they'd arrived in Beijing.

Aziguli had stayed in the *siheyuan* while Malcolm and the others had moved equipment into the tunnels. When they returned, they found a letter-sized envelope on the kitchen table. Aziguli was seated in a chair and said nothing as they entered and instead pointed to the delivery. Malcolm picked up the envelope and opened it and read out loud.

"The Standing Committee meets at eight-thirty in the East Hall," he said. "They'll be joined by the rest of the Politburo at nine-thirty and the Central Committee will get the opening address at ten-thirty in the Third-Floor Auditorium. At noon the delegates will be transported to the Jingxi for lunch and the working meetings." He stopped reading and looked up. "There we have it," he said. "Questions?"

He waited and was met by silence, so he laid the paper back down on the table.

"No big speeches," he said. "We know what we need to do. Timings are confirmed. Let's go over the maps once more to get the routes down, then sanitize this place and get some rest."

"If we can," David said.

"I guess," Malcolm said.

They set to work. Gathered around the maps and located the East Hall in the northern section of the Great Hall. Traced paths with their fingers and talked out the stairs they would climb and the rooms they would pass. Then they began to tidy so there would be no trace of their stay. Most of the gear had been prepositioned or would be carried out in the morning so there was not much left to do and within an hour the *siheyuan* was close to the state it had been in when they'd arrived.

Malcolm inspected their work and then nodded his approval and collected his jacket. "I'm going for a walk," he said. He stepped out into the alley and stood still with his eyes closed while he breathed the crisp, cold air. Reached into his pocket and felt for his crumpled picture of Amaelia and Oran and then the door to the apartment opened and David came out.

"Got a minute?" David asked.

"Sure," Malcolm said.

David glanced over his shoulder at the apartment. "Can we take a walk?" he asked.

Malcolm nodded and they moved down the alley.

"The old man wasn't kidding about Aziguli having a photographic memory," David said. "Don't know what we would've done without her."

"Same goes for Khoja, I guess."

"That's what I wanted to talk to you about," David said and came to a stop. "You think the old man's good for his word?"

Malcolm thought about that. "I think, for the moment, our interests align," he said. "Anything beyond that, we'll have to wait and see."

"Shit."

"Not what you were hoping for?"

"No," David said and ran a hand across his face. "But it's what I thought you'd say."

"Nerves?"

"Every time," David said and shook his head and then met Malcolm's gaze. "Him and Aziguli, they're quite a pair."

"Stranger than fiction."

"I know, right?" David flashed a brief smile. "I just don't want any surprises tomorrow. There'll be enough of that without the two of them adding any more."

"Maybe give him a bit of space."

"And how do I manage that? He's supposed to have my back."

"You're a good man, David," Malcolm said. "You'll figure it out."

"Thanks, boss," he said and then took a deep breath. "I'll let you get on your way."

"One last thing," Malcolm said. "Can you send Mary out? I'd like her to walk with me."

"Sure thing. Does she need anything?"

"No. I'm going to check out the Square one last time and thought we could talk through tomorrow. We'll be back by midnight."

"Got it. She'll be out in a minute," David said and headed back toward the *siheyuan*.

Malcolm watched him go and then felt again for the picture in his pocket. He held it and thought about how it would all soon be over and then leaned against a wall and waited for Mary.

He slept better than he'd expected and morning came quick.

In the pre-dawn darkness Malcolm and Mary made their way to Tian'an Men Square. They flashed their press credentials and queued with the local and foreign media in line to access the Great Hall. In the east, the sun rose distant behind a smear of low-lying smoke or smog and the filtered morning light colored the Square grey and cold. Their breath condensed in the frigid air as they slowly moved up in the line. When they reached the top of the steps into the Great Hall, they heard shouted commands from the north end of the Square and Malcolm rose on his tiptoes and spied the bobbing forage caps of the honor guard as they crossed Chang'An Avenue.

The line shuffled through the main doors and then branched to banks of walk-through metal detectors and x-ray machines. A wall of soldiers and police around the equipment. Malcolm and Mary picked a lane and each picked up an empty grey bin. They placed their phones and jackets and shoes inside the bins and then set the bins on a conveyor belt that fed into the x-ray machine. Malcolm set the case with the news camera on the conveyor belt as well and then got behind Mary in the line for the metal detector.

Mary was called ahead and walked through the thin columned frame. A soldier stopped her on the other side and took her press credentials. Stared at the card with a stern look and then thrust it at Mary and pointed at Malcolm.

Malcolm stepped through the columns. The machine stayed silent and the guard frowned. Malcolm wondered if he might get a pat down and then the guard took his credentials. Inspected them and then handed them back and called the next person.

Malcolm joined Mary at the end of the x-ray scanner. The grey bins with their belongings came out and then the news camera. Malcolm reached for the case and was stopped by a soldier behind the conveyor belt who demanded to see inside.

"Of course," Malcolm said.

He flipped the latches on the case and lifted the lid and then stepped back and put on his boots. Tied his laces and did not look at the soldier as the man peered inside the box. He watched from the edge of his vision as the soldier raised the camera and turned it over and fiddled with buttons and then set the camera down and began to poke and prod inside the case.

"What are these?" the soldier asked.

"Battery packs," he said and made sure not to meet the soldier's gaze.

"Why so many?"

"I don't want to run out."

The soldier seemed to digest the answer and then wiped the battery pack with the padded end of an electronic wand. Swabbed inside the case as well and stared at the wand's readout and then tossed the battery back into the case. "Pack this up," the soldier said.

Malcolm nodded and replaced the packs in their padded slots. Then he closed the case and fell in behind Mary and the rest of the cleared media.

They moved along with the herd of journalists into the Central Hall. Then up the stairs and into the Press Briefing Hall. The room was half full of news crews and reporters and Malcolm took a place at the back. He set down the case and checked the time and saw that it was a few minutes before eight thirty. More journalists entered the hall and the seats filled and he crouched over the case and removed the battery packs and stacked them in a pile on the floor. He checked his watch again and then looked around and saw that guards in dark suits had entered the room and stood huddled in conversation at the front. He watched them and then leaned close to Mary.

"Something's wrong," he said.

"What?" she asked.

"I don't know," he said. "But they're panicked. Look."

They watched the guards hold their fingers to their ears. Their brows furrowed. One of them nodded several times and began to point at the others and at places around the room.

"What do you want to do?" Mary asked. "It's almost time."

"Give me a minute," he said. He bent to pick up a small wireless radio from the camera case. No different in appearance than those used by the other news crews. He connected a microphone and an ear bud headset to the radio and then inserted the headset into his ear. Turned on the radio and attached it to his belt.

"David," he said.

"Anything?" Mary asked.

He tried again. Handed another radio and headset to Mary and tried David once more. "Nothing," he said.

"More guards," Mary said.

Malcolm glanced up and watched men in uniforms fill the entrances to the room. Then he crouched down and picked up a battery pack. Thumbed a small switch and the bottom of the pack fell open. He dumped the contents into the case and did the same with the remaining battery packs and the inside of the box became cluttered with white plastic pieces and a small, black rod that fit in the palm of his hand. He stuck the rod in a pocket and then his hands worked quick and sure with the white plastic and a misshapen snub-nosed pistol took form. He cleared his throat and Mary looked down and he slid the pistol into her hand.

"Sure you don't you want it?" she said.

"You're a better shot."

She took the gun and Malcolm stood and rearranged his jacket. The next time he looked at her, the gun had disappeared.

"Ready?" he asked.

"Ready," she said.

He led along the back wall, away from the main entrance and toward another pair of doors. Halfway there he looked back and saw that most of the journalists were crowded around the guards at the front of the room. The guards nearest Malcolm and Mary had edged to the front of the room as well and for the moment were obscured by the crowd.

"Let's go," he said and stepped out smooth and fast. They reached the doors and darted through and closed them fast behind them and then looked around.

"Which way?" Malcolm asked.

"Over here," she said. "Follow me."

They moved down the corridor. Took ten steps and then a stern-faced guard in a dark suit stepped in front of them and held up his hands. "This way is off limits," the guard said.

Malcolm smiled and shrugged and gestured at Mary. "She needs the bathroom," he said.

The guard pointed behind them. "Go back to the Press Hall."

"Back there?" Malcolm said and glanced over his shoulder. He put a confused look on his face and shuffled away from Mary so that he stood at the guard's side.

"I need to make a call," Mary said and pulled out her phone. Fumbled and the phone clattered onto the red carpet in the hallway. The guard glanced down with his hand on his radio and Malcolm jammed the end of the black rod into the man's ribs. Pressed a button and the guard went rigid as millions of volts of electricity coursed through his body.

Malcolm held the button for two seconds and then released it. He caught the guard as the man collapsed to the floor and then dragged him toward a small alcove set into a wall.

"Shit," Mary said. "Another one."

Malcolm glanced up the hallway and saw another guard. Thirty feet away. They made eye contact and the man froze and then reached into his suit jacket.

"Take him," Malcolm said.

"Stop!" the guard called out.

"Now, Mary!"

"Stop!" the guard yelled again and then a shot rang out. The guard's head rocked back and then came forward there was a red hole in the middle of his forehead. The man swayed and then his legs gave out and he tumbled to the ground.

Malcolm let go of the guard he still carried. Stooped and stripped the man of his pistol and gave it to Mary. "Let's get moving," he said and strode down the hallway.

"What about the others?"

"They'll be there," Malcolm said.

"And if they're not?"

He paused to scoop up the pistol from the guard Mary had shot. Felt the gun mold to his hand and then stood and walked over the body.

"Then we'll do it ourselves," he said.

• • •

Malcolm covered Mary as she led them deeper into the Great Hall's northern wing. He'd left his jacket behind and carried a pistol in hand and had another jammed into the waistband of his pants. Taken from fallen guards.

"Almost there," Mary said.

They prowled along the corridor and he scanned to the front and rear and then static crackled in his ear.

"David?" he said and halted. Pushed the headset into his ear to hear better. "Come in, David."

A broken and staticky voice replied, "En route…contact…Khoja…move."

"Catch any of that?" Mary asked.

"No. Let's keep going."

They walked on. Slowed as they approached a corner.

"What if the Standing Committee has moved?" she asked.

"That's not their drill."

"We break our drills all the time."

"They're not us."

"It's human nature."

"Even if they do, they're boxed in," he said. "Us on this side, David on the other."

The sound of gunfire came from up ahead. Then a distant explosion and a slight tremor in the walls and floor and more gunfire.

"Starting to feel like we're the ones who're boxed in," Mary said.

Malcolm took the lead as they came up on the corner. He poked his head around and pulled back into cover. Held up a hand with four fingers raised and Mary nodded, then placed her hand on his shoulder. She squeezed and he stepped wide into the corridor to leave room for Mary. He aimed at the leftmost man in a group of four soldiers armed with bullpup rifles. Twenty feet away. Dropped his target and the man next to him. He heard Mary fire and noted the soldier on the far right fall. They shot the last soldier at the same time. Advanced and put a bullet between the eyes of a man wounded in the stomach and the echo of the gunshots carried down the hall.

They paused over the bodies where Malcolm covered the corridor while Mary stripped rifles and magazines from the dead. The static buzzed again in Malcolm's ear and then cleared.

"– almost at East Hall."

"David?" Malcolm asked.

"I got you," David said over the comms.

"What's going on?"

"– compromised coming out of the tunnel. Approaching East Hall from the north."

"Our approach is from the south," Malcolm said.

"Roger, wait."

More gunfire. Closer. It did not stop.

Malcolm took a rifle from Mary and tried the radio again. Nothing. He glanced at Mary and she would not look at him. "Time to move," he said.

On down the corridor.

They wiped out two more squads of soldiers, one from the front and one that came up on them from the rear. Then the East Hall was around the next corner. They sheltered against a wall. Malcolm tried and could not raise David on the radio. They heard voices gather and grow louder along the route they'd taken and their faces became grim. Malcolm nodded to Mary and she nodded back and they took the corner with weapons raised. Face to face with twenty or thirty guards in a mix of dark suits and camouflaged uniforms.

Beyond the guards were the two sets of double wooden doors into the East Hall.

They opened fire and the din of battle filled the hall. Gunfire and shouts and the wails of the wounded. The acrid bite of burnt gunpowder. Blood and gore in the air and on the walls and the carpet and this time surprise was not enough and the soldiers fought back. Malcolm yelled and dragged Mary back behind the corner as bullets punched holes through the places where they'd stood. The air clogged with chips of plaster and wood from the roof and walls.

"Reloading," Malcolm said.

Mary's breath came ragged. "There are too many," she said and reloaded when Malcolm was done.

He tried David again and heard nothing. Waited for a lull in the shooting.

"Behind us," Mary said and fired at a policeman in the corridor.

"Can't stay here," Malcolm said and readied himself to re-attack around the corner. Mary shot at another policeman and Malcolm tensed and waited for the fire to die down. He heard a lull and moved, rifle first around the corner. Froze. The hallway littered with the dead and Khoja and Aziguli at the double doors to the East Hall.

"It's clear," Malcolm said and dragged Mary after him around the corner. Down the hallway toward Khoja and Aziguli while he scanned the corridor ahead. "Where's David?" he asked.

Khoja glanced at him and shook his head. Then the old man turned to the doors and yanked on the handles and they would not budge.

"Go explosive," Malcolm said.

"David had the charges," Mary said.

"Is he far?" Malcolm asked Khoja.

The old man looked away from the doors and then cocked his head and Malcolm heard it a second later. Shouts and yells and a tramping stampede of feet in the hallway.

Malcolm knew what he'd see before he turned.

A horde of black and green uniforms and helmeted heads. The corridor wall to wall with soldiers and police and still more around the corner. Pressed on by the weight of those behind.

"I'm on it," Mary said and walked toward the mob. Her rifle hard at work and the bullets she fired were like pebbles into the ocean.

Shouts came from the other end of the hallway and Malcolm turned with Khoja to see soldiers and police flood that way as well. He met Khoja's gaze.

"You take those ones," Malcolm said. "I'll help Mary."

Khoja nodded. Looked at his daughter. "Stay by the door," he said and then left her to join the fray.

Malcolm strode up to join Mary and they fired until their rifles ran dry and then the mass of bodies washed over them. They dropped the empty guns and fought with hand and foot. The wave broke upon them. Receded and came again. Attackers climbed the bodies of the fallen. Swarmed along the walls and fell where they stood and forced Malcom and Mary back through sheer weight of numbers.

A gunshot and then another and Malcolm knew the soldiers no longer cared if they hit each other. He fought beside Mary and there was another shot and she staggered. She began to fall and he held her up and then felt her torn from his grasp. He reached for her and the attackers carried him back. Knocked him to the ground and fell on him and others slipped past. He fought to his knees and there was a lull as the soldiers strove for the doors to the East Hall. He looked behind him and saw Aziguli at the doors and beyond her stood Khoja amid a phalanx of soldiers and police armed with rifles and batons. They streamed past Khoja on the sides of the hallway with guns aimed at Aziguli. Their mouths open, the tendons on their neck taut as they shouted, their yells absorbed in the swell of noise.

He saw Khoja knocked to his knees. The old man looked for Aziguli and held her gaze and then his free hand went to his belt and came away with what looked like a hand-held radio. Aziguli turned and stared at Malcolm and there were tears down her cheeks. Her face resolute and soldiers and police all around.

A man knocked into him and he lost sight of her. Fell to the ground and hit his face as the attackers stormed past. He pushed up and looked for her through the tangle of legs. Found Khoja instead and saw the old man push a button on the radio he held and at that moment fire and light exploded from where Aziguli had stood. The soldiers who would have been around her knocked back like dandelion tufts and then the blast wave reached him. The heat seared his face and sucked the air from his lungs. Blackness danced at the edge of his vision. He buried himself into the floor and clenched his eyes shut. Covered his head as shrapnel and debris and body parts rained down and tried not to picture Aziguli's face in the blackness.

• • •

Malcolm waited for the maelstrom to pass and then wriggled out from under the bodies. A ringing in his ears as he worked his way to his knees. When he reached his feet, the floor seemed to heave and he lurched sideways. He braced himself against a wall and then looked around in wonder at the devastation in the hallway.

He stood among severed limbs and blackened corpses. The roof and walls were misted red and the stench of burnt flesh and slaughter mixed with the tang of explosives. A few police and soldiers were left alive, writhing on the floor. Behind him he saw a soldier make it to his feet. The man's face a wreckage. The soldier staggered around and tripped on a body and landed on the floor near Malcolm.

Did not stir again.

Muffled pops broke through the noise in his ears and he looked in the other direction and saw a soldier on his knees near the doors to the East Hall. A rifle used as a crutch. The man tried to stand and then Khoja appeared behind him and shot the man in the head. The soldier fell and Khoja strode past. Fired into the chest of a plainclothes policeman who lay on the floor and then looked at Malcolm.

"You killed her," Malcolm said and his voice would not work.

Khoja said nothing. He stared at Malcolm a second longer and then moved to the double doors. The wood blackened and smoking. One of the doors hung askew on its hinges and this one Khoja kicked down and then entered the East Hall and the sound of gunfire came from within.

Malcolm let go of the wall and pitched toward the doors. Trod on hands and legs until he stumbled and fell. He picked himself up and stared at a blackened spot on the floor opposite the grand and charred double doors. Where Aziguli had been standing. The sound of shooting continued from the East Hall. Bullets hit the wall near Malcolm's head and he tore his gaze away and picked up a rifle and made entry after Khoja.

Inside the wreckage of the East Hall doors, he paused and tried to make sense of the confusion. The bodies of the soldiers who'd been nearest the entrance lay on the floor and there was paper in the air like confetti. Chairs were overturned and police and bodyguards and soldiers stood with stunned frowns on their faces. In the middle of the hall was a table that ran most of the length of the room, and on the far side of the table there were a group of older men in suits. They hunkered down on the floor while Khoja killed the security detail who'd been left behind to stop an impossible scenario. The old man methodical as he worked target to target. Closer and closer toward the men hidden behind the conference room table.

A soldier on Khoja's flank raised a rifle and Malcolm shot him.

Khoja whirled and aimed his rifle at Malcolm. Then he nodded and continued about his business.

Malcolm moved toward the old man. On the far side of the conference table he saw Vice-Premier Jiang Gaoli stand. A pistol in the Vice-Premier's hands. Malcolm shot Gaoli twice in the forehead and then ran out of bullets. He stooped to pick up a pistol from a fallen bodyguard and heard Khoja shout and looked up to see a door on the far wall burst open. Small metal cannisters sailed through the doorway and into the air to land and roll near Malcolm's feet. He turned his back to the stun grenades and shut his eyes and counted.

There was a flash of light that hurt even with his eyes closed. A series of pops and cracks and bangs and then nothing. He breathed in smoke and opened his eyes and squinted through a haze to see Khoja frozen near the head of the table. One hand in front of his eyes.

Soldiers stormed into the room, their rifles at the ready. Malcolm yelled at Khoja to take cover. The words were still on his lips as bullets found their mark in the old man's body. He stood for a long second.

Teetered like a tree cut down but not yet fallen and then collapsed all of a sudden.

Malcolm stared at Khoja's body and then looked beyond and there was Chairman Zhao Guoqiang. On his back and half shielded at the edge of the conference table. Oblivious to what was about to happen.

Malcolm raised his gun.

He breathed deep and slow. Concentrated on his aim and blocked out the screams and the shouts. He ignored the bullets in the air around him and focused on the sight picture trained on the Chairman's head. He tightened his finger on the trigger and then felt a sharp pain on the side of his head.

He stumbled and shot wide. Stars and spots appeared in his vision. He blinked back the darkness, struggled to aim the pistol that now seemed too heavy to hold and then felt another sharp pain to his head and remembered nothing more.

FIVE

18 DECEMBER 2029

Chairman Zhao Guoqiang rested his forearms on the table and stared at his interlocked hands.

"I believe you know the rest," the assassin said.

Zhao thought about that.

He thought about the reek of death in the East Hall. The air filled with dust and smoke. Empty bullet casings scattered about the floor. The cries for medical attention. The wounded with their vacant and blank stares. Shock on their faces as they bled out. The shouts of the soldiers who'd taken him by the shoulders to steer him from the room. He'd brushed them aside and staggered around, almost unable to comprehend the carnage and the corpses. Politburo members and their aides entangled in their last moments. Tears on the cheeks of Secretary Lu Weidong, of the Central Secretariat. Secretary Lu cradled his right arm and stood sentry over the bodies of Zhang Qishan, who had been Chairman of the National People's Congress, and also Xu Huning, the Chairman of the Chinese People's Political Consultative Conference. Premier Ling Chunlan's head cradled in General Chen's lap. Zhao had pushed Ling onto the Standing Committee against her protests and now her blood had stained Chen's pants wet and dark.

And Vice-Premier Jiang Gaoli, his suit jacket fallen open and his legs askew. Jiang's head faced in an impossible direction had he been alive and there were twin bullet holes above his eyes. Bereft of the dignity he had known in life. The carpet sleek and wet underneath his head and Zhao remembered he'd thought the blood would look thicker. On his knees beside Jiang Gaoli was Wang Qiao, the Secretary of the Central

Commission for Discipline Inspection. Wang clasped one of Jiang's hands at his chest and listened as the old man breathed his last.

"An impressive story," Zhao said. "Full of valor and ingenuity and Western exceptionalism." He paused and considered his words and then raised his gaze to stare at the assassin.

"Unfortunately, it is one I do not believe."

• • • • • •

Jiang Gaoli had warned him, a little over a year ago when the conditions for the attack had begun to be met. He'd voiced his concerns in private and then again at a Standing Committee session. Two of the seven-person group had sided with Vice-Premier Jiang and the others with Zhao. But not the half that counted.

"Caution and patience," Jiang had counselled. "The Americans have isolated themselves better than we could have planned and there is every indication the President-elect will continue that trend. All we need do is wait them out."

"Time is not on our side, Comrade Vice-Premier," Zhao said. "You have all seen the reports."

"Untrue," Secretary Wang said. "Our economy continues to grow."

"Not as quickly as projected, even with the new trade partnerships," Premier Ling said.

"Relative to the rest of the world, we are well off," Secretary Wang said. "Our technology strategy is working, as is our industrial policy. We will weather the coming years better than any other country."

Zhao slammed the table with both hands. "Our economy is about to shrink for the first time since the pandemic. The second time in fifty years. Tell me how that will enable us to withstand what lies ahead."

Vice-Premier Jiang cleared his throat. "This is contentious," he said. "Perhaps we should take a break to collect ourselves."

"There is no need," Zhao said and let his gaze roam over the other members. "Yes, we are better off than most. But that is no longer enough. Our financial reserves have been depleted through this ridiculous on-again, off-again trade war with the Americans. Last year our work force shrank and it will do so again."

"That will balance out," Jiang said. "The Family Planning Policy has been reversed."

"Two generations too late," Zhao said. "And birth rates have not changed."

"We have many solutions," Wang said.

"Like what?"

"In this specific case, reduce pension payments. For starters."

"Do that and the water that carries the boat will be the same that swallows it."

Silence.

Zhao snorted. "We sit here and speak of individual policies and plans as if spring arrives with the blossoming of a single flower," he said and then bowed his head toward Jiang. "Comrade Vice-Premier, you are right to caution against rashness. However, I'm sure you will concede it is also true that opportunity may knock but once. As I have explained, we have a small window of time in which to act. We must seize this opportunity to create the harmony needed for all flowers to bloom together. Should we fail, our individual challenges will reach the point that they become unmanageable in the future. This is exactly what the Americans have been working toward."

Jiang shared a glance with Wang and then nodded. "A formidable argument, Comrade Chairman. But violence is difficult to predict."

"Almost as difficult to predict as the Americans," Secretary Wang said.

"Which is why the attack is designed to minimize casualties," Premier Ling said.

"I am still not convinced an EMP strike will work," Zhang Qishan said.

"Strikes," Premier Ling said.

"Regardless," Zhang said, "the Americans began strengthening their grid against exactly this threat a decade ago."

"And promptly let the funding die in the aftermath of the coronavirus," Chairman Zhao said. "They are unprepared, comrades, as unprepared as they were for the pandemic. And they are divided. I would not be surprised if half of them welcomed us as saviors. The attack will work."

"There will be consequences," Vice-Premier Jiang said.

"As the wind blows and the clouds fly," Zhao Guoqiang said and nodded once more. "But, we cannot let that deter us from what we need to do."

· · · · ·

Zhao pushed his memories aside and considered the assassin. This man with his lank hair stuck to the caked blood on his forehead, his wrists chafed raw from the manacles that bound him to the table.

This man and his lies.

"Like all good stories, parts of yours are undoubtedly true." Zhao pushed away from the table and rose to his feet. Then he slid in the chair and stood with one hand on the chairback. "I believe you were in the Taklamakan. You found Ismail Khoja, after all. I do not believe you crossed the desert in its entirety."

The assassin's face did not change as he stared at a space in the middle of the table.

"I know this because it would not be possible to keep an expedition like the one you described a secret," Zhao Guoqiang said. "Do you think crossings of the Taklamakan occur every week? And if they did, do you think we would not know about them?"

The assassin glanced up and then returned his gaze to the table.

"It is, however, also irrelevant as it is the least of your lies. Did you expect me to believe that you simply drove into Beijing? Slipped past layers of security with a known terrorist whose face would have been recognized the moment he stepped foot in the city?"

"And yet here I am."

"You are arrogant. Like all Americans."

"My parents are from Jiaxing."

Zhao waved his hand. "That is nothing. You may have Chinese heritage, but you share none of our values. You have no respect for your elders. For your betters. This, and your arrogance, has led you to underestimate me. Why else would you tell these lies when they can so easily be uncovered? And to do so while the blood of my countrymen dries in the Great Hall above."

"Just because you don't believe we did it, does not mean it cannot be done."

"It means it cannot be done without help."

The assassin glanced up again and then looked away.

"Look at me," Zhao said.

The assassin did not move.

"I will not tell you again."

The assassin remained motionless a second longer and then raised his gaze.

"You expect me to believe that a retired soldier put together a small team that entered China in secret, crossed the most hostile terrain in the country, and then executed an attack into the most defended building in the country. Without insider help." Zhao shook his head. "It is not coherent."

"We had Khoja."

"Humor does not suit you."

"So I am told."

"By whom? This Russian you spoke of? More likely this is but one more lie."

The assassin's mouth opened and then closed.

"Your lack of composure betrays you," Zhao said. He stared at the man and then picked up the photo of the woman and child from the table. "Your family."

"*Shì.*"

"They died in the attack."

"*Shì.*"

"I regret their deaths."

The assassin glanced up and for a moment Zhao was glad for the manacles.

"I do not rejoice in death," Zhao said. "There were other options. All would have resulted in more lives lost."

"You knocked out the electrical grid during the worst winter in three decades."

"And in the aftermath, we delivered food and humanitarian supplies."

"Once we'd surrendered."

"I note that no American refused our assistance."

"We had no choice."

"There is always a choice. Your president made the right one."

"And my choice is what brought me here. We are more determined than you give us credit for."

"Although not so exceptional."

The assassin held Zhao's gaze a moment longer and then looked down.

Zhao dropped the photo back onto the table and then walked to the door of the interrogation cell. At the door he turned and said, "In time, it is possible America will recover a measure of its former glory, although unlikely. Your failure to understand the arc of history, and your country's place in it, is no less a shortcoming than your inability to understand human nature. Like asking me to believe that a man like Ismail Khoja would have helped you."

"You have no idea who Ismail Khoja was," the assassin said. "He would've killed you."

"No. You are wrong."

"You seem very sure of yourself."

"As I should be," Zhao said. "I was Party Secretary of the Xinjiang Autonomous Region during the Uighur uprising. Khoja had his chance to assassinate me five years ago and chose not to."

• • • • •

It had been the summer of 2024. Zhao had been at his home in *Zhongnanhai*, at work in his office. The house darkened and mute so his wife could rest.

He'd left a binder open at the mid-point on his desk and padded out of the study and down the hall. Outside the sitting room, he paused. Then he closed his eyes and cocked his head and listened to the dead stillness.

"Come out," Zhao said.

The shadows divided and a man emerged. A black shirt with Mandarin collar and his black hair gathered in a topknot.

"I did not expect you to be alone," Zhao said.

"She is outside," Ismail Khoja said, "attending to the guards."

"I see," Zhao said and then drew himself up to stand tall and erect. "I ask that you do not disturb my wife. She is unwell."

"This will not take long," Khoja said and then attacked.

Zhao dodged even as he marvelled at Khoja's speed and the silence with which he struck. The next strike on the heels of the first. Zhao retreated into the kitchen where he jockeyed an island between himself and Khoja. They paused and stared at each other, the air filled with the sound of their breath while the fight played out in their minds.

Zhao did not think he could win.

"This will not improve the situation in Xinjiang," he said.

"How can it not?"

"The Party will appoint another to enact its will."

"They will meet the same fate."

"The will of the Party is the will of the people."

"The people want peace."

"I agree."

Khoja frowned.

"It is understandable you do not believe me," Zhao said. "However, I can assure you that I see the same goal as you."

"Which is?"

"A government that preferences harmony over conflict." Zhao gestured to an iron teapot on the counter. "May I explain?" He waited for a response and then filled two bowls with tea when Ismail Khoja did not move. Zhao took one of the bowls for himself and left the other in the middle of the island. "To have peace, we must first have unity."

Khoja's lips pressed together in a thin line.

"You do not agree?" Zhao asked.

"Your idea of unity is flawed," Khoja said. "A musical harmony is created through a combination of different notes."

"True. However, for the harmony to work, those notes must work together and coexist. In peace."

"You preach harmony while you hold my daughter prisoner in one of your camps," Khoja said and lunged across the counter.

Zhao dropped his bowl to parry and it tumbled through the air and shattered on the floor. Khoja pressed the attack, furious and savage and

Zhao fell back against the onslaught. A wildfire that chased him from the kitchen and down the hall. Khoja's strikes began to land and Zhao fell back into the doorway of his den where he determined to give no more ground.

"Zhao Guoqiang?" a woman asked. Her voice muffled by the bedroom door down the hall.

Zhao paused and so did Khoja. They stared at each other and were silent and then Khoja nodded.

"I am here, *Chen Yu*," Zhao said. "I apologize for waking you."

"I heard you talking."

"I spilled some tea."

"You should not stay up so late. You work too hard."

"I have one or two things left to do. Please do not wait up for me."

"Would you close the door to your study? The light is bothering me."

"Of course."

Zhao straightened and then entered his office. Gestured Khoja inside and closed the door. "Shall we continue?" he asked and then turned to find his assassin stood before a small wooden altar house on a waist-high black metal stand in a corner of the room. Four carved columns supported the arched roof of the house and upon the glazed roof tiles perched six dragon-headed guardians. A porch with latticed doors ran along the front of the house and on the porch were three jade figurines and a framed picture of a young girl.

"I had thought these shrines were outlawed," Khoja said.

"They are," Zhao said.

Khoja picked up the smallest of the figurines. He cradled the *fenghuang* and glanced at the picture of the girl.

"My daughter," Zhao said.

"I hope it has not been hard to adjust to the change."

Zhao dipped his head. "It has been difficult for my wife," he said. "I accept the risk of the shrine for her."

"Then you understand how a father feels for his family."

"I understand what it's like to be a person," Zhao said, "from the viewpoint of a person."

"And do you understand the viewpoint of a people?"

Zhao nodded. "Of course."

Khoja looked at Zhao. "Then how can you persist in your actions?"

"Because I also understand the viewpoint of all under heaven."

"And what does that tell you?"

"That the interests to be considered should be the interests of all. We cannot allow individual grievances to divide us. Rather, we must all come together so we can overcome the challenges we will face in the future."

"So you will continue with your mission."

"*Shi.*"

"No matter the cost?"

"We must all add wood to the fire. To do otherwise is to let the spark of humanity go out."

Khoja turned from Zhao to stare at the *fenghuang* he held. "You are from Xinjiang, are you not?"

"My father was exiled there. It is where I grew up."

"That is why you were chosen to be Party Secretary of the region."

"It is a test to see how I would govern the country."

Khoja snorted. "The country is nothing like Xinjiang."

"That may be true," Zhao said and nodded. "But governing a large country is like cooking a small fish. I know of no harder fish to cook than Xinjiang."

"Even so, what good will it do?" Khoja asked. "We are but one country among many."

"Whoever said I would stop at unifying our country?"

When Khoja did not answer, Zhao opened the study door. Then he turned off the light and headed for the kitchen and drew up short when he saw Gul Dilmurat. She was dressed in coal-black robes, the twin braids of her hair draped upon each shoulder and the broken shards of the tea bowl crushed beneath her feet.

He stared at her and then she drew a knife from a cutting block and slashed for his throat. A cut to remove his head. The blade stopped an inch from Zhao's neck by Khoja's hand.

Gul's face spasmed. "Let go," she said and twisted in Khoja's grasp. "This man has brought death to our people."

"Judge me if you must," Zhao said. "But I will not shirk my responsibilities. I cannot, if we hope to prosper."

Gul screamed and thrashed and Khoja held her back. Grim and silent and resolute. When it became clear Khoja would not release her, Gul stilled. Khoja held her a second longer and then opened his hand and no sooner had he let go then her blade flashed and a cut opened on Khoja's cheek. His hand went to his face and it was still moving when the blade flashed again and a second cut opened on his other cheek. Her lip pulled back in a sneer and then she whirled and took flight, her robes an ebony swirl behind her.

Khoja pulled his hand from his face and stared at the blood on his fingers.

"You will need safe passage out of *Zhongnanhai*," Zhao said and offered Khoja a hand towel.

"That will not be necessary," Khoja said and walked away from Zhao's outstretched hand.

"Your daughter will be released."

"I have not asked."

"Even so."

Khoja hesitated. Produced the *fenghuang* and held it in the palm of his hand. "We must all add to the fire," he said.

"As you wish."

Khoja stood for a moment with head bowed and then the figurine disappeared into his robes and he followed his wife into the darkness.

●　　●　　●　　●　　●

Zhao Guoqiang contemplated the assassin, who had not moved. "You do not seem surprised," he said.

"I don't see how it changes anything," the assassin said. "If it's even true."

"Perhaps it is a story you already knew."

"I was told that Khoja and Gul were captured by the Central Security Bureau while infiltrating *Zhongnanhai*," the assassin said. "They escaped while being transferred to Qincheng prison and went into hiding."

"Yes, that's what the reports said," Zhao said.

"Which reports?"

"The ones Admiral Couzens gave you."

"I don't see how you could know that."

Zhao leaned over the table. Glanced at the MicroLED screen on the wall behind the assassin that displayed all the holes in the man's story. "What you believe does not matter," Zhao said. "We've known their location for years. They were permitted to live in exile on condition they renounce the Uighur uprising and sacrifice their network, which they did. As a result, conditions in Xinjiang were allowed to improve and Khoja's daughter was returned to him."

"People can change their minds."

"But not their nature."

The assassin narrowed his eyes and then dropped his gaze.

"Ismail Khoja was a worthy adversary," Zhao said. "I knew him as you never could."

"I spent months with him in the desert."

"And I fought him for years. In all that time he impressed me with his dignity and valor."

"Gul –"

"Do not talk to me about Gul Dilmurat!" Zhao shouted. He glared at the assassin and then pushed away from the table and stood. "You have told enough lies. Ismail Khoja and Gul Dilmurat would not have butchered innocents at a gas station."

"And yet those people were killed."

"By you and your team."

"No."

"Do you think us fools?" Zhao asked. "Do you think we cannot track American assets and activities and personnel?"

The assassin looked up and seemed about to speak.

"We know about your Special Operations facility in New Mexico, where the initial planning for this mission took place," Zhao said. "We allowed it to stay operational because it was so thoroughly compromised."

The assassin closed his mouth.

"We know you work for Admiral Couzens," Zhao said and then tugged on the cuffs of his shirt. "We have monitored this man's career since he was promoted to Rear Admiral. He was in charge of targeted killings in Afghanistan and Pakistan. He commanded all American special operations in Africa. He is a ruthless commander who shows little mercy or desire to understand his opponent."

The assassin clasped his hands together and the skin on his knuckles turned white.

"In April of this year, Admiral Couzens hosted representatives from the United Kingdom, NATO, Japan, Australia, Israel, and others, at this temporary planning headquarters in New Mexico," Zhao said. "Even Russia attended by sending General Yuri Alekseyev, the commander of Russian Special Operations Forces."

"Admiral Couzens is in charge of Special Operations Command," the assassin said. "His duties require him to meet his counterparts. Particularly in time of war."

"I surmise that there was one other person who was there."

"Who?"

"You," Zhao said.

The assassin glanced at him.

"It is not necessary for you to reply," Zhao said. "While no audio recording of the meeting was available, we know what was discussed. Those in attendance agreed to assist the United States in leading a retaliatory attack. Your actions were not some individual vendetta, but rather part of a coordinated international attack on my country. An attack that failed."

"Then why are you here talking to me?" the assassin asked. "Shouldn't you be planning your response?"

Zhao allowed himself a thin smile. "Assassination is a tool of the weak," he said. "I have more time than my officials think because had your country been able to mount a credible military operation, they would not have wasted time and effort on such a dubious plan."

"It didn't take much effort."

Zhao stood over the assassin and then clasped his hands behind his back. "I think I find your arrogance the hardest to accept," he said. "So little respect for your adversaries, and yet, what has your country achieved for all the gifts it has been given? Your military might, wasted on failed wars. Your wealth squandered on vanity projects and personal enrichment. Your leaders unable or unwilling to perceive or appreciate the true threats to either your country or the world. All of you lost in some imaginary past when the world needed America, when it is American leadership that has led the world to the brink of ruin."

The assassin said nothing and Zhao studied him in silence. Then he shook his head and walked to the door where he raised his hand to let the guards know he was ready to leave.

"The Russians were happy you attacked us," the assassin said.

Zhao paused with his hand in mid-air. "Of course they were," he said.

"They laughed at us, said we should never have pulled out of NATO," the assassin said. "I don't even understand how Admiral Couzens got them to attend."

"That is simple," Zhao said and turned. "They view us as a threat."

"That they do," the assassin said. "That they do."

"Why did you conceal this part of your story?"

"Why don't you tell me?" the assassin asked. "You seem to have all the answers."

Zhao stood for a moment and then walked back to the table. He stared at the assassin and thought about all the officials who'd warned him the Americans would never look at them as equals. All the advisors who'd told him America would rather be put out of its misery than submit to its own Century of Humiliation. It occurred to him as he studied the man who'd come to murder him that if even one American would show humility, then perhaps their country could yet be spared.

He did not know, however, if *this* American could admit he had been wrong. So Zhao would show him. It would not take long, and, in the process, the ideal response to the attack would no doubt become clear.

"Very well," Zhao said and sat down across from the assassin.

Then, he began to speak.

SIX

APRIL, 2029

ZHAO'S VERSION

Malcolm sat near the foot of a long conference table in Admiral Couzens's New Mexico headquarters. Recessed computers were sunk into the tabletop and microphones dangled from the ceiling. The walls of the room were ringed by a perimeter of metallic grey desks with transparent glass screens and a holographic map of east Asia was projected above the center of the table.

All the seats at the table were occupied. Lieutenant-General Stuart Fletcher from the United Kingdom and Lieutenant-General Ed Wilton from Australia were there, both in command of global operations for their countries. The German general Ødegård who was there to represent NATO, as well as Major-General Yuri Alekseyev, who headed Russia's Special Operations Forces Command. A civilian named Toshiro Kobayashi spoke for the Japanese Self-Defense Force and a woman called Meirav Arens who was possibly from Mossad spoke for the Israelis, and a Canadian general who mumbled his name.

At the head of the table sat Admiral Don T. Couzens III of the United States Special Operations Command. His bald, black, head shiny with sweat while he waited for the delegates to absorb the briefing.

The Russian general, Alekseyev, spoke first. A small man with grey-flecked hair who leaned over the table on his elbows as he talked. "Admiral Couzens," he said, "three months ago, you were certain the North Koreans had attacked your country. Now, you say it was China."

"Affirmative," Couzens said. He pressed a button on a screen to his front and the hologram over the table morphed from the map of Asia to a three-dimensional image of a containerized ballistic missile system. "As we already knew, the ships that parked off our coasts in January to launch nuclear warheads into our atmosphere were North Korean. We confirmed that when we recovered the wreckages. In the process, we identified the launchers as Chinese."

"I seem to remember MI6 providing information that showed conclusively that North Korea couldn't field a system of that sophistication," Lieutenant-General Fletcher said.

"Nor did the Koreans have the cyber expertise that accompanied the attack," the Israeli named Meirav said.

"Colleagues," Couzens said and he sat back in his chair with his hands high up on the armrests like it was a throne. "I'll grant we may have rushed things a bit."

"That's one way to put it, Don," Wilton said in an Australian accent.

"The President needed to make a strong statement."

"Well, I reckon the Koreans would agree he accomplished that," Wilton said.

"Can we focus on the matter at hand?" Alekseyev asked.

"Of course, Yuri," Couzens said and dipped his head toward the Russian. "Go ahead."

Alekseyev seemed to mull his words and then looked around the table. "With respect, Admiral, I'm confused," he said. "You did not need to bring us all the way to New Mexico to tell us this. Normal channels would have been suitable."

"That's the thing, Yuri," Couzens said. "The United States does not share that assessment."

"And why is that?" the NATO general Ødegård asked.

"Because we're not sure to what extent our communication channels have been compromised," Couzens said. "We believe the Chinese have had a quantum breakthrough."

"In what way?" Ødegård asked.

"Cryptanalysis," Couzens said.

"So they achieved quantum code breaking first," Fletcher said. "We are shortly behind."

Couzens snorted. "You're fighting the last war, Stu. The Chinese have *already* shown they can use their breakthrough to launch unopposed targeted attacks against our industrial and physical infrastructure via the cyber domain," he said. "I'm not stupid, Stu. Data breaches are one thing. Crippling our national infrastructure is another."

"I beg your pardon?" Ødegård said.

"It's the only explanation we have for the effectiveness of the cyber attack." Couzens exhaled and then leaned back in his chair and ran a hand over his head. "Shit," he said, "since I've said this much, you might as well know we're also pretty confident the Chinese are well on their way to integrating quantum sensing into their anti-access capabilities. Hell, they may already be able to track our nuclear submarines for all we know."

The room was silent. The principals at the table sat back in their chairs or looked to their aides seated behind them for confirmation and the aides shuffled through binders and briefing papers. Shook their heads and exchanged whispers with their bosses and then everyone looked to Couzens.

"Impossible," Alekseyev said. "We would know."

"You just found out," Couzens said.

"Are you sure?" Fletcher asked.

Couzens sighed. "We're still doing the forensics," he said. "But I can tell you that the cyber part of the attack that hit us was beyond anything we'd seen before. Point of fact, the nukes they exploded in the atmosphere probably weren't even required."

"That doesn't mean it was quantum," the Israeli said.

"I agree in theory, Meirav," Couzens said. "But nothing else adds up. Even assuming state of the art conventional computing power, our guys say what happened shouldn't have been possible."

"A new cyber capability perhaps, one other than quantum," Ødegård said.

"Looked at that," Couzens said and shook his head.

"Don, you're hardly in a position to do extensive analysis on a cyber attack," Fletcher said. "You don't even have power re-established across the country."

"Enough of our sites survived, like this one," Couzens said, "and what I'm telling you is there is no other explanation. And I'll go one step farther, because once you assume the Chinese have cleared this threshold, a lot of their recent actions make more sense."

"The satellite launches," Meirav said.

"That's right," Couzens said. "And the upgrades to their anti-stealth systems."

"I don't suppose your own quantum capability was anywhere close," Ødegård said.

"Let's put it this way," Couzens said, "for the moment, everyone should assume the Chinese have undisputed quantum supremacy."

"Get to the point, Admiral," Alekseyev said.

"You know where I'm going with this, Yuri," Couzens said.

"I would like to hear you say it."

"All right." Couzens sat up straight in his chair. "The United States of America is asking you all to help us take down China."

The room erupted in noise.

· · · · ·

Admiral Couzens let the ruckus continue for several minutes. At one point he caught Malcolm's gaze and winked, and then he cleared his throat and held up his hands for order. "I appreciate the enthusiasm," he said, "but why don't we all breathe through the nose for a few minutes here."

"What is there to discuss?" Alekseyev asked. "Why haven't you already attacked?"

Couzens leaned over the table and clasped his hands together. "We're not ready," he said. "As Stu pointed out, many parts of the country are only now getting electricity back."

"Bullshit," the Australian general, Wilton, said. "Your submarine fleet has more missiles than China does in its entire inventory. We're not talking invasion here."

"A submarine fleet the Chinese might now be able to track," Couzens said.

"How long?" Alekseyev asked. "Until you're ready?"

"A year," Couzens said. "Probably longer."

Alekseyev pounded on the table. "And in the mean time, China gets stronger," he said.

"You must have a plan," Fletcher said.

"Of course," Couzens said. "Officially, we'll pursue reparations through the United Nations. At the same time, we put the screws to the Chinese wherever we can to keep them overwhelmed. That'll buy us time to coordinate an attack on their quantum and second-strike capabilities either later this year or the next."

"It will be difficult to conceal an operation so large," Meirav said.

"What did you have in mind?" Ødegård asked.

"That's where you all come in," Couzens said and looked at Kobayashi. "We'd ask Japan to increase pressure around the Senkakus. Likewise, we'd ask Australia to step up your naval activity in the South China Sea and urge the Malaysians and Filipinos to do the same. We'd also like you to coordinate a multinational exercise for later this year."

"Bloody hell," Wilton said. "That's a tall order."

"I presume you wish to increase internal unrest in China as well," Alekseyev said.

"Of course. We took the liberty of compiling a detailed list of actions each of your countries can take," Couzens said and then fell silent as aides began to distribute folders around the table.

"What's Project Broken Sword?" Wilton asked, his briefing binder open before him.

Couzens nodded at Malcolm. "That would be our Hail Mary," he said.

Heads swiveled toward Malcolm.

Fletcher scowled. "I'm sorry, who is this?" he asked.

"Commander Malcolm Kwong," Couzens said. "Navy SEAL."

"Retired," Malcolm said.

"Mal's been out of circulation for a little while, but he's lost none of his edge," Couzens said. "Why don't you walk us through your plan, Mal?"

"Yes, sir," Malcolm said.

Malcolm touched his screen and the hologram in the middle of the table changed and then he began to speak. He spoke of the team he would put together and how they would get into China. He showed them the route across the Taklamakan and he spoke of Ismail Khoja and he finished by explaining how Khoja would help the team infiltrate Beijing and assassinate the Standing Committee of the Chinese Communist Party. He finished speaking in less than fifteen minutes and then sat and waited for questions in the silent room.

"Our sources indicate Ismail Khoja is no longer alive," Meirav said.

"He is," Couzens said. "Let's leave it at that."

"Even so, why would he help?" Meirav asked. "Khoja abandoned the Uighur cause five years ago."

"The man is a terrorist," Alekseyev said. "He cannot be trusted."

"All we need from Khoja is his knowledge of the Beijing underground," Couzens said and glanced at Malcolm. "We're confident we can get him to share that information. Whether he helps or not after that is irrelevant."

"Bold," Alekseyev said. "But not much chance of success."

"Doesn't need to succeed," Wilton said. "Just needs to keep the Chinese occupied so they'll hopefully make a mistake."

Alekseyev rubbed the bridge of his nose. "I would caution you not to underestimate the Chinese," he said.

"Couldn't have said it better myself," Couzens said and then cleared his throat. "Colleagues, the United States has been criticized in the past, perhaps rightly so, for going it alone. This time, we need the support of our international partners. We need your help."

"In fact, you cannot do this without us," Alekseyev said.

Couzens looked at Alekseyev for a moment and then nodded. "That's right, Yuri."

"In that case, I have to ask, what's in it for us?"

"I'm not sure I follow."

"Admiral, you've asked us to assume a high degree of risk to come to your aid," Alekseyev said and then held out his hand. "However, we are quite satisfied with the current turn of events. So, I will repeat my question. What's in it for Russia?"

"I'd have thought that'd be obvious," Couzens said. "Self-preservation."

The muscles in Alekseyev's jaw tightened. "You are in no position to give threats," he said.

"I agree," Couzens said and then smiled and looked around the faces at the table. "Plus, it'd make me one hell of a poor host. People have accused me of a lot of things, but never that."

"Then explain yourself," Alekseyev said.

"Yes, Don, I think we'd all like to know," Ødegård said and there were nods from the others.

"What I'm saying," Couzens said in a slow drawl, "is that the question you all need to ask yourselves is, who do you think the Chinese will target next? Because they sure as hell aren't going to stop with us."

Couzens watched and waited as the delegates digested what he'd said. His back erect and stiff and after what seemed a minute or two he began to nod.

"Now," Couzens said, "if we're all done sniffing each other's backsides, why don't we talk about what you all can bring to the fight."

• • • •

The team landed at Kyrgyzstan's Kant Air Force Base on a C-5 Galaxy in late August. A contingent of Russian soldiers received them and they lived and worked out of an airfield hangar for a month. They received cultural briefings from Uighur and Chinese expatriates, they sat through classes on desert survival given by a British survivalist, and they shot pigs at point blank range and then applied tourniquets and bandages while Australian medics screamed at them.

At the end of the month, a convoy of Russian light cargo trucks pulled up to the hangar in the pre-dawn darkness. They mounted the vehicles and drove all morning to the Torugart Pass. There, the team bribed their way across the border and were met by a Chinese tour company that had been paid an exorbitant amount for what amounted to one month's work. By the end of the day, the team had set up in a compound on the outskirts of Kashgar that had been secured for them by the tour company, which had since gone out of business.

The team stayed in Kashgar for four days, long enough to bribe the highest ranking local Communist Party official, a man named Zeng Huimin. This official was known to Chairman Zhao Guoqiang from the latter's time as Party Secretary for the Xinjiang Autonomous Region. Indeed, Chairman Zhao had made it known Zeng would never rise above his current position due to the man's limited competence. On the day foreign assassins infiltrated the Great Hall of the People, a notice would go out for Zeng Huimin's arrest and it would be discovered that he, too, had gone missing, presumably on a sightseeing trip with the now defunct tour company.

After four days, the team relocated to Makit to complete their preparations. A week later, they entered the Taklamakan.

• • • • •

After the first, or second, or maybe fifth day, the reality of the desert set in. At that night's camp, they tended to the camels and dug for water. The Uighurs sat in silence and cooked around a fire while the remainder gathered in a loose circle and ate pre-packaged meal packs warmed by flameless ration heaters. They tossed their garbage to the ground to be collected by the wind.

Malcolm ate his meal and then wiped his spoon on his pants. "Let's pack it in," he said and stood. "Tomorrow's a long day."

Wolf cleared his throat and spat. Watched Malcolm and lit a cigarette and then said something to Gleb that Malcolm couldn't hear and the two laughed.

"Something on your mind, Schlosser?" Malcolm asked.

Wolf dragged on his cigarette. He squinted and exhaled a cloud of smoke through his nostrils and then smiled. "Not at all, mate," he said.

Malcolm stared at Wolf until the Brit dropped his gaze and then he turned and headed for his sleeping bag.

"Well, actually, now that you mention it, there is something," Wolf said.

Malcolm paused. "What?"

"I've been thinking about this Old Lo Mein fella and whether he's worth all this trouble."

Malcolm glanced at Wolf. "You mean Khoja," he said.

Wolf's grin grew wider. "Whatever," the Brit said.

"Don't worry about Khoja," Malcolm said. "That's my job."

"See, that's the thing," Wolf said. He sucked on his cigarette and the burning tip glowed bright in the twilight. "I don't think you have the slightest idea what you're doing."

"Having second thoughts already?" David asked.

"Mate, I'm only here to get you through the bloody desert."

"Then why don't you focus on that task?" David said.

"I am," Wolf said.

"Not by talking about Khoja," David said.

"Shut it," Wolf said and pointed at David with his cigarette.

Malcolm held up a hand to David and kept his gaze on Wolf. "So, tell me how Khoja relates to you getting us through the desert," he said.

"Because he's an old bugger who, apparently, would kill us as soon as look at us," Wolf said. "Near as I can tell, that makes him the biggest threat out here next to the desert itself. The way I see it, without him, our chances of survival go way up. And if we don't need to find him, then we don't have to march through the center of the bloody desert."

"We're getting him."

Wolf shook his head. "The Uighurs hate him," he said.

"They shouldn't even know he's involved," David said.

Wolf flicked the butt of his cigarette at David. "They may be stupid, mate," he said, "but they're not deaf."

David scrambled to his feet and Malcolm blocked his way. "This isn't a discussion," he said.

"We're bloody vulnerable out here," Wolf said. "Too vulnerable to play nursemaid to some old git with a death wish."

"Leave it," Malcolm said.

"Christ, you're an ignorant wanker," Wolf said. "I don't know what's worse. That you think this is a good idea, or that you believe I'm the only one who thinks it's a bad one."

Malcolm stared at Wolf and then looked around the group.

None of whom would return his gaze.

He took a breath and looked over to the fire where the Uighurs sat. Exhaled and knelt to pick up a handful of sand and let the grains trickle through his fist to fall on the ground. "Five years ago," Malcolm said, "Khoja led an attack into *Zhongnanhai*."

"We've bloody well heard this story," Wolf said. "Through the main gate against the best soldiers the PLA had to offer. A load of tosh."

"That's not how they got in," Malcolm said. "A week before the attack, Khoja captured the wives and children of two of the guards to *Zhongnanhai*. The families lived in the same apartment complex, and when the guards came home one night, they found Khoja and Dilmurat in their homes. Their families bound on the floor. They tied up the men and Khoja made them watch as Dilmurat cut pieces off their wives."

"Bollocks," Wolf said. "They'd have told him whatever he wanted to hear before then."

"Khoja didn't ask any questions."

"What?"

"Not at first," Malcolm said. "He let Dilmurat cut up the women to let the guards know he meant business, and only then did he tell them what he wanted. A map for the underground tunnels in *Di Xia Cheng*, and access points to *Zhongnanhai*."

"The underground city is a rumor," Wolf said.

"No, it isn't," Malcolm said. He scooped another handful of sand and let it drain as he continued to speak. "Khoja had done his homework," he said, "and knew these guards could access the maps. After they agreed, Khoja let Dilmurat finish with the wives. She cut off their remaining arms and legs. Took their tongues and the old man forced the men to watch as she held her knife to the necks of their children as a warning. Then he showed them pictures of their extended family and in all of the photos, one of Khoja's men in the background."

"Bloody Christ," Wolf said. "And that's how he got into *Zhongnanhai*."

"Yeah," Malcolm said. "And he's going to help us get in the same way."

Wolf lit another cigarette and held in the smoke and then let it out. "But that's my point," he said after his second drag. "If he's such a hard case, what makes you think he'll help? Why wouldn't he just kill us instead?"

"Because I'm going to cut up his wife and daughter if he doesn't," Malcolm said.

Wolf stared at him and then chuckled. Grinned and pointed at him with the cigarette and then took a drag and scanned the faces in the group. Saw that nobody else had moved and his smile disappeared and then he turned back to Malcolm. "You're serious," he said.

"You can still back out if you want," Malcolm said. "Makit's only a few days back."

"Not if I want to get paid," Wolf said.

"Your choice."

Wolf sat and smoked. "All right then, mate," he said and then stood. "You've got me curious. So, I'll see this as far as meeting the old man."

"Just get us through the desert. That's what you're being paid for."

Wolf held out his arm in a mock bow and then walked off toward his bedroll.

Mary and David came and stood at Malcolm's side and together they watched the Brit disappear into the darkening night.

"Think he believed it?" Mary asked.

"Doesn't matter," Malcolm said. "He's doing what I want."

"You should have told the rest of the story," David said.

"What good would that do."

"Put the fear of God into him. Khoja's not going to come quietly."

Malcolm thought about all the parts of the story the Chinese reports had left out. How Khoja and Dilmurat had exited the tunnels in *Zhongnanhai* to be confronted with battalions of Central Security Bureau soldiers. How the two had fought through and almost killed Zhao, who was then the Provincial Party Secretary for Xinjiang and a newly established full member of the Central Committee. Already marked for greatness and summoned to *Zhongnanhai* for a meeting of the Standing Committee. Zhao had been spared by Khoja for no known reason and soon after the Uighur uprising died.

It was the modern version of a fairy tale to scare security analysts before they went to bed. Smoke and mirrors and magic beans.

Except Malcolm had seen what Khoja had done in the Middle East and Africa.

"You all right, boss?" Mary asked.

Malcolm blinked. Glanced at Mary and then looked at David.

"Let's get some rest," Malcolm said. "Early start tomorrow."

• • • • •

The expedition reached Khoja's mountain on the thirteenth day in the desert.

They stood at the base of the peak with the sun late in the sky and watched the shadows lengthen and grow among the cliffs and crannies. The outline of a path snaked back-and-forth up the mountain's rocky approach and there was no sign of footprints or recent use. Malcolm ordered the Uighurs to unload the camels and set up camp and then gathered the rest of the group.

"Grab a bite to eat and whatever you need for the night," he said. "We climb in fifteen minutes."

"What about ropes and gear?" David asked.

"Don't need them," Malcolm said.

"Are you daft?" Wolf asked. "That's at least a two-thousand-foot climb."

"Khoja gets up it somehow. We'll take that route."

"I hate to say it, but I agree with Wolf," David said. "Let's check out the slope today and climb in the morning."

"The mountain's not going anywhere, boss," Mary said. "And it'll be dark in a few hours."

"Mary's right," David said. "Being stuck on the side of that hill at night won't be fun."

"Then we'd best get going so that doesn't happen," Malcolm said and headed for the camels to collect his pack.

"What's the bloody rush?" Wolf called after him. "It's not like he knows we're coming."

Malcolm stopped. Turned to face the group and did not like the weakness and indecision that he saw. "He's been watching us the past two days," he said.

• • • • •

Ismail Khoja watched the group of five trek up the southern approach to the mountain. The gentle slope was bare and scoured down to jagged rocks in between which snaked the trail. A faded line among the browns and reds.

The group stopped where the approach merged into the steep sides of the mountain and the leader looked up at the top of the mountain. The man remained that way for several seconds and then looked back over the ones stretched behind him on the traverse. In the camp far beneath, the camel handlers had paused in their labors and clustered around the cairn that marked the trailhead.

Observing.

Then the group began their climb and passed out of Khoja's sight.

The edge of the sun touched the western horizon when the climbers reappeared on a scree-covered stretch of trail. Khoja watched them scramble around the mountain base to follow the path up the eastern face where the route was shrouded in shadow and dark. The sound of a curse carried up the side of the cliff face and Khoja wondered whether they might turn back and then heard them continue on.

He lost sight of them again and was yet able to track their progress. They climbed like pigs. Grunts and complaints and a cacophony of displaced rocks and noise. They continued around the cliff-face to the north where the path narrowed to a small ledge and then terminated at a series of ropes and chains. A make-shift bridge secured to the face of the mountain.

Khoja moved to stand beside a pile of rocks and stones that loomed over the route up the mountain. A piece of wood he could break in his hands was all that held back an avalanche that would scrape the face of the mountain clean. He heard footsteps and said nothing as Gul Dilmurat came to his side.

She stood for a moment and peered down into the gloom and then put her hand on the lever that would release the rocks. Then she looked at him and the wind on top of the mountain caressed her black robes. Swirled the fabric around her body except where it was pinned to her shoulders by her twin ebony braids. The lines of grey-steel wound through her hair paired with the hard-won lines of her face.

His opposite and his equal.

Khoja returned her gaze and then he shook his head.

Her face did not change. It did not need to for her to register her disapproval. She cocked her head and left her hand on the lever. Listened to the racket from the side of the mountain and studied him and then the thin line of her lips became a bit thinner and she walked away. Left him on the edge of the mountain while the sun sank into the horizon and the sky deepened through pinks and oranges and purples.

· · · · ·

Khoja left the edge of the clifftop when it became clear the climbers would summit and entered the remains of an ancient fort built on the mountain top. A compound with walls half again as tall as him and a squat building down one side of the courtyard. A stone tower jutted up from the northwest corner of the compound. He built a fire in a low brazier in the middle of the courtyard and smoothed his white robes beneath him and sat on the ground to wait.

They appeared out of the night in the open space beyond the courtyard gates. Dark shapes that coalesced at the edge of the firelight where their five shadows merged into one. Their voices low and indistinct. Khoja waited and did not move and then one of their number advanced.

The man who'd led them up the mountain.

He was covered in dirt and sweat. Strands of tied-up greasy hair had broken free to hang in his face and there were pools of black where his eyes should have been. The man entered the courtyard and advanced toward the brazier. Then he laid his pack beside him and knelt and stared at Khoja through the flames.

"You are Ismail Khoja," the man said. "Who the Arabs called, *You Hun Ye Gui.*"

"He is called that no more," Gul Dilmurat said from the doorway of the squat building.

"And you are Gul Dilmurat," the man said. His gaze on Ismail Khoja.

Gul joined them at the brazier and stared at the man. The firelight reflected in her eyes.

"My name is Malcolm Kwong," the man said. "I've come a long way to find you."

"Then you have wasted your time," Gul Dilmurat said. "We have nothing for you."

"I'll decide that for myself," the man said and then dragged his pack onto his lap. He unfastened the snaps and his hand disappeared into the main compartment of the bag.

Khoja poked at the coals. "The wise discern all in their mind but speak simply," he said.

The man's gaze met Khoja's through the sparks of the fire. Burned with an intensity Khoja had not felt in some time and they stared at each other while the light flickered and shadows danced on the compound walls.

"I suppose you will claim to hear in the silence?" Khoja asked.

"Nothing like that," the man said and pulled out a piece of wood from his backpack. "I wish only to suggest some common interests."

Khoja stirred the fire once more and then sat back. "Speak," he said.

The man nodded and then drew a knife from his belt and began to carve.

"When you're done," Khoja said, "you may leave."

The man bowed his head and began to talk.

• • • • • • •

Malcolm spoke long into the night. Gul sat beside Khoja and listened and would get up every so often to feed the fire. When Malcolm had finished, he handed Khoja the carving and then waited to see how the old man would respond.

The fire had died down and the old man sat in dim light. The carving of the snake coiled around a dragon's neck in his hands. Gul stood and laid more coals into the brazier and then took her seat again and still the old man said nothing.

"You can finish what you started," Malcolm said.

Khoja rotated the carving and studied at it from a different angle. "That was a long time ago," he said. "Much has changed."

"Not as much as you think."

The old man glanced up to stare at Malcolm through the smoke of the fire.

"I came through Kashgar," Malcolm said. "The government continues to persecute your people. The re-education centers –"

"They are not my people," Khoja said.

"I see," Malcolm said. "Then they are not what brought you to Syria?"

Khoja dropped his gaze to the carving.

"To Africa?" Malcolm asked.

"Why should I listen to an American?"

"We share great ambitions. It is natural that we would confer."

"I wonder," Khoja said. "I do not recall that being the case when you pursued me across Africa."

"There are no constant conditions in war," Malcolm said. "We walk the same path, now. There is no shame in helping each other."

"We are not friends," Khoja said. "Nor does America have much to offer, from what I have heard."

"We remain strong."

"But far away," Khoja said. "It is difficult to see how your strength could be brought to bear in this place."

"You misunderstand," Malcolm said. "Our strength is not measured by our arms alone, but through our singular unity of purpose and deed. A unity of intent that we share with you. Once we have committed to helping each other, iron bolts could not keep us apart."

"I wonder," Khoja repeated.

Gul shifted. "Enough," she said. "You have already made your decision."

"He asks the impossible," Khoja said.

"You once promised to bring me the moon and stars," Gul said. "And when you looked up, the heavens trembled. Where is that man now?"

"The stars belong where they are," Khoja said.

"This is not *Zhongnanhai*," Malcolm said. "All we need is to get in. We can do the rest."

"You will not even make it out of the desert," Khoja said.

"If not for the Uighurs, then for the rest of the world," Malcolm said. "There will be war if the Chinese are not stopped. Many will die."

"Save your breath," Gul said and then stood. "This one has left the world behind."

"There will be war even if you succeed," Khoja said. "Perhaps most especially if you succeed. It is the one constant."

Gul's face twisted and she spat on the ground at Khoja's feet. "Coward," she said. "As always, you will do nothing."

Khoja glanced at her and then tossed the wood carving into the brazier. Sparks and embers shot into the air and the old man turned to Malcolm. "You may leave," he said.

Malcolm watched the flames consume the carving. The fire grew and crackled and he glanced at Khoja and wondered who would win were they to fight while overhead the stars marched through the sky in their celestial cycle. Oblivious or uncaring to what happened on the earth below.

Then Malcolm whistled. A sharp keen that pierced the night.

There was silence and then the whistle was answered by a muffled cry that came from the building on the far side of the courtyard.

"You've been up here too long," Malcolm said. "You've gotten sloppy."

His team materialized out of one of the building's darkened doorways, except when they fanned out in the courtyard, there were five shadows instead of the four who'd come up the mountain with him.

"Aziguli," Khoja said and rose to his feet, Gul beside him.

"That's far enough," Malcolm said and waited until the old man dropped his arms to his side. Then he nodded at David, who led the group. "Bring her here," he said.

The group came forward and the light illuminated a young woman held between Wolf and Gleb. Her long black hair pinned up with blue flowers over her ears and her porcelain skin and white flowing robes glimmering orange in the light of the flames. David led the group to Malcolm's side and then he pulled out a knife and held it to Aziguli's throat.

"Father!" Aziguli screamed.

"Be calm, child," Khoja said.

Gul sneered at Malcolm. "You're bluffing," she said.

"Like hell he is," Wolf said.

Malcolm shrugged and then turned to David. He saw a droplet of blood on Aziguli's neck where the knife blade cut into her throat and then he nodded.

David moved the knife from Aziguli's throat to her hand. Held it against her pinky finger and then looked to Malcolm.

"I think you know how this turns out," Malcolm said.

Khoja did not move.

"Do it," Malcolm said.

David dragged the blade along Aziguli's finger and she screamed.

"Stop," Khoja said. "Your fight is not with her."

"Then do as I say."

"It will do you no good."

"Wrong. Killing the Standing Committee is going to do the whole world a lot of good."

"It will not end the way you think."

"Have it your way," Malcolm said and raised his hand to David and Aziguli screamed.

"Enough," Gul called out. "We will help."

David stopped and Malcolm's eyes narrowed as he turned his gaze to Gul. "Both of you?" he asked.

"Yes," she said.

"I want to hear it from him." Malcolm watched Khoja and the old man did not move.

Gul took Khoja's hand in her own. Stared at him and then walked to stand in front of him. "Five years we have lived in this desert," she said. "Five years to reflect on your decision to spare Chairman Zhao's life."

"I do not regret my choice," Khoja said. "It is not weakness to protect the future."

"I did not agree," Gul said, "but in that time, did I ever ask you to change your mind?"

Khoja stood silent.

"Did I ever question you, or complain?"

Khoja shook his head.

"Now I do, because you ask too much. I will not be separated from Aziguli again."

Khoja met her gaze and then glanced at Malcolm.

"Zhao has had five years he should not have had," Gul said. "Do not punish Aziguli so he might have a few more."

Khoja stared at Malcolm and then turned back to Gul and closed his eyes. "Very well," he said.

Gul placed a palm to Khoja's cheek and then placed her forehead against his. They stayed that way for a minute and then she turned to Malcolm.

"Let my daughter go," she said. "We will do everything you ask."

"Good," Malcolm said and then turned to Mary. "Do it."

Mary stepped forward and held up a padded strap the size of a small belt to Aziguli's neck. The girl saw the strap in Mary's hands and began to kick and thrash.

"Hold her," Gleb said and the muscles in his arms tightened.

"A real tiger by the tail here," Wolf said.

"What are you doing?" Gul asked. "We agreed to help."

"And I appreciate that," Malcolm said as Mary fitted the strap around Aziguli's neck. "But we can't hold a knife against her throat for the entire trip, so that thing Mary's putting around your daughter's neck is our insurance policy. It's small, has enough explosives to separate her head from her body, and has an anti-tamper rig, in case you were thinking about how to remove it." He reached into a pocket of his cargo pants and pulled out a small black fob that he held in front of his face. "And this," he said, "is a remote detonator. The two of you do as I say, or her head comes off."

"Then we will kill you," Khoja said.

Malcolm smiled. "Let's cross that bridge when it's time," he said. "You have until morning to collect whatever you need."

• • • • •

Malcolm led them back down the mountain in the morning. A brief respite to collect the caravan and then back into the desert until they came across the ruins.

Khoja implored them to go around. Instead Malcolm halted for the day despite it being mid-afternoon. They set up camp near the remains of a small building at the bottom of a sand-encroached plateau and half the camels had yet to be picketed when Wolf dragged off three Uighurs armed with shovels and bags.

"Good luck," Malcolm called out as he watched the scavengers skulk off to loot whatever artifacts had been preserved in the ruins. He said nothing when David came to his side.

"Camp isn't set up yet," David said.

"Let them go."

"Probably isn't anything here anyways."

"No harm looking if it keeps them happy."

"And her?" David nodded at Aziguli. Alone and headed into the ruins as well.

Malcolm considered the girl and then shook his head. "She can't go anywhere," he said.

They finished with the camels and then Malcolm explored. Mounted a dune and passed the ruins of several buildings. Nothing left but skeletal wooden poles that jutted out from the sand. He approached a clay and brick building that still had its roof and from inside he could hear Wolf. Hoots and yells about an ancient bow and quiver and how much he'd get for them in London.

Malcolm walked on.

At the far end of the plateau he found three near intact buildings. Their walls of brick and baked mud hard and unblemished. The interiors of the buildings were divided by screens of decayed rattan and there were pottery shards strewn about the floors. In the third of the buildings he found Aziguli, kneeling on the floor with a hardened clay tablet in her hands.

She glanced up when he entered and then sprang to her feet. Waited with head bowed and hands clasped at her waist.

"What do you have there?" he asked.

She did not answer.

He walked up and took the tablet from her. Traced a finger over the carvings etched into the wood. "You like history?" he asked.

She stood for a moment and then nodded.

"I was never partial to it," he said and tossed the tablet to the sand-covered floor where it broke in half. He left her to gather the pieces and paced around the room. "History just ties our hands," he said.

"My father says history can teach us."

He snorted. "Everyone says that," he said and gestured around the room. "If it's so true, then tell me what there is to learn in a place like this."

"It is ancient. Older than China itself," she said. Her voice low and tentative and then it picked up strength. "It was an outpost of the Tibetan Empire. A people who –"

"Where is this empire now?" he asked.

She met his gaze and said nothing.

"There isn't one," he said. "They're dead. They've got nothing to teach us."

"There was an inland sea here, a –"

"And now it's gone, and so are they," he said. "Both swallowed by the desert. The one, useful lesson from history. Everything has to end, sometime."

"Why are you here?"

He stared at her and considered his answer. "I'm a soldier," he said. "I follow orders."

"The Chinese –"

"Need to be put in their place," he said. "And unlike your dad, I fight for those I love."

"My father –"

"Your father hid in the desert for years. He forced you to do the same."

"He told me –"

"What, that he was protecting you?" he asked.

She met his gaze and he saw in her eyes that he was right and then she turned away.

He walked up to her and raised her chin with the tip of a finger. "You think it's right that he forced you to hide? While those who persecuted you walk free?" he asked. His voice close to a whisper. "He's the one who messed up. Why should you have to suffer?"

"It is for the greater good."

"Another thing everyone always says," he said. "I'm sick of hearing about the greater good. What about what's good for you?"

She stared at him and did not answer and then the silence grew heavy and she broke away. Put her back to him and strode as far from him as she could get in the room.

"Where I come from," he said, "we don't pay for the sins of our fathers."

"Is that so."

"It is," he said. "We make others pay for the sins they inflicted on us."

• • • • •

Malcolm left her, alone, and walked out of the building. Shielded his eyes against the sun's glare and spied Wolf and two Uighurs headed in his direction. He nodded at them and then went deeper into the ruins toward a rectangular shaped building with a large domed roof. A still intact waist-high wall formed a sort of courtyard around the building and in the open space towered a single petrified tree where Khoja and Gul stood. Their hands were clasped together and their heads were bowed and penitent.

Malcolm climbed through a hole in the courtyard wall and moved up behind them. Thought nothing of the hallowed ground upon which he trod or the restless dead who'd walked this place in all the centuries before him. A few paces behind the couple, he stopped and waited. Studied the pair from behind as the wind gusted and whistled through the stunted branches of the petrified tree. When Gul raised her head and glanced back at him, he smiled and then watched her walk off to enter the temple, Khoja left behind.

Malcolm moved up beside Khoja. "What was that all about?" he asked.

The old man did not look at Malcolm. "An old conversation," he said.

"About what?"

"My humble position in the kingdom."

"You've had too much sun," Malcolm said. "China hasn't been a kingdom for a long time."

"That is not what we were not talking about."

"Then which kingdom do you mean?"

Khoja glanced at him. "The only one that matters," he said. "The one that has existed through all the ages and to which all things under the heavens belong."

"You all are awfully concerned about the past," Malcolm said.

A woman's scream came from the ruins behind them. Carried faint on the wind like some forgotten memory dredged up by their presence. Both men turned and saw one of the Uighurs outside the building where Malcolm had left Aziguli.

Wolf nowhere in sight.

Another scream pierced the ruins. Louder. Full of distress. The remaining Uighur disappeared into the structure and the voice cut off.

Khoja began to walk toward the building.

"Just be careful her collar doesn't get set off," Malcolm called out to him. "The electronics are sensitive."

Khoja came to a stop. Hands balled into fists.

"You know, the way I see it, there's only one thing the past teaches us," Malcolm said and glanced back at the petrified branches of the tree and the temple beyond. Saw nothing except dead wood and decayed mud. Testaments to the power of the desert. Then he turned and walked up beside Khoja. "Take what you want, when you can get it," he said. "Because any minute could be your last."

Khoja stared to his front. Blinked when another scream came from the building but did not move. "This will not bring your family back," the old man said.

"I never thought it would."

"Then why do it?"

"Because this is what happens when kingdoms and empires fall," he said and then clapped Khoja on the shoulder. "But I'll put a stop to it," he said. "For you." He walked off toward the screams and then called out over his shoulder. "Just don't forget you owe me."

· · · · · ·

They continued the next day. Aziguli on a camel, propped up in turns by Khoja and Gul. Over the course of the next week they ran low on water and when they came in sight of a gas station along the S165 highway around noon on the eighth day, Malcolm decided to try their luck.

Malcolm halted the caravan a mile out from the road so they were still hidden in the dunes. He had the Uighurs hobble the camels and ordered three hardcase plastic boxes unloaded. From one of the boxes came personal radios and a ruggedized tablet and a remote controller. Wolf closed this box and set the tablet on top of it and then picked up the handheld controller. Manipulated the controls and a swarm of microdrones hovered up out of one of the other boxes. Wolf buzzed the drones over top of the caravan and the camels started and strained at their pickets.

"Quit fooling around," Malcolm said.

"Just a wee bit of fun," Wolf said and skimmed the drones over the sand to the east.

The last of the boxes contained guns. Pistols for Mary and Malcolm, a bullpup submachine gun for David and a takedown rifle fitted with a scope for Gleb. They handed out the weapons and the radios and then huddled around the tablet to watch the microdrones locate the gas station in the middle of a belt of trees and bushes that paralleled the highway.

Nothing moved.

Wolf handrailed the drones along the road to the north and south of the gas station. "Unfucking believable," he said.

"What's that?" David asked.

"Only communist China would have the slave labor and apathy to waste time planting trees in the middle of a desert," Wolf said.

They watched the road for half an hour until a truck lumbered down the highway followed within seconds by another. Then nothing. Wolf brought the drones over top of the gas station where they saw a man come out of a large building with a billboard on top that they took to be the main store. The man walked to a long, squat building covered in metal siding on the side of the site and spoke with a woman who stood in the doorway. The pair talked and then the man left her and returned to the store and there was again nothing.

"Think there are others?" Malcolm asked.

"Maybe a kid," David said. "Nothing we can't handle."

"Agreed."

Malcolm waited until late afternoon and then ordered the team to move. There had been no vehicles on the highway in over an hour. He set Gleb up on a dune that overlooked the gas station and left Wolf with the caravan to control the drones and keep tabs on Khoja and Gul and Aziguli. Then he led Mary and David through the sand on foot. Himself in the lead, Mary and David on his flanks.

They made for the rear of the long, squat building. Lined up against a wall with weapons at the ready while Malcolm thumbed his mic. "Any update?" he asked.

"No movement," Gleb said.

"Negative," Wolf added. "Place is fucking dead."

"Got it," he said. "Mary and David will take the quarters. I'll take the store. How copy?"

"Acknowledged."

"Rog."

He sent Mary and David to their entry points while he loped to the front of the store. The proprietor had his head buried in a tablet at the counter when Malcolm entered. The man did not look up until Malcolm could have touched him with his gun and by then there was nothing he could have done. Malcolm shot him in the head and then stood over the body and radioed to the others that the store was secure.

"Send update," he said.

"Quarters secure," Mary said. "One woman and a baby."

"Copy," Malcolm said. "You stay there, send David to my location."

When David arrived, Malcolm had him drag the body out back and then he radioed Wolf to bring the caravan into the rear of the gas station.

"On our way," Wolf said.

• • • • • •

Twilight darkened the small oasis by the time the caravan had gathered at the rear of the gas station. Malcolm set David and the Uighurs to unload jerry cans and fill buckets with water so the camels could drink. Mary ransacked the quarters for food that would not spoil while Malcolm did the same in the store. Through the store windows he glimpsed Khoja walk to the front of the gas station and stand near the fuel pumps and then he returned to his task.

Wolf's voice sounded in his ear. "Lorry heading south to north."

Malcolm thumbed his mic. "Got it," he said. "Gleb? You see it?"

"Not yet," the Russian said. "Okay, eyes on."

"We'll watch and see what it does."

The seconds passed and then Wolf spoke. "It's slowing down," he said. "It's going to stop."

"Understood," Malcolm said and peered out the front of the store. He watched a red cabover truck pulling a trailer with two sea containers make a laborious turn off the highway and stop by a bank of fuel pumps in a cloud of dust. The truck sat there for a minute and then a bell rang from a computer screen that served as the cashier. Malcolm moved to the counter and glanced at the screen and then looked back outside to see a squat Chinese man in a white t-shirt and ballcap climb down from the truck's cab and begin to pump gas.

"Truck has stopped and driver is filling up," Malcolm said into his radio mic and then the bell rang again.

"What do you want to do?" David asked.

"Hold for now. Maybe we can get him fueled up and on his way," Malcolm said and frowned when the driver glanced up to stare at the corner of the gas island.

Where Khoja stood.

Malcolm thumbed the mic again. "Confirm location of Dilmurat and Aziguli?"

"With me," Mary said.

"Keep 'em there," he said and then rested his hands on the counter. Observed the driver and considered what the old man might do. He ignored the bell at the computer screen when it rang again and the minutes passed and then the driver replaced the fuel hose in the pump.

"Truck is fueled," Malcolm said. "Let's see if it leaves."

The driver waited at the pump and glanced at the store. Began to pace and his face grew dark and then he stomped past Khoja toward the building.

"Driver is entering the store," Malcolm said. "Standby."

The man yanked the front door open and stormed inside the store. He hesitated when the door did not shut and turned to find Khoja behind him with the door propped open. The driver flinched and then hunched his shoulders. Waved a hand at Khoja and swore at him and then clumped through the aisles to grab a bag of melon seeds and a bag of snack shrimp. Up to the counter where he shoved the purchases in Malcolm's face.

"Hey. Are you stupid?" the man asked. "Why didn't you bring these out to the truck?"

Malcolm smiled and dipped his head. "Of course, let me ring those through for you."

"Only the dummies work out here," the man said and pointed at the screen. "I paid from my truck. All you had to do was bring these out."

"I apologize," Malcolm said. Bowed his head once more. "Safe travels."

The man lowered the bags. "You're new here," he said.

"I am. Just started," Malcolm said. "Please, come again."

"Where is Liu Wei?"

"He is sick."

"I want to talk to him. He needs to know about your incompetence."

"I'll tell him myself."

The driver paced along the counter toward the side of the store. Peered through a side window at the residence building. "I'll tell Li Jing, then."

"I assure you, I will let them know."

"I don't believe you. Stay here." The driver whirled and stalked for the door.

Malcolm drew his pistol and aimed at the driver's head. The trigger half depressed and then Khoja stepped in the way. "Get out of the way, old man," he said.

Khoja did not move.

"What?" the driver asked. Came to a stop and began to turn. "Liu Wei will hear about this," he said. "I'm younger than –"

"Shut up," Malcolm said. He hopped over the counter and angled for a clear shot and wherever he moved, Khoja appeared.

"How dare you," the driver said and then saw the pistol. He stared at the weapon in incomprehension and then his eyes widened and he threw up his hands. Fell to his knees and gibbered nonsense.

"Got a problem," Malcolm said into his mic. "David on me."

"This man does not deserve to die," Khoja said. "Neither did the store owner."

"Deserve's got nothing to do with it," Malcolm said. "Just the wrong place, wrong time."

"If an accident is what brought him here, then let him leave."

"Can't risk him talking," Malcolm said. "Same reason I killed the store owner."

"This is not the way."

The front door swung open again. Relief on the driver's face until he turned and saw David and the machine gun in David's hands. The man sat back on the floor with his hands in front of his face. "Don't shoot don't shoot don't shoot," he said in rapid-fire Mandarin. He scuttled crab-like on the floor away from David and then flipped onto his belly and scrambled for one of the aisles.

"Shoot him," Malcolm said and pointed at the driver with his pistol.

David aimed and then Khoja stood over the driver where he could block both shooters. Hands held up as if to ward off the bullets.

"Enough, old man," Malcolm said as he and David circled. "Get out of the way."

The door opened again and Gul entered. Her blood-red robes blown about by the wind so that they filled the doorway around her. Khoja hesitated and glanced at her and the driver continued to crawl on the floor and that moment was all Malcolm needed.

He fired and Khoja lunged. So fast Malcolm wondered if it was possible the old man could catch the bullet and then the driver collapsed on the floor. A small hole in one side of the man's head and a big hole on the other. Blood and skull and brains on the white floor.

Malcolm keyed his mic. "Mary, this is team lead," he said. "Execute the prisoners."

Khoja shouted from where he knelt on the floor. Rose to his feet and yelled again and then came to a stop when Malcolm aimed the pistol at him. He stood and opened and closed his fists and then paced like a wild animal until Dilmurat glided across the floor to stand in front of him. He stilled and they stared at each other and then she slapped him with the back of her hand. Slapped him again and this time he kept his face turned.

"Compose yourself," she said. "There was nothing you could do." She glared at him a moment longer and then disappeared the way she had come.

Malcolm kept the pistol on Khoja and spoke into his mic. "Where are we at for water?" he asked.

"Nearly there," Wolf said.

"Good," he said. "I need this truck moved out back, then we finish up and get out of here."

"What about the bodies?" Mary asked.

"Dump them out back," he said and then he headed for the exit. At the door he stopped and considered Khoja and the old man would not return his gaze. He wondered if he'd been wrong about the old man and then walked out of the store.

• • • • •

Malcolm drove them on. Grim and relentless through the unending dunes and heat.

A sandstorm hounded them on the tenth day out from the gas station. Formed up in dark clouds on the western horizon and mushroomed out across the sky. First Wolf and then David said they should stop. Ride out the storm.

Malcolm would not listen and forced the caravan on.

The wind picked up and the desert lashed them with sand. The air so thick Malcolm walked with his compass in hand. His head buried in the compass mirror so he could shoot bearings on the move until David emerged out of the haze and grabbed him by the shoulder.

"We need to stop," David said and his breath was ragged and broken.

"No."

"The caravan is going to split."

Malcolm glanced behind. Squinted and thought he could still make out the second group of camels. "Have the packets close up," he said and bent to the compass once more.

"We're going to kill a camel. Maybe more than one."

"Are you finished?" Malcolm stood and waited for an answer that did not come. "Then fall in," he said and left David behind.

They marched another hour. Malcolm half-blind when he stumbled over the slipface of a massive dune to find himself on the edge of a valley. He caught his balance and shielded his eyes to stare across the gorge and then dropped his gaze and spied a rectangular copse of trees on the valley floor.

"Water," he said, his voice an unrecognizable croak through the *shemagh* over his face.

He waved at the packet behind him. Gave up when he saw the animals had ground to a halt. Two camel handlers idle and unaware. He dropped back to curse and beat the lead camel over the dune and down its leeward slope. The Uighur handlers morose as they clung to the ropes that tied the camels together as if they were ring buoys.

At the bottom of the valley he heard a faint cry followed by thuds and clunks as of boxes banging together. He peered up into the blown sand that had followed them into the valley and could make nothing out. Then the wind carried more cries and these were joined by shouts and swearwords in Uighur and Russian and English.

Malcolm halted the caravan and trudged as fast as he could down its length. Back up the dune past camels and people who stood dumb and gaped at him until he reached the third packet. The lead camel sat in the sand chewing its cud, the load it had carried a wreckage strewn down the side of the dune. Malcolm scanned through the haze and spotted a huddle of people farther up the dune. He stalked up to the group and shouldered his way into the middle. "What's going on here?" he asked. "Why isn't the camel being loaded?"

"You stupid twat," Wolf said. The Brit did not look at him and Malcolm followed his gaze to see Dilmurat on the sand in the middle of the group. Her right arm snapped above the elbow. The bone white and jagged where it had broken through the skin. A rasp in her breath he could hear over the wind and her chest rose and fell at the same time as she breathed. Khoja on his knees with her head cradled in his hands.

"What happened?" Malcolm asked.

Wolf shoved him and Malcolm fell back. "What happened is you didn't fuckin' stop," he said. "The lead camel tripped and went ass over teakettle down the dune. Took the others with it, right over top of the stupid old bitch."

Malcolm lay on his back and stared up at Wolf. "How bad is it?"

"How the fuck should I know?" Wolf shouted. He stood over Malcolm and ran his hands through his hair and then yelled and stalked off through the haze to where the lead camel still sat.

Malcolm got to his feet and met Khoja's gaze. "Can she move?" he asked.

"We'll need a litter," Khoja said.

"I'll send Mary back to take a look at her," he said. "We'll camp on the valley floor and reassess when the storm dies down." He turned and began to make his way to the front of the caravan.

"You've killed her, you know," Wolf said as he walked by the camel where he sat.

Malcolm stopped and half-turned and then kept moving down the dune.

•　•　•　•　•　•

They got Gul to the valley floor and into a tent. Malcolm had Mary and Khoja tend to Gul while the rest of the team sheltered from the storm.

Night fell.

Around midnight the wind died down. Malcolm poked his head into the tent that held Gul and considered her pale and sweaty face. Listened to the old woman's breath rattle in the closeness and shared a look with Mary and then left. He stood outside and stared at the stars until Mary came out of the tent and pulled him aside.

"How bad?" he asked.

"She'll die without treatment," she said.

"How long?"

Mary shrugged. "A week? Give or take."

"We have at least two to go."

"She won't make it. She might die anyway, to be honest."

"Well," he said. He dug out a canteen and rinsed his mouth and spat into the sand.

"We could go south," Mary said.

"Why would we do that?"

"Qiemo Town's only a few days from here."

"There's nothing for us in Qiemo Town," he said.

"There's a hospital."

He took another sip from his canteen. Held the water in his mouth and then swallowed. "It'll take too long," he said. "We're short on time as it is."

"Split the caravan."

"We need all the camels."

"We're almost across. We can spare two or three."

"No."

"Wolf and Gleb can take her," Mary said. "They're only with us until we're out of the desert anyway. What difference does it make if they leave now?"

"They're the ones making sure the camels can keep going, Mary." He tilted his canteen and dribbled a trickle of water onto the sand. "Who's going to do that if they're in Qiemo Town?"

"We don't need them for that anymore," she said. "We've been in the desert for six weeks. I can do it myself."

"You're a medic, not a vet. Unless you're telling me you got a veterinary degree when I wasn't looking. Is that what you're telling me?"

"Of course not. That's not what I meant."

"The Economic Conference is in less than a month, Mary," he said. "We can't be wasting time fucking around with camels in the desert. We have little enough as it is, and that's why we brought Gleb and Wolf in the first place."

"I understand all that."

"Do you? Then why are you recommending we send off our camel experts on a fool's mission? We should leave her behind and be done with it."

"Perhaps we should," Khoja said.

Malcolm squinted into the darkness and saw the old man emerge from the direction of the treatment tent. He walked up and bowed his head to Mary and then turned to Malcolm.

"I will take care of the camels," the old man said. "And I will ensure you reach your destination in time."

"I don't believe you," Malcolm said.

"Nonetheless, it is true."

"Why?"

Khoja inhaled and squared his shoulders. "My wife has made me swear it," he said.

Malcolm sipped from his canteen and spat onto the sand.

"And I will get you inside the Great Hall," Khoja said. "Although, I will not kill for you."

"To do the first, I think you'll find you won't have a choice with the second," Malcolm said.

"No matter. It will be done. What you do then will be up to you."

Malcolm stared at the old man and then nodded. "All right," he said. "We'll split up tomorrow." He turned and headed for his tent.

"My daughter will go with my wife," Khoja called after him. "You no longer need her."

Malcolm thought about that. "No," he said and then turned and disappeared into the night.

·　·　·　·　·

In the morning, Malcolm split the caravan.

He placed Gleb in charge of the group that would go to Qiemo Town. Gave him Wolf and two Uighurs and three camels to carry food and water and the artifacts Wolf had stripped from the desert. Wolf complained they needed more camels and Malcolm told him to be glad he'd be out of the desert in three days and then left to see that his orders were followed.

Mary and Khoja fashioned a litter from a ripped tent and tied it to the quietest camel of the lot. They secured Gul inside the litter and then helped load the animals while Malcolm had the rest of the team strike camp. Within an hour they were on the move, past the grove of dead trees and up the opposite side of the valley.

When the entire caravan had escaped the valley, he went and found Gleb. He clasped hands with the big Russian and let his gaze roam over the small packet of three camels. The litter on the sand behind the last camel and Khoja and Aziguli on their knees to either side.

"You got everything you need?" Malcolm asked.

"Probably too much," the Russian replied and followed Malcolm's gaze to where Khoja and Aziguli held Gul's hands in theirs.

"Feel free to dump the dead weight," Malcolm said.

Gleb glanced at him and said nothing and then looked back to where Gul lay in the litter.

"I understand," the Russian said. He clasped hands with Malcolm a last time and then walked to the lead camel and wrapped his fingers through its halter and gave a yank. "We go now," he said and began to march.

Malcolm watched them go. He said nothing to Wolf when the other man walked past. A cigarette in the Brit's mouth and his wrap-around sunglasses pulled low so he could squint at Malcolm over the top.

No words of good-bye.

Gleb led the small caravan due south, over the crest of a dune where he passed out of sight. Malcolm observed the litter dragged behind the last camel and the shallow ruts it left in the sand. He saw that the grooves had already begun to fill in and then the hair on his arms rose and he glanced over to see that Khoja watched him. The old man's face hard and resolute.

After a few seconds, Malcolm looked away.

By this time Gleb had reappeared. He climbed a dune and paused at the top and then turned and raised a hand in salute.

Malcolm raised an arm in return. Held it aloft until Gleb continued on and then watched the desert swallow up the small caravan while he resigned himself to the day's march.

• • • • • •

Malcolm had marched the caravan due east for an hour when David came to tell him Khoja was gone.

"What do you mean?" Malcolm asked. "Where would he go?"

"I could take a guess."

Malcolm cursed and then broke out a radio. He tried to reach Gleb and got no reply.

"What do you want to do?" David asked.

"Keep trying to raise Gleb."

"Should we call a halt?"

He scanned back along the line of camels and saw that Mary walked beside Aziguli at the head of the second packet. An ivory-white scarf around the girl's neck and the ends trailed out behind her in the wind.

"No," he said. "We'll keep going."

"What if he doesn't come back?"

"He'll be back," he said and began to walk.

"He might not be able to find us," David called after him.

"Then he'll lose two people today."

They marched on.

The day went on and the sun rose high and then slipped in its slow arc down to the horizon. Malcolm halted an hour before sunset to set up camp. They had finished supper and were sitting around a fire they'd made with wood scavenged from the petrified forest when Khoja walked up and squatted beside the flames.

Malcolm did not look at the old man. "I was wondering when you'd be back," he said.

Khoja shifted on his haunches.

"In fact, I wasn't sure if we'd see you at all," Malcolm said. "Or if I'd just wake up with my throat cut."

Khoja glanced up from the pot and Malcolm saw that the front of the old man's white tunic was dotted dark red. Like someone had flecked paint at him.

"Did you get there in time?" Malcolm asked. "Or had they already done it?"

The old man spooned a mouthful of supper into his mouth from a pot beside the fire. "I was too late," he said.

"And the caravan?"

"Your friends have joined her," Khoja said and then took another bite of food. "The camels and what they carried I presented to the Uighurs. For their troubles and for what they saw."

"I see," Malcolm said and slid his hand to the hilt of the sheathed knife at his hip.

"That will not be necessary," the old man said. "I gave my word."

"Even so," he said, "we'll set a watch tonight."

"As you wish," Khoja said and then lay down in the sand on the edge of the firelight.

But the night was uneventful and the next day they marched on.

Two weeks later, they exited the desert.

•   •   •   •   •

Malcolm strode past the bodies that littered the red carpeted hallway and keyed his mic as he walked. "Delta," he said, "this is team lead. Send status."

The earset was silent.

He stooped to collect a discarded bullpup rifle and reloaded the weapon and then held up at a corner in the hallway, Mary behind him.

"David?" he asked into the mic and then met Mary's gaze. He stared at her and then shook his head and she looked away. He put a hand on her shoulder and squeezed.

"You ready?" he asked.

She met his gaze and her eyes were moist and hate-filled and then she nodded.

"Stay close," he said and listened to the sounds of shouted commands and gunfire from deeper into the north wing of the Great

Hall. Then he squeezed Mary's shoulder again and together they launched around the corner.

A troop of soldiers in camouflage uniforms guarded the massive double doors of the East Hall. The soldiers stood with their backs to Malcolm and Mary, their weapons aimed at two people who stood at the opposite end of the corridor.

Aziguli and Khoja.

Aziguli's white robes hung limp around her and Khoja had his hand on his daughter's shoulder. Khoja's other hand was raised in the air beside his face. The pair stood still while a tall, athletic man with an officer's gold stars on the lapels of his uniform ordered them to come forward.

Malcolm eased toward the man, his steps slow and quiet. Mary on his right flank. They closed to about twenty yards or so while the officer yelled at Khoja and Aziguli and then they opened fire. Too close to miss and the soldiers did not get a single shot off in return. Within seconds the soldiers lay dead or dying, their groans and cries mixed with the echo of gunfire. Malcolm moved up to the entrance of the East Hall and left Mary to execute the ones who still moved.

When he reached the doors into the East Hall, he pressed an ear to the polished wood. He held his breath and heard the muffled voices that he'd come to silence and then he sensed Mary at his back.

"Where's David?" Mary asked.

Malcolm pulled his head from the door and turned to see Khoja and Aziguli on their way toward him. The old man met Malcolm's gaze and said nothing.

"Where's David?" Mary repeated. She waited for Khoja to reach them and then put her face in his. "Where is he?" she asked again, louder.

"Mary," Malcolm said and put a hand on her shoulder.

"Don't touch me," Mary said. She shrugged out of his grip and he grabbed for her again and then she wrenched his wrist and arm against him. Pain shot up Malcolm's arm and shoulder and drove him to his knees and then Mary released him and went back to berating the old man.

Malcolm stood. "That's enough, Mary," he said. He reached for her again and this time when she went for him, he was ready. Locked her up in his arms and held her while she thrashed and screamed and fought.

"We don't have time for this," he said and then she became still. He let her go and watched her for a second and then turned to Khoja.

"I have done what you asked," Khoja said. "Zhao is in this room."

"Don't know that until we get inside," Malcolm said.

"Release my daughter."

He stared at Khoja and then glanced at Aziguli. Her eyes moist and large and unflinching. She held her chin high and stood tall despite the weight of the explosives strapped to her chest beneath her robes. Then he turned back to Khoja. "When we're done," he said and pounded a fist against one of the double doors into the East Hall.

"We will go no farther," Khoja said and then stopped and cocked his head.

A low rumble came from either end of the corridor. The sound became louder and then coalesced into the tramp of boots, the shouts and clamor of soldiers driven to battle.

Malcolm faced Khoja. "Hold them off and I will release her," he said.

"Do it now," Khoja said.

"No time," he said and then soldiers and police flooded the hallway from each end. Charged toward them amid bloodlust shouts. Malcolm looked at Mary. "You got that side?" he asked and nodded in the direction from which they'd come to the East Hall.

"Yes," she said, already in motion.

Malcolm watched her go and then headed in the opposite direction.

"I will stop those who make it through," Khoja said from behind him.

Malcolm half-turned. "Stay close to her," he said and nodded at Aziguli. "Close to the doors."

"Of course."

The muscles in his jaw clenched and then he left Khoja and Aziguli and advanced toward the charging front rank of soldiers and police. The hallway filled with attackers as far as he could see and then the mob crashed over him and battle was joined.

He punched and kicked and gouged from one attacker to the next. Gave out ten hits – twenty – for every strike he took and it was not enough. The soldiers pushed him back, swarmed past him to attack the old man. He snatched a quick look behind and saw Mary fall and then he staggered and lost his balance and his feet were pulled from under him. He fell to the ground and from between the legs of the soldiers, watched the horde fall upon Khoja and Aziguli. They pressed Aziguli up against the doors of the East Hall and her white-clad arms stretched out over their heads to clasp her father's hand as he was pulled from her and then she screamed.

"Father!" Aziguli called out.

Malcolm found himself punched and kicked and stomped on. Hands grabbed him and he flung his elbows and knees to clear space, fought to free an arm so he could pull the remote detonator from his pocket. Bodies fell on top of him and he held the detonator in front of his face and closed his eyes.

"Fire in the hole, Mary," he whispered. "Fire in the hole."

And then he blew up the bomb he'd strapped to Aziguli's chest.

· · · · ·

Malcolm wormed out from under a pile of bodies. The stink of seared flesh and explosives acute in the confines of the hallway. He pushed to his feet and collected a discarded rifle and then weaved through the scorched and decapitated remains toward the East Hall's entrance. He slowed long enough to shoot a soldier who still moved in the back of the head and then moved on until he came to a severed leg. A woman's shoe on the foot and singed white cloth wrapped around the calf. He stared at the limb and then glanced up and down the hallway. He saw that nothing moved and so he stepped over the leg and walked until he stood before the double doors of the East Hall.

One of the great wooden doors hung by a single hinge. Crooked and blackened and smoking. The other door had blown into the East Hall and come to rest against an immense table that ran two-thirds the length of the room. A man's suit-clad legs pinned beneath the bottom of the door and the red carpet. Malcolm shouldered past the remaining door and shot a soldier near the table who'd started to come to his feet.

He penetrated deeper into the room and scanned for targets. Worked quickly through the soldiers and bodyguards who'd been nearest the explosion and were mostly dead or unconscious. Those farther away dispatched with methodical and well-placed shots.

A man in a suit tried to crawl underneath the table. A piece of wood was lodged in the man's thigh and his face was contorted and tear-stained when he looked behind him. Malcolm recognized the man as a member of the Standing Committee but could not remember his name. He shot him between the shoulder blades and then again in the back of the head.

"Fool," a man said from near the head of table.

Malcolm zeroed in on an old man with closely cropped hair and recognized Vice-Premier Jiang Gaoli. Trapped in his chair by the body of a soldier who'd fallen on top of him.

"What have you done?" Jiang asked and coughed.

He stared at Jiang and then shot him in the chest. Shifted his point of aim and put a bullet between the Vice-Premier's eyes and then worked his way around the head of the table. He executed a suit-clad civilian he took to be an aide and another Standing Committee member who he shot in the side of the face.

And so on, until he stood over Chairman Zhao Guoqiang.

Zhao's eyes were half-open and he had blood on his forehead. The Chairman mumbled and reached for Malcolm's foot and Malcolm kicked away the hand and then took aim at the man's head. Tightened his finger on the trigger and then glimpsed movement to his side and turned to bring the rifle to bear.

Too late. His attacker was almost upon him and so he dove to the side. Came to his knees ready to shoot and hesitated a second when he saw Khoja. Then he pulled the trigger and clipped Khoja in the arm.

The old man twisted as he ran and then crashed into Malcolm. The pair fell to the floor and Khoja scrambled on top of Malcolm's chest. His lips pulled back from clenched teeth. Silent and savage and no trace of humanity. He knocked the rifle away and pummelled Malcolm about the head and then his hands wrapped around Malcolm's throat.

Malcolm grabbed on to the old man's wrists. He thrashed and writhed to no avail and the edges of his vision darkened. His heartbeat drummed in his ears and the old man's fingers had sunk deep into the soft flesh of his neck. He noted faint bangs and flashes of light on the edges of his vision. Then Khoja's iron grip let up enough for him to turn his head to the side and he found himself face-to-face with Zhao. He saw soldiers in the doorway beyond Zhao and realized he'd run out of time.

He took a breath and then bucked his hips. He was able to push Khoja up and then bullet holes appeared as if by magic in the old man's chest and his hands loosened and went limp. Malcolm pushed him away. Gasped for breath and twisted on the floor to grab his dropped rifle. He brought it into position and looked at Zhao through the sights and then the soldiers rolled over him and darkness descended.

SEVEN

18 DECEMBER 2029

C hairman Zhao Guoqiang fell silent. His mouth dry and an ache behind his eyes. He ran his tongue along the inside of his lower lip and considered the assassin.

"Like all good lies," Zhao said, "your story has elements of truth."

The assassin continued to stare at a point on the table between the two of them. The same point he'd stared at this entire time.

"However," Zhao said, "we must remember that one ant hole may collapse a thousand-li dyke. And your tale, such as it is, is riddled with gaps much bigger than ant holes."

The assassin met Zhao's gaze.

"You are an American agent," Zhao said. "Assisted by a number of other countries and individuals, all of whom sought to humiliate my nation. Again."

The man's jaw muscles clenched and unclenched.

"You could not have crossed the border, or the desert, so simply or without assistance," Zhao said and then his eyes narrowed. "Or, for that matter, gained access to the Great Hall."

"Do you have so little regard for our skill?" the assassin asked.

"It is because I have such great regard for our own," Zhao said. "There is nothing that happens in Xinjiang that we do not know about. We would have detected your team the minute you crossed the border."

The assassin's lips pressed together in a thin line.

"To have evaded detection, you must have compromised our security agencies. The question is to what level."

"I assure you, that's beyond my abilities."

"Perhaps," Zhao said and became silent. His voice quiet and firm when next he spoke. "In any event, your lies dishonor a noble adversary.

The Ismail Khoja I knew was not the callous savage you made him out to be, but rather a principled, though formidable, foe."

"I did not force Khoja to do anything."

"While you betrayed him in the end by killing his daughter, you misjudged him," Zhao said. "You had thought to kill him as well. But he survived, and, no doubt driven insane by the death of his daughter, sought his revenge on you."

The assassin dropped his gaze and began to shake his head.

"Thankfully, in doing so, he prevented you from killing me," Zhao said. "And in the process, he gave our soldiers the time to neutralize you both before you could kill anyone else."

"You have not listened."

"You are an eloquent liar," Zhao said and straightened his back, "but in the end, facts surpass eloquence. You have attempted to confuse me, but all your lies have done is help clear the water."

"And what do you see?"

"That I have not examined myself."

• • • • •

Chairman Zhao remembered the conversation with Jiang Gaoli. About one year ago in Zhao's *Zhongnanhai* office.

Vice-Premier Jiang had come on his own and Zhao had paused his work and called for tea. He sat with Jiang and exchanged pleasantries while they waited for the servers to depart. When the tea had been poured, he studied Jiang's venerable face over the lip of his tea bowl and waited for the real meeting to begin.

"This old man has become a worrier," Jiang said, his tea bowl cradled in his lap.

Zhao bowed his head. "Unlikely," Zhao said and then gestured with a hand. "On my behalf, will you share what has you worried?"

Jiang resettled himself in his chair. "We have come far these past few years."

"You have seen much in your time."

"We are well on track to achieve Chairman Xi's Chinese Dream by the second centenary."

"By the fortune of our ancestors."

Jiang smiled. "It is ironic, don't you think?" he asked. "The American Dream dominated the past century, and now that it has died, it will be replaced by a dream of our own, one of collective harmony."

"Things return to their natural order," Zhao said. "May it last longer than a hundred years."

"Yet there remains apprehension about our motives," Jiang said. "America's traditional allies remain suspicious."

"This is natural. Although they must realize that America is the single biggest source of instability in the world today, it will take time for them to accept a model of world governance organized on universal values and cooperation as opposed to the nation-state and competition."

"Time which you have said we do not have."

Zhao gave a small smile that did not reach his eyes.

"Comrade," Jiang said and set his tea bowl on the table, "I dare not climb up high to you. At this time, all I look forward to is the continued ability to offer my service."

"Please," Zhao said, "bestow your wisdom."

"I will speak plainly," Jiang said. "We risk moving too fast. We stand on the brink of a deep gulf, and should move with caution."

Zhao sipped his tea and thought. "I do not fear the Americans."

"It is not the Americans who concern me," Jiang said, "it is whether our own house is in order."

Zhao's gaze darted to Jiang's face.

Jiang raised a hand and smiled. "As I said, this old man worries."

"Old, and respected."

Jiang nodded. "Because I examine myself daily," he said.

"As do I," Zhao said. "Have I been disloyal? Untrustworthy? Have I practiced what I preached?"

"*Shi.*"

"Then you agree that the treasure created by heaven and earth is limited? And that the people's desire is not?"

"I do," Jiang said.

"Then there can only be one conclusion," Zhao said. "We must take the Americans place at the center of a new world order based on collective harmony to ensure that humankind is not destroyed. We saw how they handled the coronavirus pandemic, what more proof is needed?"

"And yet for all our discussion on the Americans, I also believe that when we focus on the far, we ignore the near."

"What do you mean?"

Jiang sighed. "There are many officials – Chinese officials – who do not share your diligence for serving the people. Despite our best efforts, we have been unsuccessful at rooting out corruption."

"Go on."

"Your strategy is a bold hypothesis, but there are bound to be unforeseen developments, errors that, while unavoidable, may cultivate the perception that you have lost the mandate to rule. These officials, who we know exist, may seek to leverage those developments for their personal gain, to the point that their actions further undermine your plan. Our adversaries will take advantage of that, you can be sure."

"What do you suggest?"

Jiang sipped his tea again while Zhao waited in silence. Took his time and then set the cup on a side table and stood. "We cannot allow our desire for external order to blind us to the need for internal stability," he said. "Please, go slowly."

Zhao stood. "Well do I know the risks."

"Then I implore you to take every opportunity to carefully validate your strategy," Jiang said and bowed. "You can not afford mistakes that suggest you have lost the mandate of heaven."

• • • • •

Zhao Guoqiang pushed back from the table and stood. "It would seem General Fan's fears were valid," he said. "You have attempted to waste my time, but in doing so, you have revealed more than you anticipated." He pushed in his chair and rested his hands on the chair back. "Vice-

Premier Jiang was right. My assumptions have been flawed." He shook his head. "I cast the net wide, and yet, I took my foundation to be secure."

He stayed like that for a few seconds and then straightened and stepped back from the table. "You have my thanks," he said.

The assassin glanced up. "For what?"

"As I explained how you were able to conduct this attack, it became clear to me that there is no way you could have achieved what you did without significant help from officials in my own regime. In doing so, you have laid bare our defences and shown me the nature of my vulnerabilities," he said and tugged on the cuffs of his shirt. "In a way, it is an honor so many countries banded together to stop us. It is a sign of the seriousness with which they take the threat. And yet, the true threat is not from the failed state that is America, but from within."

Zhao walked to the door and raised his hand to bang on the metal. Then he paused and looked back at the assassin and his face grew hard. "Still, I will not lose sight of the global view. Once I have dealt with the dissidents in the Party and secured my position, my attention shall return to America and its allies."

Zhao turned and drew back his arm to bang on the door and then stopped.

The assassin had begun to laugh.

· · · · ·

Malcolm could not control the laughter.

The laughter came so hard his sides hurt and his eyes watered. He leaned over the table to wipe his eyes with his manacled hands and laughed all the harder at the perplexity on Zhao's face. Even to himself the laughter sounded manic and scary and he realized it would get him killed. So he breathed deep and dug his fingernails into his palms. Bit the sides of his cheeks and forced himself to meet the Chairman's fury with a straight face.

"I meant no disrespect," he said.

"Your opinion does not matter to me."

"And yet you did not leave."

"I would know what amuses you about this situation."

Malcolm snorted. Looked around the cell and then back at Zhao. "Only that you think countries around the world were falling over themselves to help the United States."

Zhao did not move.

"If that was the case," Malcolm said, "do you think we'd have risked everything on a small team crossing the Taklamakan?"

"An attempt which almost succeeded."

"Sometimes a Hail Mary works out."

"You can explain that to the interrogators at Qincheng."

"I guess."

"And years from now, when I've unified the world in peace, we shall see if you are still able to find humor in your fate." He turned to the door.

"So you will not stop?" Malcolm asked.

Zhao stood still and then spoke. "From the top of a mountain, all appears small," he said, "and it becomes difficult to think of anything else except this single, great aspiration. That has not changed." He faced Malcolm and his voice grew calm. "Though I must attend to the near fight for the foreseeable future, when that is complete, I shall return as a riotous cloud, sweeping past swift and tranquil. It will take longer, but your actions have shown the futility of moving with too much haste. I only hope the lesson has not been too costly. There is not much time." He returned to the door.

"You were right," Malcolm said. "About some things. Couzens recruited me."

Zhao stopped.

"And we had agents in your government."

Zhao half-turned. "Who?"

"Stay. I'll tell you."

"Why should I believe you won't lie again?"

Malcolm stared at him and then drew a breath. "Because while I may have underestimated you, there is someone that *you* underestimated."

Zhao's eyes narrowed. "Who?"

"Aziguli."

Zhao stood and said nothing and then pulled out the chair and sat down. "Speak," he said.

EIGHT

APRIL 2029

MALCOLM'S VERSION REDUX

Malcolm remained seated while the delegates filed out of the converted conference room. Cracked paint on the walls and a film of dust ground into the chipped and broken floor tiles no matter how many times they were swept. Cords and cables ran along the bases of the walls and were taped haphazardly across the floor. The decrepit headquarters had been left vacant for a reason. It would have stayed that way had it not ran off a hardened power source that had survived the Chinese attack.

Major-General Alekseyev from Russia left without speaking to anyone. Kobayashi, the civilian from the Japanese Self Defence Forces, was close behind. Ødegård, the NATO general, exchanged a few words with her British counterpart, Lieutenant-General Fletcher, while the Australian, Wilton, spoke with Admiral Couzens. Malcolm sat too far away to hear what was said between the Admiral and the Australian, so he read the conversation in Wilton's head-shakes and hunched shoulders. Then the men clasped each other's shoulders and Wilton exited the room. Ødegård stepped in, gave Couzens a perfunctory good-bye, and then departed with the Israeli spy and Couzens was left to speak with Fletcher. The British general was stiff and proud where the Australian had been amiable, though Malcolm guessed that the message was the same. Within fifteen minutes, the room had emptied, the delegates in their pressed uniforms or tailored suits already in cars and SUVs that would whisk them out of the waste and debris of a nation under attack. A nation many of them had said had already lost.

Couzens stood for a moment after the last delegate had left, and then sat down at his place at the head of the table. "So," the Admiral said, "what do you think?"

"Could've been worse," Malcolm said.

Couzens snorted, then glanced at an aide who stood on the threshold to the room. "What is it?" he asked.

"Sir, Secretary of State Bains is on the line," the aide said.

"That was quick," Couzens said.

"Do you want me to buy time?" the aide asked.

"No, I'm coming." Couzens inhaled and seemed to summon his strength and then rose. "Gimme a minute, Mal," he said and walked out.

Malcolm moved to a seat nearer the head of the table and then sat and waited. He flipped through his green notebook and jotted a few notes and then Couzens reappeared. "That was short," Malcolm said.

"Yeah."

"Is that a good or bad thing?"

"Well since there aren't any good options left, let's call it less bad," Couzens said and took his chair. "You know Bains?" he asked as he leaned back and propped his boots up on the table.

"Only from what I've seen in the news," Malcolm said.

"He holds his cards tight."

"Tighter than you?"

"Shit, Mal, I'm not in the same *league* as him," Couzens said and flashed a grin.

"I don't know about that," Malcolm said. "I thought you would've mentioned the negotiations with the Chinese to your colleagues, but you didn't."

"And how long do you think those negotiations would have stayed secret if I'd brought them up?"

Malcolm thought about that and said nothing.

"Hell," Couzens said and ran a hand over his bald head, "half of those 'colleagues' are probably talking to their Chinese counterparts right now."

"Does POTUS know?" Malcolm asked.

Couzens's eyes narrowed. "Does POTUS know *what*?"

"About the Chinese negotiations."

"What do you think?" Couzens asked. "You think I'd be helping Vice-Premier Jiang stage a coup in China if POTUS didn't know?"

"I'm not sure."

"Good answer," Couzens said. "Then let me rephrase the question. How long do you think this POTUS could keep something like that quiet?"

Malcolm shrugged. "Not long," he said.

"Damn rights," Couzens said. "Not long."

"So this is between you and Secretary Bains?"

"Does it matter?"

"Not really," Malcolm said. "Do you trust Jiang?"

Couzens scowled. "Hell no," he said. "Would you?"

"He's right to worry that we'll never stop fighting."

"Course he is," Couzens said. "But make no mistake, Jiang doesn't need us. This is a power grab, pure and simple. Besides," he said and shook his head, "no man who says he wants peaceful coexistence can be trusted. That's not the way the world works."

"Then why go through with it?"

"One, it buys us time," Couzens said. "A couple of years if we play our cards right, which is more than we have now. Two, Mr. Vice-Premier is going to find we have a few tricks up our sleeve. The Communist Party will be in a fight for its life when we're through."

"Dangerous game, sir."

"You don't know the half of it, Mal," Couzens said and then took his feet off the table. "I take it you were reading the room."

"Of course."

"So, who's going to help?"

"Nothing from NATO," Malcolm said. "Same for the Japanese and the Australians, although I hate to say it."

"The Aussies might share some intel," Couzens said.

"Maybe. The Canadians are in, but there's nothing they can really do."

"What about the Israelis?"

"I'd say they're in. The Brits, too, possibly some technical expertise."

"Alekseyev?"

"He'll do what he said. No more."

"You think?" Couzens asked.

"If for no other reason than to jerk around the Chinese."

"God the Russians are assholes," Couzens said and shook his head. "Any others?"

"No, sir."

"Yeah, that's what I thought," Couzens said and then sighed. "Where does that leave you?"

"I need a few more people."

"Gunfighters? I could have a lineup in here tomorrow morning."

"I've got two in mind."

"Who?"

"Couple of people I've crossed paths with over the years. One's a Russian, the other's a Brit."

"Huh," Couzens said. "You trust 'em?"

"To do what I need them to. Not more than that."

"I guess beggars can't be choosers."

"They won't work for free."

"You can't appeal to their sense of patriotism?"

"No."

"How much?"

"Six figures, maybe seven."

"Shit." Couzens winced. "Congress'll have my ass, if they ever find out."

"If you've got better options, sir, I've love to hear them."

Couzens snorted. "Leave it to me," he said and then leaned back in his chair and clasped his hands behind his head. "I'll make it happen."

"I appreciate that, sir," Malcolm said.

"Lot of work ahead of you. Need anything else?"

"You got a couple of days?"

"You know I don't."

"Then there's nothing."

"All right then," Couzens said. "Go on and get out of here."

Malcolm rose and headed for the exit.

"What odds do you give this mission, Mal?" Couzens asked from behind him.

Malcolm came to a stop. "I'm not a betting man, Admiral."

"Not what I asked."

There was silence while Malcolm thought. "One in twelve," he said. "Maybe a bit higher."

"Good thing you're not a betting man. Too optimistic by half."

Malcolm waited to see if Couzens would say more and was about to continue on when the Admiral spoke again.

"What would Mel would think about all this?"

"Sir?" Malcolm asked and half-turned.

"I'm sorry. Amaelia," Couzens said. "What do you think Amaelia would say? Would she approve of what you're doing?"

"I'm not sure how that's relevant, sir."

"That's for me to decide."

Malcolm stood and thought about that. "You know what she'd say, Admiral," he said. "She'd want me to save the world. Not stand by and watch it burn."

"That's about what I thought."

"Anything else, sir?"

"You know, you don't have to do this," Couzens said. "Mary could lead the team. She's more than capable."

Malcolm thought of Amaelia. And Oran. He thought of times spent sailing his father's 26-foot daysailer and hikes in the Appalachians. "That's for you to decide, sir," he said.

"This shit is only beginning, Mal."

Malcolm looked at the Admiral and it occurred to him that Couzens and the conference room were one and the same. Gaunt and old. Relics. "I know," he said.

"These next few years are going to be rough," Couzens said.

"You think it'll be over that quick?"

The Admiral's jaw clenched. "No," he said. "And your country could use you."

Malcolm thought again of his dad's yacht. Planted in the roof of a coastal house by Hurricane Shary in '23. And he thought of his mom, dead in the heat wave of '24. The hottest year on record. Until the year after and then the year after that. He began to think of Amaelia and Oran and then buried their faces deep inside where they couldn't escape. He turned from the admiral and spoke over his shoulder.

"The world's moving on, sir," he said.

The Admiral said nothing and then Malcolm heard the fake leather of the Admiral's chair squeak as the old man shifted. "Yeah," Couzens said. "I guess."

Malcolm waited once again except Couzens seemed to have run out of things to say.

• • • • •

The team arrived at Kant Air Force Base in Kyrgyzstan in late August of that year. They flew in not on one of the new C-5 Galaxy cargo planes, but on an aged Gulfstream 37A jet that had entered service with the U.S. Air Force in the 1990s, been retired in 2020, then reactivated that year. The plane shuddered and banged through the landing so that it reminded Malcolm of the decrepit Mi-17 helicopters he'd flown around Africa.

They taxied to a stop and the door dropped and Malcolm stepped into a wall of humidity. His shirt drenched in sweat by the time he reached the bottom of the stairs, Mary and David on his heels. There was nobody to receive them. The crew unloaded their gear and they shouldered their bags and walked to the nearest hangar where they were met by Gleb.

Malcolm stood in front of the Russian and gestured around the emptiness of the airfield. "Still have a way with the locals," he said.

"And you still can't help sticking your nose where it doesn't belong," Gleb replied.

Malcolm smiled.

They stayed at Kant Air Force Base for two weeks. Confined to an isolated hangar with sporadic power to acclimatize and plan and wait for the temperatures to cool. They were surveilled at all times by Russian and Kyrgyz soldiers and by the end of the two weeks the weather was hotter and dryer than when they'd arrived.

At the end of the two weeks they departed the Air Force Base in a pair of run-down Hyundai passenger vans provided by the Kyrgyz. It was mid-September and the mercury had not dipped below 24 degrees Celsius the night before. They had not slept. All the way to the Torugart Pass they were tailed by three olive-drab SUVs and a six-wheeled Ural-4320 troop carrier. Their 'escort.' Soldiers with Russian flags on their uniforms crammed into all of the vehicles.

The route to the Torugart Pass took them through four checkpoints. They had to bribe their way through each one. The guards at the third checkpoint aimed their rifles at them and forced them to empty the vans while the Russian officer in charge of their 'escort' stood by his vehicle and smoked and ignored their calls and Gleb's curses.

They did not reach the Torugart Pass until the sun had begun to set and were told by the border guards that the crossing had closed for the day. So they drove back to Naryn where Gleb and Malcolm placed calls throughout the night to their Kyrgyz and Chinese contacts to rework the timings for the following day.

Their 'escort' left.

The next morning, they were the first vehicles at the border crossing. They waited an hour and then the Kyrgyz guards called them up and allowed them to cross-load equipment into several vans. When they'd moved their gear, the two vehicles picked their way along the gravel road to the Torogart Pass.

The gate was closed and locked.

Malcolm and Gleb spoke to the Chinese border guards and then waited beside one of two grey pillars that marked the border. Great concrete slabs set in red marble bases and the pillars were engraved with the number '51' beneath a Chinese crest. A convoy of three vans arrived from the Chinese side at noon and disgorged a group of soldiers and a man in a suit. The delegation entered the tower on the Chinese side of the border and it was another hour before a guard was dispatched to open the gate. Malcolm and Gleb were brought through at gunpoint and ushered into a small office where the man in the suit was seated.

"You are late," the man said.

"The Kyrgyz held us up," Malcolm said.

"That is not my concern," the man said. "What is important is that I had to reschedule the arrangements. There are costs associated with those changes."

"We have been more than generous," Malcolm said.

"It is not enough."

Gleb began to stand. "I had arranged –"

Malcolm grabbed Gleb's arm. He dragged the Russian back into his seat and kept his gaze on the functionary. "How much?" he asked.

"Triple."

"Triple?" Gleb's face turned red.

"Be reasonable," Malcolm said. "Triple is ludicrous. Fifty percent more."

"You are in no position to bargain," the man said.

Malcolm stared at the man and saw how it was. He nodded in response and two soldiers took him back to the vans to collect the man's payment.

The man forced Malcolm and Gleb to wait while he counted the money. Then he closed the ruggedized case that contained the money and stood. He took the case in hand and gave a curt order and then the soldiers began to yell for them to put their bags into two of the Chinese minivans. Within minutes they'd loaded and departed the crossing on the Chinese side of the border.

The convoy was waved through a number of Chinese checkpoints. They travelled for two hours along winding mountain roads until they reached the Chinese immigration and customs building at the intersection of roads that lead back to the Torugart Pass and the border crossing in Irkeshtam. The vehicles stopped and the man in the suit ordered them to remain in the vans. Then he disappeared inside the building with one of the soldiers.

They waited and waited and waited.

The insides of the vehicles baked and they asked to walk around to stretch their legs. They asked to use the washrooms and to get some fresh air and the Chinese soldiers aimed their rifles at the vans and ordered them to shut up. So they waited some more. They waited until Wolf peed into an empty water bottle and flung the filled bottle through the window at the customs building. At which point the soldiers surrounded their vans and yelled at them. They yelled back and shortly after, the soldier who'd entered the building reappeared and the convoy was on its way once more.

They reached the outskirts of Kashgar as the sun sank beneath the mountains to the west. The west-facing tops of the buildings painted orange by the setting sun. The vans deposited them at the Radisson Blu Hotel where a contingent of uniformed police watched in silence as they unloaded their bags. Then the vans were empty and drove away.

Wolf shouldered his duffel and shoved past Malcolm into the hotel's lobby. "Great fuckin' start," he said. "Absolutely bloody great."

Malcolm eyed the police and then hefted his own bags and followed Wolf into the hotel.

• • • • • •

They stayed in Kashgar for three days and then relocated to Makit.

David found them a compound near the camel market which they moved into and it was here where they got their first glimpse of the Taklamakan. Stands of Euphrates poplars with their foliage bright orange and unending hills of sand. Malcolm stared at the desert as the sun dropped beneath the horizon and shadowy tendrils grew out of the trees to shroud the land in dark.

Then he went inside and set to work.

On their second day in Makit, they were visited by a man called Zeng Huimin. Malcolm and David were stood at the edge of a small courtyard in the compound, watching Wolf badger the Uighur camel handlers, when they saw Mary stalk across the courtyard toward them. Puffs of dust kicked up from the dirt under her feet.

"She's in a hurry," Malcolm said.

They waited for her to join them and then David asker her what was the matter.

"We have a visitor," she said.

"Who?" Malcolm asked.

"A man who says he's Zeng Huimin."

"The local Party official?"

"Yes."

"He's not supposed to be here."

"I told him that."

"What does he want?" Malcolm asked.

"He says we don't have permits," she said.

"Gleb was supposed to pay off the local cadres," Malcolm said.

"He did," David said.

Malcolm drew a slow breath and let it out through his nose. "Okay," he said to Mary. "I'll see what he wants."

He walked with Mary to the front of the compound. Stopped at the gate and peered into the street at a grey-haired Chinese man in glasses and a short-sleeve button-up shirt and suit pants. Five police officers in black uniforms stood behind the man, all of them clad in tactical body armour and armed with automatic weapons that seemed an extension of their hands.

"Can I help you?" Malcolm asked.

The man in civilian clothes spoke through the rusted steel bars. "I am Zeng Huimin," the man said. "Party Secretary for Makit and Kashgar."

"Of course," Malcolm said. "I am honored that you would visit."

"There have been reports of suspicious activity at this compound," Zeng Huimin said. "I have come to inspect."

"We're tourists preparing for a desert expedition," Malcolm said. "As I believe you know."

"I need to see your permits."

"You have copies."

"Those are no longer the right ones."

"One of my people will come with you to get new ones."

"That is not sufficient. You must stand aside and let us into the compound."

"Surely this does not require your personal attention."

Zeng Huimin smiled and clasped his hands together at his waist. "We receive very few tourists in this part of the world," he said. "Particularly ones as ambitious as your expedition." He spread his hands and shrugged. "It is natural for there to be problems in these situations. I would not want to be remiss in managing affairs such as these before they become, shall we say, chaotic."

Malcolm said nothing. Glanced behind him to the compound full of tents and sleeping bags and water cans and then turned back to Zeng.

"Give me a second," he said. "And then we can talk."

• • • • •

Malcolm and Zeng Huimin sat at a small table on the edge of the courtyard. They watched David assemble a tent and waited for Mary to fetch tea while the five police officers milled around in the sun. Their faces moist with sweat. Malcolm studied them. Noted the ease with which they carried their weapons and how they stood far enough away to not intrude on the conversation yet near enough that their presence could not be overlooked.

Mary arrived with a tea pot. She filled their cups and then set the tea pot on the table and straightened. Waited with her hands clasped at her waist. Malcolm nodded a silent thanks to her and she took a step back and then Malcolm motioned for Zeng Huimin to help himself.

The Chinese official sat perpendicular to the table. His legs crossed and one arm draped over the chair back. He waited for Malcolm to offer again and then picked up his cup and continued to survey the courtyard while he sipped his tea.

"Your men look hot," Malcolm said.

"It is always hot in Xinjiang," Zeng said.

"Perhaps they'd like to sit down. Have some water."

"They will be fine," Zeng said and set his cup on the table.

"How long have they been in Xinjiang?"

"Not long enough to get used to the heat."

"And yourself?"

"I have been here since before the uprising."

"That is a long time."

"Indeed," Zeng said and then took in the compound with a wave of his hand. "Let us talk about why you're here."

"As you wish."

"You say that you are tourists."

"*Shì.* We're preparing for an expedition."

"Into the Taklamakan, yes," Zeng said. "You are taking Uighurs with you."

"We need camel handlers."

"So many."

"We have a lot of camels."

"The Uighurs are forbidden from assembling in groups larger than five."

"I was unaware."

"That is irrelevant. There will be consequences."

"For us?"

"For them. For their families."

"They seem harmless enough," Malcolm said. "All they'll be doing is working with camels."

Zeng Huimin sipped his tea and then folded his arms at the wrists and rested his hands on a knee.

"How is this related to the permits?" Malcolm asked.

"They were incomplete," Zeng said. "An expedition that requires so many handlers must be accompanied by a government escort."

"I was not aware of that."

"That is no matter."

"I doubt my sponsors would agree," Malcolm said. "Or yours."

"I understand," Zeng said and the corners of his mouth rose. "Should your sponsors wish to back out now, they could hardly be blamed."

"I did not say that," Malcolm said. "However, it will take time to discuss this new development."

"As you wish," Zeng said and shrugged. "However, I would not delay too long. It will be end-September soon. By the end of November, the Taklamakan will be too cold to cross. Two months is not a long time when it comes to permits."

Malcolm stared at Zeng and then stood. He glanced at Mary and moved to lean against a nearby pillar. "Is there a way to expedite the permits?" he asked. "We could compensate you."

"It would depend," Zeng said. He sipped his tea and then resettled his glasses and Malcolm was about to repeat himself when he spoke. "It is a great risk for me."

"I'm sure my sponsors would be comfortable with a transfer equal to the cost of the original permits."

"I fear that amount would be poor compensation were it discovered I broke Party protocol."

"Then what would be acceptable?"

Zeng Huimin was silent. "Five times the original cost," he said after several seconds had gone by.

"Out of the question," Malcolm said. "Three times."

"Four."

"Three and a half."

"It really couldn't be any less than four."

"That is a lot."

"There is a lot it must pay for."

"And that would be enough?" Malcolm asked and then sat back down at the table. "We wouldn't need, say, additional permits at some point in the future?"

Zeng met Malcolm's gaze and his eyes sparkled. "Yes, I think that amount would cover a one-time special issuance. As for additional permits, I cannot say."

"Why not?"

"I do not plan to be here. However, I judge that scenario unlikely."

"All right then. We'll deliver the payment tomorrow."

"I will, unfortunately, need to take possession of the payment today. Right now, in fact."

Malcolm stared at Zeng and the man did not drop his gaze. He contemplated the Chinese official for several more seconds and at the same time he noted how the police escort had moved closer to the table. Then he nodded at Mary. She raised an eyebrow and Malcolm's expression did not change and then she left to collect the payment. When she'd gone, Malcolm turned back to Zeng. He refilled the man's cup and replaced the tea pot on the table and said nothing.

Zeng picked up his tea and balanced the cup on his knee. "I've never understood one thing," he said. "Why go into the desert at all? I would think it would be easier to go around it."

"I couldn't afford that many permits," Malcolm said.

"I suppose not," Zeng said. "In that case, as well, I suppose you would miss what you're hoping to find in the desert."

"Such as?"

Zeng shrugged. "All the sites of interest."

Malcolm glanced at his tea cup. "I'm sure there is lots to see, but once we enter the desert, we can only spend so much time there."

"I see," Zeng said. "The clock is ticking, as you might say in the West."

"*Shi.*"

"However, it is not impossible to survive in the desert for more than a few months," Zeng said. "In fact, it is rumored that a man has lived in the Taklamakan for five years now. He went in and never came out."

"I'm sure he must be dead by now."

"For a time, this man was the most dangerous person in Xinjiang. Perhaps in all of China."

"Better if he's dead, then."

Mary returned from inside the residence, a ruggedized plastic box the size of a briefcase in her hands. She handed the box to Malcolm and he set the case on the table and then slid it toward Zeng. Flipped the latches and opened the lid.

Zeng stared at the contents of the box and then smiled and nodded. Malcolm closed the lid and Zeng took the case by the handle and then stood. "I hope you have a pleasant expedition," he said.

Malcolm stood and walked with Zeng toward the gate. The police officers in step behind the Chinese official and Mary on their flank. When they reached the gate, the police officers exited and formed up in the street while Zeng paused and then turned to Malcolm.

"Ismail Khoja is a dangerous man," he said. "His re-emergence will make life more difficult for the Uighurs. There is bound to be unrest."

"Does that worry you?"

"Hardly," Zeng said and stepped through the gate. Then he turned and nodded to the case in his hand. "As I said, I do not plan to be here when that happens."

"Then what do you care?"

Zeng stared at him and then resettled his glasses. "I thought you might be interested in knowing the consequences of your actions," he said. "I did not plan on spending so much time in Xinjiang. Nor did I expect to grow so accustomed to the Uighurs." He stood in silence and then dipped his head. "However, if there's one thing I've learned, it is to avoid meddling in systems when we don't know the precise consequences of our actions."

Zeng stood for a moment longer and then walked to street to join his police escort.

"Then why are you doing this?" Malcolm called out after him.

Zeng paused and then looked back. "Call it a gift to the man who sentenced me to spend the rest of my career here," he said and then walked off, the police officers close behind.

•   •   •   •   •

The caravan entered the Taklamakan a week later.

Malcolm gathered the team in the courtyard of their compound. An hour before dawn and the sky above a deep sapphire blue. The faces of his teammates were dark and their eyes were bright as they waited in the shadows that still gripped the land. He nodded at them and then shouldered his pack and walked into the street.

The cobblestoned alley outside the compound was deserted and carried the echoes of Malcolm's boots. He walked with his head down and did not look around. It was not until he turned onto the road that took them to the stables that he saw the crowd.

Silent Uighurs lined both sides of the street. Shoulder to shoulder and ten-deep. The women in bright colored dresses with baggy sleeves and silk scarves and embroidered caps. Old men in long coats bound by cloth bands around their waists. Flags and banners in turquoise and yellow and blue stretched between the buildings overhead and when Malcolm looked up there were Uighurs on the roofs. Their faces grave and serious and not a few whose cheeks glistened with tears.

A bell tolled and Malcolm's pace faltered. To his left he saw the spires of a local mosque, where an imam had stepped out to beseech the blessings of Almighty Allah. Malcolm walked past the man and did not look back. A low chant had begun in the crowd and Malcolm's stride shortened as he cocked his head to try and make out the words.

"*Khayr khosh! Khayr khosh!*" The first word a solemn murmur and the emphasis on the second so that the pair sounded like, "*Hosh. Hosh.*"

Goodbye. Goodbye.

Malcolm led the team down the street, through clouds of confetti thrown from the buildings. Their steps in time to the chants, all the way to the stables.

Zeng Huimin waited for them at the edge of town. He and his escort of police in helmets and body armor and rifles stood in the middle of the road, on tendrils of sand that writhed into the streets. The town in a slow battle with the desert at the edge of civilization.

Malcolm stopped in front of Zeng, Mary at his back. "Take everyone inside and get the camels ready," he said and waved for her to go around.

"You got it, boss," she said and came up on Malcolm's side to be blocked by the police.

Zeng stood for a moment and then nodded. The police escort made a gap through which Mary led the team.

Zeng watched the team pass and then half-turned to Malcolm. "So, today is the day."

"*Shi.*"

"I hope the cadres know what they're doing."

Malcolm said nothing. He met David's gaze as he brought up the rear of the procession and then the police closed ranks and Malcolm was left alone with Zeng.

"The Uighurs are a proud people," Zeng said.

"*Shi.*"

"And what do you think will happen to them now?"

"I don't see how that's related," Malcolm said.

"Don't you?" Zeng said and stepped aside. "They believe you're going to bring back Khoja so he can lead them to independence."

"I never told them that."

"The truth does not matter. This is what they believe. You have given them hope. It will have to be eradicated."

Malcolm shifted from foot to foot and tried to ignore the chants that continued to fill the air.

"I cannot wish you luck," Zeng said, "so instead let me say good riddance."

Malcolm dipped his head. Glanced once behind him at the Uighurs who remained on the street and then turned his back on them and entered the stables.

• • • • •

Malcolm halted the caravan in a horseshoe canyon deep within the rocky hills. The sun a reddish-orange ball low in the western sky and Khoja's mountain skylined to the east. He stared at the peak and waited for the other packets to arrive. Shadows fell along the floor of the canyon when he glimpsed a speck of white near the top of the mountain. A glimmer of reflected light. The hairs on his arms raised and he stood as still as the mountain itself and watched but did not see the movement again. He stared at the mountain for several more minutes and then shivered and rejoined the caravan.

He had Musa and the other Uighurs oversee the camels and the search for water while he gathered up the remaining team members. They formed a semi-circle around him and dropped their bags at their feet, their faces weathered and haggard.

"We'll camp here tonight," he said. "Tomorrow, I'll go up the mountain."

"You mean we," David said.

"I said what I meant."

"I don't think splitting the team is a good idea," Mary said.

"I agree," David said. "What if it's not a friendly reception?"

Malcolm shook his head. "The more of us there are, the bigger threat we'll pose."

"And what if he decides we're a threat anyways?" David asked. "What if he comes to us before we can get to him? Like he did with the militias, in Sudan."

Wolf dragged on a cigarette and its cherry glowed bright red. "Let him," the Brit said. "He'd be daft to come down that mountain at night."

"Mary?" Malcolm asked.

Mary glanced at Wolf and then back to Malcolm. Her lips pressed tight together. "I agree with David," she said. "You know what Khoja's capable of."

"I hope so," he said. "Otherwise we've come this whole way for nothing."

"What's that supposed to mean?" Wolf asked.

"It means set a watch."

"What, like all night?" Wolf asked.

"Is there any other way?" Mary asked.

Wolf took a last drag from his cigarette. "You're a real bitch, you know?" he said and then flicked the butt at Mary's feet. A burst of sparks like fireflies when it hit the ground. "Have it your way, Mum. I'll take first shift," he said and walked away.

"You can have midnight to one," David called after him.

Wolf stuck out his hand with the middle finger raised.

• • • • • •

Malcolm rose before dawn to find Mary and David already awake. They offered him oatmeal they'd cooked over the fire and he took it and ate. He cleaned out his bowl and began to pack his bag for the climb when he felt their gazes on him.

"No," he said and did not bother to look up from his bag.

"You haven't heard what we were going to say," Mary said.

"Surprise me, then."

David cleared his throat. "We think it's a bad idea to split the team."

"I told you to surprise me."

They were silent then and he knew they were looking at each other. Wondering how best to proceed. He stood and faced them.

"We've been over all this," he said.

"At least take Wolf," David said. "He's a first-rate mountaineer."

"And what will I do with him when I get to the top?"

"Make him promise not to talk."

"No," he said and slung his pack and then headed for the hardened path at the base of the mountain.

"Boss, how will we know if you succeeded?" Mary called after him.

He paused and half-turned. "If I'm not back by tomorrow night," he said, "leave."

"Where do we go?"

"Wherever you want," he said.

The sun had grown into a half-circle on the eastern horizon when he reached the trailhead. Angry and red. The path climbed out of the shadows cast by the nearby rocks and the ground became craggy and scree-covered beneath his boots. He inched along until he stood on a thin ledge that ended in a chain and rope traverse anchored to the side of the mountain. He tested his foot on the bottom chain and then backed off. Studied the bridge and the cliff face and several hundred feet up the mountain he spied an overhang of rocks and stones. Enough to pull the rope and chain and anyone who happened to be climbing into the abyss below.

He shielded his eyes with a hand and squinted at the top of the mountain. There was nothing to see and so he turned back to the bridge and then looked back the way he had come. There did not seem to be another way and so he grabbed the top rope and stepped out onto the chain. Shuffled along around the east side of the mountain until he came to another ledge. The sun was overhead now, the air still and hot like the inside of an oven. He paused for water and resisted the urge to look up and then continued his climb.

The path widened as he neared the top. Rough-cut steps appeared out of the rock and he paused at the base of the stairs and then climbed slow and deliberate. He came out onto a rock-strewn plateau and staggered in a sudden gust of wind. On the far side of the mesa stood a small compound made of dried brick and in front of the compound walls were two figures in white robes that flapped in the wind. The man with long grey-streaked hair and a thick and unkempt goatee and the woman with two twin black pony-tails draped over her shoulders.

Malcolm stared at the couple while the wind blew and pushed him back toward the stairs. He held his ground and got his feet under him and then presented his right fist against his left palm. He stood and waited and the pair stared at him and then the man returned the salute. Held his hands for a few seconds and then disappeared into the compound behind him. The woman watched Malcolm a moment longer and then followed the man.

• • • • •

Malcolm held out his hands. Cupped them together while the daughter, who he knew to be named Aziguli, poured water over them from a pitcher. The warm liquid trickled between his palms and fingers to drain into a basin set on the ground before him. He nodded his thanks and Aziguli handed him a towel and then moved on to do the same for the wife, Gul, while Malcolm dried his hands.

Khoja sat on the other side of a small fire and watched Aziguli pour tea into small bowls and offer them around. When she was done, he waved for her to sit and then gestured at several bowls of nuts and dried fruit.

"We do not have much," the old man said, "but what we have, we share with you."

Malcolm bowed his head. "I didn't come empty handed," he said and from his pack he produced packages of pastries and nougats that had been purchased in Kashgar. He offered them to Gul and she took them and handed them to Aziguli to put onto plates which were then passed around.

"We have watched you for days now," Khoja said.

"I know," Malcolm said. He held his bowl in his hand and swirled the tea in small circles.

"How did you find us?"

"It was not so hard," he said. "I knew where to look."

Khoja grunted. "You are American."

"Yes."

"All of you?"

"No. We have an Englishman and a Russian. And the camel handlers are Uighurs, of course."

"Of course."

Aziguli disappeared into one of the buildings and re-emerged with pots of rice pilaf and laghman and naan bread which were set around the fire. Khoja waited until Malcolm had filled his plate and then continued.

"Why have you come?" the old man asked.

Malcolm chewed slowly. "To request your help," he said.

"I am in exile."

"Self-imposed."

"Is it?"

"If you wanted to, you could leave."

Khoja snorted. "The character does not change the nature."

"It might. If the circumstances were different than you thought."

"Doubtful," Khoja said. "But possible."

"Earlier this year, the Chinese attacked my country."

"I have heard of this. Artfully done."

"The Chinese leadership will strike others. They are a threat to world security."

"You seek revenge."

"It is more complicated than that."

"Like a defeated fighter, your country is embarrassed."

"If it helps you to think of it in this manner."

"What is it you plan to do?" Khoja asked.

Malcolm waited while Aziguli refilled his tea and then picked up the bowl. "I'm going to finish what you started," he said.

Khoja stared at him. The flames flickered and Malcolm ate in silence and ignored the look that Khoja and Gul exchanged. After several minutes Khoja spoke. "Please explain," he said.

"My target is the Standing Committee."

"The entire Standing Committee?"

"Yes."

"That is a difficult proposition."

"There is a faction working with us," Malcolm said.

"I'm sure they are," Gul said and her voice was sharp and abrupt.

"Let him finish," Khoja said.

"This faction seeks to take power from Chairman Zhao," Malcolm said. "And they will help us gain access to the entire Standing Committee."

"And then you will kill them all," Khoja said.

"Yes."

"I see," Khoja said. "Who is it that seeks Zhao's downfall?"

"Perhaps I should start at the beginning," Malcolm said.

Khoja and Gul glanced at each other and then Khoja nodded.

"Thank you," Malcolm said. He set down his plate and reached for his pack. Pulled out a piece of wood and took up the knife he wore at his belt and began to talk while he carved. The sky grew dark and the air turned cool and when he had finished, the wood had transformed into a carving of a snake wrapped around the neck of a dragon. Malcolm passed the carving to Gul and she turned it over in her hands and then gave it to Khoja.

Khoja held up the dragon and studied it by the light of the fire. Lowered the carving and glanced at Malcolm. "You have captured the essence," he said.

"Thank you," Malcolm said.

"You are skilled," Khoja said and handed the dragon to Gul, "but that will not be enough. I could have killed Chairman Zhao five years ago and did not. Why would I help you now?"

"Because of the Uighurs."

"What about them?"

"Since your attempt, their situation has become worse."

"That is true," Gul said and glanced at Aziguli, who sat with her food untouched.

"Killing Zhao will not change that," Khoja said. "If anything, it will make the situation in Xinjiang worse."

"That may be," Malcolm said. "But it may prevent other people around the world from experiencing the same fate."

Khoja snorted. "So they can live as proud, individual peoples."

"If they so choose."

"With life, liberty, and freedom to pursue individual happiness."

"If that is what they choose, yes."

"And the freedom to die as individuals, as well."

"I'm not sure what you mean."

"It is said that fools notice differences," Khoja said, "while the wise notice what is the same. Also, a fool seeks people with different ideas, a sage seeks those who share common interests."

"I would need to think about that."

"Common interests, or the interests of all, are the interests that must be considered."

"That is what we have done."

"You have not. You have considered the interests of a small number of politicians and governments. You have considered the interests of the powerful."

"Peace is in the interest of us all," Malcolm said. "It is equilibrium, and it has worked for decades. Chairman Zhao and the current Chinese leadership seek to upset that harmony."

"Bah," Khoja said. "The equilibrium you speak of is based on the pettiness of individual differences. It will see the world's nations and peoples divided while the planet leaves us behind."

Malcolm picked up his tea. "I thought you might say that," he said.

"Then why did you waste your time?"

"To present my case to her," Malcolm said and turned to Gul. "You would have killed Zhao five years ago. I can help you finish what you started."

Gul raised her chin and her face was fierce in the firelight. "What makes you think I would help?"

"You hate Zhao."

"What do you know about hate?" Gul asked.

Malcolm's face grew hot. "My family died in the Chinese attack on America."

"Your family," Gul said and then stared into the flames. "Who in your family?"

"My wife and son."

Gul's lip curled in a sneer. "I have lost generations of family," she said. "Culture. Tradition. Language. Speak to me about hate when you have lost as much as I."

Malcolm drew a breath. "That is why it is you who I ask for help," he said.

"And what do you offer in return?" she asked.

"Revenge."

"What will I do with that?"

"Fill the emptiness inside."

Gul snorted. "What else?"

"I offer a warrior's death," Malcolm said and gestured around the courtyard of the darkened compound. "A chance to shake the foundations of the earth instead of starving in the wilderness."

"Is that what you think I want?" Gul asked. "Or is that what *you* want?"

Malcolm said nothing and did not move.

The fire had died down and Aziguli began to pick up the dishes and carry them into the building. When she came back out, Gul stood.

"Unfortunately, this old fool is correct," she said. "I will not help you." She handed the carving back to Malcolm and then picked up the teapot and disappeared into the building.

Malcolm sat and watched Gul leave and then turned to Khoja. "Perhaps if you had some time to think about it," he said.

"We have thought about this for the last five years," Khoja said.

"Then one more night is a small request."

Khoja stared at him as the last embers of the fire died and then stood. "You may stay the night," he said. "I will show you to your sleeping area."

Malcolm stood. "Thank you," he said.

"I will speak with Gul, and in the morning, she can discuss it with you, should she wish," the old man said. "As always, she makes her own decisions."

"That is all I can ask," Malcolm said and followed Khoja into the dark.

•　•　•　•　•　•

Malcolm dropped his backpack onto the floor of the tiny room where he would spend the night. An oil lantern hung from the ceiling and shone light on a simple cot in one corner. The carpets on the walls and floor were worn. He pulled his micro sleeping bag out of his pack and unrolled it on the cot and then straightened. Then he grabbed his pack and hurled it against a wall and stalked out of the room before the bag could fall to the floor.

He entered the courtyard and inhaled deep of the night air. The moon had not yet come out and the black sky was pierced by millions of pinprick stars. He gazed up into the darkness until a clatter came from the other corner of the compound. Gul's sharp voice carried across the courtyard and he thought he could make out Khoja's voice as well. He walked in the opposite direction, outside the compound to stand at the edge of the stony plateau where he stared out over the pitch-dark ocean that was the desert.

"You came all this way for nothing," a girl's voice said out of the night.

Malcolm half-turned and watched as Aziguli stepped into view. "They might change their minds," he said.

"They won't," she said and stood beside him. So close he could feel the heat of her body.

"Then I'll go on without them," he said.

"And you'll fail," she said. Her fingers found his and he tensed. He moved to extract his hand except she held on and linked their hands together. "I could help," she said.

"This isn't a game."

"And I'm not a little girl."

She traced a line along his forearm with her free hand and he shivered despite himself.

"Enough," he said and grabbed for her wrist. His hand closed on air and then his wrist wrenched back on itself and pain shot up his arm. He stepped into her to break the hold and a whiff of apricots tickled his nose. Then the pain in his arm doubled and drove him to his knees. His free hand reached for the ground and came down on the edge of the mountain. Stones tumbled over the side and he felt sick and then the pain eased. Steady enough to hold him in place and no more.

"You don't need them," she said.

He gritted his teeth against the pain. "They know the way," he said.

"So do I," she said. "He's told me countless times how he and my mother assaulted *Zhongnanhai*. It would be as easy as walking around this mountain."

"Let me go."

Pain electrified his arm and he felt himself move closer to the mountain's edge. He braced against the rocks to fight back. Knew in the best case he would lose his wrist and summoned all his strength and then she released him. He stayed on his knees for a moment and then rose and she placed her hands on his chest and leaned close so her lips almost touched his. He stumbled back and struggled to keep his voice steady and quiet.

"What do you want?" he asked.

"My father has forgotten what it means to be a warrior."

"He cares for his family."

"Then he would avenge us. Like you are doing."

"You know nothing about me."

"It is good that your whole family died. There is nothing to hold you back."

"Stop."

"My father has let fear own his heart. He cannot see the pain this causes me, or my mother."

"And what about his vision? That Chairman Zhao will unite the peoples of the world?"

"A dream, nothing more," she said. "This world will never be anything except a place where the strong take what they need to survive." She wrapped an arm around his neck and placed her lips near his ear. "Take me with you and you will get what you want."

"Your parents will not allow it."

"They cannot stop me. Leave tomorrow and wait for me two days to the east."

And then she let him go and disappeared into the night.

• • • • •

Malcolm collected his things at dawn and sought out Khoja. He found the old man in the courtyard and stood transfixed in the shadows of the compound while he watched Khoja's body trace lines through the air. The courtyard painted in grey and ash as the morning sun peaked over the compound walls and the old man's grace unlike anything Malcolm had ever seen.

When the old man had finished, Malcolm raised a hand in a greeting that was not returned. He dropped his arm and he strode out to where Khoja waited, the old man's hands buried in the sleeves of his robe.

"Have you decided?" he asked.

"We discussed your proposal long into the night," Khoja said.

"And?"

"We have not changed our minds."

"I see," Malcolm said and dipped his head. "I appreciate that you listened."

"What will you do now?"

"I'll leave," he said and hefted his backpack. "The others need to know."

"Eat before you depart."

"I have eaten enough of your food already," Malcolm said. He bowed to Khoja and then headed for the courtyard gate.

"And what of your mission?" Khoja called from behind him.

Malcolm paused. "We will continue it without you," he said and half-turned to find Gul at Khoja's side. Her robes bright yellow at her feet and deepening through orange near her waist to become blood-red at her chest so that she appeared to be on fire.

"We cannot allow that," Khoja said.

Malcolm thought about that. "You feel that strongly?" he asked.

"We do."

"Both of you?"

"Of course," Gul said.

"This is unexpected," he said and adjusted his pack.

Khoja waved a hand in dismissal. "You may return to your camp to talk about it with your team," he said. "We will meet you at sunset to hear your answer."

Malcolm paused. "And should we not be there?"

"Then we will pursue you," Gul said.

"I apologize," Khoja said. "But we must know that you will not jeopardize what we have worked to accomplish."

"I see," Malcolm said and then dipped his head. "Very well." He shouldered his pack and spied Aziguli in the doorway of the main building and then headed down the mountain.

• • • • •

The descent went quicker than the way up and Malcolm reached camp by late-morning. He called the team together and put to them Khoja's ultimatum.

"Let me get this straight," Wolf said. "This bloody old fool who we trekked across the Taklamakan to ask for help is now going to try and kill us?"

"He didn't say that," Malcolm said. "He gave us the option to abandon the mission."

"Great choice," David said.

Mary's eyes narrowed. "You haven't told us everything," she said.

Malcolm glanced at her. Scanned the faces of the group and then turned back to Mary. "I saw him move this morning," he said.

"And?"

"He's good."

"Come on," Wolf said. "It's five against one. He can't be that good."

"Five against two," Mary said.

"That's right," Malcolm said. "And if Gul is half as skilled as him, then we're in trouble."

"Then what are we waiting for?" Wolf half-turned and called to where the Uighurs sat on the ground. "Hey! You there! Round up those other tossers and get the camels ready to move."

"We're not going anywhere," Malcolm said.

"What?" Wolf asked. His face was contorted in confusion. "Did I hear you right?"

"He'll follow us."

"With what?" Wolf looked from Malcolm to the others, a deep crease in his brow. "A fuckin' magic carpet?"

"I hate to side with Wolf, boss," Mary said, "but he may be right this time. We can be miles away by sunset. If he follows, we ambush him."

"Bloody well right," Wolf said. "Fight on our terms, not his."

"And where would we do this?" Malcolm asked.

Wolf flung a hand at the mountains. "From the fucking hills, man."

"He knows this land better than us. We would be the ones at a disadvantage, not him."

"I can't believe what I'm hearing." Wolf ran his fingers through his hair.

"You're welcome to leave," Malcolm said.

Wolf flung out a hand. "Yeah, great choice, that. While we're stuck in the middle of the bloody desert."

"Gleb, you too," Malcolm said. "This wasn't what you signed up for."

The Russian stared in silence into the ashes of the camp fire.

"Boss, if these two are as good as you say, we'll need everyone," Mary said. "Even Wolf."

"Let's put it to a vote, shall we?" Wolf asked. "I say we leave. Now. What about you, Mary? Come on, speak up."

David held up a hand. "Wolf, calm down."

"Like hell I will. Come on, girl, speak up."

Mary stared at the ground. "Leave."

"Right. And you, Gleb?"

"Leave."

"I thought so. David? Come on now."

"Shit." David looked at the ground and put his hands on his hips. "It'd be better to pick ground of our choosing."

"Leave, then?"

"Yes, goddamnit. Leave."

"Well, there you have it," Wolf said and held out his hands. "Leave it is."

"I say we stay," Malcolm said.

"Four to one," Wolf said and shrugged. Turned and yelled at the Uighurs. "Hi! Musa. Get these camels loaded!"

"Come sunset, be ready," Malcolm said. He turned to walk away and a hand grabbed his shoulder.

"Don't you walk away from me," Wolf said. "We all –"

Malcolm spun and punched Wolf in the throat. Then he grabbed the Brit by the neck and choked him and felt the hand on his shoulder let go. Wolf gagged and rose on his tiptoes and Malcolm leaned close. "Stay or leave," he said. "Your choice. But question my authority again and Khoja will be the least of your worries."

He held the Brit a moment longer and then loosened his grip and let Wolf slump to the sand. Stared at him and then at each member of the team.

"Sunset," he said and then walked off to prepare.

· · · · ·

Malcolm watched Khoja and Gul descend the mountain.

The late afternoon wind swung from the west to the east and whipped their robes about them as they moved along the path. Two rolling stones called back to the lowly earth. The sun dropped lower in the sky and one by one the others joined him to wait. Silent and alert. He'd sent Musa and the Uighurs deeper into the hills to set up another camp to the east and there was nothing to do but wait.

The wind died as the pair started down the sandy approach to the mountain. The air hot and still and heavy. Malcolm stood and waited for them where the path entered the sheltered box canyon. Khoja stopped a stone's throw away and Gul stopped beside him, her body bladed toward them.

Malcolm heard footsteps on his flanks. Mary and David come to stand at his shoulders. Gleb farther back and as for Wolf, he had no idea. He turned his attention to Khoja.

"Welcome," he said.

"You decided to wait."

"Of course."

"I was unsure whether you would flee."

"What would be the point?"

"You will not abandon your mission," Khoja said and his voice seemed full of sadness.

"No."

They stared at each other and then Malcolm gazed up into the sky. Clear and colored in shades of dark blue and indigo. The sun abed on the western horizon in a maelstrom of oranges and reds and purples. He drew a breath and looked back at Khoja.

"Would you like food before we begin?" Malcolm asked. "Water?"

"No."

"Then let's get this over."

"It is not yet sunset," Khoja said. "If you need more time to prepare."

"No," Malcolm said. "Let us begin."

Khoja cupped his right fist in his left palm. Held them in front of his chest and then struck.

It was almost over before it began. Malcolm so bewitched by the utter absence of wasted effort in Khoja's movement that he nearly forgot to evade. He wouldn't have believed it possible to cover as much ground and as quick as the old man. His instincts were all that saved him.

He recovered, however, and began to press Khoja. Forced the old man to retreat up the mountain's slope, always on the edge of Malcolm's strikes. The thickness of a sheet of paper away. They circled and as they did, he tried to keep track of the broader fight. Mary and David against Gul. Him against Khoja. Gleb and Wolf outmatched, hanging around on the periphery of the fight to watch for openings and give the pair something to think about. This became impossible as the wind picked up and night fell, each element an additional combatant in its own right.

Then the fight consumed him and he lost focus on anything except the old man.

The wind gusted and Malcolm knelt and threw sand into the old man's face. Stared agog while Khoja whirled and merged into a gale of dust and grit. A dervish that harnessed the wind and hurled the airborne sand back to scour Malcolm's face and his eyes. He squinted and Khoja connected with a kick and then it was he who had to give ground. Back toward the camp.

A cloud of sand blotted out the sky, kicked up and carried aloft by the tempest that howled around them. Malcolm could barely see Khoja anymore. The old man fought like a ghost and seemed to land strikes at will. Another attack and he fell to his knees. He dove to the side and rolled. When he came to his feet, he saw that Mary and David were pressed as hard as he was, and then Khoja drove him back once again. Unrelenting. As he began to gasp for breath, it became harshly clear he could not survive much more and then the wind stilled and the sand hung in the air. Khoja emerged from the gloom to his flank and Malcolm understood he would not be able to evade the old man's attack. He twisted away even as he steeled himself for the blow, so committed to the motion that he could not stop when the strike never landed.

He lost his balance and tumbled to the sand. Flipped onto his back and all he could do was stare and gasp for breath. Unable to comprehend how Aziguli had come to stand in the way of the old man. A double-edged *jian* sword in her hand, the blade's tip held steady at her father's throat. A midnight black tassel dangled from the sword's pommel. Aziguli cut a circle through the air with the sword and the blade and tassel whipped around and blurred and then lashed out against Khoja.

The old man stepped out of range and a strand of his hair fell to the ground. Aziguli struck again and again and he ducked and dodged and cuts and slits opened in his robes as each slash dismembered the space he'd once stood.

"Fight back," Aziguli yelled at him.

Khoja contorted his body to evade the tip of the sword and did not speak.

"Fight back!"

"Stop this, Aziguli," Gul said and came to Khoja's side. Turned sideways to avoid a slash that would have opened her from head to belly and stepped on the flat of the sword's blade to ground the weapon in the sand. "We don't want to hurt you," she said.

The girl's face twisted in a snarl and she yanked the sword out from Gul's foot. Redoubled her assault while the old woman tumbled through the air to land on her feet beside Khoja. Aziguli attacked them both now and her blade blurred and hummed, so fast it created a sword wind that cleared a path through the sand that hung like fine mist in the air.

For all that, Malcolm saw that it would not be enough.

Khoja and Gul fought like they were one. Each purposeful dodge taking them on an invisible and divergent arc that enveloped Aziguli on both sides. The girl's focus split front and back. She swung at Gul and Malcolm saw Khoja move in from behind.

Malcolm attacked.

He landed a strike on the old man's back and across the sand he saw Mary kick out Gul's legs. David joined in and along with Mary they drove a wedge between the pair. Malcolm hit Khoja again and again and the old man turned to face him and then dove back from Aziguli. He recovered quick and lunged at Malcolm. Adjusted his attack to evade Aziguli's sword and Malcom grabbed his wrist and then the old man was on his back in the sand with the tip of Aziguli's sword at his throat.

The night became quiet and still. Khoja and Aziguli locked in silent combat.

"Aziguli!" Gul yelled. She brushed off Mary's hand and strode toward Khoja.

"Not one step closer," Aziguli said and a drop of blood appeared where the sword touched Khoja's neck.

Gul stopped. "Aziguli!"

"You have learned well, daughter," Khoja said.

"By necessity," Aziguli said.

"You fight with too much emotion," the old man said. He put the palm of his hand against the side of the sword. "I could still beat you."

Aziguli shifted her weight and the drop of blood at Khoja's neck turned into a trickle. "You would have to kill me," she said.

"Do you think I won't?"

"Aziguli!" Gul called.

"I know you won't."

"Aziguli! Stop!"

"Then go ahead, daughter," Khoja said.

The words still on Khoja's lips and Aziguli leaned into the sword.

"Stop!" Gul screamed and fell to her knees. "I'll help you!"

Aziguli paused and Khoja's gaze flickered to the old woman.

"What are you doing?" he asked.

"I will help," Gul said. "Let him live."

"Help me do what, mother?" Aziguli asked.

"I will help you kill the Chinese."

Aziguli stood and contemplated her father. Pinned by her sword to the ground beneath her. "And you, father?" she asked. "What will you do?"

Khoja stared up at her and then his hand left the blade of the sword. "I will not help," he said. "But nor will I stop you."

"Then tomorrow we leave," Aziguli said and pulled the sword from Khoja's neck. Glanced at Malcolm and then walked off into the night.

Gul crawled to Khoja. Knelt at the old man's side and clasped his hands in hers.

Malcolm moved away and then turned to look back at the pair. He did not move when Mary came to stand beside him.

"You should have told us about the girl," she said.

"I had no idea," he said.

"Well, now we know."

"I guess."

"It'll be nice having her on our side,' Mary said.

"Is she?" Malcolm asked and peered into the darkness where Aziguli had gone.

"Is she what?"

"On our side."

• • • • • •

Back into the desert.

Within days, Khoja and Gul and Aziguli had settled into the team's routine. The girl kept to herself, and would range far in front of the lead camel during the day. She did not talk to Malcolm and all the same her presence prodded him to go faster. He forced himself to plod along in the echoes of her footprints and sometimes he imagined the scent of lavender on the breeze.

He followed Khoja's directions to a resupply on the Hotan River where they replenished their water and food from another caravan. They crossed the G217 highway the same day and then pushed on another six miles. The days were a blur of sand and sun and heat, and the camps were mute and somber as the travelers recuperated from the daily toll of the desert. The newcomers tended the camels and dug for water, whatever the nightly routine demanded, with one small adjustment.

Wherever Khoja was, Aziguli was not.

The old man seemed in turn perplexed and resigned at his rejection. As if he knew, but could not accept, that it was deserved. He would walk beside her in silence, he complimented her sword technique, even offered facts about the desert and oddities about the camels, like how they had three lips. Anything to draw her into conversation.

Aziguli rejected every attempt.

There was a night, the highway three days behind them, when they'd set up camp and begun supper. All but Khoja were seated around a fire David had made from scavenged pieces of petrified wood collected on the day's march. The old man ladled food onto his plate and then sat beside his daughter as he did every night. The silence around the camp fire deepened as all waited for Aziguli to stand up and leave.

Malcolm stared into his plate, unwilling to watch Aziguli rebuff her father once again. He picked at the slop and glanced up when he heard Mary snort and choke. When he looked at her, he saw that she was all right and then he followed her gaze to Khoja. The old man with a chopstick stuck out of each nostril and his face contorted so that one eye was hidden and the other almost popped from his face. Malcolm was halfway to his feet and then stopped as Khoja's face split into a wide grin.

The old man smiled at his audience. He picked up a piece of meat and fumbled it into his mouth, then grabbed his throat and pretended to gag. Mary giggled and Khoja added groans and moans. Gul began to laugh also as Khoja swayed where he sat and then his food slopped off his plate and onto his lap and he sprang to his feet and cursed and then David and Gleb were laughing and Malcolm could no longer contain himself. He sat and struggled to keep his own food on his plate as the laughter overtook him.

Aziguli stood and walked away from the fire. Across the sand to eat by herself.

As she did every night.

Khoja's gaze followed her and his face grew serious and then it contorted once more as if he was choking. He swayed again and held onto his throat as the laughter around the fire died. Then the mask dropped once again. He gave up and took the chopsticks out of his nose and sat back down. Gul took her place beside him and put her hand on his knee and he flashed her a brief smile and they finished their meals in silence.

• • • • •

The next day they found the ruins.

It was late afternoon when Malcolm stopped. They set up camp and then the team explored the site. Malcolm went his own way into the ruins until he came across a large tree in what might have been a courtyard. Beyond that lay a building with a domed roof. He stood beneath the tree and placed a hand on its gnarled and twisted trunk and did not move when Aziguli appeared.

"How old is this place?" he asked.

Aziguli snapped a branch off the tree and Malcolm started.

"Who cares?" she asked. She snapped pieces from the broken limb and tossed them to the sand. "Everything here is dead."

"It has survived," he said.

"Has it?"

"Look around."

"I am."

"Then tell me what you see."

Her red robes whipped and billowed in a gust of wind and she gazed around the ruins.

"Empty buildings," she said. "Lost memories. Forgotten dreams and forgotten people."

"It has endured who knows how long?" he asked.

She turned to him. "I thought you were different," she said. "But you are like them."

"You don't know anything about me."

"Trapped in memories that no longer exist," she said and walked up to him. "I've seen you stare at the picture of your family taped to your compass. Like it's a star that guides your way, instead of an anchor that prevents you from seizing greatness." She stood so close to him that her airborne robes curled around his arms and legs. "Why do you cling to them so?"

"It's all I have," he said and the words sounded as lifeless to him as the ruins in which he stood.

"And they are all dead."

"I remember times we shared together. I remember their sacrifice."

"They had no say in it," she yelled into his face. Beat on his chest and drove him back.

He stumbled away from her sudden fury. Held up his arms to fend her off while she thrashed and screamed.

"They were used! Sacrificed for someone else's goal!"

"No," he said and his face reddened as she beat him around the ears.

"Enslaved," she yelled, "and at the end, cast aside. Left to die in a world that will itself die."

"Stop."

"Just as the world has left my people to die. My generation. Me. You did that."

"No."

She hit him again. "You, and the Han," she said. "And my father. All the same. All words and talk and none of you with concern for anyone but yourself."

He grabbed her wrists. Held her at arm's length while she fought and cried.

"Even now, all you care about is who will rule this dying world," she said. "Your silly countries will fight until nobody is left!"

He pulled her close, his fingers white where he squeezed her arms.

"Who will be king of the compost heap?" she shouted in return.

"Aziguli." Khoja spoke from the entrance of the domed building. "Control yourself," he said.

She stilled. Bottled up her fury so suddenly that Malcolm staggered forward and she leaned close to him so that her lips grazed his ear.

"Do not let him trick you into thinking any of them can be trusted," she said. "They all deserve to die."

"Aziguli," Khoja called.

She wrenched free from Malcolm's grasp. Stepped back and stared up at him and then glanced at her father and stalked off into the ruins with the wind at her back.

Malcolm took a step in her direction and then Khoja's hand was on his shoulder.

"Let her go," Khoja said.

He hesitated, tense under the old man's touch.

"She was not always like this," Khoja said and then released him.

He stared after Aziguli for a few seconds longer and then glanced back at the old man. "What happened?" he asked and followed Khoja to stand outside the entrance to the domed building.

The old man was silent and it occurred to Malcolm he might not answer.

"I did," Khoja said and then entered the temple.

Malcolm stood in the doorway and watched Khoja move to a mural on a far wall. "What did you do?" he asked.

"I abandoned her."

"Why?"

The old man clasped his hands behind his back and stared in silence at the mural.

"I asked you a question."

"Because my daughter is correct about one thing," Khoja said and turned to look back at Malcolm. "The world is dying. And precious few have the ability to stop it."

"You, I suppose."

"No. Nor you. All we can do is adjust the timeline," he said and faced the mural once more.

Malcolm entered the building and let the silence envelope him.

"This site was conquered during the reign of Mangsong Mangtsen," Khoja said while Malcolm walked. "Lost during the reign of Tridu Songtsen to the Tang dynasty, the high point of Imperial China. The emperor Taizong laid the foundation for the empire to flourish for centuries and in that time, China led the world in both culture and technology."

"And then lost to the Mongols," Malcolm said.

"All empires fall," Khoja said.

"Then what do you care?"

"Do you know how they rise?"

"Power," Malcolm said. "Strength. Good decisions. Luck."

"All true," Khoja said. "But the most important component is unity. This is the greatest gift that came from the Qin dynasty. It allowed China to achieve things only dreamt of by others."

"For a time."

"Once again, true. The mandate of heaven was lost," Khoja said and then looked at Malcolm. "But it has come again."

"They attacked my country. Killed my family," Malcolm said and then flung an arm at the door. "Your own daughter is proof of how they treat people."

"And what is the suffering of one person compared to the suffering of all?"

Malcolm stared at the old man.

"Or the suffering of one people compared to all people?"

"I have my orders," he said.

"And will your mission accomplish what you want?"

"Yes."

"It will bring back what you've lost?"

Malcolm's voice was quiet. "What do you know about that?"

Khoja stared at him. "Nothing," he said and headed for the door. Then he stopped and glanced back. "Except that only a man with nothing to lose would undertake a mission into the Taklamakan. A mission from which there will be no return."

Malcolm kept his gaze on the ancient mural. "You know, I've been in this position before."

"Alone?"

"Yes," he said. "Before Amaelia and Oran, before –"

"Before you knew me."

Malcolm glanced back. "Yes," he said and then turned back to the mural. "What you're selling, it's a pipe dream. Impossible. All I want now is to kill Zhao for what he's done."

"A cold victory."

"Maybe," he said. "But it won't stop me from saying Hallelujah when he's dead."

"That does not have to be the future," Khoja said. "You have time to avert your path."

"It's too late for that."

"It is only too late for the dead."

Malcolm glanced back. "Does that extend to your daughter?" he asked.

The old man contemplated him and then stepped into the door. Paused with one hand on the doorway and spoke over his shoulder. "The past seeks to trap us all," he said. "I can only do what I can to ensure it does not succeed with my daughter."

"Sounds like a cop out to me."

"Perhaps," Khoja said, "but have you considered how *your* past traps you?"

Malcolm turned his back. "Like I said, I have my orders."

"And who gives them?" Khoja asked and then walked out.

· · · · ·

Another seven days on the march.

Seven days of sun-drenched heat and blisters and strained muscles and parched throats. Seven days where the holes they dug at night either turned up dry or surrendered brackish water unfit to drink. Malcolm reduced the daily ration of water to one liter per person and gave the rest to the camels. Wolf would drink all his water in the morning and then badger the others for sips the rest of the day. David lied. Told the others he had no water left and snuck his last mouthfuls when he was alone.

On the fifth day, Malcolm asked Khoja to spell him off at the front of the caravan so he could walk the line.

"Are you sure you can trust him?" Mary had asked when he told her what he'd done.

"He knows better than I do where we are," he'd said. "Where we're going."

The old man had not argued. Instead, he'd glanced at the sun and then stepped off without a word.

Malcolm slowed his pace and fell in with the first packet. Spoke with Gul and Aziguli and then dropped back and spent several silent minutes of peace with Gleb and Mary in the second packet. He walked with David and Wolf for almost thirty minutes at the rear. Endured Wolf's rants and could not get David to say more than a few words. He gave up and fell in beside Mary on his way to the front of the caravan.

"What's going on with David?" he asked.

"I think the medical description is sand in his vagina," she said and then looked at him. A wry smile that the fatigue on her face could not erase. "Sorry, did I say that out loud?"

"You did."

"He goes through these funks now and then," she said and then frowned. "Although this one is lasting longer than normal."

Malcolm glanced back and shielded his eyes with a hand. "He's different than I remember," he said.

"He's tired. We all are."

"It's more than that. He's more on edge."

Mary studied Malcolm and then offered him her canteen. "He's scared," she said.

"Of what?"

"The usual. Dying. Failure. Most of all, though, I think he's scared of this desert."

He wiped his mouth and handed back the canteen. "Because we might not make it through?"

"Because it gives him too much time to think." She took back her canteen and stowed it.

"About what?"

"Mostly about how he wishes he'd gotten out of the military. Like you."

Malcolm glanced at her. "I never knew he felt that way," he said.

"Don't let it bother you," she said. "If he'd left, he would've missed working with me." She smiled. "We all know how that turned out."

Malcolm paused and looked back once more. "And now I'm taking that away," he said. Behind them the third packet was stalled and he could hear David and Wolf's yells as they wrestled with the lead camel. Then he turned around and saw that Mary had left him behind.

• • • • • •

Another waterless camp that night.

In the morning, Malcolm led the caravan due east toward the S165. They stopped at a dune a few miles out and he glassed the highway until he located a gas station among the rows of trees and brush that lined the road. There was a red canopy with the PetroChina logo over the gas island, a concrete building with a billboard he took to be the main store, a long, squat structure covered with metal siding, and a blue shed the size of a large shipping container near the back of the site. He watched for the better part of the afternoon and then signalled for the caravan to proceed.

The sun was already flirting with the western horizon when he led the way into the gas station. He scoped out the water supply while the packets straggled in and then tracked down the proprietor, a man in a red baseball hat, yellow shirt, and blue pants. He offered the man a wad of bills and the man's eyes widened, then he took the money and disappeared into the store.

While David supervised the water resupply, Malcolm went out front and leaned against a fuel pump. He gazed across the highway at the line of trees and bushes and wondered how far the shelterbelt extended.

"Impressive, isn't it?" Khoja said.

Malcolm took a sip from his canteen. "You know," he said, "for someone who led an uprising against the Chinese, you come across as an awfully big fan."

Khoja snorted. "I grew up in the Cultural Revolution. None who lived through that time will forget the horrors inflicted by the government."

"Then how can you defend them? How can you defend Zhao, knowing what he's done?"

"His experience of those times is not so different from mine. He was a child then."

"What about Xinjiang, then?"

"He did what he felt he had to do. I have respect for his capabilities."

"Which he won't hesitate to use against you."

"I do not worry about floating clouds blocking the gazing eye," the old man said. "For the foreseeable future, Chairman Zhao and I share a common enemy."

"Amaelia would've loved you," Malcolm said and shook his head.

"Your wife?"

"Yes."

"What makes you say that?"

"She was as stubborn as you."

"It is okay to be stubborn if you are right."

"That's what she would've said."

"What did she do?"

He glanced at Khoja and then went back to his contemplation of the shelterbelt. "Environmental scientist," he said.

"Then she would have appreciated this," he said and gestured at the trees and bushes. "Similar reclamation work takes place at the edges of the desert, building off the expertise developed in Kubuqi."

"I try not to think about it."

The old man stood silent and then placed a hand on Malcolm's shoulder. "I hope that one day you will adjust to the change," he said.

Malcolm thought about Amaelia and Oran and how all he had to remember them by was the picture taped to his compass. The hurt that picture caused him, which had not slackened an ounce after all these months until the pain had seemed to solidify into one more thing to carry around the desert. He tried to acknowledge the old man's kindness and found he could not trust his voice. So he stood and watched the eastern sky darken through shades of deep blue until the wind picked up and then he turned.

"We'd best finish up," he said and headed toward the store.

"Killing Zhao will not bring back your wife," Khoja said.

Malcolm paused. "I know that."

"Or your son."

"I know that, too."

"Do you?"

He glanced back at the old man.

"You have spoken of your wife, what would she say?"

"She's dead."

"Do you not know?"

"Of course, I know," he said and the words cut through the air. "But this is all I'm good at, so it will have to do."

"A true warrior," Khoja said. "But is the calling of a warrior only to kill? Or is it also to bring peace?"

"Go to hell," he said and headed for the convenience store.

"Who does a warrior serve?" Khoja called after him. "Themselves? Or others?"

Malcolm paused. Looked down and made fists of his hands.

"Boss!"

Malcolm looked up and saw David in the gap between the residence and the gas station's main building. "What is it?" he called.

David's gaze flicked to Khoja and then back to Malcolm. "I'll tell you on the way," he said.

He nodded and headed for David.

"And what about that?" Khoja called out.

Malcolm glanced back to see a red cabover semi-truck turn into the gas station. He watched it head for the pumps and then looked at Khoja. "Move him along," he said. The old man nodded and Malcolm fell in beside David.

David led him around the back of the site.

"Want to tell me what this is about?" he asked as they walked.

"It's Aziguli," David said. "She broke into the residence and won't leave."

Malcolm met David's gaze and knew it was bad.

They found the door to the residence ajar. Malcolm barged in to a tiny foyer and followed the sounds of a woman's sobs, through a cramped living room to the kitchen where he elbowed past Mary to find Aziguli. A woman he didn't recognize knelt on the floor and stared up at Aziguli, who held a baby in her arms.

"I tried to stop her," Mary said.

"It's all right, Mary," he said. Then he held out a hand to Aziguli. "Give her back the baby."

Aziguli glanced at him and then looked at the baby. "I could raise it," she said as she let it suckle on her pinky finger. "Teach it all the terrible things the Han have done."

The mother wailed and held her hands to the sides of her head, her cheeks wet with tears.

"We don't have time for this," Malcolm said. "We need to load up the caravan and get back into the desert."

"That would be fitting wouldn't it?" Aziguli asked and met Malcolm's gaze. "To turn the children of the Party against it?"

"These people aren't Party officials, Aziguli. They run a gas station," he said. "The child belongs with its mother. Please, give it back."

"You're right," she said and then looked at the baby. Withdrew her finger from its mouth and wrapped her hand around its throat.

Malcolm froze. Unable to move while Aziguli's other hand covered the baby's face. The baby screamed and the noise broke his paralysis. He lurched for them and had not even cut the distance in half when she wrung the baby's neck.

"No," he whispered as Aziguli cast the body onto the floor in front of the mother. The woman screamed and wailed, scrambled on her hands and knees to scoop up the body and clutch it to her chest. Her face twisted inside-out with grief.

Aziguli brushed past him and he grabbed her arm. "Why?" he asked. Yanked on her arm when she did not answer and yelled in her face. "Why?"

She stared at him and her face was blank and impassive. "They can't change," she said. "They will never change."

He glared at her and thought about his dead son and then she slipped from his grasp. Flatfooted once again when he saw the knife in her hand.

Aziguli wrapped a hand in the mother's hair. She pulled the woman's head back and dragged the blade across her throat and then held her upright while blood spurted out to cover the dead baby and the floor. A wet gurgle escaped the woman and Aziguli let her go and then wiped the blade on her shirt and walked out.

Malcolm stood over the bodies. Rooted to the floor.

"Boss?" Mary asked.

The baby cradled in its mother's arms. Almost like Amaelia used to hold Oran.

"Boss?" Mary asked. "You in there?"

He blinked and then turned to Mary. "Get the others," he said. "We have to go."

• • • • • •

Malcolm ran to the front of the gas station, where the semi-truck was parked beside the fuel pumps. Khoja waited near the front of the rig with his arms clasped behind his back and the driver stood with his back to Khoja as he pumped gas.

Aziguli was nowhere to be seen.

Malcolm went to the main building next and entered the store. He let the door shut behind him and faced off against Aziguli, who stood behind the service desk. The body of the attendant on the floor at her feet, half-hidden by the counter with only the legs visible.

He walked toward her. "Enough," he said.

"We could not have left him alive."

"These people didn't deserve this."

She came out from behind the counter. "Does anyone?" she asked and came to a stop in front of him. Then she nodded at the door. "Does *he*?"

He turned as the door opened and in walked the truck driver. Khoja behind him.

The truck driver took three steps and then glanced at the body of the attendant behind Aziguli. He came to a stop and then saw the knife in Aziguli's hand. The man's eyes widened and his face paled. He looked at Malcolm and fell to his knees, held his hands by his ears and pleaded for mercy.

Aziguli strode toward him.

"Stop this," Malcolm said and grabbed for her arm.

Aziguli sidestepped him and stood at the edge of his reach. She held the knife in front of her and then shrugged. "As you wish," she said and then sent the knife through the air. End over end to bury the blade in the truck driver's chest. The hilt of the knife quivered and the truck driver looked down as if to wonder how it had got there and then the man fell onto his side.

Khoja knelt beside the man and eased him onto his back. When he glanced up at Aziguli, the pain in his eyes was as if she had stabbed him instead. They stared at each other for a second and then Aziguli walked up to him. She stooped and pulled the blade from the truck driver's chest and then wiped the blade on the man's shirt. She took her time to sheathe the knife and then her upper lip curled and she left the store.

Malcolm watched her go. Unable to comprehend what he'd watched her do. Then the door slammed shut and he looked at Khoja.

"Help me," the old man said.

Malcolm knelt on the opposite side of the truck driver. He pulled up the man's shirt to access the wound and saw blood bubble out through the hole. Pinkish red and tinged with foam and a hissing sound when the man drew breath.

Malcolm shook his head. "There's nothing we can do," he said.

"We can seal the wound."

"Then what?" Malcolm asked. "He needs surgery."

"There is a hospital in Ruoqiang Town."

"That's at least an hour away."

"Forty minutes."

"He'll be lucky to make it fifteen."

"I will take him."

Malcolm met Khoja's gaze and saw that the old man knew it was impossible. "You know you can't," he said. "None of us can."

"He has done nothing wrong," Khoja said.

"I know," Malcolm said. "He just had poor timing."

Khoja stared at him and then looked down at the truck driver. "Yes," he said. "Poor timing."

Malcolm stood. "We need to go," he said.

"We cannot leave him like this."

"We have to."

"But not like this," Khoja said and then looked at Malcolm's belt.

Malcolm followed the old man's gaze to the knife sheathed at his hip. He thought about what Khoja had suggested and then nodded. Unsheathed the knife and knelt once more beside the truck driver.

"I'll do it," he said.

"No," Khoja said and held out his hand. "It is my responsibility."

Malcolm hesitated and then offered the knife. He felt Khoja's hand brush his own when the old man took the blade and then watched as Khoja positioned the knife's edge by the truck driver's throat. The man flailed and Malcolm pinned him down the shoulders and looked at Khoja.

"Do it," he said and his voice was soft.

But Khoja did not move.

"Do it," he repeated. "It's not going to get any easier."

"I misled you earlier," Khoja said.

"What?"

"When we spoke about suffering."

"I don't understand."

"I asked you about the suffering of one compared to the suffering of the many."

"We can talk about this later."

"The truth," Khoja said, "is that I cannot bear the suffering of my daughter."

The knife shook in the old man's hand and when he met Malcolm's gaze, his eyes were moist. "The truth," he said, "is that I would sacrifice the entire world to spare her the pain she feels."

Malcolm stared at the old man and then covered Khoja's hand that held the knife with his own. Steadied the blade against the truck driver's neck.

"Help me save her," Khoja said.

He shook his head. "Do you think you can?" he asked.

A thin smile crossed Khoja's face. "I would at least have the opportunity."

They stared at each other and then Malcolm sighed. "I can't promise you anything."

"All I ask is for your consideration."

Malcolm thought about that and then nodded. "All right," he said.

Khoja looked at him and then nodded in return. Then he dropped his gaze to the truck driver and pressed the blade into the man's throat. The man strained and began to thrash and Malcolm held him down and then Khoja cut the man's throat.

• • • • •

Malcolm forced the caravan on long into the night.

They put six miles between them and the highway. Then Malcolm had them stop and set up a hasty camp and they collapsed into sleep, most of them in their clothes and with their boots on. He sat on his rolled-out poncho liner, the last one awake, and glanced around the dark shapes on the sand that were sleeping bodies and realized he'd set no watch. He mulled this over and decided they'd gone far enough. Then he dragged his sleeping roll apart from the others so he would not hear them snuffle or snore as they slept. When he lay down, he stared up at the stars and wondered if he'd be able to sleep in the few hours left before dawn.

He drifted off and dreamed of Amaelia. The moonlight on her bare shoulders. He tried to tell her he was sorry. Tried to tell her that he knew she wasn't real and that he'd be with her soon and then she knelt and put her hand on his chest and her beauty overtook him.

He woke to a blade at his neck.

Aziguli.

He could hear her breath. Deep and strong.

She knelt in the spot where he'd dreamed of Amaelia and he moved to sit up and she pushed the knife into his throat and forced him back.

"You were dreaming," she said. She threw a leg over his body and straddled him and then leaned down so that her chest touched his. Her mouth by his cheek so he could feel her breath on his face. Warm with a hint of cardamom.

He stared up into the night and then she straightened. Her hair in his face and her eyes two black holes in the dark.

She began to grind her hips into him and he hardened and then she reached down with her free hand to his belt. Contemplated him as she tugged the free end out of the buckle. Then her hand moved to the button of his pants.

He closed his eyes.

She stopped. "Look at me," she said.

"No."

She ground the blade up under his chin and a trickle of blood ran down his neck.

He opened his eyes.

She stared down at him. Remote and statuesque and cold in the starlight. "Pathetic," she said.

He said nothing and she bent close. The knife between them.

"The man you hunt is protected by the mandate of heaven," she said. "To kill him, you must be prepared to die."

"I am."

She was silent and then said, "I think you lie. You still believe you have something to live for."

They stayed like that for a second longer and then she pulled the blade from his neck and stood. "You wouldn't have survived a day in the camps," she said and then walked away.

He lay there on the sand and put a hand to his throat. Held his compass at his heart with his other hand and thought about Amaelia.

• • • • •

He sat up with a gasp and looked around.

A sliver of red and orange on the eastern horizon. The rest of the sky black and indigo and the desert grey in the pre-dawn light. He saw that a handful of camels had broken free in the night and that nobody else was awake.

He rose to his feet and straightened his clothes, then headed toward the sleeping bodies laid out on the sand. When he was about there, he paused and glanced to his side to see Khoja sat on a dune. He stared at the old man and his jaw muscles flared and relaxed and flared again and then he looked away and walked on.

"There is nothing to be ashamed about," Khoja said.

Malcolm stopped. He kept his head down and clenched his hands into fists while the old man stood and approached and he could not look Khoja in the eyes.

"You were not prepared for her," the old man said.

"We need to get going," he said. "We're still too close to the highway."

"You were not prepared for any of this."

"What do you want from me?" Malcolm asked and met the old man's gaze.

"To consider the path she walks."

"I said I would think about it."

"Not for me," Khoja said. "For you. You walk the same path."

Malcolm thought about that and then looked away. "I have to wake the others," he said.

He took three steps toward where the others slept and then looked back to see Khoja with his hands buried in the sleeves of his shirt. They gazed at each other and then he turned and began to shake and kick the others awake.

• • • • • •

They continued on.

Malcolm walked more and more inside his own head. Mary would have to come to the front to tell him to stop whenever there were breaks in the caravan, or to suggest he adjust the direction of march. He would listen to her and nod. Then he'd stop and wait if that's what she wanted, or pretend to shoot a new bearing while he gazed at the photo of his dead wife and son instead.

The rest of the team he saw as if through one-way glass. David sullen and drawn into himself. Wolf's sarcasm and jokes left behind in the desert. He didn't know where. Gleb silent and robotic, an automaton who would walk himself into the ground. He kept his distance from Khoja and Gul lest he become in thrall like them to the girl.

Aziguli, who he tried not to think about.

Mary held them together. She broke up the arguments over who would dig the empty water holes and who would cook and who would picket the camels. He realized she'd assumed his role, knew he'd let her down, and took it as permission to retreat even more.

• • • • • •

The sandstorm overtook the caravan on the tenth day out from the gas station.

Malcolm ignored Mary's pleas to stop and forced them to continue. He dragged the entire caravan through the dirt blizzard because the sole place he could be alone with his family was out front on the march. Then he'd led them into the valley, where the screams and yells had intruded upon his ruminations. He turned back and found everyone gathered around Gul, her head cradled in Aziguli's lap and Mary and Khoja on their knees in the sand at her shoulders.

He unfurled the *shemagh* from around his face. "What happened?" he asked.

Mary glanced at him. "A camel fell on her," she said and took Khoja's hands and placed them on the Gul's chest.

Wolf lurched up, grabbed Malcolm by the shirt and shoved him. "This is your fault, you fucking git," the Brit yelled. "What did you think would happen by marching through a sandstorm?"

He let Wolf push him once more and then punched the Brit in the gut. Left him on his knees in the sand and squatted beside Mary.

"How bad is it?" he asked and watched Gul's chest move in three or four places as she breathed in and out.

"Bad," Mary said.

"She's as good as dead, more like it," Wolf said from where he struggled to his feet.

Aziguli looked up from her mother. Her eyes dark and her lips pulled back from her teeth.

"Can we move her?" Malcolm asked.

"We don't have a choice," Mary said. "Whether she'll survive it is another question."

"Pray that she does," Aziguli said and kept her gaze on Wolf.

"Don't look at me," Wolf said and pointed at Malcolm. "He's the one who led us into this valley."

"And you are the one who spooked the camel," Aziguli said.

"I had to," Wolf said. "It wouldn't move."

Aziguli sprang to her feet. "And you never thought to check where everyone else was!" she screamed.

"I never –"

"Stop talking, Wolf," Mary said. "She doesn't care."

"He's the one she should be angry at," Wolf yelled and pointed at Malcolm. "He's the –"

"You're right," Malcolm said. He looked at Wolf and saw that the Brit's face was pale beneath his tan, the whites of his eyes visible as his gaze darted around the group. "You're right," he repeated. "It's my fault. I wasn't paying attention."

"That does not excuse this one's actions," Aziguli said and continued to stare at Wolf.

Wolf returned her gaze. He opened and closed his mouth and then shook his head. "You crazy bitch," he said, then backed away and stumbled off down the dune.

*   *   *

They built a litter and used it to drag Gul to the valley floor. Got her into one of the bigger tents so Mary could tend to her and then Malcolm sheltered with David to wait for the storm to blow itself out.

They sat in silence while night fell and the wind whipped the sides of the tent. A strangled cry caused them both to look up. A deep and sonorous quiver half-mangled by the gale. They stared at the door of the tent until the moan died and then looked at each other.

"Camel," Malcolm said.

David nodded.

"I don't know any other animal that makes those types of sounds."

"We shouldn't have come here," David said.

"I'm sorry," Malcolm said. "I know I've been distracted since the gas –"

"I meant we shouldn't have come to China."

Malcolm glanced over but David would not meet his gaze. "You've been talking to Khoja," he said.

"No," David said and then snorted. "I mean yeah, but that's not why I said that."

Malcolm waited.

"Have you spent much time with the Uighurs?" David asked.

"Every day."

"I mean talked to them."

"I talk to Musa all the time."

"To make sure they can keep going. Like we do with the camels," David said and then met Malcolm's gaze. "I mean talk to them as people. Listen to what they have to say."

Malcolm said nothing.

"Right. How could you?" David asked. "You're always at the front."

"The Uighurs aren't why we're here."

"Got it. No, I got it," David said and nodded. He glanced away and wiped his mouth and then looked back at Malcolm. "They're not stupid, you know," he said.

"I never thought they were," Malcolm said.

"Wolf thinks so, but they're not," David said. "You know what they think is going to happen?"

"No."

"They think the Chinese will round up every last Uighur in Xinjiang. They'll put them in camps, only this time they'll kill them."

Malcolm held David's gaze.

"You know why Musa and the others are doing this?" David asked. "Helping us?"

Malcolm shook his head.

"Because they think we can get their families out," David said. "They think we're going to bring them stateside when this is over."

Malcolm stared at David and then dropped his gaze.

"You knew that," David said.

"I've never told them that."

"You just let them believe it."

David waited and when Malcolm didn't answer, he shook his head. "Hell, at this point it probably doesn't matter if we succeed," he said. "The Chinese will kill them all regardless. And for what? What are we really going to accomplish?"

"You know what."

"Right. Get the Chinese off our backs," David said. "Buy time and space to regroup. Rearm."

"That's right."

"And then what?"

"And then what?" Malcolm asked and then frowned. "Isn't that enough?"

"What, you think the Chinese are just going to roll over after this?" David asked. "That they'll say, 'sorry, our bad' while we ride off into the sunset?"

Malcolm looked down and said nothing.

"But you don't care about that," David said. "Do you?"

Malcolm thought about that. "I guess," he said.

"You guess." David stared at him and then shook his head. "Well, the next time you're off daydreaming," he said, "maybe you should take a guess at whether this whole thing is worth it. Or whether we're just going to make things worse."

Malcom met David's gaze and then the door to the tent unzipped from the outside, Khoja's head in the gap.

"May I come in?" Khoja asked.

"Yes," Malcolm said.

"I'll go," David said and scuttled toward the door.

"You don't have to," Malcolm said.

"Yes, I do," David said. He crawled out of the tent and then Khoja came in and sat cross-legged on the floor.

"How is she?" Malcolm asked.

"She cannot go on," Khoja said.

"I'm sorry."

"She understood the risks."

"That doesn't make it any easier."

Khoja grunted.

Malcolm pulled out his map and spread it out between them. He pointed to a dot on the southern edge of the great brown spot that was the Taklamakan.

"Qiemo Town is almost due south of us," he said. "A couple days march."

"Yes."

"It's big enough to have a hospital. We could take her there."

"It would add a week in extra distance."

"We could get vehicles there," Malcolm said. He traced a line on the map that led east out of the town. "If we got on the highway in Qiemo, we could be in Beijing sooner. We'd need –"

"The arrangements you had in place in Kashgar and Makit do not extend to Qiemo Town," Khoja said. "If you lead this caravan there, your mission will be over."

Malcolm studied the map. "Qiemo Town is still part of the Xinjiang Autonomous Region."

"It is a different prefecture," Khoja said. "Huimin's influence does not extend this far. And, in any event, he has no doubt already fled the country."

Malcolm traced the border lines that separated the districts. Saw that Kashgar lay over six hundred miles to the west across the expanse of the Taklamakan. "What about a small group?" he asked. "We could send her with a few of the Uighurs, maybe even Gleb or Wolf."

"I cannot ask for that."

"But would it work?"

Khoja shrugged. "Perhaps."

"Then it's settled."

"Thank you." Khoja bowed his head and reached for the tent zipper.

"You know, you could go as well," Malcolm said.

The old man paused. "I cannot," he said.

Malcolm drew a breath and let it out slow. "Aziguli," he said.

"*Shì.*"

"You think you can stop her?"

"*Shì.*"

"Like you stopped her at the gas station?"

Khoja sat silent and still and Malcolm began to think he would not answer. "Look," he said, "there's got to –"

"I will not let her kill Zhao."

"What if you have to choose? Her or him?"

"Then I will accept that I have failed as a father, and I will stop her," Khoja said. "But I will do everything in my power to avoid making that decision until it is absolutely necessary."

"You won't be able to stop her," he said. "Not at that point."

"It will be harder, yes," Khoja said. "But not impossible. This is a fundamental problem to understand."

"What is?"

"This business of turning from our errors and advancing toward what is good," Khoja said and when Malcolm did not answer, the old man continued. "I see that you are confused, but give it time," he said. "Fundamental problems are simple to comprehend, difficult to act upon. But when we grasp the fundamental problems, we also understand the minor ones."

"I see," Malcolm said.

"No, you do not," Khoja said, "but you will." Then he dipped his head and crawled out the tent door. When he had begun to zip up the tent door, he stopped and poked his head in the flap. "By the way," he said, "It does not work the other way around. Understanding a minor problem does not allow you to grasp a fundamental one." He stared at Malcolm a moment longer and then zipped up the tent door and left him alone.

• • • • •

The next day they worked all morning to rig the litter and prepare the three camels for the trip south to Qiemo Town, then said their good-byes in the early afternoon.

Gleb stood morose and quiet when Malcolm found him.

"I have decided I don't like the desert," Gleb said.

"That's why I thought you'd be happy to leave," Malcolm said.

"Except no one will remember my part in this," Gleb said. "I will die an unknown. Like my father."

"Chin up, big guy," Mary said and hugged the Russian. "The rest of us'll know. We couldn't have made it this far without you."

"That is true," he said and held her. "But you will all be dead." His hands slipped from her back to her ass and he squeezed and then darted away before she could hit him. He nodded to Malcolm and then picked up the rope of the lead camel.

Wolf was next, his eyes bloodshot and puffy. He stared at Malcolm's outstretched hand, took it and squeezed. Then he walked to the rear of the small team of camels where Khoja and Aziguli knelt by Gul's litter. He stood behind them and spoke and none of the three acknowledged him. He waited a moment when he had said his piece and then turned to walk back up the caravan. He'd taken maybe five steps when he paused and began to look back.

Then Aziguli stood and plunged a knife in the back of his head.

"No," Malcolm said and sprang forward. He watched Aziguli wrap an arm around Wolf's neck and kick out his legs and put her mouth close to the Brit's ear. She whispered as the Brit's body stiffened and then went limp. Then Khoja pulled her off and Wolf collapsed. Malcolm caught him and eased his body to the sand and the Brit blinked and tried to talk but his body would no longer respond.

Mary knelt beside Malcolm. She ran her fingers over Wolf's head and pulled out the knife. Then she stood and stalked toward Aziguli. "No more," she said.

Khoja put himself between them. "Stop," he said.

"No more," Mary said and slashed at Aziguli.

The old man held Aziguli behind him and backpedaled. Not far enough and the blade opened his cheek. He stumbled and held up a hand. "Stop," he said. "She is all I have."

Mary held the knife before her. "Get out of the way," she said and raised the knife to cut again and then Malcolm grabbed her wrist.

"Enough, Mary," he said.

She beat him with her free hand and he stood there and would not let go.

"Enough," he said.

She hit him some more and then stilled and glared at him. When he released her wrist, she struck him one more time and opened a cut above his eye.

"We need them," he said.

"Like hell we do," Mary said. She looked at him with contempt and then turned and flung the knife at Aziguli. Buried the blade in the sand at the girl's feet and then walked away.

Khoja stared at him and then bowed his head. "Thank you," he said.

"Shut up," Malcolm said.

• • • • •

Eight more days until they put the desert behind them.

Then on to Beijing, enormous and chaotic after the desolation of the desert. They got lost on their first night in the city, ended up in the *Chaoyang* business district where they were dwarfed by the China Zun tower and the China World Trade Center. On into *Chaoyang* North, where the skyscrapers intermixed with tree-lined routes and parks, and the vehicles competed for space on the roads with pedestrians and electric autonomous trackless trams. Massive tower cranes on a dozen different buildings, their booms lit in red and yellow. Malcolm's team insignificant as they ground their way through traffic jams in their old van. They drove half the night to find the right residential district, then spent the remainder of the night lost in a *hutong* in search of their *siheyuan*.

Over the days and nights of the next week they travelled to Tian'an Men and *Di Xia Cheng* to learn the terrain. They grew familiar with the streets of their *hutong*, enough to locate landmarks they remembered when they became confused. The weight of old Beijing was all around, thousands of years of unbroken civilization not so much seen as experienced while they went district to district in search of schedules and security details and weapons. The Temple of Heaven, where a police officer in the shadow of the triple-gabled Hall of Prayer for Good Harvests handed off itineraries for the Politburo Standing Committee members, and the temples and pavilions of Beihai Park, where a woman who might have come from a fashion shoot slipped them journalist credentials that would gain them access to the Great Hall.

Their accents, absent the hard r's at the end of their words, marked them as foreigners, among other things. They needn't have worried. In a city of immigrants and newcomers, where native Beijingers were outnumbered at least two to one by those from other parts of China or farther afield, they fit in as outsiders. Yet even strangers like they could feel the tension between old and new, the traditional shops and restaurants bricked up to make way for high-end boutiques and skyscrapers. Beneath everything, a smoky aroma as of generations of Beijingers with their old bird cages and palm leaf fans, crammed into shoe-box sized apartments. Not so different from the scents Malcolm remembered at the house of his grandparents, who'd been first-generation Americans.

The locals were distant and preoccupied and where David interpreted this as arrogance, Malcolm came to understand it as anxiety. The more he talked to the street vendors and tuk tuk drivers and others, the more they seemed to share the same concerns as Americans he knew. Preservation of their way of life, food and clothing, a decent place to live, a lifestyle that would neither drive them to an early grave nor leave nothing for their children. He wished he could ask Amaelia what she would have thought.

Then he realized he already knew.

One people, regardless of nationality.

· · · · ·

And then it was the night before the attack.

Malcolm held a final team meeting and then took Mary with him to walk the ground one last time. They left the *siheyuan* behind and followed the streets north and east, hands jammed in their pockets from the cold. Street lights came on as night fell and then they broke into an open area and stood across an open expanse from *Zhengyangmen*. The base of the building was lit-up stark and bright and its upper levels were shrouded in darkness.

They approached the archery tower until they reached a brass marker laid into the ground. Here, they stood on each side of a large wheel with spokes in the cardinal directions and sixty-four dots on the perimeter. A black tortoise at the north point and a vermillion bird by the south point. A large zero in the middle of the plaque.

"So, this is the exact center," Mary said.

"That's what they say," Malcolm said.

"The center of China? Or the center of the world?"

"More like the center of the universe, I think."

"How do you figure?"

"*Tianxia*," he said. "All under heaven."

"Huh," Mary said and then lifted her head to stare up at *Zhengyangmen*.

"So, what do you think?" Malcolm asked.

"I think it's pretentious as hell to believe you're the center of the universe," she said.

He smiled. "That's not what I meant."

"I know," she said and fiddled with the buttons of her coat.

"Nerves?" he asked and nodded at her hands.

"Every time."

"Me too," he said and felt the weight of the archery tower loom over him in heavy silence.

She placed her hand in the crook of his elbow. "If it means anything," she said, "for the first time in my life, I'm glad I'm not in charge."

"If you were, what would you do about Khoja?"

"He's full of surprises, isn't he?"

"That's what has me worried."

"That he'll do something you don't expect?"

"No," he said. "That he's right about Zhao."

"Then doesn't that answer the question for you?"

He glanced at her and then turned back to the tower and she adjusted her grip on his elbow.

"I mean, if there's even a possibility Khoja's right, doesn't that mean you should at least give Zhao a chance?" she asked.

"It doesn't change what happened."

"No," she said. "But it will change what comes next."

He said nothing and they shivered in the cold.

"Whatever you decide," she said, "we're with you."

He smiled and nodded and they stood on the zero point and gazed up at the front gate of *Zhengyangmen*. Malcolm wondered if he would be able to do what needed to be done and then a patrol officer rounded the corner of the tower.

"Better head back," Malcolm said.

"I wish I could be more help," she said when they'd begun to walk.

"You told me what I needed to know," he said and glanced at her. "And for what it's worth, we'd probably all have been better off if you'd been in charge."

She gripped his elbow tighter. "You don't need to say that," she said.

"It's true, though," he said. "Wherever you go, you make that place better."

"Right now, I want to go home."

"We all do."

"Do we, Malcolm?" she asked and then paused and looked up at him. "Do you?"

He stared at her and did not answer and then she dipped her gaze.

"I shouldn't have said that," she said and took a step.

He held onto her and pulled her to a stop. "You're not wrong," he said.

Her breath condensed in the cold air between them. "I'm sorry," she said.

"Don't be."

"You must be lonely."

"I am," he said and tried on a smile and then gave up the attempt. "Most of all," he said, "I'm tired."

She held on to his hand and left him to his thoughts. When he looked up, he saw that her eyes glistened moist in the neon lights of the city.

"No need for that," he said and tried another smile for her sake and this time mostly succeeded. "Besides, you've helped me make my decision."

"Oh, yeah?"

"Yeah," he said. "I'm going to try and be like you."

"How's that?"

"I'm going to leave places better than how I found them."

A tear rolled down her cheek and then she smiled and reached up to wipe her face. "Don't tell anyone I cried," she said.

"Your secret's safe with me," he said and he waited for her to compose herself and then gave her his elbow and they walked back to the *siheyuan*.

· · · · ·

The assault began much as they'd planned. Their infiltration of the Great Hall under journalist credentials. The underground access through *Di Xia Cheng*. Even the detection of David's team and the confusion it caused in the Press Briefing Hall which allowed them to slip past the guards.

It was when –

NINE

18 DECEMBER 2029

General Fan Qiliang stood outside the interrogation cell and watched soldiers flood into the tiny room. He entered the cell last and let the door close behind him. Soldiers armed with telescopic batons and pistols lined the walls, their weapons aimed at both of the figures seated at the table and Fan paused to savor what he took to be surprise on the Chairman's face.

"What is the meaning of this?" Chairman Zhao asked, his hands clenched into fists on the table.

"I apologize," Fan said. He pointed at the assassin and a soldier walked up and struck the man in the head. "There has been a breach of security."

Chairman Zhao frowned. "Then handle it while I finish."

"I'm afraid I cannot allow that," General Fan said and came to stand at Chairman Zhao's side. "There have been enough stories for one day." He picked up the assassin's photo from the table and stared at it and then tucked it into an inside pocket of his tunic. Then he unlatched the holster at his belt and drew his pistol.

The Chairman's eyes narrowed. "You." He addressed the soldiers. "Guards. Arrest General Fan."

None of the men moved.

"Guards!" Chairman Zhao's voice rang in the small room.

"Do not make this harder than it has to be," Fan said.

Zhao rose to his feet and scanned the faces of the soldiers. Then he pointed at General Fan. "Arrest this traitor!"

Fan snorted. "Allow me to explain the nature of the security breach," he said and then nodded to the soldier who had hit the assassin.

The man grasped the assassin by the head and then a second soldier came and pinned the assassin's hands to the table.

Zhao stood for a moment with his hand outstretched and then lowered his arm. "What are you doing?" he asked.

"Earlier today, an American assassin was taken into custody," Fan said. He produced a key from his pocket and gave it to a soldier beside him. "Against our best recommendations, you decided to interrogate the man. Alone."

The soldier with the key approached the table and bent over the chain and manacles that bound the assassin to the table. There was a click and then all that held the assassin were the two guards.

"Unfortunately, the assassin was resourceful," Fan said. He leaned across the table and laid his pistol down in front of the assassin. "He escaped, and was able to arm himself and complete his mission." Fan stared at the man and then lifted his hand from the gun and stepped back.

The guards who lined the walls trained their weapons on the assassin and waited. Ready for anything.

"In turn, the assassin was killed in a gun battle," Fan said.

"I thought you'd had enough stories," Zhao said.

"The difference is that this one is true."

"I give you one last chance to stop this, Fan."

"Comrade Chairman, the time to stop passed long ago," Fan said and then nodded at the two guards who held the assassin. "Let him go."

      •   •   •

Malcolm circled his wrists. His fingers were numb and the feel of the shackles was yet on his skin. The pistol lay inches out of reach. All he had to do was stretch out and claim the weapon.

He rose to his feet.

The soldiers who'd held him down stood one on each side. They pulled out telescopic batons which locked into place with a metallic clink. The rest of the soldiers with their guns pointed at his chest or batons held cocked and ready to strike.

He kept his gaze on the pistol on the table.

"Pick it up," General Fan said.

Malcolm inhaled and then reached for the gun. He settled his hand on the grip and noted the anticipation ripple through the soldiers around him. Their weapons held before them like shields. He straightened and held the pistol in the working space near his chest, and then checked whether the gun was loaded.

It was. One round in the chamber and no magazine.

"This is what you came for," Fan said. "Complete your mission."

Malcolm met Zhao's gaze, noted how the man stood tall and composed.

Resolved.

The general pointed to the two soldiers nearest Zhao and barked a command. The men lowered their weapons and pinned Zhao's arms to his side.

"Do it," Fan said and snarled when Malcolm didn't answer. "Follow your orders!"

Malcolm aimed the pistol at Zhao's head. He focused on the sight picture and wondered if Zhao might speak, might try to reason with him. But the man did not. Instead, Zhao swayed in the grip of the soldiers and Malcolm understood that the men were unnecessary.

Zhao would have stood like a statue had they not been there.

"Do it!" Fan yelled and spittle flew from the General's mouth.

Malcolm tightened his finger on the trigger and then shifted his aim and shot the soldier who held Zhao's right arm in the face.

• • • • •

Chairman Zhao Guoqiang's ears rang.

He had blood splatter on his cheek and shoulder, and he and everyone else in the room seemed gripped in a stupor. Spectators all.

Except for the assassin, who'd already turned to the men at his sides.

Then the soldier who'd been shot collapsed to the floor.

General Fan began to shout, the words unintelligible. Soldiers nearest the assassin fell on the man with their batons. Fan continued to shout and a soldier near the door aimed his rifle at the assassin. Zhao shoved the man who still held him into the soldier with the rifle and the gun fired up into the ceiling. Everyone in the room ducked at the gunshot and then a soldier along the back wall of the cell clutched his neck. Blood between the man's fingers. A struggle broke out inside the doorway and Zhao tripped and fell to the floor.

More soldiers streamed into the room. They trampled Zhao, knocked aside the soldier who'd held him in their haste. Those closest to the assassin beat him with their batons and the man shielded his head and chest with his arms. He pushed into a group of soldiers so they had no room to swing their batons and then began to lash out with his feet. Bodies fell to the ground and General Fan shouted for backup, his cheeks red and a swollen blood vessel on his forehead.

Zhao covered himself as additional soldiers stormed the cramped cell. He made no noise when they trod on him and when it seemed no others would come, he crawled out the door. In the hallway, he stumbled to his knees and scanned the corridor to find himself alone.

For the moment.

He pushed to his feet and lurched along a wall. Around a corner he went, where he heard the clomp of boots from farther down the hall. He stopped, opened his mouth to shout and realized he had no idea who he could trust and so he opened the door to an adjoining cell and entered the room. Then he eased the door shut and waited for the footsteps to pass.

His breath loud in the dark.

• • • • •

General Fan stooped to recover his pistol, dropped when the latest rush of soldiers had entered the cell. From his knees, he loaded a magazine into the pistol and aimed at the assassin, buried amid a mass of soldiers. Fan saw that there was no safe shot. He pulled the trigger anyway. A soldier screamed and clutched the small of his back and fell to the ground.

The assassin fought on, armed with two extendable batons he'd taken from fallen soldiers. The metal rods became a black blur that beat the limbs and heads of the soldiers, pummelled all the parts of their bodies that weren't protected by body armor.

Fan angled for a better shot at the assassin and took aim again. Then a baton flew at him. He ducked and the weapon rapped off his elbow. He cursed and clutched his arm, put his back tight to the wall as more soldiers entered the cell. Then he sidled along the wall until he reached the doorway where he tumbled out of the room. In the hallway, he bent over, rested with his hands on his knees. He could not seem to catch his breath and his heart pounded in his ears and he wondered when this day would be over.

Then he realized he had lost track of Chairman Zhao.

He strode back into the cell. Shoved soldiers out of the way and scanned the corners and beneath the table. He did his best to see through the tangle of bodies around the assassin even though he knew there was no way the Chairman would be in that mob.

Nothing.

He backed out of the cell and stood for a moment in the hallway. Then he resettled his glasses and scanned the corridor in both directions. Nothing. He shouted Zhao's name and then yelled for more troops. No answer to any of his cries. He held his pistol at his chest and stared at it and then grimaced and began to follow the corridor that would talk him back to the Great Hall.

He'd taken two steps when a set of keys landed at his feet.

The general spun, had the pistol half-aimed when a pair of hands gripped the weapon. He struggled and pulled the trigger and a bullet hit the corridor wall and ricocheted down the hall with a whine. Then the pistol twisted, the general's finger caught in the trigger guard. He screamed and then his finger broke and the pistol was stripped away.

• • • • •

Malcolm punched General Fan Qiliang in the face.

The general stumbled back, and when he reached for his broken nose, Malcolm hit him in the gut, then kicked out his legs. Fan fell to the floor, clutched his stomach and moaned.

Malcolm crouched beside him. "Let me know when you're done," he said and then waited.

Fan grew silent, then rolled over and glared at Malcolm from where he lay on the floor. "You've made a mess of things," he said.

Malcolm thought about that.

Fan pushed up with his elbows. "*Xīshēng xiǎo wǒ, wánchéng dà wǒ,*" he said. "You know this?"

Malcolm nodded.

"We are both soldiers," Fan said, "and soldiers must be loyal. That is the highest value of our profession. Although everyone is responsible for the rise or fall of the country, soldiers are held to a higher standard. Our honor depends on this."

Malcolm shifted a bit farther away when Fan sat up.

"The good of our countries must come before our own, or before the interests of any individual," Fan said and coughed. "This is natural. It is how we protect our compatriots." Fan held up his non-injured hand and raised a finger. "Chairman Zhao's actions have jeopardized *Zhongguo Meng*. His removal is necessary to revitalize the collective effort that enabled our nation to reclaim our greatness and prosperity, and which in turn has created stability."

Malcolm glanced at the interrogation cell. The bodies visible through the door.

"You do not know this," Fan said and his lip curled in a sneer. "You are naïve. Idealistic. A powerful China, supported by a strong military, is as beneficial for the United States as it is for the people of China. America's best successes have been when it was locked in confrontation with a formidable opponent. In fact, it is changes to that equilibrium that cause the chaos you see around us, and it is Zhao Guoqiang who initiated these actions. That is why he must be removed. In this way, harmony can be achieved. Your leaders understand this, even if it is lost on you."

Malcolm returned to his contemplation of the general.

"You see, assassin," Fan said, "there are those in both countries who understand their duty. Unlike you."

Malcolm shifted his weight from side to side.

"And now what will you do?" Fan asked. "Flee, no doubt. Leave your betters to set things right."

Malcolm dropped his gaze to the floor and did not answer.

"Say something."

Malcolm looked up and then grabbed Fan by his lapels. "I don't care about your excuses," he said. "You have something of mine. And I want it."

Fan's eyes narrowed. He began to snarl and yell and then the crack of a gunshot came from down the corridor. A bullet whined overhead and both men ducked.

There was another gunshot and then Malcolm dragged Fan back up to a sitting position and crouched behind him. Peeked out over the general's shoulder at a small group of approaching soldiers.

Eight men armed with rifles and clad in helmets and riot gear.

"Up we go," Malcolm said and pulled Fan to his feet. He twisted one of the general's arms behind his back, used the man's body as a shield and began to advance toward the soldiers.

The soldiers slowed as Malcolm drew near and their rifles wavered, as if unsure where to aim. One of the soldiers held up a hand and the group came to a stop. The soldier who'd raised his hand yelled at Malcolm to release the general and lie down on the ground.

Malcolm pushed Fan before him and continued to walk.

Another soldier spoke. The first soldier silenced him and then called once more for Malcolm to get on the ground.

"Kill him!" Fan yelled.

A few of the soldiers flinched and the ones in front tried to back up to create space except their comrades behind them had not moved. The general screamed at them again and the soldiers clustered together and yelled at each other to get out of the way and then Malcolm was on them.

He shoved Fan into the center of the group and fell on the soldier closest to him. It was tight quarters in the hallway, so he hit and kicked the soldiers into each other to take away their shots. He crushed the throat of one soldier with a baton and gouged the eyes out of another and sensed the others freeze in place. Unprepared for the onslaught. He ignored their cries and cut them down and it was not until he stood among their broken bodies that he became aware General Fan was not one of the fallen.

"Assassin."

The voice came from behind him. He hesitated and then turned to face General Fan, who stood in front of the doorway to the interrogation cell. The general held a pistol, which was aimed at Malcolm's chest.

They stared at each other and then Malcolm stepped over a body toward the general.

"That's far enough," Fan said.

Malcolm took another step, his gaze on Fan as he picked a careful path through the fallen.

The general fired and a bullet whined past Malcolm's head. "I said, far enough."

Malcolm slowed and then came to a stop. Too far away to close the distance.

"Everything I have done, I did for the greater good of my country," Fan said.

"I don't care," Malcolm said.

"I have sacrificed the small self for the great self. As it should be."

"I'm not going to kill you."

"That is what concerns me."

They continued to stare at each other and then Fan held the pistol to his temple. "Who upon this boundless earth decides whether I should fall?" he asked and then pulled the trigger. His head rocked to the side as the gun shot echoed along the hallway and his body defied gravity for a second and then slumped to the ground.

Malcolm walked up and stood over Fan's body. He stared at it and then crouched and reached inside the general's tunic, then pulled out his photo of Amaelia and Oran. He held the tip of a finger to his lips and then placed it on Amaelia's face. Did the same for Oran and then rose to his feet and placed the photo in a pocket.

He stepped over the general's body and then looked down the hallway. Silent as the concrete upon which he stood. There was a bend in the corridor up ahead, and the hallway was lit with harsh white light. He figured the route would take him deep into *Di Xia Cheng*, and that within an hour's easy walk, he could find a hundred exits into Beijing.

His breath was loud in the hallway and he felt for the picture in his pocket, let his fingers toy with the crumpled edges of the photo. Then he stooped and picked up the pistol from beside Fan's body. He waited for a second, then tucked the pistol into his pants at the small of his back. When he straightened, he cast one more look at the way out, then turned and headed up the hallway in the direction that would take him back to the Great Hall, pausing long enough to take up a discarded rifle dropped by one of the fallen soldiers.

• • • • •

Chairman Zhao Guoqiang waited in the cell until the footsteps had passed and then stepped back into the hallway. The sound of gunfire came from the direction of the assassin. Then yells and what sounded like General Fan's voice and Zhao decided he had to move. He walked in the opposite direction with one hand on the wall. His other hand pressed against a stitch in his side. When he came to a t-intersection in the corridor, he stopped and frowned. He could not recall if he'd passed through this section of *Di Xia Cheng* and realized he had not paid attention when his aide had led him to the interrogation cell.

He suspected he might be lost.

A single gunshot sounded from behind him. He turned and squinted down the hallway, wondered who had killed whom. Then the tramp of boots on concrete came from the opposite direction.

More reinforcements.

Zhao searched for a place to hide and then decided he'd played this game long enough. He moved into the center of the hallway and waited for the troops to appear and when they did, he focused on the officer.

"You. Captain." Zhao pointed at the third man in the group. "Come here."

The officer's eyes widened. "Comrade Chairman," he said.

"Come here."

"*Shì.*" The officer fanned the soldiers out behind him and stood before the Chairman with his gaze lowered.

"What is your name?" Zhao asked.

"Bo Xilai, Comrade Chairman."

Zhao studied the man and then pointed down the hallway to where he'd last heard gunfire. "The American assassin is that way," he said. "Stop him."

"*Shí*." The captain snapped to attention. Nodded and nodded again and began to bark orders.

"Captain," Zhao said and the man froze and then looked at him.

"Yes, Comrade Chairman?"

"Captain, where is the Great Hall stairwell?"

"Up ahead, Comrade Chairman," the captain said and waved down the hallway in the direction from which he'd come. "I will detail an escort." He turned to the soldiers closest to him. "You four –"

Zhao held up a hand. "Two is sufficient," he said.

"*Shí*, Comrade Chairman," the captain said and pointed at two of the soldiers.

"That is all," Zhao said.

"Of course, Chairman." Captain Bo snapped to attention and then shouted at the soldiers and they barreled down the hallway.

Zhao watched the officer depart and then nodded at his escort and followed them up the corridor.

· · · · · ·

Malcolm stood calm and patient and aimed the rifle down the hallway. When the soldiers came around the corner up ahead, he pulled the trigger. He ran the gun dry and then scanned the dead and wounded in dispassion. From around the corner came shouts and the stomps of boots and he knew that more soldiers were on the way and he advanced to meet them.

They came around the corner at the same time.

He swung his rifle like a club. Knocked one soldier back and then took a hit in the ribs. Another in the small of his back. He hissed in pain and went to the ground. The soldiers stood over top of him and stomped and kicked until he began to chop at their legs with the rifle. Two soldiers stumbled back and one fell on top of him and he stripped the man of his pistol. Killed him with a shot under the jaw and then shot the remaining soldiers from where he lay. Then he clutched the pistol to his chest and closed his eyes.

He was tired.

He got to his feet amid the moans of the fallen. Leaned against a wall to catch his breath and then scavenged weapons and ammunition and a radio from one of the wounded soldiers and continued on.

Zhao was up ahead.

He patrolled up to an intersection and peeked around the corner. Bullets zinged past and he pulled back into cover. He waited for a lull in the gunfire, then sprayed bullets down the hallway in return. Another barrage drove him back. He knelt by the corner and then pulled out a thick cannister taken from the last group of soldiers. Pulled the pin and waited. At the next pause in the battle he released the spoon, counted to two and then banked the cannister off the opposite wall and down the hall.

Panicked yells came from around the corridor followed by a loud hiss.

"It's only smoke," a man's voice said. "Fire into it so he can't use it as cover."

The gunfire began and Malcolm pulled out two more grenades. These ones small and lightweight, pineapple shaped. By now smoke filled the hallway around the corner and he yanked the pins from the grenades and lobbed them one after another into the thick haze. The gunfire so intense he didn't hear the grenades strike the concrete floor.

The explosion tore the air from his lungs.

When he came around the corner, there was nobody left standing. Knee-high smoke lingered in the hallway, and he began to ease his way through the half-concealed carnage. He tripped over a leg and a rifle clattered on the concrete floor and then a groan came out of the smoke further ahead. He stalked toward the noise and kicked a pistol away from a soldier with lieutenant's rank, then held the barrel of his rifle under the lieutenant's chin.

The man glared up at him. Blood at his ears and nose and his face contorted in pain.

"The Chairman is safe," the lieutenant said.

"You saw him?"

"I was honored to secure the stairs for him."

"Where?"

The lieutenant moved to grab the muzzle barrel and Malcolm stood on his arm.

"Where?" Malcolm asked. The man did not answer and Malcolm left him on the floor and continued down the hallway. Around the next corner he found a door, which opened it into a stairwell. He stood at the base of the stairs with the rifle aimed up into the gaps between the spiralled landings and heard the echo of footsteps on the concrete steps.

"Chairman Zhao," he called out and the footsteps paused. "Chairman Zhao, you should know that Vice-Premier Jiang Gaoli was the one who betrayed you."

•   •   •   •   •

Zhao Guoqiang stood with one hand on the railing. On the next landing there was a door that exited to the main floor of the Great Hall. He stared at the door and considered what the assassin had said and could not reconcile it with the Jiang Gaoli who had mentored him. The Jiang Gaoli who had waived his own opportunities to be Chairman.

The Jiang Gaoli whom the assassin had killed.

"You were right that we had help," the assassin said from below, his voice faint and diffuse in the stairwell. "It was Vice-Premier Jiang. He contacted Secretary of State Bains. Made sure we could get across the border and that we could access the Great Hall."

Zhao clenched his teeth and began to climb the last flight of stairs.

"He sent us the agenda for the economic conference."

"You killed him," Zhao shouted into the stairwell. He gripped the railing so hard his knuckles turned white.

"He let us know where the Standing Committee would meet. How else do you think we were able to get that information?"

"Khoja," Zhao said, unable to stop himself.

"Not even Khoja could have gotten that agenda."

Zhao Guoqiang drew a breath. "Jiang would have been a fool to trust you," he said and resumed his climb.

"He didn't." The assassin's voice was closer, perhaps only a few flights of stairs below. "My team wasn't supposed to be involved in the assault. Our role was to find Khoja and Gul and get them inside the

Great Hall, they would have done the rest. Jiang knew Khoja was honorable from his assault on *Zhongnanhai* five years ago, he felt Khoja could be controlled and would only kill you."

"Then it would seem you went off mission."

"Admiral Couzens changed the mission profile, but he underestimated Khoja," the assassin said. "And he didn't account for Aziguli. But then, we're all guilty of that."

Zhao placed his hand on the door that led into the Great Hall and paused. He looked back down into the stairwell and then yanked open the door and strode into a hallway on the north side of the Great Hall. He spotted a cluster of soldiers headed in the other direction and called out to them.

The soldiers spun, their weapons levelled at him and it occurred to Zhao he'd made a mistake. Then the officer in charge straightened. The man yelled at the other soldiers to lower their guns and then hurried to Zhao's side.

"My apologies, Chairman," he said as he kept pace with Zhao. "We did not –"

"The assassin is in that stairwell," Zhao said and pointed at the door behind him. "Stop him."

• • • • •

Malcolm took the steps two at a time and reached the top landing as the door opened from the other side. The muzzle of a rifle appeared in the gap and he dashed up and wedged his shoulder against the metal door. He pushed against the door and was shoved back and pushed again. He wrestled for a moment and then the rifle was pulled out of the doorway and a pistol appeared. Malcolm grabbed the barrel, twisted the pistol around and back through the gap. A man screamed from the other side of the doorway and Malcolm held down the trigger and a shot rang loud in the stairwell.

The pressure on the door eased and Malcolm yanked it open and came face-to-face with two soldiers. The soldier closest to Malcolm held his right hand cradled by his chest. The other with a gunshot wound in the shoulder. Malcolm grabbed the second soldier by his body armor and dragged him toward the stairwell. Slammed the man into the door frame and then through the entrance and the man tripped and fell and tumbled down the first flight of stairs. Landed in a heap at the landing below and did not move.

Malcolm knocked the soldier with the wounded hand backward into several other soldiers who'd come up from behind. They fell into a tangle of helmets and limbs and guns. Farther down the hallway were yet more soldiers, their eyes wide and unbelieving, their weapons held useless in their hands.

For the moment.

Malcolm dove into the hallway. Tucked and rolled and came up to bound off a wall and launch a kick into a soldier who'd drawn a baton. The soldier stumbled and Malcolm stripped away the baton and then took a hit in the head. Stars in front of his eyes. He floundered around and was hit in the side. A cracked rib. Soldiers closed in and he flailed out with the baton. His vision darkened and he fought on and when he'd struck air three times in a row he came to a halt. Panted and stood with his arms limp at his sides and realized he was the last one upright in the hallway.

He propped himself up against a wall. Every breath a jagged pain. He glanced once at the doorway that led into the stairwell and wondered whether it was still an option to slip away. Then he picked up a rifle and staggered down the corridor.

He came to a corner and did not stop. He found the hallway clear and kept on until he heard voices up ahead. Then he leaned against a wall and closed his eyes to listen. Picked out Zhao's voice mixed in to a cacophony of shouts and yells and he continued down the hall until he came to a pair of double wooden doors. From within he heard Zhao's voice and he staggered up to the doors and into the room, took two or three steps and then stopped. Swayed on his feet while the voices died away and he stared at Zhao Guoqiang across the room. In conversation with a man he recognized as Wang Qiao, the Secretary of the Central Commission for Discipline Inspection.

In every other part of the room stood soldiers and police.

A soldier with colonel's rank moved to Zhao's side. The man pointed at Malcolm and the chairman turned and met Malcolm's gaze.

They stared at each other and Zhao opened his mouth to speak and then Wang Qiao stepped in front of him and began to clap.

· · · · ·

"Thank you for your determination," Secretary Wang Qiao said, his voice deep and smooth. "It has saved us the trouble of hunting you down."

The assassin walked deeper into the room, his rifle held in one hand by the pistol grip. The man's other hand was pressed to his side inside his shirt.

Wang barked a command and soldiers closed ranks around the assassin until the man disappeared in a sea of uniforms and helmets.

"Bring him," Wang said.

A space opened and the soldiers passed the assassin forward until he stood on the edge of a large red carpet in the center of the meeting room. A soldier clung to each arm and they held the assassin so that the toes of his boots were on the floral pattern that bordered the carpet.

Wang clasped his hands behind his back and considered the assassin by the light of the massive chandelier hung from the ceiling. This man who had caused so much trouble.

The assassin's shoulders were hunched and he stood not so much held by the soldiers as propped up. His head was down, there was a rattle in his breath and his hair hung lank and limp across his pale and gaunt face.

"You do not look like a man who should have made it this far," Wang said.

The assassin glanced at Wang and then dropped his gaze.

"No matter," Wang said. "Your mission ends here." He gestured around the room and spoke so that all could hear. "The soldiers and police before you come from our finest units. The ones who protect members of the Politburo. They are eager to make your acquaintance." He faced the assassin and smiled. "I should think so, considering their failure earlier today."

The assassin stood with his downward gaze and did not move.

"What lies do you have now?" Wang asked.

The assassin glanced at Wang. "None for you," he said.

"I thought as much. Only a –"

"I'm not here to talk to you."

Wang stepped forward and raised his hand to strike.

"That will not be necessary, Secretary Wang," Chairman Zhao said.

Wang paused with his hand in the air and then stood aside to make room for Zhao.

The chairman stared at the assassin, the man's face unreadable. "You ask me to believe that Vice-Premier Jiang Gaoli betrayed me," Zhao said. "A stalwart of the party. A fierce comrade who survived the cultural revolution and numerous other intrigues and who wanted nothing more than the returned glory of our country. A mentor. This is the man you ask me to believe was a traitor."

"*Shì.*"

"How can you ask me to believe this?"

"He disagreed with your assessment of China's strategic position."

"That is no secret," Wang said. "Diversity of ideas is a strength."

"Then he disagreed more than you realized," the assassin said. "He offered a collaboration to our Secretary of State. That in return for removing the senior cadre of the Politburo, he would install a Chairman and President who would enter a non-aggression pact with the United States. Under his watch, both China and America would focus on regional dominance, and America would have the time to rebuild."

"America was always going to be allowed to rebuild. That is why we chose a method that avoided physical force," Zhao snapped. "Had we desired otherwise, we would have pressed the attack, not handed out food and medical supplies."

"Secretary Bains did not share that assessment," the assassin said. "And neither did Admiral Couzens."

"And after all that, you killed Jiang anyways," Zhao said.

"*Shì.*"

"Why?"

"Isn't it obvious?" Wang said. "Americans can only be trusted to consider their own interests."

The assassin glanced at Wang and then dropped his gaze.

"I suspect this man's orders were always to kill the entire Standing Committee," Wang said. "A man like Admiral Couzens would have felt there was more to be gained."

Zhao moved in front of the assassin. "Tell me, why should I not kill you?"

"There are parts of the story you have not heard."

"I have heard enough," Zhao said and the muscles in his jaw clenched. "My hope had been to unite the world through mutual accord. To overcome the advantages of situation afforded by the Earth to achieve strength of unity and harmony."

"Attacking the United States is a strange way to unite the world," the assassin said.

"Is it?" Zhao asked. "There is no nation that lives more in the past then your own. No country more committed to preserving a world order unsuited to the future."

"And none with a shorter memory," Wang said. "Unable to even comprehend the thousands of years in which Chinese civilizations provided peace and harmony in accordance with the mandate of heaven."

"Indeed," Zhao said. "I had hoped to use a minimum of force, but you have shown me the only tongue people understand is fear and violence, and so I shall have to be fluent in that language. I shall have to strike America while it is weak lest its former allies feel emboldened. I shall have to eradicate thoughts of independence among the Uighurs to send a lesson to any others who seek to disobey. But first, I shall have to cement my position as Chairman, lest all progress be lost."

"Ismail Khoja –"

"Remember your place in what has happened," Secretary Wang said and placed himself between Chairman Zhao and the American. "Ismail Khoja was a treacherous assassin. Like you, nothing he said or did could be trusted. He has paid his price. So shall you." He stared at the man and then nodded at a soldier. "Take him to Qincheng," he said and then turned to look back at Zhao. "With your concurrence, Comrade Chairman."

The Chairman considered the assassin and then nodded. "*Shì.*" He watched for a second longer and then turned and headed for the exit, an escort of soldiers on his heels.

"Comrade," Wang said and then faced the assassin. He waited to see if the man would say anything and then began to speak. "Vice-Premier Jiang was a great man," he said. "But he was a fool to think an American assassin could succeed, even supported by one such as Ismail Khoja. Our might is simply too great." He held out his hands and turned about the room. "What say you?" he shouted.

"Hail!"

"What say you?" Wang shouted again, the tendons taut on his neck.

"Hail!" A shout from every mouth in the room that resounded and echoed.

"What say you?" The words inaudible even to Wang among the voices.

"Hail! Hail!"

Wang smiled and then stepped close and put his mouth to the assassin's ear. "Now it falls to me to clean up your mess," he said and then pulled back and spoke to a nearby officer. "Kill him on the way to Qincheng," he said and then followed after Zhao.

· · · · · ·

Malcolm waited for the soldiers to take him away. He kept his gaze on Secretary Wang and one hand inside his shirt, pressed against what felt like a broken rib.

A primed grenade inside his fist.

The soldiers who held him began to jostle him around and flex cuffs appeared. The next time he was shoved, he shouted and out came the grenade. He held it above his head and the room became quiet. A silence that rippled out until it reached Wang, who'd almost reached the doorway leading out of the room. When he sensed the silence, Wang seemed to waver and then looked back. He met Malcolm's gaze and then glanced at Malcolm's upraised hand.

Malcolm opened his fist.

There was a metallic click and the grenade's spoon soared into the air. A collective gasp passed through the room and then soldiers scrambled in all directions. Some toward Malcolm and some away from him and amid the confusion Wang stumbled out of the room, hustled away by his security detail

Malcolm lobbed the grenade into the air and then dove in the opposite direction. He hit the floor and crawled through legs and then the grenade exploded, the blast muffled by the bodies closet to the explosion. Soldiers fell around him and he rolled onto his back and grabbed his last grenade. This one a shiny metal cannister with red lettering in both Chinese and English.

CS-1 Gas.

He came up to his knees, took a breath and held it. Then he pulled the grenade's pin and thick grey smoke began to billow out. A soldier grabbed him and Malcolm smashed the grenade into the man's face. More soldiers closed in and he thrust the grenade at them and then slipped away, moved through his enemies while gray ribbons of gas streamed out of the grenade. Malcolm's eyes began to water and his hand burned and by then, half the room was shrouded in misty fog. He dropped the grenade and kicked it away from him and then fought his way through the choking mist to the door.

•   •   •   •   •

Secretary Wang Qiao's protective detail manhandled him down the hallway. Hands were on his arms and his shoulders and pressed inside his suit jacket to his chest to see if he was injured. A soldier stood in front of him and the man's mouth moved and Wang could not hear over the ringing in his ears. He squinted and the soldier began to yell and Wang held up a hand and pushed him away.

"I'm fine," he said.

The soldier pushed back. "Comrade –"

"I'm fine," Wang repeated. He shook off the hands and resettled his suit jacket and then peered around the corridor to make sense of the chaos.

Soldiers filled the corridor. They flowed down the walls and around the tight circle of his protection detail. All toward the room that held the assassin. Tendrils of smoke seeped out from between the double doors and as Wang watched, a soldier burst through the doors and propped himself up against the opposite wall. The man coughed and choked and pressed his hands to his eyes, a slurry of tears and snot and mucus from his nose and mouth.

An acrid smell wafted down the hallway and Wang's eyes watered. He could hear now, muffled coughs and screams. Gunshots. Yells as more soldiers ran down the hall. They stopped at the entrance to the room and donned gas masks and then entered.

No sign of the assassin.

"– you to safety," a voice said from beside him.

A hand gripped Wang by the elbow and he resisted. The pull grew stronger and he turned to face the soldier who'd spoken to him earlier. He recognized the man now. An officer from Chairman Zhao's security detail. Wang swallowed and then spoke in a steady voice. "Enough," he said and shook off the grip. "Let me think."

"We need to move away from the gas," the soldier said.

Wang glanced back at the room and nodded and then followed the soldier farther down the corridor. His own security detail formed a circle that moved with him. He saw Zhao's man speak into a radio, heard the man report that Secretary Wang Qiao was secure. Then the man spoke Chairman Zhao's name as if it were a question. Wang didn't hear the response, but the man nodded and then continued to escort Wang down the hallway.

Wang stopped and the man turned to look at him. "Where is Chairman Zhao now?"

"I don't know," the man said.

"You don't know," Wang said.

The soldier did not reply.

"Find him," Wang said.

"Secretary?"

"I said find him."

The soldier stared at Wang and then looked to the others in the security detail.

"Where was he last seen?" Wang asked.

"On the way to the Central Hall."

"Take me there."

"Secretary, my orders are to take you out the back of the Great Hall."

Wang stared at the man and then extended his hand. "Give me your pistol."

"Secretary?"

"Give me your pistol!"

The man flinched and then pulled out his pistol and offered it over. "Thank you," Wang said. He stood for a moment and then scanned the faces around him. All men from his own security detail. Men who'd worked for him for years. He turned back to the soldier who'd given him the pistol. "You are relieved of your task. These men will escort me to safety," he said and then began to stride down the hallway.

"Secretary," the soldier said from behind him, "my orders are to –"

Wang stopped. "Your orders are to go after the assassin."

"Comrade secretary –"

Wang turned and shot the soldier in the head. He stared at the body and then nodded at his soldiers. "Come with me," he said. "We need to find Chairman Zhao."

•　•　•　•　•

Malcolm stumbled around the room.

His eyes burned and he lost his balance and a beast of a man tackled him to the floor. Lay atop him and pummeled him while he coughed and retched in Malcolm's face. Malcolm reached for the soldier's eyes. He dug his fingers into the man's eye sockets and pulled him off and then fought back to his feet.

Other soldiers replaced the fallen. The newer ones in gas masks. He took one of these down and stripped off the man's mask, put it on and then a baton struck him on the thigh. He fell to a knee. Teeth clenched against the pain. He rolled into his opponent and punched him in the throat. Ripped off the soldier's gas mask and then stood and staggered toward the door on one leg that no longer seemed able to hold his weight.

He didn't know how he ended up in the hallway.

He held on to the doorframe and cast a look back over the fallen that seemed to cover every inch of the floor. It would be so easy to lay down among the bodies and slip into darkness. He shed the gas mask he'd taken and then he reached into the pocket that held his picture of Amaelia and Oran and pulled it out, brushed his fingers over the photo. It had never felt so real, like he could curl a lock of Amaelia's hair around his fingers and drag her toward him for a kiss.

But not yet.

He let go of the doorway and staggered on down the corridor.

· · · · ·

Chairman Zhao Guoqiang studied the hallway from the safety of a door frame. The Central Hall up ahead and beyond that the front entrance of the Great Hall.

Safety.

Voices carried to him from the Central Hall and he tucked himself farther into the doorway in which he hid. He'd ordered his security detail to stay behind and prevent the assassin from following. Even as he'd done so, the assassin's words had been in his head, so that he wondered who he could trust if he hadn't been able to trust Vice-Premier Jiang. Then he glimpsed police in black uniforms in the Central Hall, crowded around a bald man in the blue uniform of an Air Force general.

General Chen Jihua, a man Zhao himself had installed as Vice-Chairman of the Central Military Commission.

Zhao observed General Chen from the safety of the doorway. The general waved his arms in the air as he spoke and Zhao thought about General Fan Qiliang and questioned to whom the People's Liberation Army remained loyal. When Chen pointed down the corridor in his direction, Zhao backed into the small and darkened conference hall and eased the door almost shut.

He waited for the police to pass. Held his breath when General Chen's voice grew louder and listened to the general urge the police to find Chairman Zhao and Secretary Wang. Then the general's voice faded and with it went the noises of armed troops.

There was silence now and Zhao waited another minute to see what would happen and then pulled open the door. He poked his head into the corridor and scanned both ways to find the hallways vacant. The visible parts of the Central Hall empty as well and so he exited the conference room and made his way closer to the Great Hall's front entrance.

•　•　•　•　•

Malcolm covered his mouth with a hand. He stood in a doorway and muffled the rattle in his breath while the troop of police and the Air Force general hurried through a T-intersection in the hallway up ahead. A sharp pain stabbed him in the side of his chest whenever he inhaled. When the police had moved on, he limped down the hallway. After three or four steps, his thigh muscle seized and he fell against the wall.

While he massaged his leg and waited for the spasm to subside, he looked around and realized he knew this part of the Great Hall from the walking tour with Aziguli. If he continued on his way – the way the general and the police had come from – he'd reach the Central Hall and the main entrance.

He considered whether to take a different route. There would be nowhere to hide in the Central Hall and he guessed there would be more soldiers. Then he thought about where his quarry might be headed and steeled himself and let go of the wall. Lurched farther down the hallway and around the corner.

The corridor was clear and he crept along until he came to another corner where he leaned against a wall and checked the pistol he carried. Then he inched his head around the wall. The hallway was clear and he rounded the corner and then froze at the sight of a man in a suit up ahead on the threshold of the Central Hall.

Chairman Zhao Guoqiang.

Malcolm tightened his grip on the pistol and hastened down the hallway.

• • • • •

Secretary Wang Qiao strode along the corridor while his security detail trotted beside him. Their helmets and armor and tactical vests an encumbrance he did not share. It occurred to him that none of this equipment had helped against the assassin and then he frowned and walked faster and the clatter of the troops doubled as they struggled to keep pace.

He arrived at a T-junction and scanned both directions and cursed. There was no trace of Chairman Zhao. The soldiers panted and their equipment rattled and distracted him and he told them to be quiet and then cursed again.

"Follow me," he said and took the route that lead to the Central Hall. "Keep up."

He drove the soldiers onward, past a troop of police that he ordered out of the way. The men huddled to one side of the corridor and Wang and his soldiers moved on. When they arrived in the Central Hall, Wang marched onto the brilliant red carpet laid across the marble floor. He stopped in the center of the hall and stood amid the pillars and the chandeliers while his soldiers formed a perimeter around him. He looked around and spotted a lone figure among the columns on the edges of the hall.

Wang Qiao grabbed the soldier nearest him and pointed him at the person. "Fire!"

The soldier brought his rifle up and a gunshot rang out and then the figure dropped.

• • • • •

Chairman Zhao Guoqiang tucked up against a pillar, the echoes of the gunshot still in the hall. He made himself small and waited to hear if there would be more shots. Then he peeked out and saw a lone man laid out on the carpet at the edge of the hall.

The assassin.

Several soldiers in riot gear came into view and Zhao inched back into the cover offered by the pillar. He tensed and then recognized the uniforms and swagger of troops from the Central Guard Regiment, soldiers selected to defend the inner members of the Politburo and the VIP quarters in *Zhongnanhai*. He stepped away from the pillar and then Secretary Wang appeared amid the soldiers and approached the assassin. Wang stood over the man and spoke, too far away for Zhao to make out the words. Then Wang aimed a pistol at the assassin's head.

"Secretary Wang," Zhao said and moved into the open space of the Central Hall.

Wang's security detail spun and aimed their rifles at him. Then one of them barked a command and they lowered their weapons and Wang turned his head. He kept the pistol aimed at the assassin and nodded at Zhao as he walked across the floor.

"Chairman," Wang said.

Zhao stopped at the edge of the carpet where the assassin lay. He considered the assassin for a moment and the man did not return his gaze and then he looked at Wang. "I'm happy to see you, comrade," he said.

"As am I," Wang said. "As am I."

•　•　•　•　•

The assassin struggled to get off the floor. He made it to his hands and knees and then Secretary Wang put his foot on the assassin's shoulder and shoved. The man flopped onto his side and rolled off the carpet runner and onto the marble floor. Clutched his shoulder and left a red stain on the floor.

Wang walked up and ground the toe of his Oxford shoe into the bullet hole in the man's shoulder. The assassin writhed under his foot and Wang smiled. "No more options," he said.

The assassin reached for Wang's leg and Wang kicked him in the face. Then he crouched down beside the man with the pistol held loose in one hand. "All you can do now is die."

The assassin coughed and rolled to his side to spit out a wad of blood. "Then I can choose how to meet that death."

"You already did," Wang said and he stood and aimed the pistol at the assassin. Then Chairman Zhao knelt near the man's head.

"Move out of the way, Comrade Chairman," Wang said.

Zhao did not move and instead stared at the assassin. "You have been a worthy adversary," Zhao said. "However, you have been defeated. I had thought to keep you alive to extract any further information you might have, but I fear you may be too resourceful for that. Like Khoja, it is possible you would find a way to return, and to ensure the country has discipline, I must deliver punishment in accordance with the crime. I allowed mercy to override my judgement before, I cannot let that happen again." He stared at the assassin a moment longer and then stood.

"Your mercy is the reason you're still alive," the assassin said.

"*Shì*," Zhao said. "Although Khoja would not have needed to stop you had he been executed five years ago."

"You are mistaken." The assassin coughed and spat up more blood. "It is I who stopped Khoja."

"Enough," Wang said. He shouldered Zhao Guoqiang aside to get a clear shot at the assassin. "This ends."

"Wait," Zhao said and knelt once more beside the assassin, his back to Wang. "What do you mean that you stopped Khoja?"

"As you wish, Comrade Chairman," Wang said and aimed the pistol at the Chairman's head.

• • • • •

Malcolm pushed up off the floor, knocked Zhao back into Wang and the pistol fired over the chairman's shoulder. The bullet struck the floor behind Malcolm and peppered his back with chips of marble. He grimaced and then scrambled forward and wrapped up Wang's legs. Wang struggled, and Malcolm pulled him down and wrestled with him for the pistol. When he could not free the weapon, he flipped around onto Wang's back, clinched his arms around Wang's neck. Around them, the soldiers shouted and closed ranks, unable to shoot lest they hit Secretary Wang.

Malcolm tightened his hold and when Wang began to go limp, he dropped the choke and went for the Secretary's pistol. He kept Wang on top of him like a shield and used his heels to pivot in a circle on his back while he fired into the soldiers at point blank range. Half the soldiers fell before the rest had begun to move and then the pistol ran dry. Malcolm clubbed Wang in the head and rolled his body off and toward the remaining soldiers. They stumbled back and Malcolm dove after. Came up and grappled with a soldier. They fell to the floor and then there was a gunshot and the soldier's head exploded.

Malcolm clung to the dead man as a shield while bullets chewed up the floor around him. He rolled around and kicked out the legs of another soldier and then there were three left. He came to his feet. Then his injured leg gave out and collapsed to his knees and the soldiers were on him. They butt-stroked him to the floor and then one got too close. He grabbed the man, stripped his rifle from him and cut down the other soldiers. Hot casings on his arm and the smell of burnt flesh in the air.

A shout came from behind and he twisted, saw too late that Wang had regained consciousness. Then Wang's fist struck him in the jaw. His vision blurred and he let go of the soldier and fell to one side as a flurry of kicks followed the punch.

Malcolm fell back under the assault toward the pillars on the edges of the room. He almost made it when Zhao blocked his path. He hesitated and then Wang and the remaining soldier closed in.

The two men maneuvered Malcolm back into the middle of the Central Hall. Wang's attacks were no longer furious and undisciplined but calm and resolute. "There is no way you could have stopped Khoja," Wang said. "You are not half the fighter he was."

"How would you know?" Malcolm asked.

"I was there during his assault on *Zhongnanhai*. I escorted Vice-Premier Jiang to safety."

"But you weren't in the East Hall today."

"No," Wang said and struck Malcolm in the face and then again in the gut. "Jiang would not have it."

Malcolm backpedaled. "It was you," he said. "You were working with Jiang."

"You have it mixed up," Wang said and drove Malcolm back. "Confused."

"That's why you weren't in the East Hall," he said, his blocks slow and clumsy.

"Soldiers should do what they're told and leave thinking to their betters," Wang said and then tagged Malcolm with a kick that knocked him back. He advanced without pause, his words punctuated with blows that did not fail to meet their mark. "You have stopped nothing. You are alone, your team dead. Tell me, who do you think will come to your aid?"

Malcolm dragged his feet and gasped for breath. His shoulders slumped in the face of Wang's triumphant smile, and he lowered his hands and then Wang lunged for his head. A punch that would level a mountain. When he could almost feel Wang's knuckles, he sidestepped and Wang's hand passed by his temple. The width of a sheet of paper away. Then Wang stumbled and exposed his back and Malcolm fell on him from behind. They grappled and Malcolm maneuvered so that Wang was between himself and the soldier.

"Kill him!" Wang screamed and spit flew from his mouth.

The soldier threw a tentative punch at Malcolm's head and Malcolm twisted so that Wang's hand batted away the strike. The soldier punched again and Malcolm mirrored the movement on the other side. Then the soldier's face contorted in a scowl and he drew an extendable baton and attacked in earnest. All of the blows blocked by Wang's body. When the soldier backed off, Malcolm shoved Wang toward him. The two fell to the floor and the baton skittered to a stop at Malcolm's feet and he picked it up and clubbed the soldier in the head.

Then he stood over Wang, the end of the baton pointed at Wang's head.

"You weren't helping Vice-Premier Jiang," he said. "It was the other way around."

Wang's gaze flickered to the side and Malcolm dropped. He lashed out with the baton as he fell, had time to recognize Zhao and then the baton connected with the Chairman's arm. Zhao cried out and something clattered to the floor and then Malcolm reached out and dragged Zhao toward him. Kicked out the man's legs and flung him into a heap on top of Wang.

Malcolm watched the men struggle and then knelt and recovered the pistol Zhao had dropped. He almost collapsed as he regained his feet and then righted himself and waited with the pistol aimed at Wang and Zhao as the men separated themselves and stood to face him.

• • • • • •

Chairman Zhao Guoqiang stood to his full height, raised his chin and stared at the assassin. "Go on then," he said. "Do what you came here to do."

The assassin swayed on his feet. He waited for Secretary Wang to stand and then motioned with the pistol for the two men to stand closer together. Wang did not move and the assassin aimed the pistol at the man's head and the gun was the one thing about the assassin that did not shake or move.

"It seems Admiral Couzens chose well," Wang said and then moved to Zhao's side.

"You know him?" the assassin asked.

"I'm familiar with his work."

"He's often wrong," the assassin said, "but never in doubt."

"I do not understand."

The assassin stood in silence and then nodded and said, "Good."

The assassin stared at Wang and then put his free hand in a pocket of his pants. His eyes closed for a long second and then he opened them and stared at a point between the two men. Unfocused.

"My story's not done," the assassin said.

Wang snorted. "More lies?" he asked.

"No," the assassin said and turned to Zhao. "I didn't come here to fool you."

"Arrogant," Wang said. "There will be no victory march for you."

"Never wanted one," the assassin said. "They're lonely."

Zhao drew a breath and then let it out. "What do you want?"

The assassin seemed to think about that. His eyes took on a far-off look and he glanced first at Wang and then back to Zhao. "It's all gone wrong," he said. "But when I leave here, there will only be one word on my tongue. Which means I have to finish my story."

Noise rattled from the far end of the hall and General Chen stormed into the Central Hall. A troop of soldiers in front and all around him.

"Opportunity has slipped away from you," Wang said with a sneer. "General Chen!" he called out. "Kill this man!"

The soldiers ran up into an extended line. All with their rifles aimed at the assassin. All with a clear shot.

"What are you waiting for?" Wang asked. His face a snarl.

"General Chen," Zhao said and his voice echoed throughout the hall. "Do not fire until I give the order."

"Comrade Chairman –" General Chen began.

"I said, do not fire until I give the order," Zhao repeated, his gaze on the assassin. "This man has earned the right to speak."

The assassin hesitated and then nodded.

· · · · · ·

David's voice broke in Malcolm's ear.

"– barricaded. No way in, over."

Malcolm leaned against a wall and let Mary take the lead while he spoke into his mic. "What about door charges?" he asked.

"No time. Wait –"

Mary took down a soldier and then glanced back. "What's going on?" she asked.

"The entrance on David's side is barricaded," he said. "He can't get in."

"Tell him to make for the entrance on our side," Mary said and pointed to the wooden double doors farther down the hallway. On the other side of a wall of soldiers and police.

"Delta," Malcolm said into the mic. "Delta, this is team lead. Send –"

A muffled explosion rippled through the building. The lights flickered on and off and puffs of plaster and debris fell from the ceiling to land on their shoulders.

"Delta."

"What was that?" Mary asked, her voice strained.

"Delta, come in."

"Boss, what happened?"

"I don't know," he said. "Delta, come in."

"Boss —"

Malcolm glanced up to tell Mary to be quiet and then he saw how she stood. Stiff and rigid, her hands pressed to her abdomen where a red stain had begun to appear.

"Mary," he said. He caught her as she fell. Her body limp and he tried to ease her to the floor and then the soldiers were on top of him and he had to let her go.

He could not say for how long he fought. Soldiers and police all around. Shouts and yells and cries of pain. Mary dead at his feet and he had to protect her body and then there was a pause in the fight and he realized he could hear Aziguli.

She stood outside the double doors that led into the East Hall. Farther down the hallway, Khoja fought with a mob of soldiers. She ignored him and wrenched on the doors, braced her foot on the wall and pulled with her whole body. The massive slabs of wood would not budge and Aziguli began to beat on them with both hands.

Malcolm walked toward her. More soldiers streamed around the corner up ahead and enveloped Khoja and for every one the old man took down, two more appeared. A few slipped past and headed for Aziguli and they were joined by a few more and then it became a flood.

Malcolm began to run.

"Father!" Aziguli screamed.

The old man sunk beneath a deluge of human flesh. His head would surface amid the soldiers and he would seek out Aziguli and then he would sink beneath the tide once more, dragged down under the helmets and armor.

"Father!"

Malcolm pushed himself on. He slowed to take down a soldier who had run past Aziguli and he wondered why they had bypassed her and then another soldier was upon him. He took this one down as well and moved on, stopped when he saw a circle of soldiers around the double doors. Aziguli stood in the center of the circle with her shirt was open and her chest covered in explosives.

A detonator in her hand.

"Father!"

"Aziguli," Malcolm said and then soldiers engulfed him from behind. They carried him off his feet and threatened to crash him into the shield wall around Aziguli and he realized they could not see what she was about to do.

"Father!"

He twisted among the hands and arms, looked down the hallway and saw Khoja at the far end. A soldier on every limb and another around the old man's neck. His face was calm and pale and his eyes heart-rending as he peered out from under the soldiers at Aziguli.

"Father!"

Khoja's mouth opened and then the soldiers nearest Aziguli lunged for her.

"No!" Malcolm shouted.

Aziguli pressed her body against the double doors and let the soldiers close in. The tips of their fingers teased by stray wisps of her hair.

And then a sun exploded in the hallway.

Fire and light and noise so loud it could not be heard so much as felt. Bodies bowled him over, pressed down upon him and when he regained consciousness, he had to fight free from the mass of flesh under which he lay.

He could not process the devastation. The dead in rows on the floor like trees around a blast crater, a charnel house of blood and gore on the walls and ceiling and the doors to the East Hall askew on their hinges. He staggered over the blackened bodies, through the smoke and haze and the plaster that fell from the ceiling and came across Khoja outside the entrance to the East Hall.

The old man knelt in the center of the hallway. On the edge of a coal-black circle charred into the carpet. His face covered in grime. Ash in his hair and a severed leg with a woman's shoe in his lap.

"Khoja," he said.

The old man's lips moved but there was no sound. Voices began to carry through the fog from inside the East Hall and both ends of the corridor. Cries for help and commands and Malcolm knew there wasn't much time.

"Khoja," he repeated.

The old man did not move.

"Khoja," he said again and then a soldier emerged from the smoke inside the East Hall. The man bled from his ears and carried a rifle in one hand and Malcolm shot him down and then turned back to Khoja.

The old man's gaze centered on the fallen soldier. A spasm twisted his face and then he let Aziguli's leg roll off his lap and onto the floor and rose to his feet. He stood in the center of the blackened circle and then flowed across the threshold into the East Hall.

Malcolm grabbed the old man's shoulder as he passed. Felt himself become weightless as Khoja launched him through the air and then landed on his back. He gasped for breath, flailed around until he made it to his hands and knees and then glanced into the East Hall. The old man a dervish in the center of the room and a trail of death and ruin in his wake.

Malcolm rose and rushed into the room. He zeroed in on the soldiers and bodyguards along the far wall, gunned one down after another. He spotted Khoja near the end of the table and beyond the old man a group of people who cowered among overturned chairs. He recognized them as Politburo members and in the center of this group was Chairman Zhao Guoqiang on his hands and knees.

A guard attacked Malcolm from behind and he fought him off and then shot him in the gut. When he turned, the Politburo members had dispersed and left Zhao on the floor.

A sacrifice for the old man.

"Khoja," Malcolm called.

The old man oblivious to anything but Zhao.

An older man on the far side of the table raised a pistol. Malcolm shot the man twice in the chest and once in the head and held the sight picture on the man's face and realized he'd killed Vice-Premier Jiang. The man's features marred by the bullet hole in his forehead. He left Jiang where he fell and tackled Khoja as he was about to strike Zhao.

Khoja recovered first. He flipped Malcolm over and straddled him, pummelled him with fists and elbows.

Malcolm called but the old man would not listen. He hit Malcolm again and again and Malcolm's vision began to turn black and then there was a gunshot and Khoja stiffened. One hand in the air and the other around Malcolm's windpipe. A blood-red spot in the center of the old man's chest.

Khoja lowered his hand. He stared at Malcolm while the tension drained out of his face and then there was another gunshot and another red dot on the old man's chest. He wheezed and swayed and then toppled over to lay beside Malcolm on the floor.

Malcolm coughed. "Khoja?" he asked and it hurt to talk. He leaned over Khoja and the room spun in and out of his vision and then he pulled open the old man's shirt and stared at the wounds and knew that Khoja would die. Shouts and cries came from all around and he looked up and then a hand pressed against his face. He hesitated and then met Khoja's gaze. The old man's face calm and resolute.

"My fault," Khoja said.

"No," Malcolm said. "Not yours."

Khoja coughed and blood appeared on his lips. "A house divided cannot stand," he said. "That's what is said, correct?"

Malcolm nodded. "*Shì.*"

"Neither a kingdom."

"Rest."

"Tell him," Khoja said.

Malcolm said nothing.

"Tell him."

"He won't listen to me."

"That is not your concern," Khoja said. "Tell him. Tell him also that when rulers rejoice in the joys of their people, they, in turn, rejoice in the joys of the ruler."

"He won't –"

"Tell. Him."

Malcolm stared at the old man and then drew a breath. "I will," he said.

Khoja nodded and lowered his hand from Malcolm's face. His hand disappeared into a pocket of his robes and then pulled out what appeared to be a tiny, jade figurine.

"And I will tell him also that when a ruler grieves with the people, they, in turn, grieve with the ruler," Malcolm said.

"*Shì*," Khoja said and nodded and then went still.

Malcolm held vigil while the life disappeared from Khoja's body. Shadows gathered behind and above him and the last thing he remembered before the pain and the blackness was watching the jade figurine tumble from Khoja's limp hand.

• • • • •

Malcolm aimed the pistol at a point between Chairman Zhao and Secretary Wang. The Central Hall came in and out of focus and he wondered how much longer he could remain on his feet.

Zhao had not moved or spoken while Malcolm had talked. He'd made a sound in his throat when Malcolm had finished and inhaled and then closed his eyes.

"Comrade Chairman, this man is a liar," Wang said. He clenched his fists and his upper lip in a sneer. "He is an assassin sent to bring back the century of humiliation. An enemy who would reverse what we've accomplished over the last fifty years."

Zhao opened his eyes and stared at Malcolm.

"He allied himself with a known terrorist, and together they murdered our comrades on the Standing Committee." Wang's voice was loud and forceful and it carried throughout the Central Hall. "Ling Chunlan. Zhang Qishan. Xu Huning. And Jiang Gaoli. All butchered because America cannot accept our rightful place in the world."

Malcolm glanced at Wang and waited.

"Kill him," Wang said. "Show our adversaries what happens to those who stand against us. And then –"

"Be quiet, Wang," Zhao said.

Wang's eyes narrowed. "If you do not have the strength to do what must be done, then it falls to me," he said. "General Chen. You have heard enough to make your own decision. Do what you should have already done and shoot this man down like the mangy dog he is."

"Stay your hand, General," Zhao said.

"Only a coward would fail to act." Wang's face contorted in a snarl.

"I said, be quiet."

Zhao considered Malcolm and then raised his chin and clasped his hands behind his back. "Tell me," he said, "why did you not share this story before?"

"Would you have believed me?"

Zhao grunted. "Perhaps," he said. "Perhaps not." He took a breath and met Malcolm's gaze. "Is there anything else you wish to tell me?"

"I would like to ask you a question."

"You have earned the right."

"What will you do if I let you live?"

Zhao said nothing for a moment and then nodded. "A fair question," he said. "I will finish what I have started."

"Are you sure?"

"More than ever. Our countries must be united in harmony if we hope to overcome the challenges of the future. Today's problems know no borders."

"Your actions will commit millions to death."

"Billions will die if I do nothing."

"That might happen regardless."

"*Shì.*"

"And what of those who come under your rule? Will they end up like the Uighurs?"

"We must have peace so we can concentrate our energy and work together."

"And if you succeed? When good harvests have returned, will you forget to save food?"

Zhao did not answer and the Central Hall became silent. Then his lips spread in a small smile. "I see now, assassin, the full meaning of Khoja's message," he said. "True harmony embodies the virtue, values, and happiness that come from the unity of humankind. And the sweetest harmonies are those with the biggest variety of notes."

Malcolm stared at Zhao and then nodded. "Then we share the same aspirations," he said. "If every family is united, society will prosper."

"One kingdom under heaven."

"*Shi.*"

Zhao nodded. "It gives me pleasure to know my greatest enemy is the one who understood me most."

"Tell him, when you see him."

"I am ready."

Malcolm considered that and then aimed the pistol at Zhao.

A clatter passed through the soldiers as they took aim at Malcolm. The red lights of lasers painted on his chest.

"Lower your weapons," Zhao said.

"Comrade Chairman –" Chen began.

"Do it, General Chen," Zhao said. "Do not shoot unless I give the word."

"And if he kills you?"

"Then you will no longer need to follow my orders."

General Chen said nothing and then barked at the soldiers and the red dots moved off Malcolm's chest.

Malcolm met Zhao's gaze through the sight picture of the pistol. He stared at this man he'd travelled around the world to kill and tightened his grip on the trigger and then aimed at Wang and fired.

The bullet struck Wang between the eyes. His head rocked back and his body continued to stand. As if it refused to acknowledge what had happened. It stood erect and still and then his head dropped and the eyes were vacant and then his body collapsed to the floor.

Malcolm stood with the pistol held out. When he glanced down, the red dots had returned to his chest. He lowered his arm and let the pistol clatter to the floor and then looked at Zhao.

"There is one last thing I think Khoja would want to tell you," he said and glanced at Zhao.

"Please share."

"The water that supports a ship, can also sink it."

Zhao was silent and then nodded. "As I told you," he said, "I can only do my best until I die."

Malcolm stared at him and then bowed his head. "Hallelujah," he said. Then he straightened and turned and limped past the soldiers toward the Great Hall's main entrance.

• • • • • • • •

Chairman Zhao Guoqiang watched the assassin depart and did not move when General Chen came to his side. Nor did he move when the soldiers aimed their rifles at the man, his back painted with red dots.

"Comrade Chairman," General Chen said, "he cannot be allowed to leave."

The assassin had reached the wall of flat arches that separated the foyer from the Central Hall. He stopped and leaned against one of the pillars when it seemed he might fall. Waited and put one hand into a pocket of his pants and then staggered past the rows of x-ray machines and metal detectors. Out the doors onto the top of the landing.

General Chen gave a curt order and the soldiers dashed after the assassin. Through the foyer they ran and out the doors while the general moved in front of Zhao. "Comrade Chairman," he said, "this man plotted to destroy the party and the government. To let him go will be interpreted as weakness."

Zhao continued to stare after the assassin.

"Comrade Chairman."

Zhao stooped and picked up the pistol the assassin had dropped.

"Comrade Chairman," Chen said, "Give the word and the soldiers –"

"An easy life is not the way to cultivate greatness, General Chen," Zhao said. "The burden must be mine."

He stared at the pistol and felt the cold press of metal in his hand and then passed through the foyer and out the doors. The soldiers stood in a line at the top of the landing with their rifles aimed at the assassin and they made a hole for him in the middle of their number. He took up his spot and stared down at the assassin. A third of the way down the wide stairs. One slow step at a time.

Chairman Zhao Guoqiang cast his gaze out and over Tian'an Men Square. Guangchang West Side Road had vanished beneath barricades upon barricades erected at the base of the Great Hall's stairs. The square itself was filled with soldiers and police, still and somber beneath the lights that kept back the dark. To the north, the illuminated Gate of Heavenly Peace shone like a beacon in the night. The rest of the square's monuments, decorated in like manner, were even more beautiful.

He breathed in of the cold air and then turned his gaze to the assassin. The man whose name was Malcolm Kwong. He watched Malcolm descend another step and then raised the pistol and took aim.

"One day," he said, "we shall skim the waves. Blown by the wind, with sails hoisted high across the vast ocean."

Then he squeezed the trigger.

• • • • •

Malcolm did not hear the shot that killed him.

The world went white as the bullet entered his brain and he collapsed and tumbled down several steps and came to rest on his back. One hand on his chest. The hand that held the photo of Amaelia and Oran askew on the stairs of the Great Hall.

He did not feel pain from the hole in his head that had killed him quick.

Nor the one in his heart that had killed him slow.

Instead he felt light. As if a weight had been removed.

As if the warm sun shone on his face.

He held on to the crumpled photo long after any conscious thought directed his body to do so. And when he died, and finally let go, the picture remained for a moment in his open palm. Flitted in place and then soared up into the air on a gust of wind.

Not to be seen again.

• • • • •

Chairman Zhao Guoqiang stood at the top of the stairs.

Dwarfed by the massive columns of the Great Hall.

He tore his gaze from Malcolm Kwong's body and let it roam once again. Out over the soldiers and police packed into Tian'an Men Square. So many that the Monument to the People's Heroes and the Chairman Mao Memorial Hall seemed to rise out of the bodies. The streets and sidewalks beyond the Square filled with civilians as far as he could see. To the north, a phalanx of soldiers guarded the Gate of Heavenly Peace, shoulder to shoulder with people crammed into Chang'an Avenue.

All silent.

All eyes on him.

A blast of cold winter air blew up the stairs and struck him head-on. He did not look away. Nor did he shield his face. Instead he let the wind's chill pierce him and returned the stares of the people in the crowd.

He had no illusions about what was to come.

Although he could not foresee the future, it was not a matter of whether the journey would be smooth or arduous. It was a question of how difficult it would get and whether they would succeed.

His eyes began to water and he dropped his gaze and considered Malcolm's body. Crumpled in a heap halfway down the stairs. Then he closed the hand that did not hold the pistol into a fist. Raised it over his head and called out a single word.

"*Tianxia*."

The word reverberated out over the Square and was met with silence.

He called out again.

"*Tianxia*."

The echoes began to die and he called out one more time.

"*Tianxia*."

He remained as he was a moment longer and then dropped his hand and as he did, the word returned to him from the crowd.

Tianxia.

Low and murmured.

Then again. Stronger.

On the third time the word was on the lips of every person he could see and it continued to grow in strength. Three more times until the pillars of the Great Hall seemed to shake.

Zhao Guoqiang waited until silence once more fell upon the assembled and then he turned and entered the Great Hall. He handed off the pistol to General Chen, stationed inside the Great Hall's entrance. Through the foyer he walked, past paintings of the Yellow River and of blooming cherry blossoms and cranes.

On and on, his footsteps confident and sure. Up the grand staircase where he came to a stop.

He stood for a moment and then went to stand before a painting of a river among mist-covered mountains. The tiny houses of several villages nestled amid the merger of land and water.

He stared at the painting and then reached into his suit jacket and pulled out the jade figurine he'd found beside Ismail Khoja's body. He held the *fenghuang* in his hand and then nestled it on the ledge of the painting's frame. Then he stepped back and contemplated the green mountains and the people homebound in the evening mist.

All united under heaven.

THE END

ACKNOWLEDGEMENTS

This story would not have been possible without a hell of a lot of help.

Above all, my family, for their patience, support, and amused tolerance.

Those who've gone before me, who both inspired the story and provided the material needed to bring it to life. First and foremost are Zhang Yimou's 2002 movie, *Hero*, as well as Charles Blackmore's *Conquering the Desert of Death*, an engrossing tale about his 1993 expedition across the Taklamakan. For research on China, I dug deeply into books like, *When China Rules the World*, by Martin Jacques, *Chinese Visions of World Order*, edited by Ban Wang, Zhang Fenzhi's *Xi Jinping: How to Read Confucius*, and a number of others. I also discovered many Chinese authors, like Ma Jian, Gao Xingjian, and Yu Hua. I hope their influence brought a degree of authenticity to the work.

Those who helped with the writing. I tend to overwrite, and this novel became a chance to work on word selection, brevity, and minimalism in general. Cormac McCarthy was a primary influence here, although I also turned to MacKinlay Kantor and many other authors noted for distinct prose, including Brian Francis Slattery, Peter Heller, and Claudia Casper. Minimalism also ended up being a central part of a research project I completed through the University of Gloucestershire while writing this novel, and I'd like to thank Dr. Martin Randall for his suggestions and advice. I'd also like to thank Shannon O'Neill, who edited the manuscript.

Lastly, those who've read this story. Your time is the biggest investment you could make, and if you've chosen to spend yours reading about Malcolm and Zhao, then I hope I used your time wisely. I hope that you can overlook my limited ability as a writer and any errors within these pages.

I can only strive to do my best until I die.

ABOUT THE AUTHOR

Alastair Luft writes out of Ottawa, Ontario, Canada, where he lives with his wife and two daughters. He is the author of two other novels, *The Battle Within*, and, *Jihadi Bride*, which was a finalist in the 2020 ITW Thriller Awards. A 25-year veteran of the Canadian Armed Forces, Alastair is also an accomplished speaker who has given TEDx talks on how violence begets violence, and the importance of art.

NOTE FROM THE AUTHOR

Word-of-mouth is crucial for any author to succeed. If you enjoyed *One Kingdom Under Heaven*, please leave a review online—anywhere you are able. Even if it's just a sentence or two. It would make all the difference and would be very much appreciated.

Thanks!
Alastair

Thank you so much for reading one of **Alastair Luft's** novels.

If you enjoyed our book, please check out our recommendation for your next great read!

Jihadi Bride by Alastair Luft

"A timely edge-of-your-seat terrorism thriller that plays on every parent's worst fears. This cinematic thriller is destined for TV."

–*Best Thrillers*